He stood, slightly crouched, with the naturi dagger in his hand.

Screaming, I slashed and kicked wildly. There was no holding back anymore—I wanted death; his death and maybe even mine.

Backing Danaus against the wall, I kicked the dagger free. It spun through the air to crash against the stone wall. With my right hand, I threw a ball of blue fire at the blade. I encased the dagger in flames hot enough to cause the cement to sizzle and pop. The room grew hot as I poured all my anger and hatred into the fire, willing the metal to bend and melt. . .

I stared at the naturi blade and started to laugh; high-pitched and a little mad.

The blade was completely untouched. The metal had glowed red, but it was unchanged. I could do nothing to it. The charms on it were impenetrable.

As long as the naturi existed, so would this blade . . .

By Jocelynn Drake

NIGHTWALKER
The First Dark Days Novel

nightwalker
The First Dark Days Novel

JOCELYNN DRAKE

An Imprint of HarperCollinsPublishers

This is a work of fiction. Names, characters, places, and incidents are drawn from the author's imagination or are used fictitiously and are not to be construed as real. Any resemblance to actual events, locales, organizations, or persons, living or dead, is entirely coincidental.

EOS
An Imprint of HarperCollins*Publishers*
10 East 53rd Street
New York, New York 10022-5299

Copyright © 2008 by Jocelynn Drake
Cover art by Don Sipley
ISBN 978-0-06-154277-0
www.eosbooks.com

First Eos paperback printing: August 2008
First Harper special printing: March 2008

HarperCollins® and Eos® are registered trademarks of Harper-Collins Publishers.

Printed in the U.S.A.

10 9 8 7 6 5 4 3 2 1

To Mom and Dad
You believed in me first.

Acknowledgments

The road here has been long, and at times ugly. The list of people who have helped me get here is equally long, and I want to thank everyone who laughed with me, held my hand when the dark closed in, and shared their lives with me, even if it was only nervous small talk in a slow-moving line. You've shaped me and in turn shaped my words.

However, there are a few people I need to thank specifically. Thanks to my brilliant agent Jennifer Schober. Your patience, endless enthusiasm, and belief in me have meant more than you will ever know. Thanks to my amazing editor, Diana Gill, for taking a chance on a newbie and demanding that I be the writer I always wanted to be.

A special thanks to Kim Harrison, Rachel Vincent, and Joseph Hargett. For years you have been my personal cheering section, editors, friends, champions, and when I needed it, a valuable reality check. Thanks for putting up with me.

And thank you to my family. Thanks, Stephen, for reminding me cartoons and video games are still an essential part of living no matter how old I get. Thanks, Nate, for always making me laugh, even when I thought it was impossible. Finally, thanks, Mom and Dad, for pointing out that I would be much happier as a writer than a chemical engineer. You just may have saved the world.

nightwalker

ONE

His name was Danaus.

And what I remember most were his eyes. I saw them first by lamplight; a flicker of dark cobalt as he paused a distance from me. His eyes were the color sapphires were meant to be, a grim sparkle of pigment. I stared at those eyes, willing time to slow down as I slipped into those still, stygian depths. But it wasn't the waters of the Styx I swam in, but a cool lagoon of Lethe where I bathed in a moment of oblivion.

He stopped on the deserted street outside the edge of a pale pool of light thrown down by a wrought-iron lamp, his eyes darting up and down the empty expanse. He drew in a deep breath. I think he could sense me watching from some perch but could not peg my exact location. His right hand flexed once at his side, and to my surprise he stepped forward into the light, his night vision momentarily destroyed; taunting me with the bait he dangled before my eyes.

I slowly ran my tongue over my teeth. Not only was he impressive to look at, but there was a confidence about him that begged my attention. I was half tempted to step away from the shadow of the chimney and allow the moon to outline my slim form. But I hadn't survived for more than six centuries by making careless mistakes. Balanced on the ridgepole of the three-story house across from him, I watched as he continued down the street. His black leather duster flared as he walked, snapping at his heels like a chained wolf forced to follow its master.

The truth was, I had watched him for more than a month. He'd blown into my territory like a cold wind and wasted no time destroying my kind. In the past weeks he had killed nearly half a dozen of my brethren. Almost all had been fledglings, with less than a century to cut their teeth upon, but it was still more than any other had dared.

And these killings had not been spineless daylight stakings. He hunted each nightwalker under the caress of moonlight. I had even watched some of these battles from a hidden perch and barely kept from applauding when he knelt, bloody, over each of his prey, cutting out the heart. He was speed and cunning. And the nightwalkers were bloated on their own inflated sense of power. I was the Keeper of this domain, entrusted with protecting our secret; not protecting those who could not protect themselves.

After weeks of watching my would-be prey, I thought it was time for formal introductions. I knew who he was. More than just another Nosferatu hunter. Something wonderfully more, with a vibrant power all his own. I wanted a taste of that power before he died.

And he knew of me. In their final seconds some of the weak ones had mewled my name, hoping my identity would buy them a last second reprieve. It hadn't.

I sped silently along the rooftops, leaping over the gaps and landing with the sure-footed grace of a cat. Slipping past him and down two more blocks to the outer edge of the historic district, I stopped at an abandoned home with a widow's walk and worn red brick that would serve as a nice meeting place. Its single turret and dark windows gazed out toward the river like a silent soldier.

The night air was warm and thick despite the fact that we hadn't had any rain for more than two weeks, leaving the brown lawns struggling from yet another rough summer. Even the crickets seemed to put forth only a halfhearted effort with their chirping, burdened by the oppressive heat. The light breeze that blew in from the sea carried with it more moisture, thickening the air until it carried a weight all its own. I had come to Savannah more than a century ago, seeking anonymity, an escape from the world that had consumed me for nearly five hundred years. I loved Savannah's grace and history, the ghosts that seemed to haunt every shadowy corner and rambling house. Yet I could do without her oppressive summers. I'd spent too many years in cooler climes.

The abandoned house was half hidden behind enormous oak trees dripping with Spanish moss, as if guarded by a pair of grand dames swathed in antique lace. The front of the property was lined with a tall, spike iron fence ending in a pair of stone pillars that flanked the path up to the house. I sat on the top of the left pillar with my legs crossed, waiting for him. The subtle throb of my powers tumbled from my body. I wanted him to follow the trail until he came to me, like the pied piper trilling his merry tune for the children of Hamelin.

Danaus stopped when he reached the edge of the property to my left and stared at me. Yes, it was brazen, and maybe even a little overconfident on my part, but I didn't want him to grow too sure of himself. He would have to work for his blood tonight.

With a slow smile, I rolled off the pillar, disappearing behind the spike fence and into the deeper shadows of the overgrown yard. I cut through the air as if I were made of the night, disappearing through an open window on the second floor at the back of the house.

Waiting in a former bedroom, I listened. Anticipation coiled in my stomach, my body tingling with the thrill of the hunt, so rarely had I the chance to pit myself against something that could actually destroy me. I'd killed my share of human hunters, but they hadn't been a real challenge, waving their silver crosses about and praying to a god they had abandoned until that moment of final judgment. After so many long centuries, there were too few ways in which to feel that rush, to dance along the razor's edge and remember, even if only for a breath, what it had meant to be alive. Danaus would help me remember.

This hunter was different. He was as human as I was. His body was only a shell, barely capable of restraining the power that seemed to pour from him like a river.

Downstairs, the front door exploded open, banging against the wall. I smiled; he knew I was here waiting for him. I strode across the hardwood floor, moving into the master bedroom, the heels of my boots echoing through the empty house. Now he knew exactly where I was, too.

Peace, Mira, I reminded myself. *No reason to rush this. You haven't hunted him for more than a month to snap his neck in a careless moment.*

No, I would put an end to his destruction of my race and enjoy it as I did so.

Once in the bedroom, my steps quieted until I didn't make a sound as I crossed to the far side of the room. I leaned into the empty corner, letting the shadows fold around me like a cloak, falling into the darkness that had long whispered secrets of the night and death. Around me the old house creaked and sighed as we both waited.

Danaus finally appeared in the doorway, his shoulders so wide they nearly brushed the sides of the entry. I stood silent for a moment, enjoying the slow, even rise and fall of his chest. He was perfectly calm. He was tall, maybe six feet, with raven black hair that hung wild to his shoulders. His cheekbones were high and his jaw strong and hard like granite. Along the way he had shed his black coat, and his right hand gripped a six-inch silver blade that caught the moonlight.

"You are the one they call Danaus," I said. My voice slithered out from the shadows while my body remained hidden. His head jerked toward me, his eyes slits of blue in the darkness. "They say you killed Jabari in old Thebes."

I stepped forward, the shadows sliding their arms about my body, and paced across the room so he could see me clearly for the first time. In the soft light that poured through the windows, my pale skin glowed like white marble. I moved no closer to him, giving him a chance to size me up.

"But you missed Valerio in Vienna," I said, curiosity lifting my voice. "And Yuri waits for you in St. Petersburg, though he is not half as old as Jabari."

"There's still time." His voice was like a growl in the back of his throat.

I paused, staring at him for a moment. I couldn't place the accent, and I'd heard many over the centuries. It was old, very old. Not nearly as old as Jabari's Egyptian lilt, but something that hadn't been uttered in ages. It would be something to ponder, but I had more pressing queries.

"Maybe," I conceded with a slight nod. "But instead you came to the New World. While I may be one of the oldest here, I am far younger than Valerio. Why travel such a distance?"

"Aren't you called the 'Fire Starter'?"

I laughed, a deep throaty sound that curled through the air and brushed like a warm hand against his cheek. The ability to touch another with your voice was an old trick that came naturally to some nightwalkers. It had few real uses, but was great for unnerving your opponent. Danaus shifted from one foot to the other, but his expression never changed.

"Among other things." I walked back toward the opposite wall, but this time I moved a few steps closer to him. His muscles tightened but he didn't step backward. It was enough for me to brush against the circle of power that enveloped him, rubbing against my bare skin like warm silk. It also gave him a better taste of my own power. By the time I reached my original corner, something had changed in his eyes.

"You were at the Bonaventure cemetery three nights ago," he said.

"Yes." The word came out a whispered hiss.

"I killed two vampires that night." He said it as if it should have explained everything.

"So? Since entering my territory a month ago, you have killed five nightwalkers."

"Why didn't you try to stop me?"

I chuckled softly, with a slight shake of my head. *Try.* Were we both truly this arrogant? I lifted my shoulders in an indifferent shrug. "They were not mine to protect."

"But they were vampires."

"They were fledglings without a master," I corrected him. Pushing off the wall, I started to walk toward him. "A master you killed more than a week ago." Of course, I'd been planning to kill Riley myself, but Danaus beat me to it. Riley had been expanding his own little family without my permission, and a balance had to be maintained in order to preserve our secret.

Danaus moved, mirroring me as he stepped out of the doorway. He turned so his back was to the wall as we circled each other. His steps were graceful and fluid, like a dance. The knot tightened again in my stomach and my body hummed with energy.

I took a single step forward, testing him, and Danaus lashed out with his right hand. Jerking away, I kept the blade from slashing at my face. Yet, he surprised me when he immediately spun back around, lifting his left hand to reveal a Saracen blade curving up the length of his arm. His first move had been a feint to get me to expose my throat. I dropped into a spin kick, clipping one of his feet before he could move. The hunter stumbled as he backed away, but remained standing. Balanced on the balls of my feet, I pressed my fingers to the dusty hardwood floor.

"Nice sword. Gaelic runes?" I inquired, as if making idle small talk, but my eyes were locked on him. The hand holding the sword tightened. It was an exquisite blade, with a line of runes etched down the side. I couldn't read them, but I would have wagered that they were more than just decoration.

He grunted, which I took for an affirmation to my question.

"Thanks for not coming at me with a stake," I said, standing. He looked at me, his dark eyebrows briefly meeting over the bridge of his nose. "It's so cliché." The right corner of his mouth twitched before he could stop it.

"You would have set it on fire," he said stiffly.

"True." I waited a heartbeat, then crossed the distance between us, hitting him in the chest with both hands. Air exploded from his lungs. The blow threw both of his arms involuntarily forward as he stumbled back. I kicked out with my right foot, hitting his left hand. The impact loosened his grip and sent the scimitar spinning across the floor, to clatter against the far wall. Unfortunately, he recovered faster than I expected and swung his right arm forward, grazing my cheek with the dagger.

The unexpected stab of pain screamed through me, and I jerked back out of arm's reach. I hissed at him, fangs bared, my body hunched as if prepared to spring. Yeah, I know. The hiss was even more cliché than a wooden stake, but the grating sound erupted from my throat before I could think about it, let alone come up with something a little more civilized. I'm 603 years old, not an Ancient.

Again I forced myself to stand and relax. Danaus drew in a few ragged gulps of air before his breathing evened out. Breathing would be painful for a while, but at least he still could. I lifted my left hand to my cheek and then moved my fingers into my line of sight; my eyes never leaving his tense form. Blood covered two fingers. Slowly, I licked them, letting the copper taste coat my tongue. The pain in my cheek was already gone and I could feel the wound closing. In another moment there would only be a smear of blood.

That bit of blood had been enough. The taste lit the lust, sending it burning through my veins. Sure, it had been my blood, but it was all the same; vampire, human, and even whatever Danaus was. It all pulsed with power from the soul, the very essence of life, and I knew this time it would be his I tasted.

I rushed him again, but Danaus was ready. He swung the blade at me, once again going for my throat. I easily caught his hand. He swung his left fist at my face. I batted it away. Squeezing his right hand, I tried to force him to drop the dagger without breaking his hand, but despite the pain, he wouldn't drop it. Out of the corner of my eye I saw his left hand go for another weapon at his side.

"Fine." The single word escaped in a growl as I grabbed his left wrist. I swept my leg beneath his, throwing us both down. Lying on top of him, I pinned both of his hands against the floor. Sure, he was heavier than me, but even with all his muscles, I was still stronger. Vampirism has its perks. Sliding along his body, my leather pants slipped along his legs until I was straddling him. I smiled down at him, rubbing against the hard bulge in his pants. He didn't carry a gun. Unless you put a shotgun in our mouths and pulled the trigger, you really couldn't kill a nightwalker with a gun. It generally didn't even slow us down.

"I thought you were glad to see me," I purred, unable to keep the laughter from my voice. Danaus glared at me, his eyes hardening into cold gems. I knew better. The violence turned him on, not me. The thrill of the hunt.

He stared at me, his mind turning over thoughts I wished I could hear. Something about me bothered him. Sure, I was beautiful, but all nightwalkers were a pretty face and a nice body. If his attention was that easy to catch, he would have been dead long ago.

The question that flickered in his eyes was the only reason I think he had not actually tried to kill me yet. We'd taken a few nice stabs at each other, but no killing blows. The other fights I watched had been quick. Each of his attacks were precise and efficient, planned to end the battle and take down the nightwalker. Maybe we were still sizing each other up, enjoying the building tension, but it felt like there was more hanging unsaid in the ether.

With my hands still locked on his wrists, I pulled backward, lowering my face until my chin rested on his sternum, my eyes locked with his. I could feel the muscles in his body tighten beneath me, but he didn't jerk or try to throw me off. Despite the fact that my lips were barely an inch from his chest, I couldn't bite him at that angle. We both knew this, so he lay still, waiting.

Drawing in a deep breath, I let his scent fill me. I could smell sweat and that certain musky scent of man, but there was more, the wind, a distant sea, and best of all, the sun. The scent was so strong I could taste it, conjuring up ancient memories of basking naked in the midday heat.

I needed to get off of him, to put some distance between

us. I was becoming giddy on his power as it wrapped its
arms around my cool flesh. Giddy, along with other things
I knew would serve us no good tonight, except maybe kill
him a little faster. And I so wanted to do this slowly, to enjoy
the fight that he offered.

"I didn't come here to destroy you," he said, his voice
rolling through the silent room like a rumble of distant
thunder.

A bubble of laughter escaped me as I moved forward so
my face hovered above his. "And that is supposed to stop
me from killing you? You come into my territory, kill my
people, and then you say you're not here to destroy me. No,
Danaus, I plan to dig around inside of you to find out where
that little ball of power is hiding." I smiled at him, broadly
enough to expose my fangs.

Danaus was moving before I even had a chance to react,
rolling so he was now on top of me. But I was still holding
his wrists. I pushed him backward, throwing him off me
and across the room. The hunter landed on his back and slid
a couple of feet. When he was standing again, I was on the
other side of the room.

I leaned back into the corner, balanced on my heels, with
my shoulders braced against the two walls. After letting his
warm powers wash over me, I forced myself to slow down.
I had never encountered a creature with powers that felt like
his. We had acquired a new, dark threat. I needed to discover
who or what he was, and if there were more like him. We
had not spent countless centuries fighting, and finally defeating, the naturi, only to find ourselves faced with a new
foe. One free to walk about in the daylight hours.

I forced a laugh, sending the sound dancing around the
room until it finally skipped out the open window to my
right. My laughter seemed to put him more on edge than my
straddling him. Or maybe it was the fact that he had enjoyed

being pinned. I doubted he'd ever allowed any nightwalker get that close to him without putting up a fight.

Staring at him now, something else caught my eye. "Where's your cross, Danaus?" I called across the distance, hooking my thumbs on the front pockets of my leather pants. "All good hunters have a cross dangling about their necks. Where's yours?"

"How can you control fire?" he demanded. His face was grim and half hidden in the shadow of his hair as it fell forward. "It's forbidden." He took a wary step forward, the gritty floor crunching under his foot.

I gracefully rolled to my feet, as if I was a marionette pulled up by my strings. There was nothing human about the movement, and I was pleased to see it still unnerved him even after all his years of hunting us. He took a half step back before he could stop himself, his frown deepening.

"Forbidden?" I repeated. "Has someone written a book of rules on nightwalkers that I don't know about?" *Information.* Could that be the reason he had come hacking and slashing into my domain? He was curious and seeking information?

"No vampire has ever been able to control fire."

"Few have ever hunted us without the protection of a silver cross," I countered.

Danaus stared hard at me. I had a feeling he would have growled at me, but I think he was leaving the animal-like noises to me. He turned the knife handle around in his hand, weighing his options. How important was this information to him? Enough that he would finally be forced to divulge some of his own? Of course, he could then kill me and that would be the end of it.

When the hunter spoke again, the words seemed dragged from his throat. "A cross cannot protect one who is already damned to Hell."

A dozen new questions rushed to my lips, but I had my answer and knew he wouldn't willingly give up any more. At least, not without my answer to his question, and I was willing to play, for now.

"We all have our gifts," I said with a shrug. "Yuri can call wolves to his side. Seraf can raise the dead."

"But fire . . . " His voice drifted off.

"Doesn't quite seem fair," I said. "The one thing that is supposed to kill us all, and I am completely immune. But it has nothing to do with being a nightwalker. I could control fire before I was reborn. Somehow, I retained the gift."

"Like the naturi," he murmured.

"I am nothing like the naturi!" My temper flared to life instantly and I took a step toward him with my fangs bared. All I saw was a quick flick of his wrist, faster than I had ever seen any human move. But that was my fault. I was still thinking of him as human.

The blade flashed for half a second in the moonlight before burying itself in my chest. I stumbled backward, my back slamming into the wall behind me as my hand closed around the knife. It was an inch below my heart, clipping the side of my left lung. With his skill, I guessed he missed my heart on purpose. Even a blow to the heart wouldn't have necessarily killed me, but weakened me enough so he could stroll over and take my head off. It was supposed to be a warning, and if I wasn't so angry, I might have heeded it.

I pulled the dagger from my chest, gritting my teeth as it rubbed against bone and sliced more muscle and flesh. Pressing my left hand against the wound, I tried to slow the flow of blood as it moved like warm fingers down my stomach. The dagger fell from my fingers and clattered to the floor. The sound echoed through the house like shot across an empty plain. I glared at him, finding he had already pulled another knife and held it clenched in his right fist, waiting for me.

This time I walked across the room. I wanted him to see me coming. The movement pulled and twisted the cut in my chest as the flesh struggled to mend. I'd worry about that later. I kept the faint smile on my face, burying the scream of pain deep in my chest.

He slashed at me with the same speed he'd thrown the knife, but I expected it as I watched the twitch and flex of muscles play below his skin. I knocked his hand away, feeling the crack of bone in his wrist as my arm connected. The knife fell to the floor as his fingers spasmed under the flash of pain. He kicked out with his left leg, trying to keep a safe distance between us, but I caught his leg with my right hand and threw him back into the wall. I grabbed his arms, slamming them against the drywall with enough force to dent the surface, keeping them raised above his head. My left hand pressed a bloody handprint into his forearm, and I crushed my body against his with enough force that he grunted. I was done playing nice.

I was shorter than him even in heels, but I could still reach his neck without tiptoeing. I smiled, displaying my fangs. His heart skipped faster, pounding against my chest with its intoxicating warmth. His scent came back to me, the sweet kiss of the wind sweeping over dark waters and the bright sun.

"What are you, Danaus?" I whispered, peering into his eyes. His lips were pressed into a firm, tight line. He was furious. I smiled and leaned into him, close enough that he could feel my words caress the tender flesh of his neck. This time he struggled, muscles straining up and down his body as he tried to rid himself of me, but he was trapped. In a battle of strength, he knew he couldn't win.

My breath brushed across his ear. "It doesn't matter." My

lips dipped down to graze his neck, and I could feel a chill skitter across his sweaty flesh. "You'll tell me one day. Before I'm through, you'll even trust me."

I released him and jumped backward, landing easily on the other side of the room. No reason to give him another chance to put a knife in my chest. I had a feeling that this time he wouldn't miss. I stared into his eyes, and there it was this time: fear. A deeper look of uncertainty and doubt. I had finally shaken him down to his core; touched something no one else had. It made him infinitely more dangerous, but then again, I had just become infinitely more dangerous to him, threatening him with something far more horrible than a painful death.

"We're not finished," he said, one hand holding his fractured wrist.

"Oh, you're right. We're not finished by a long shot, but tonight's fun is over," I announced, tilting my head to the side.

"I didn't come here to kill you."

"Really?"

One corner of his mouth jerked into a half smile as he watched me. "Not this time."

"Just remember that your business is with me. Touch another nightwalker and you'll be dead before you even know I'm there." I let my hands fall to my sides, palms facing him. Drops of fire tumbled from my fingertips like water. The flames pooled at my feet for a moment, then shot out like something alive, surging toward the walls and across the hardwood floors. My eyelids drifted lower until my eyes were barely open. I could see him watching me, but my focus was on the fire that had slipped down through the floor and was quickly seeking out both of the exits.

With one last smile I darted out the open window to my right and landed in the yard. I jogged across the lawn and only paused to look back when I was in the middle of the street. The house was engulfed in brilliant orange and yellow flames. I knew he would get out. Men like Danaus didn't die so easily. I was half tempted to remain behind to see him run from the building, but there wasn't time. The night had grown old and I needed to feed to replace the blood he'd spilled tonight. I would finish killing the hunter later.

Two

The sand has run out on more than six centuries for me. I have seen the rise and fall of kingdoms, the discovery of new lands and peoples, and acts of cruelty by humans that chill even my cold blood. But across the ages and changing face of man, I have to admit that the twenty-first century is by far my favorite. In these times, people can shed their past and appearance like a snake slithering free of its dead skin. The world is covered in a new Technicolor facade that has been built over the old realm, blotting out the sky and the earth.

Now there is no need to stalk my victims through dark alleyways and gaze down from hidden rooftops. Lost souls dot the landscape like daisies, waiting for me to pluck them up with promises of release. They stare up at me with empty eyes and broken hearts like I am their saving angel. I slip into their lives to deliver them briefly from an existence that has no direction or greater meaning.

In an effort to blot out this vast void, these poor people have decided to fill it again with the primitive. In the dark corners and hidden clubs, the comfortable mask of civilization has been ripped away and they indulge in a feast for the senses. This new age of decadence has these creatures drowning in a wellspring of sensations, bathing in new tastes and smells. But my favorite is the glorious sense of touch. No matter where I go, there always seem to be hands reaching out to caress, to fondle, and to connect.

After centuries of covering our flesh from the tops of our heads to the soles of our feet, clothes have shrunk and become a type of second skin. In fact, I've never seen a people with a greater fascination with leather. That wonderful material has been cut, stretched, and stitched into so many amazing shapes that it can now cover every inch of the body or just the social essentials.

Upon waking with the sinking sun, I decided to go to one of my favorite haunts not far from the river. The Docks was an old, derelict building that had been converted into a nightclub. I strolled through the city streets, enjoying the warm caress of a late July breeze. The area hummed and throbbed with life. It was a Friday night and people were rushing toward one distraction or another. Weaving through the random herds of people gathered here and there, I listened to the steady cadence of my heels clicking against the cracked and dirty sidewalk, echoing up the sides of the flat brick buildings that lined the city landscape.

At the corner, I paused. I had been about to turn north when I sensed a nightwalker at Forsyth Park. This giant green space lies in the historical district, dominated by a great white fountain bathed in the glow of yellow lights. Among the various races, Forsyth was a type of demilitarized zone. Within the boundaries of the park, there was no hunting, no fighting, and no spell casting. Anyone who broke this truce forfeited his or her life. It was here that most of my kind requested meetings with me. Of course, I could ignore the request. Unfortunately, the young nightwalker's tension was thick in my thoughts and polluting the air. Such things were never good for keeping the peace.

Threading an errant lock of red hair behind my ear, I continued west to the white fountain that rose up in the center of the park. The night was thick with the scent of flowers that overflowed from their beds. Despite the ongoing drought, this favored spot was well-tended by city officials, determined to maintain its verdant perfection. The soft splash of water hitting stone danced in the air, nearly overwhelming the steady swish of cars headed toward the hot spots along River Street.

Joseph lounged on the low marble wall surrounding the fountain. His long legs were extended and crossed at the ankles. He wore a pair of dark dress slacks and a burgundy dress shirt open at the throat. Barely more than twenty years old, Joseph was still a baby among my kind. He had been a member of Riley's flock, but at least was brought over with my approval. Only recently had Riley begun creating nightwalkers with careless abandon. Since Riley's demise, Joseph stuck to the outskirts of my domain, determined to find his own way. He had also been wise enough to avoid me. I didn't tolerate the young well.

"This isn't your part of town," I said as I entered the park. He slid easily to his feet, but anxiety tightened like a rubber band in his frame. I could feel his emotions as clearly as if they were my own. Older vampires learned to shut the door of their mind. Joseph was still struggling.

To make matters worse, I had surprised him. I shouldn't have been able to, but his attention was divided at the moment. There was only one thing I could think of that would drive a fledgling vampire to seek me out: Danaus.

"The symphony lets out in a few minutes. I thought I'd visit with the blue bloods tonight," he said. He shoved his hands in his pockets, trying to affect a casual stance, but his legs were spaced wide apart, ready to run or fight.

"Running low on funds?"

Other than a slight twitch of his right eye, his bored expression never wavered. We all started out that way, a mix of bloodsucker and pickpocket. Most didn't appreciate being reminded of it. Joseph's normal hunting grounds were the narrow strip that housed most of the nightclubs as well as the scattering of bars not far from the university. Aesthetically speaking, those areas were more pleasing to the eye and generally more entertaining. Unfortunately, the college crowd wasn't the greatest source of income.

"We're not all as lucky as you," he said.

"Everything comes with a price." I strolled closer, vaguely aware of the scattering of people spread about the area. However, none were close enough to overhear our conversation. The steady rush of traffic flowing past us also kept our words muffled against the curious. I stopped before him, gazing into his hazel eyes. The gentle tug of his powers teased at my mind as he tried to enthrall me. He couldn't help it. He had not yet learned to control it. Humans would fall to his every whim, but if he encountered anything else, it would most likely rip his throat out in irritation.

I ran my left hand up his chest and was starting to wrap it around his throat when he jerked away. It was an instinctive move, showing a distinct lack of trust. I had to only arch one eyebrow at him in question before he returned to my side, tilting his head to offer up his throat. Seizing his neck, I forced him to sit back on the low wall.

"You are pressing your luck." I struggled to keep from gritting my teeth as I spoke, keeping my cool, patient facade in place for any onlookers.

"The truce," he said, reminding me needlessly that we were still standing in the park.

I smiled down at him, exposing my pearly white fangs. "The truce keeps us from fighting. It does not save you from punishment." Beneath my hand the muscles in his neck stiffened as a new fear entered his mind. His hands tightened their grip on the rim of the fountain.

The life of a nightwalker was about power and control. Those at the top of the food chain had all the power and wielded absolute control over anything below. Those weaker had to bow or be broken.

Joseph had come to me, and I needed to see a little subservience if he wanted to stay in my good graces. I wasn't the type that needed an assortment of toadies following me about. But to maintain my position as Keeper of the city, I would be feared.

"Lucky for you, I have no interest in toying with you tonight," I said. "Let's get on with business. Why have you requested this meeting?"

"They say you fought the Butcher," Joseph said.

I released his throat and slid my fingers under his chin in a gentle caress before my hand fell limp to my side. "Butcher" was what many of the young ones were calling Danaus; understandable, given that he'd carved up several of us like so much meat.

"We have met." I shrugged, ambling a few feet away, my arms swinging loosely at my side. Two couples strolled across the park, their loud laughter drifting through the open area as they headed toward any one of the several bed and breakfast hotels that surrounded the park.

"But he's still in town." The poor boy sounded so confused. He obviously expected me to either eject Danaus from my domain or kill him. That was all part of the plan, but I wasn't about to burn through such a great opportunity in one quick fight. Unfortunately, Danaus had become more of a problem that just an efficient hunter. He had come to my domain specifically looking for me. Nightwalkers aren't exactly listed in the phone book. We're notoriously difficult to locate unless you are a nightwalker yourself, or a member of our trusted inner circle. Before killing Danaus, I needed to know what he was and how he came to find me. And if I was being honest with myself, I wanted to know what he knew of the naturi. There was more to his offhand comment, considering very few even knew the name, let alone anything about the race.

Pushing those concerns aside for a moment, I turned my attention back to the fledgling. "Are you questioning my methods?" My tone came out light and innocent sounding, but Joseph was no fool.

"No! Of course not!" He lurched to his feet and hurried to my side. "I'm young. I'm still trying to learn our ways. I want to understand." He took my left hand and pressed it back to his throat, offering himself to me. Smooth, diplomatic, placating, with just a hint of humility. He was good. There was hope for him yet.

He was a few inches taller than me. Pulling him closer, I pressed a kiss to his jugular vein with my lips parted so my fangs grazed the skin. Dragging my lips up his throat and across his jaw, I deepened the kiss when I reached his lips. I ran my tongue over his fangs and for a moment my blood filled his mouth, letting him taste me. A shudder ran through his frame as I stepped away, but he did nothing to hold me there. Joseph had shown me a moment of absolute trust and for that I rewarded him.

"You may not understand our ways, but you are learning quickly," I said with an appreciative smile. I walked back to the fountain and sat down. "Has the hunter killed anyone since my meeting?"

Joseph blinked twice as if waking from a dream. "No."

"Nor will he unless provoked. His business is with me."

"Yes, Mistress," he said, bowing his head.

Rising from the fountain, I stretched my arms. "Now if you will excuse me, I seek a bit of amusement for the evening. Enjoy the symphony."

"I always do." Joseph smiled and the tips of his fangs poked from beneath his pale lips. He darted away, moving so fast that he seemed to disappear. Across town the curtain was falling and the house lights were coming up. Soon Joseph's prey would be stepping into the warm summer air and his cool embrace.

Three

I strolled toward River Street, heading slowly northwest to the Docks. The River Walk area housed the majority of the city's nightlife entertainment. For most of the year the front doors would be thrown open and the sweet sounds of jazz and blues trickled out onto the street, drawing people into the dark confines of the various bars. However, at the far western edge of the street the neighborhood turned a little darker and grittier. People shrank back into the heavy shadows that clung to the buildings and followed me with slitted, calculating eyes. They watched but never moved, as if they could sense that I was somehow *other*. Or at the very least, more than the easy prey I appeared to be.

I nodded to the large, heavily muscled man who stoically guarded the front door to the club. He nodded back, one corner of his thin mouth quirking in a half smile as he let me in ahead of the line. The Docks was one of my regular haunts, and the manager seemed to appreciate my business. Pulling my wallet from my back pocket, I grabbed a twenty and laid it on the chest-high counter as I walked in. The cover charge was only five dollars, but the little extra was part of a silent agreement that ensured the doorman wouldn't ask for my ID and they wouldn't try to put one of those silly paper wristbands on me indicating I was over twenty-one.

With a smile and a wink, I slipped my slim leather wallet into my back pocket. The entryway was open, with a scattering of tables and a large bar taking up residence against the right wall. A network of televisions hung from the ceiling, playing rare and independent music videos that no one could hear over the cacophonous roar of music tumbling from the other end of the building. A winding maze of walls and partitions blocked the main dance floor from the rest of the bar. The lighting at the front of the club was nearly nonexistent, with only the occasional spotlight and stuttering strobe cutting through the smoky haze of shadows.

Scanning the midnight crowds, I wandered toward the dance floor. Even without my powers, I would have felt the looks running up and down my body. Swathed in my typical attire of black leather pants that fit like a second skin and my matching black leather halter top that stopped at my midriff, I felt like a ghost from an SM dream. My only concession to my unnatural abilities was a pair of gold-rimmed, red-tinted glasses balanced on the bridge of my nose. My eyes had a tendency to glow in a heated moment, potentially scaring off my hard-won prey.

I was on the dance floor when I finally sensed him. Sandwiched between a pair of strong, healthy male bodies, I let the thunderous beat of the music wash over me. Their hands roamed my body, slipping from slick leather to cool flesh and back to leather. Sweat beaded on their skin and their heartbeats vibrated against my body in their own hypnotic rhythm.

And then somehow above it all, I felt a new pulse ripple through the crowd. I cracked open my eyes and scanned the darkness. Something new and strong had entered my domain. Danaus stood on the edge of the dance floor directly across from me, arms folded across his chest, legs braced wide apart, as he stared.

He was early. I knew he would seek me out, but I had guessed that it would be another night or two before our paths crossed again. I also hadn't expected him to confront me at the Docks. We couldn't try to kill each other here. Too many potential witnesses, too many people who could easily get hurt in the fight. The secret existence of nightwalkers hadn't remained intact over so many years because we fought our battles around scores of humans.

Danaus could have easily waited outside, watching for my departure—maybe this strange creature was telling the truth when he said that his goal wasn't to fight me. But I had my doubts. Unfortunately, I was still waiting for word from my contacts in Europe regarding the hunter. If someone else had information on Danaus, I could remove his head and put the whole messy business behind me. But if he represented something no one knew about, I couldn't get rid of the hunter until I had gotten a little info out of him. I would have to string him along until I heard from the Old World.

Smiling at Danaus, I leaned back into the young man who danced behind me. I lifted my left arm and lay it behind his neck, my long fingers threading through his brown hair. He put one arm around my waist, his hand grabbing my side. His warmth seeped into my body and I absorbed it like a sponge. In fact, if I spent the night on the dance floor with a man wrapped about me, I would finish the evening with a nice flush to my cheeks without ever having to feed. I could suck in their warmth, their vitality. It would give me the look of the living, but I still needed blood to sustain my existence.

When the next song started, Danaus's frown deepened. He finally caught on that I wasn't going to leave the floor just because he was lurking on the fringe. I turned my back to him as he approached, wrapping my arms around the neck of my dance partner, grinding my hips into his. Leaning into him, I ran the tip of my tongue up his neck. I had just reached his earlobe when Danaus's hand clamped on my right shoulder.

"Enough," he growled in my ear. "Come with me."

I turned my head enough to look at him over my shoulder, my eyes barely open. My wide smile had faded to one of languid pleasure. "I'm a little busy." I looked back at my dance partner and the lovely expanse of his neck when a sharp object was suddenly pressed into my back, biting through the leather halter.

"Now! I have a knife in your back and I have no problem putting it in you while on the dance floor."

"Is that the slang for it now?" I laughed. Reaching back with my right hand, I grabbed his hip. I started to slide my hand toward the front of his pants, but Danaus released his hold on my shoulder and grabbed my wandering hand. Then he thrust my hand away and turned, stalking through the crowd, which seemed eager to jump out of his way. His black leather coat flared as he walked, making me wish he wasn't wearing it. It would have made watching him storm off more enjoyable.

Curiosity demanded that I follow. I had to know what would make this man follow me not only to this lonely ring of the Inferno, but out onto the dance floor. What would make a vampire hunter seek me out for anything other than to kill me? I leaned back into my dance partner, running my tongue over the pulse throbbing against the surface of his skin, promising myself I would find this tasty little bit later.

I strolled off the dance floor, my arms swaying at my sides. My gaze casually traveled over the pockets of people gathered along the black walls and in remote corners. Some looked up, their eyes following me as I passed, but most seemed oblivious to my presence, lost to whatever escape they had sought for the evening. I paused for a moment when I entered the bar area at the front of the club, wondering where my little stalker had disappeared to, when I felt him just behind my shoulder. Turning, I found him sitting on a bench against the wall. He leaned back, one hand resting on the table while the other lay on his upper thigh, inches from where I guessed a knife was sheathed near his waist.

Biting my lower lip to keep from smiling, I walked over, placed a knee on either side of his hips and sat in his lap. If he could have jumped up, I believe he would have been hanging from the ceiling in his attempt to be free of me. But all he could manage was sitting up a little straighter, his back pressed into the wall as if he wished to merge with the wood and gypsum.

"Did I interrupt dinner?" His low voice rumbled up from his chest. His teeth were clenched and the muscles in his jaw strained against his skin. Narrowed blue eyes glittered at me, catching the pulsing white light that tripped from the dance floor.

"No, just an appetizer, as it were. Have you come to offer me a warm meal?" I asked, wrapping my arms loosely around his shoulders. He remained silent, staring at a point somewhere behind me. I leaned forward and lay my head on his shoulder, touching the tip of my nose to his throat. "I'm so glad to see that you managed to escape without being singed too badly."

"Get off."

It was a struggle to keep from saying the first crude thing that came to mind, but I finally succeeded. "I can't. The music is too loud in here. We'd never hear each other speaking if I moved away." I sat up so I could look into his face.

His eyes narrowed at me, his muscles stiffening. "You could hear me from across the room if you wanted."

"But could you hear me?"

His lips pressed into a tight, thin line of anger and frustration. What could he do? I honestly wondered. I sat here in his lap, with his aura wrapped around me like a fleece blanket. What could he do with all this strength and power? Of course, he wasn't going to volunteer the information.

The soft throb of power washing over me felt all wrong for the typical rabble of witch or warlock. And a warlock wouldn't rely on a sword when hunting nightwalkers when he could use magic. Lycanthrope? Maybe. He didn't have the same rich earthy scent as most weres, or their amazing strength, but he definitely had their speed and agility. I mentally shrugged. The quandary would be nice to figure out, but it wouldn't stop me from killing him.

"What do you know about the naturi?" he asked.

My thoughts were a sudden train wreck, ideas and images lying broken and derailed. I stared motionless at him for a long time, my mind unable to fathom why he would bring up such a topic. While few knew of the existence of nightwalkers, even fewer knew that the naturi actually lived and breathed. The other races had spent countless years wiping away all accounts of their existence. Of course, some tales had become embedded in the human psyche, which we could not destroy. From the naturi grew the stories of elves, fairies, and many other magical creatures that could not be explained away with the cold, hard logic of science.

But the naturi weren't the only ones we attempted to erase from history. After humans were created, the old stories stated that the gods created two guardian races to maintain the balance. The naturi were guardians of the earth, while the bori were guardians of all souls. The naturi existed in five clans—water, earth, animal, wind, and light.

On the other hand, the bori existed as a single clan with their own dark side, as they worked to become the one dominant power on the earth. From the bori, the legends of demons and angels were born.

Unfortunately, the powers and strength of the two races were dependent upon what they protected. As humanity flourished, the earth weakened. So the wars started.

"Sorry," I said. "I don't know what you're talking about." No one talked about the naturi. They were gone, for the most part, banished centuries ago to another reality, similar and forever linked to this world, but always locked away, hopefully.

"The naturi; guardians of the earth. Sometimes referred to as the Third Race, the Seelie Court—the Sidhe," he corrected.

"They're nothing more than fairy tales." I leaned back down so I could rest my head on his shoulder while I ran my fingers through his dark hair. It was softer than I had initially expected, almost silky in texture. "Where do you come from?" I whispered in his ear.

He was silent for a minute, and I listened to the sound of his breath slowly enter and leave his chest. "Rome."

"It's been years since I was in Rome. Boniface IX had just been named Pope. Beautiful city, even before Michelangelo painted the Sistine Chapel. Have you seen it?"

"The Sistine Chapel? Yes."

"Is it as lovely as they say?"

"Better."

"I guessed as much." The Sistine Chapel was one of the many things that I would never see. Whether I believed in a one great God didn't matter in the grand scheme of things. I could never step foot into a church. Trust me, I've tried—it was like running into a brick wall.

"Tell me about the naturi, Mira." His voice softened for the first time to something less than a growl. It wasn't what I would call an inviting or pleasant tone, just one not honed to an angry edge. His right hand settled on my left knee for a moment before falling back to the bench, but the brief touch was enough to send a wave of heat through my leather pants. I pulled away from him so I could look him in the face, my eyebrows bunched over the bridge of my nose in surprise. It was the first time he had used my name.

"So you know about the naturi; bully for you," I said. The topic of conversation was beginning to grate on my nerves. "Vampires too much of a challenge for you, so you thought you'd go after a naturi or two?" The taunt was childish, but I didn't want to think about the naturi, let alone talk about them. I wanted to forget about that whole horrible race. A part of me wanted to get up and return to the dance floor, to drown in the warm flesh and let the angry grind of music pull me under.

"Tell me."

"Tell you what?" I snapped, but quickly got my voice back under control. "They were here, but now they are gone. That's it."

The naturi wanted nothing more than to rid the entire earth of all humans and nightwalkers. For them, protecting the earth was only possible through removing its greatest threat—mankind. But it was more than that. I had my own painful past with the naturi, memories overflowing with pain and white-gray stones splashed with my blood in the fading moonlight. And worse yet, a return of the naturi held whispers of a potential return of the bori. A tug-of-war that offered no victory. For nightwalkers, the naturi represented extinction, while the bori represented an eternity of slavery. The naturi and the bori had to remain in exile, never to be spoken of.

With his right hand, Danaus reached into the interior pocket on the left side of his jacket and pulled out a sheaf of papers. He dropped the pile on the table behind me. I twisted in his lap to look at what turned out to be a pile of high gloss, color pictures. My whole body reflexively stiffened and what little warmth I had gained on the dance floor flowed out of my body, leaving a sharp chill to bite at my tensed muscles.

I reached out, forcing myself to touch the top picture. With a little pressure, the pictures spread out across the scarred tabletop. They were all of trees with symbols carved deep into their bark. My eyes skimmed over them, vaguely noting that each curling symbol was etched into a different type of tree. It was the language of the naturi. I couldn't read it or speak it, but I had seen enough to know that I would never forget it.

A knot in my stomach tightened and I fervently hoped I wouldn't vomit in the mix of fear and horror that was replacing the blood in my veins. Somehow I managed to keep my expression bland and noncommittal, but that's what nightwalkers did. We kept everything hidden beneath a mask of boredom and beauty. Danaus was watching me, peering deep, as if trying to read my thoughts.

"Trees. Nice, but not exactly my thing," I said, proud of the fact that my voice didn't crack. "I don't know why you sought me out. I don't know anything about the naturi or trees." With one hand braced on the wall to the right of his head, I slowly unfolded my body from around his and stood. Turning my back to him, I started to walk away. I needed to leave and wash down the terrible memories with blood.

Out of the corner of my eye I saw Danaus rise, his left hand locking around my wrist. "What about this?" There was an ominous thunk on the wooden table beside me. Something in me screamed, *Run*. All the survival instincts left in my brain were screaming for me to keep going, but I had to know.

In the center of the table, piercing the pile of pictures,

was a dagger. It was a unique dagger—one I was sure no living human had ever set eyes upon it. Slim and slightly curved, the silver blade straightened an inch before the tip. It was designed this way so it slid nicely into the body and at the same time caused the most amount of damage when worked around the vital organs. On one side of the blade, symbols similar to the ones in the pictures were etched into the metal. The handle was wood, stained dark from the blood that had soaked in over the years.

I knew that blade. Not just its type, but that particular blade. The metal shiv had sliced sinew and carved hunks of flesh from my body. I'd spent seemingly endless hours developing an intimate knowledge of that blade and the many-faceted layers of pain it could cause.

I spun and grabbed Danaus's shirt below the collar, slamming him into the wall. The hunter grunted. "Where did you get that?" My fangs peeked out from beneath my drawn lips. I'd drain him to the very edge of death that second in order to get my answers.

Around us, people scrambled away, trying to keep a safe distance and yet still be able to glean something from our conversation. It had to be a strange sight. A woman was pushing around a man twice her weight and size like a rag doll, while a dagger stood straight and tall in the table beside them. They would have paid less attention if I'd just pulled out a gun and shot him.

"From a naturi," Danaus said. His voice was calm and even, completely unshaken by my explosion of temper.

"What naturi?" My grip on his shirt tightened and I was vaguely aware of the fact that he had released my wrist. He could have been going for another knife, but at that moment I don't think I would have felt it even if he had buried the blade straight into my heart.

"Nerian."

"You lie," I snarled, slamming him into the wall a second time. Desperation was starting to crowd my thoughts. No one could have told him of Nerian except for a select few, who would have killed him on sight. "He's dead."

"Not yet."

"Where?"

For the first time, a cold smile lifted his lips, revealing a hint of white teeth. His eyes danced with a dark light that almost made me growl.

"I'll crush you now, Danaus. Tell me where he is!"

He stared at me for a long time, obviously enjoying the fact that the tables had been turned and I was at his mercy. "I'll take you to where I have him," he said at last.

I released him suddenly, as if he had burst into flames. He had Nerian? How? It didn't seem possible. It had to be some elaborate trick.

Stepping away from him, my eyes swept over the crowd. Everyone scurried out of my line of sight, returning to his or her conversation. Their world had shuddered to a stop for a moment and stood balanced on the edge of a knife. But with a jerk it all started again, and they banished what they thought they'd seen. They weren't ready for my kind and all the others lurking in the shadows.

It was coming, I knew that. And if Nerian was still alive, it might be sooner than I'd originally thought. Of course, if Nerian were still alive, I had to wonder if I would live to see mankind's Great Awakening.

Beside me, Danaus pulled the dagger from the table and slipped it back into a sheath on his left hip. His nimble fingers swept over the table, gathering the pictures into a single pile. As he placed them back into the interior pocket of his coat, I looked toward the dance floor. One of my favorite songs had started, the lead singer promising that he would not let me fall apart. His low, whispered cry settled my nerves and I reluctantly smiled. I had often toyed with the idea of seeking out this human, with his raw emotions set loose for all the world to see. But I had learned the hard way that my kind often had an ill influence upon the artists of the world, and I liked his music the way it was. Tonight I would take his promise with me as I visited an old shade from Hell.

FOUR

The night air was thick and still, as if the city held its breath, waiting for something else dark and creepy to slip from the shadows. I stepped outside the Docks, resisting the urge to roll my shoulders and relax the tension from my body. There were a lot of questions hovering in the silence and no answers. Like how the hell did Danaus capture Nerian? The naturi fought to the death, and had no intention of ever being held captive. Was Nerian using Danaus to get to me? The hunter didn't strike me as the type to serve anyone's purpose but his own.

I tried to keep from frowning as I followed him down the street into an even darker part of town. Through the trash-cluttered and crumbling streets, we angled north, trudging farther from the heart of the city and tidy parks. The street lamps were fewer and spaced wider apart here. The houses sagged, almost leaning into each other as they sought support under the weight of years of neglect. It was only a couple hours after midnight, but the streets were deserted.

We were a few blocks from the club when I stopped. Danaus halted beside me, his hand sliding up to his waist near one of his sheathed knives.

"You pull that naturi dagger and I'll rip your arm off." Each word squeezed past my clenched teeth. Out of the corner of my eye I saw him give a quick nod before his hand shifted to the small of his back. "We're being followed."

I had sensed the poor fool when we left the club, but didn't stop until the nightwalker closed the distance significantly. No one else needed to know about the naturi just yet. I wanted to determine for myself what was going on and how bad the damage was before word spread. There were still a few naturi wandering around, lurking in the forests and jungles of the world, keeping far from humanity when possible. No reason to start a panic when this could be nothing more than a random sighting.

Not wanting to waste any more valuable time, I stretched out my senses. The power washed through the buildings, sending back slight vibrations of the people lying huddled in their beds. Throughout the city, I could feel the other nightwalkers in the midst of their nightly activities. For a breath, they paused at the slight touch of magic, then returned to their amusements. They knew I wasn't searching for them.

The second I located my prey, he sprang. He crossed the remaining two blocks between us in a heartbeat. I had opened my mouth to warn Danaus but it was already too late. The vampire was a blur of shadow and gritty color as he pounced on the hunter.

Danaus hit the ground but used his momentum to fling the vampire off him as he rolled back to his feet. The blond vampire regained his feet and would have attacked again if I had not stepped between the two combatants. I didn't have the time or patience for this nonsense. First Joseph muddled up my night, and now Lucas—I had more important problems on my plate at the moment.

"Stop!" I shouted, holding up my hands to keep the two creatures apart. Lucas glared at Danaus before straightening from his half crouched position and looking at me with a smug expression. My fingers twitched and closed into a tight ball as my hands dropped back to my sides. I longed to knock the look from his face.

Lucas stood at roughly five feet three inches, with blond hair that curled loosely around his ears and jaw. With his slim figure and soft features, there was something almost feminine and delicate about him. But this angelic guise was ruined by the cold cruelty he could not keep from his Nordic blue eyes.

"So, the rumors are true," he said with ill-concealed amusement, unable to keep his smile from widening to reveal fangs. "You've abandoned your own kind for the hunter."

Damn, the grapevine was fast among vampires. But then again, we were telepathic. I should have expected this. Every nightwalker in the city knew of my confrontation with Danaus. I had enjoyed it too much to not share flashes of the encounter with my kind, letting them savor the emotions and the violence like a fine wine. Yet, two nights had passed since that introduction, and many of the young ones were surprised to find the hunter walking the streets of the city. I had been waiting for more information from the Old World before killing him, having learned to be cautious over the years. Information was its own power, and held more value than a quick snap of the neck when all was said and done.

Furthermore, I'd watched Danaus long enough to know that he had enough of a sense of honor not to hunt further in my domain until our business was completed.

A weary sigh escaped me as my shoulders slumped. "You're mad."

"Then stand aside and let me enjoy my kill," he said, making it sound like we were arguing over who got the last piece of chocolate cake.

"He belongs to me. His life is mine to enjoy when I so

choose." My voice hardened to the cold, hard edge of tempered steel. I took a step toward the vampire, but he held his ground, the smile crumbling from his face. Lucas was always a bit of a fool. "The other nightwalkers of this city know not to touch him unless he attacks first. And you can't kill him. If I didn't have more pressing matters, I would stand aside and let him cut your heart out."

I was standing so close our noses nearly touched. In my boots, I was four inches taller than him, just enough for me to look down at him. Lucas's eyes darkened with anger, his irises expanding, nearly blotting out the pale blue of his eyes. A ripple of his power washed through me like a cool breeze and remained trembling in the air. I had nothing to fear. This blond-haired monster with the angelic face was only a few centuries old and had more ego than real strength.

"Why are you here?" I demanded when he finally took a step back.

"I was sent to check on you," Lucas said. The smug smile returned to his lips, while his irises shrank to let the sky slip back into his eyes.

"Why haven't you presented yourself before now? You've been in my city for more than a week."

He gave an indifferent shrug of his shoulders as he slipped his hands into the pockets of his black slacks. "I am the Companion of Macaire. I go where I please."

I crossed the distance in a single step and grabbed the front of his red silk shirt, twisting it slightly around my fist so I could be sure I had a good grip on him. A bubble of laughter nearly escaped me when I saw the brief look of surprise that flooded his handsome features before I threw him across the street and into a dark alley. I wandered across the street, following the sound of the metal trash cans colliding with Lucas. He had just picked himself up off the ground, a low growl rumbling from the back of this throat at the sight of me. He roughly brushed bits of trash and rotting food off his slacks.

It was a while since I'd had the opportunity to fight something that could take a good beating. Danaus had been fun, but extremely brief. Lucas, on the other hand, could go a few rounds and still come back for more.

The vampire lunged at me, his fingers out like claws. I caught him by the throat with one hand and slammed him into one of the brick walls that lined the alley. Behind me, Danaus entered the alley, his footsteps nearly silent on the trash-strewn concrete. Under normal circumstances I would have worked Lucas over until he was nothing more than a quivering ball of raw flesh in the corner. Unfortunately, I had other tasks to complete tonight. Naturi business and preserving the secret always came first.

"I don't care if you are the newest toady for Macaire. I am still Keeper of this domain and you will give me my due." I raised my free left hand, cupping it slightly with fingers spread. My pale flesh was bathed in the glow of dancing blue flames.

Lucas immediately began to struggle, shrinking away from the fire as his fingers clawed my hand holding his throat. *"Per favore, Mira! Mia signora!"* he said, unconsciously slipping into Italian. Lucas wasn't Italian. I hadn't a clue as to what he was other than his slight accent, which seemed vaguely Slavic. However, the Coven was based in Italy, and eventually all nightwalkers learned to beg in Italian. "I—I was sent by the Elders. They're concerned."

"About what?" I asked. Did they know about the symbols as well? A sick fear twisted in my chest. Coming to the attention of Ancients was never an enjoyable experience.

"The humans—they're beginning to ask too many questions."

"They've always asked questions. That hasn't changed."

Mankind had speculated about the existence of nightwalkers for centuries, but never truly believed the tales to be true.

"But they have proof now," he said, falling back into English.

An uneasy feeling added to the weight of my earlier fears and I went still. "Proof? How?"

"Bodies were found in California two nights ago, and another in Texas last week."

"I heard."

"The Daylight Coalition is claiming it's proof that we exist."

"They're just a fringe group." I extinguished the flame from my hand but didn't release Lucas. "No one believes them. The police claimed it was a hoax."

"It doesn't matter. They are winning over more followers. The number of hunters has more than doubled during the past few decades. The Elders think we're running out of time."

"So why come here?"

Lucas stopped trying to pry my fingers loose and went still. "They want to know who left the bodies. You're one of the oldest in the New World."

"I didn't come here to babysit, nor will I clean up after every kill." My grip on his throat tightened and I leaned closer. "I don't know who made the mess." Releasing him, I paced over to the other brick wall in the narrow alley. There were already more pressing matters on my mind. I didn't need to worry about the Elders and their flunkies invading my territory.

"They will find out who has caused this ripple among the humans." Lucas said. "If he or she is still in the New World, it will be your job to mete out the punishment." His hand absently rubbed his throat.

"I do not jump for the Elders." But even I knew that statement was only partially true. I was stronger than most night-walkers my age, and it was more than just my ability to use fire, though that unique gift kept many at a distance. I had destroyed more than my fair share of Ancients, earned every bit of my dark reputation through centuries washed in blood and death.

I didn't feel the need to jump for the Elders, because of Jabari. He acted as a buffer between me and the rest of the Coven, giving me my freedom. The oldest and most power-ful member of the Coven, Jabari had earned my unwavering loyalty. He had only to ask and I would perform nearly any task for him. But Jabari was missing now, my buffer gone.

"You will obey if you wish to keep your domain and your life," Lucas said, his eyes narrowing to thin slits.

I stared at him, willing myself not to rip his head off. He was a pathetic creature. Less than three hundred years old, I knew he probably wouldn't survive to see another century. Those who served as Companions to the Elders rarely lived long lives, but the reward during those short years was the ability to bask in the amazing power the Elders wielded. Once you were selected as a Companion, other nightwalk-ers could not touch you without risking the wrath of the El-der. Of course, if you failed your caretaker, which inevitably happened, your existence was forfeit. And from what I'd heard, your death was always slow and painful.

"Leave here, Lucas. Return to your master and tell him what you have found."

"Like your defense of the hunter?" His gaze flicked over to Danaus at the mouth of the alley then back to me.

"Like how I spared your life," I said with a smile that was all fangs and menace. "You've delivered your message. Be gone before the sun touches the earth or I shall introduce you to a whole new realm of pain."

Lucas glared at me for another second before turning and

walking down the alley, back toward the street. I watched him go, his body nearly brushing against Danaus, who didn't flinch. A vampire like Lucas was easy prey for Danaus and not worth such worries. Of course, Lucas was also the mouthpiece for something much larger and scarier.

From the entrance to the alley, Lucas turned back to look at me. "The Elders are not the only ones concerned. The others are watching as well," he called, then disappeared into the night.

"Shit," I whispered into the darkness when I was sure Lucas couldn't hear me. I had enough to worry about without having the Elders and all the others breathing down my neck. I doubted Macaire would come after me for roughing up Lucas, but I certainly didn't need to be on his bad side if the Elders suddenly decided to hand over a sacrificial lamb to the humans.

In the nightwalker hierarchy, we kept things simple. The top dog was Our Liege, who ruled all nightwalkers. Below him was the Coven, which consisted of four Elders. Below the Coven, it was just whoever was the strongest and the smartest. Of course, Ancients—any vampire more than one thousand years old—were their own special bundle of trouble. And I was asking for trouble.

It was one thing to talk big while standing in a dark alley in my own domain, but I had never faced all of the Elders at once. I had maintained a comfortable distance from the group. I'm sure some of my actions caught their notice and made them frown on more than one occasion, but I'd done nothing to endanger our secret.

Unfortunately, on more than one occasion I had flaunted my total disregard and general lack of subservience for the group. So far they'd let it slide, and I knew I had Jabari to thank for it. Yet, if things started to get out of hand here in the New World, the Elders would use it as an opportunity to either bring me to heel or serve my head up to the humans.

I saw Danaus put his dagger back in its sheath in the small of his back. Of course, this creature was yet another problem to figure out before I had the Ancients on my soil.

"Nerian," he said in his usual deep growl.

And back to the more pressing of the problems. Lucas and the Elders could wait. So could Danaus's death.

Five

My teeth were clenched when my gaze fell on the two-story house with the peeling, pale blue paint three blocks from where we encountered Lucas. I frequently hunted in this part of town. The inhabitants here struggled to eke out a living, and the air smelled thick of sweat and despair. Their lives were simple and harsh, with hopes that stretched no further than thoughts of food and warmth. Not so different than the village where I'd been born more than six centuries ago.

The street lamps at the top and the bottom of the road were out. Danaus had most likely seen to the darkness when he moved in. Thick, velvety night oozed around the houses and filled the street like heavy tar, making it easier to slip in and out of the neighborhood without being noticed.

A light breeze stirred from the south, rustling leaves on a sickly scattering of trees. The harsh, dry summer left them covered in only thin foliage that had already begun to brown. Most of the broken-down houses crowded on the street were dark except for a handful that leaked a blue glow thrown down by television sets. A high-pitched whine stole down the block as the wind blew open the gate of a sagging chain-link fence.

As I mounted the crumbling stone steps, I reached out again with my powers, running my senses through every inch of the house. Danaus was the only other creature I could pick up. Unfortunately, I couldn't sense the naturi. I could be walking into a house full of them and wouldn't know it until the dagger was already in my back.

The hunter looked back at me, his hand on the doorknob. He felt me use my powers as well.

"Open it," I said with a nod of my head, relieved that my voice didn't betray my concern. For all the world, I sounded as if I was actually looking forward to seeing Nerian, like a reunion of old friends. Hardly. My only hope was that I didn't kill him on sight, but I had serious doubts as to whether that was a realistic thought.

Danaus pushed open the door, which moaned in angry protest. The hunter stepped inside first and moved so I could follow while he closed the door. Once inside, I turned to face him, keeping my back to the wall. I didn't trust him or this situation. With his hands open at his sides, he walked in front of me down the main hall. The floorboards creaked and screamed under the weight of our footsteps. The walls were cracked and crumbling, and the scent of some long-dead animal lingered in the air. A dark staircase ran along the left side of the hall, leading to a silent second floor.

Stopping halfway down the hall, Danaus pulled open a door under the staircase. He flipped on a light, revealing a set of plain wooden stairs that led into the basement. I was surprised. Most homes in Savannah didn't have basements, due to the height of the water table. I had one in my own home, but it was added at great expense. Of course, underground was the only safe place to be during the daylight hours.

A single bare bulb dangled from the ceiling above the

stairs, fighting to push aside the shadows that inhabited the dark corners of the subterranean room. I followed him down the stairs, my heels echoing like gunshots off the wood. Neither of us was trying to be quiet. The scent of blood on the damp air brought me to a sharp halt on the landing. It was the first bit of proof that someone else was in the house, but I still couldn't sense anyone. I continued down the stairs, my eyes quickly scanning the room.

The walls were made of gray concrete, covered in a spiderweb of cracks and fissures that now leaked water from the ground outside. The floor was the same cold concrete. It was completely empty except for a furnace squatting in the far corner and a network of pipes and wires overhead. The air was musty and damp, filled with mold and the faint tang of blood.

It took me a couple seconds to actually see the hunched form. Maybe it was because my mind didn't want to see him, didn't want to know that he actually was still alive. But once I did see him, rage flooded my senses, blotting out all rational thought. The muscles in my body involuntarily clenched and knotted as if I'd been hit. When I looked at Nerian, I didn't see him standing against the wall, his wrists and ankles chained in iron manacles. I saw him standing over me more than five centuries ago, with that dagger covered in my blood. I heard him laughing in my mind and my scream.

And then I realized I really was screaming. I kept screaming, clamping my hands over my ears as I tried to push the memories from my mind. The sound only stopped when the rawness of my torn throat finally overcame the images. The silent night air had been shattered by the wretched sound and was left cringing in some dark corner.

I blinked, my screams still echoing in my brain. Both Danaus and the naturi were staring at me. Nerian was smiling with that same horrible smile, basking in my pain.

"You remember me!" he exclaimed. He tossed his head back and laughed, the sound somehow managing to be both musical and maniacal at the same time. I shivered, clenching my teeth against the sound as a fresh onslaught of memories danced through my brain. My knees turned to jelly and for a moment I thought I would fall, but the wave passed.

"Thank you, human," Nerian continued. "Seeing this parasite again is a real treat. Though I'm surprised she had the sense to stay alive this long. But even cockroaches are known for their resilience."

"I see you managed to pull yourself back together," I said. My voice was choked and rough, failing miserably to portray my usual bravado. I finally descended the last couple of wooden stairs and stood in the basement. "I imagine it was difficult to get your intestines back inside your skin."

At Machu Picchu so many years ago, Jabari had given me the gift of killing Nerian. We fought and I eviscerated him, leaving him curled on the ground, clutching his stomach and intestines. But the sun was rising. My own strength was failing me in the growing light. I was forced to run to find shelter before the sun finally broke above the horizon. If I had thought it was at all possible that Nerian would survive, I would have stayed and finished him, meeting my own end.

"Unshackle me and I will happily show you how difficult it was." His tone was still light and full of amusement. There was some veiled enticement lying hidden between his words as his voice tried to work a spell over my will.

"No." The silence settled back between us for a moment as my eyes ran over his blood-encrusted wrists, battered face, and stained clothes. "I think I like you better this way; trapped by a human."

Nerian was of the animal clan, resulting in his shaggy mane of brown hair and the hard, aggressive bone structure of his face. His vibrant green eyes were vertically slitted, like that of a cat. The iron manacles were the only thing keeping him from calling for assistance from any other naturi or animals. The old tales of iron and its harmful effect on the fey were actually true. It kept the naturi from performing any kind of magic.

His taunting smile crumbled from his face. "Hardly a fair fight."

"What do the naturi know of fair?"

"What do we care of fairness when dealing with vermin?" His voice had changed from one of enticement to that of a cold, hard glacier. "Both vampires and humans are beneath contempt. You should never have survived so long, but at least humans have their uses. Vampires are just parasites."

With my teeth clenched and fists at my sides, I closed the distance between Nerian and myself. I felt more than saw Danaus take up a position behind my right shoulder. His arms were folded over his chest, his legs spread wide.

I stared at Nerian, only inches between us. In all this time, he hadn't changed. Yet, it felt like something should have been different. He should have been scarred in some way. When I'd last seen him, both his legs were broken and he was struggling to keep his intestines in his body. I had left him for dead. He should be dead. But instead he stood before me, his wrists bloody from pulling against the iron manacles. His brown leather jerkin was splattered with blood. His sharp, wide face was smudged with dirt and blood, his thick brown hair dirty and matted. And still he smiled at me, dark amusement glinting in his green eyes.

I don't know how long we stood there staring at each other. It could have been hours or seconds. Time had become a thing that existed outside this small, damp basement, twisting and contorting into something I no longer recognized.

"Has the seal been broken?" I demanded at last. I had

no more energy for verbal sparring with him. My voice sounded rough, as if it had been dragged along the lower levels of Hell before finally reaching my ears.

I didn't think it was possible, but his smile widened, revealing a perfect set of white teeth. "Rowe has spoken with the sun," he said in a lyrical voice. Without words, it whispered of clear streams and green woods. That voice had bewitched scores before the slaughter. "The dawn is coming."

There was no clear thought after that. My body throbbed with rage and all I felt was anger and fear. Enough fear that I could taste it in the back of my throat. Enough that I was drowning in it. A kaleidoscope of brutal memories flashed through my brain. The naturi held me captive for two weeks at Machu Picchu, torturing me each night until I finally escaped consciousness with the rising sun. Their hope had been to wear me down until I agreed to serve them as a weapon against the nightwalkers. They wanted me for protection as they opened the door between the two worlds, freeing the rest of their kind. But I knew they could never be free. It would mean the destruction of everything I loved.

My hand shot out and closed around his throat, squeezing until I felt my fingernails tear through skin and muscle. I squeezed until my hand was filled with his warm flesh, and then I pulled. He gave one last gasp as his throat was ripped from his body. I dropped the squishy clump of flesh at my side, but chunks of it remained buried under my nails. I stood there, letting his warm blood spray over my face and shoulders, closed my eyes as the blood ran down my arms and coated my bare stomach. A scream rose up in my throat again, but I stood silent, listening to the gurgling sounds he made as he struggled to breathe without an esophagus.

When I could no longer feel his blood raining on me, I opened my eyes. Nerian sagged forward, held up by his arms, which were still chained to the wall. His head had fallen against his chest and his body was now covered in blood. Stepping back, my mind stumbled out of the blinding haze of anger. I could taste his blood in my mouth, and a part of me panicked. Naturi blood was poisonous to nightwalkers. I spit and raised my arm to wipe it off my lips, but my arm was covered with his blood as well. A little taste wouldn't kill me, but it was enough to send an anxious chill through me. It didn't taste like other blood. It was more bitter and unnatural.

Turning, I suddenly found myself facing Danaus. For a moment I had forgotten he was there. He stood in a crouch, the naturi dagger in his hand. I don't know if he'd purposefully drawn that dagger or instinctively reacted when I tore out Nerian's throat. It didn't matter. My emotions were still too raw and violent for me to think clearly. I lunged at him, my hands going for the dagger. He swung it at me, causing me to jerk backward. Screaming, I slashed and kicked wildly. There was no holding back anymore. I wanted death; his, and maybe even mine. Anything so I could be free of Nerian's smile. Backing Danaus against the wall, I finally kicked the dagger free. It spun through the air and crashed against the cinder-block wall.

The monstrous piece of metal held me in its bloody thrall, and I had to be rid of it . . . for good. I turned my back on Danaus, heedlessly, and stalked over to the blade. With my right hand, I threw a ball of blue fire at it. I encased the dagger in flames hot enough to cause the cement to sizzle and pop. The room grew uncomfortably hot, but I poured all my anger and hatred into the fire, willing the metal to bend and melt.

Exhausted, I sank to my knees, extinguishing the blaze. Then I stared at the naturi blade and started to laugh, high-pitched and a little mad. The blade was completely untouched. For a moment the metal had glowed red, but it was unchanged. I could do nothing to it. The charms on the blade would keep it from ever rusting, chipping, or melting. As long as the naturi existed, so would this blade.

Turning my head, I narrowed my gaze on Nerian. I might not be able to get rid of the dagger, but I could wipe his existence off the earth. Instantly, his body became engulfed in beautiful yellow and orange flames. The stench of burning flesh and hair filled the air, but I didn't care. I kept the flames on him until the body crumbled to a small heap of white ash on the floor. The smoke filtered up through the warped boards of the ceiling to fill the upper part of the house. I didn't care if anyone noticed. I'd be gone from this place soon enough.

Nerian was gone, but his memory would never leave me. For the first time in centuries I longed for Jabari. He had saved me from Nerian and his kind once. He had helped to keep the horrid memories at bay. Now I longed for the feel of his strong arms around me and his calm, cool presence in my brain, cradling my thoughts.

But Jabari was gone; dead or just absent, I didn't know. It also didn't matter. Nerian was dead at last. I had stood on my own two feet for more than four centuries. I would continue to do so no matter how weary I became.

The sound of a foot scraping along the cold concrete floor drew my attention back to Danaus. Gazing at him over my shoulder, a soft sigh rose from me. I felt a little freer than I'd been in a long time. A ghost had been sent back to Hell where it belonged; where I knew it would wait for me. But that wasn't now.

I was more than a little surprised that Danaus had not tried to kill me when I attacked him. He'd defended himself, but nothing more. He had not needed me to kill Nerian for him; the naturi was at his mercy. To keep me alive, Danaus must have still needed something from me. However, I was coming up with fewer reasons to leave the hunter alive. Right now I only needed to know how he captured Nerian and if there were any more naturi.

"What do you know of the naturi?" I inquired, turning to face him. I held up my right hand and a small yellow flame danced on the palm.

Danaus stood against the far wall, a bead of sweat running from his temple down along his hard jaw. His dark blue eyes were narrowed in the faint light. With his right hand, he grabbed the right side of his leather coat and held it open. He reached over with his left hand and pulled a folded piece of paper from the interior pocket. With a flick of his wrist, he sent the paper across the room, to land less than a foot away from me. Extinguishing the flame, I leaned forward and picked up the paper. It was another high-gloss, color picture.

This one was distinctly different from the others. It was of a woman lying naked on reddish-brown paving stones. Her arms were thrown over her head. The skin on her chest had been peeled back and all of her organs removed. The little piles of black ash around the body had been her various pieces. Her blood pooled beneath her, but on the ground several feet away from her, symbols similar to the ones carved into the trees were drawn with her blood. Her face had been turned toward the camera, her mouth forever frozen in a scream that no one would ever hear. She had been alive during the ceremony. I imagine she was kept alive and lucid right up until her heart had been removed.

"When?" The single word floated through the room like a white wraith. The momentary peace I'd found with Nerian's death had shriveled up in the pit of my stomach.

"Three months ago, night of the new moon."

I nodded. I understood enough about magic to know that you started new magic under the new moon for the maximum potency. The full moon was used for breaking old spells, curses, and for binding. The naturi were just getting started.

"Where?"

"Konark."

My head snapped up, eyes locking on his grim features. The muscles in my body clenched painfully. "Where?"

"Konark. The Sun Temple in Orissa, India."

"I know it's in India," I said irritably, straightening up. My brain was struggling to take in this information. They had started making the necessary sacrifices in order to break the seal and open the door between the worlds. There were twelve sacred locations scattered around the world that could hold enough power for the naturi to perform the necessary spells. But how could they be doing this now? It didn't make sense. It had been roughly five hundred years since they had last attempted this. Why now?

"There will be more," Danaus said. It was more of a question than a statement.

I looked up at him, weighing my options. "Two more." My earlier relief slowly leaked from my soul and I tried to organize my thoughts.

"You asked about a seal. What did you mean?"

My gaze fell to the floor for a moment as I thought back to the stories my maker, Sadira, and my beloved Jabari had told me. My own memories of Machu Picchu were sketchy and fragmented, but I knew the old "ghost stories." I'd read our histories and the journals written by other nightwalkers detailing all we knew of the naturi.

"Centuries ago, before my time, before the time of any nightwalker that still exists, the naturi lived on Earth. Vampires forced them to another world. One that was similar and connected to this world, but different. A nightwalker triad closed the door and fashioned a seal on this side to bar them from returning. It's like an elaborate magical lock."

"So, the seal has to be protected."

"That's only part of it. The naturi have other locations they can use to make the other two sacrifices. We have no idea where and when they will strike."

"I might."

Wiping off a drop of blood that was running down my cheek, I narrowed my eyes at Danaus. "How?"

"I am part of a large organization, spread around the globe. We will know if something is happening." The hunter dropped his hands into the pockets of his leather duster, a faint smile tugging at the right corner of his mouth.

"Like you knew about Konark? Or the symbols on the trees?"

The would-be smile disappeared instantly. "We didn't know we should be watching for something at the temple. We know there will be at least two more sacrifices and that they will likely happen around certain phases of the moon. We can watch for signs."

"It's more than the moon phases," I grumbled, shoving my right hand through my hair, trying to ignore that it was now cold and sticky. "They could also use seasonal holidays or even any of the holidays from the dead religions. It's hard to say when they will attempt the second sacrifice, or even where."

"But vampires are limited to only night surveillance. My people are not."

I frowned. I hated to admit it, but he did have an edge in that arena, and help in this matter was necessary. We couldn't call in the lycanthropes for daytime assistance because they would be too easily enthralled by the naturi, their former masters. And working with witches and warlocks was always sketchy at best and never particularly reliable.

"You seem to be very well informed," I said, cocking my head as I took a couple steps closer. Danaus removed his hands from his pockets and bent his frame as if preparing for an attack. "You knew of the naturi, you knew of the symbols in the trees, you knew where to find me and even some of my past."

"The organization is very well informed. We have spent many years watching your kind."

I shook my head, placing my hands on my hips. "Oh, this is more than just watching. Someone has been giving you information about nightwalkers and our world."

"We are well informed, but not strong enough to directly take on the naturi. I was sent to find someone who defeated them at Machu Picchu."

"Yes, I was at Machu Picchu, but the triad defeated the naturi."

"Where is the triad?"

I just smiled in return. Did he honestly think I was going to tell a known hunter where to find three of our most important nightwalkers? But in truth, one was already dead and a second was missing, possibly dead. I didn't have a lot of good news to offer on this front.

"I thought I had earned it. I gave you information on the symbols and the sacrifice. I also gave you Nerian," he continued, taking a step closer.

"It's a good start."

"We're also offering to watch the other sites for you."

"Mmmm . . . yes, very altruistic of you."

Danaus snorted, closing the distance between us. "I would love nothing more than to see both naturi and nightwalkers wiped from the earth. However, I realize that the naturi are the bigger threat, and we need your assistance. But you also need our help. I am offering a temporary truce. We eliminate the threat of the naturi and then we can get back to the natural order of things."

"Back to killing each other?"

A smile danced in his eyes. "Exactly."

I nodded once and took a step back from him. "I need to think about this. Meet me at Orleans Square at Hull Street and Jefferson tomorrow night at ten o'clock." I turned to leave the basement, but paused as another thought occurred to me, my right foot resting on the first stair. "Before coming, drop that in the river," I said, pointing to the naturi dagger against the opposite wall. "It will not help you."

I headed up the stairs and outside without looking back. A breeze rushed from some secret hiding place, rubbing against my body. I suppressed a shiver as it chilled the blood still coating my skin. I was a mess, but no one noticed me as I walked down the street. It was a weak entrancement spell that all nightwalkers could perform from the moment they were reborn. It worked on most, though witches, warlocks, and psychics were somewhat problematic. At that moment I really didn't care. I was covered in the blood of a naturi, something I never expected to happen again. With the exception of a few dozen left in hiding, the naturi had been wiped from the earth and sealed away.

Yet, on the silent street in the middle of my own domain, I wondered how many naturi were lurking nearby. Was there one hiding in the shadows, watching me, waiting for the opportunity to strike? Or worse, follow me back to my private lair, where he would stake me during the daylight hours? And who was this Rowe that Nerian had mentioned? Was he the one who sought to free the long-lost queen of the naturi? Too many questions . . . and there were no easy answers to be had.

But the path was clear. I had to discover who this Rowe was and stop him from making any more sacrifices. And the only way to do that was to locate the triad, or at the very least, what was left of it.

Six

My plan for the rest of the night was simple. I would return home, shower, and then hunt. I could even hunt first, and then return home to shower. I was flexible. But those plans were pitched out the window. The acrid smell of smoke tainted the air a couple blocks away, along with a rising wave of fear. This was worse than a random house fire in the early morning hours that claims the lives of the unwary. Something had stirred up the natives in an ugly way.

I ran the last blocks to the fire, to find a trio of bright red fire trucks positioned outside the Docks. Firefighters were pouring water on the flames, which were still jumping out the front door. The hoard of people standing beyond the trucks was covered in smoke and soot and blood. Women were weeping hysterically, while more than a few men were pacing, pulling at their hair in a sort of impotent rage. And others stood still, eyes staring blindly forward in numb shock, their minds refusing any further information.

This was more than just a fire cause by a carelessly dropped cigarette. I dipped into one scarred mind after another to find that several people had been murdered. Someone had come among this hardened, jaded group, cutting down people at random before setting fire to the place.

Turning my attention to the fire, I closed my eyes and quickly extinguished the flames. In a matter of a couple minutes the last tongues of fire were completely gone. It would have looked a little odd to the experienced firefighters, but no one would question their sudden good luck. I needed to get in there to find out what happened, and the fire was destroying evidence.

Pulling aside one stunned man, I convinced him to give me his shirt. Without his eyes ever drifting from the blackened building, he pulled the T-shirt over his head and handed it to me. I wiped off the naturi blood that still covered me and scanned the crowd for a familiar face. Off to one side stood Jonathan, surrounded by a small contingent of friends. His black tights were torn and his plaid skirt and white button-up blouse blackened with soot and splashed with blood. His blond wig was missing and his face was streaked with mascara-tinged tears. He would have made an attractive woman if he weren't built like a linebacker.

With the man's shirt waded up in my left hand, I walked over to Jonathan, who had been attending the Docks for years and knew all the regulars. His friends stepped aside at my approach, their lost gaze seeming to hold me for only a moment before drifting back to the building.

"Hey, Little John," I said when he looked up at me. "What happened here?"

"Oh, MiMi," he sighed, rubbing his left eye with the heel of his left hand. "There you are. They just started killing us." His voice was surprisingly soft despite his large barrel chest, but it held a mountain of sorrow.

"Who? Who did this?"

"I—I don't know," he said with a shake of his head. "I had never seen them before. Two men came in. No, it was two teenagers with long brown hair and green eyes. They were . . . they were . . . " Jonathan paused and stared straight ahead, blinking rapidly for a moment as if trying to clear his vision, or maybe just his memory. "They were looking for someone. Nathan somebody, I think. We didn't know this person, so they started—"

"It's okay," I said, taking his large hand in mine as his voice cracked. I could guess at what happened, but there was no way a pair of teenagers could cause this kind of damage and create this level of fear. Not even if they walked in with Uzis, and not once had I picked up the image of gunfire in anyone's thoughts.

There was more to this tale. I didn't think Jonathan was lying to me. His mind was just struggling to make sense of what he'd seen. Carefully, I slipped into his thoughts, reviewing his memories. Two slim, graceful figures waltzed in. Their longish blondish-brown hair fell around their faces, but I could see their almond-shaped green eyes and catch glimpses of high cheekbones. It was a safe bet that Jonathan's mind had already blurred the sight of anything else that didn't quite make sense to him. Naturi, possibly from the wind clan, from their graceful movements. However, their use of fire to consume the place made me wonder if one of them was from the light clan. If members from either of the two upper clans were out searching, this was serious.

"Nerian," I whispered.

Jonathan's hand jerked in my grasp and his gaze jumped back to my face. His brown eyes widened. "Yes, that's it. Nerian. Do you know him?"

"He's dead."

Jonathan took a step away from me, pulling his hand from my grasp. "They'll be pissed, Mira!"

"I'll handle them."

As I slipped away from Jonathan, I raised the enchantment

back around me and wiped his memory of our conversation. Weaving through the crowd of onlookers, firefighters, medical workers, and police, I slipped unnoticed into the Docks. The walls and ceiling in the main bar were blackened by the fire, but the worst of it appeared to be toward the back.

Around me, bodies were strewn about, their limbs lying at strange angles. Some had died quickly with their necks broken. Others had been stabbed and left to bleed to death. More than a dozen were killed. It appeared that after the naturi failed to get the information they wanted, they set fire to the room that held the dance floor, and several had died in the chaos and ensuing stampede.

Walking back toward the dance floor, I paused at the table Danaus and I had sat at only an hour ago. It was blackened but unburned. Around the scar in the wood from the naturi dagger, several symbols were written in blood. More symbols from the naturi language. I was willing to bet they were tracking down Nerian through the blade.

By now they would know that he was dead. If Danaus was as good as he seemed, he would be able to take care of a couple of naturi. Besides, the naturi had been gone for a while now, and the night was wasting away. The hunter was on his own.

Turning away from the table, I slowly gazed around the room. Faces I had seen on a regular basis during the past few years were being covered with white sheets. For so many, I didn't know their names or histories, but they had been a part of my domain, a part of my home. The naturi had stolen them from me.

Destruction, death, and fear; that was all the naturi had to offer both nightwalkers and humans. I knew vampires weren't a great alternative, but at least we had learned to coexist. If the seal was broken and the door opened, the naturi would reduce the world to a blackened shell much like the

Docks. From that, they would build their world, one exclusively for the naturi.

As I walked back toward the front door, the table burst into flames. No evidence could be left behind of their existence. When I returned home, I would burn the T-shirt I'd used to wipe off the naturi blood. Things were beginning to spiral out of control and it was all starting in my domain—this I would not allow. I had to make plans fast if I was going to crush the naturi once again.

Seven

The Dark Room was more than a mile south of my current location, within the confines of the Victorian District, with its elegant stained-glass windows and gingerbread trim. It was the only nightclub in the region. It was also the only nightclub that catered almost exclusively to the *other* races, and for very good reason. When the various races got together, accidents tended to happen. During my reign in Savannah, I had burned down two other incarnations of the Dark Room because of fights and human deaths. We had finally learned to play nice together, as well as come up with some rules that worked, which included allowing the lycanthropes in the club except during the week of the full moon. Humans were allowed inside, but they had to be accompanied by nightwalkers.

I quickly walked to the Dark Room, where I knew I would find Knox. Along the way, I made several calls on my cell phone, making preparations as best I could before arriving at the club. Turning the last corner, I found a long line standing outside the club, consisting mostly of humans. Two large men with black T-shirts stretched across their muscled chests guarded the front door. One was a werewolf and the other a vampire, there to make sure that both races were treated fairly and allowed into the club.

As I approached, the eyes of the nightwalker flared slightly in surprise and he stepped away from the door to let me pass. "Mira," he whispered. "It's been quiet, I swear."

I swallowed my rude comment and walked wordlessly past him and the crowd, which was now grumbling at my entrance ahead of them. Regardless of whether it rankled my nerves, I understood the bouncer's comments. The last time I'd shown up at the Dark Room, I had to dispose of two nightwalkers who broke some of the more basic rules of the club—no feeding immediately outside the club and no turning a human on the premises.

I quickly passed through the narrow hall that held two empty coat check rooms and paused before the main floor. The Dark Room was a sanctuary of decadent luxury within the city. The main floor was dimly lit with small sconces around the room, casting a thick red light. The walls were lined with deep booths partially hidden by thick velvet curtains. The center was a massive dance floor, where creatures now swayed and writhed to the low, almost hypnotic music that swelled in the air. Where the Docks had been filled with fast and hard beats that created an almost frantic need within its occupants, the Dark Room was a slow seduction of the senses. The Docks was made for humans who wanted to pretend to be dark predators; the Dark Room was made for predators who didn't want to hide what they were.

My eyes skimmed the room while I lightly reached out with my powers to search for Knox. The small bar on the left side was relatively empty, but that was normal. The only ones who ever used it were the lycanthropes and the human companions of the nightwalkers. Alcohol consumption was not what kept this place open. It was an exclusive club. All nightwalkers and lycanthropes that entered the club were on a members' list and paid annual dues. Furthermore, if they ever brought in guests, there was a second set of dues that had to be paid. Attending the Dark Room was a status symbol, a sign that you had not only achieved *other* status, but also acquired some wealth. And the more guests you brought, the more money you had.

Of course, paying your dues didn't guarantee you admittance on any given night. If the place reached capacity—which was relatively low, in an effort to avoid confrontations—you couldn't be admitted. Also, if you had recently pissed me off, you were on the no-admittance list until I said otherwise.

I stood at the entrance to the main room for only a moment before a tall, lean nightwalker stepped out of a shadowy booth and stared at me. I hadn't told Knox I was coming, so my presence at the nightclub naturally surprised him. He tilted his head to his right before turning and walking in that direction. I cut across the dance floor, weaving through the crowd, to meet him as he opened a door at the back of the building. There were several private rooms in the club that were used for feeding and other activities. However, feeding was the only thing specifically outlawed in the main room.

As I stepped past Knox, he ran an index finger down my bare arm, wiping away some of the blood I had missed. "Looks like you've had an interesting evening," he slowly drawled. "The Butcher?"

I roughly seized his wrist as he raised his finger to his mouth, halting him in the act of tasting what he assumed to be a very messy meal. "Naturi."

Knox stumbled backward from me, jerking his wrist from my grasp. He frantically wiped his hand and wrist on his dark slacks while a string of low German curses escaped him. I gave him a few moments to collect himself.

At just under six feet, Knox had a lean, narrow build, a

mix of bone and hard muscle. He was nearly two centuries old, still somewhat young, but very powerful and intelligent for his age. But that was no great surprise considering his maker. Valerio very rarely converted a human, but when he did, it was always with a great deal of care.

Knox moved into my domain less than two decades ago, and has served as my nightwalker assistant almost that long. While we had no official name for it, he served as a type of second-in-command. His mere presence helped to maintain the peace. Yet, I never used him as an enforcer. While he was more than strong enough for the task, I preferred to handle such things personally.

"The Butcher is in league with the naturi?" Knox asked when he was finally calm again.

"Actually, the naturi was a gift for me," I said with a light shrug. I turned and walked past the black leather sofa and matching chair to the far wall. Putting my back against the wall, I slid down until I was seated on the floor with my knees bent before me. I was tired and needed a few moments to think.

Knox pushed the ottoman closer to me with his foot and sat on the edge. "He comes into your domain, kills five nightwalkers, and then gives you naturi as a gift. Forgive me if I'm slow, but what the hell?"

"It's more complicated than that," I murmured, dropping the bloodstained T-shirt I'd been carrying next to me. I threaded my fingers through the thick charcoal-gray carpet that stretched through the room and helped to muffle our conversation.

"I sincerely hope so," Knox said.

Resting my head against the wall, I looked up, watching him brush some sandy blond hair from where it fell across his forehead. I had grown accustomed to his dry wit and calming influence during the past few years. It took a great deal to rattle him, but it appeared that the naturi was one of those things, given the lines of strain around his mouth. I was grateful Valerio had at least taken the time to educate Knox on that dangerous bit of history.

"I have to leave town for a while," I said, pulling my fingers into a loose fist. I hated not being here if the naturi were running around my domain, but they had to be stopped, and the answers I needed could not be found here.

"Are you leaving because of the Butcher or the naturi?"

"Both. While I am gone, spread the word that I want everyone pulled close to the city. No one is to hunt alone until I return or send word that it is safe. And do not mention the naturi. I don't want a panic."

Knox rubbed his temples and forehead with one hand, staring off into space for a moment. "This will make things . . . difficult."

I knew what he meant. While we frequently congregated at the Dark Room, nightwalkers were solitary, independent creatures by nature. Forcing vampires to stay within close proximity for an extended period of time was asking for trouble. But telling them that the naturi were close would only make matters worse.

"I hope to get this taken care of as quickly as possible. Where is Amanda?"

"Concert at SSU," Knox quickly replied, referring to Savannah State University. The college was relatively small, but frequently played host to a variety of bands, both known and unknown. The college also made for a great feeding ground for nightwalkers. "Do you want me to summon her?"

"No, talk to her after the concert, fill her in. Get her to help you keep the peace."

While they looked nothing alike, I frequently referred to them as my Doublemint Twins because they both had the same shade of blond hair. Amanda wasn't quite fifty years old, but had taken to vampirism like a fish to water, seemingly without the struggles many her age went through. I had no idea who her creator was. She had simply appeared in my domain ten years ago and seemed to instantly fit in. Of course, her sunny yet positively brutal personality won a special place in my heart. Despite her youth, she managed to keep a tight rein on some of the younger nightwalkers. If Knox was considered my second-in-command, then Amanda had managed to quietly attain a type of sergeant-at-arms position.

"What about the Butcher?"

"He will be gone from my domain before I leave." I hadn't yet decided how I would take care of the hunter, but I would not leave him here while I was away. Right now, he was balanced between too dangerous to leave alive and too important to kill. I was still waiting for the scales to finally tilt in one direction.

Knox opened his mouth to say something, but the words were halted by a knock at the door.

"Show him in," I called, quickly pushing to my feet. I had sensed the approach of the bouncer and knew he would come to that room for only one reason—my invited guest had arrived.

"Use your best judgment." By the finality in my tone, Knox knew he was being dismissed. The blond vampire nodded once and then left the room as Barrett Rainer entered.

Given his broad shoulders and somewhat stocky build, it was no surprise that Barrett Rainer was a werewolf. The man was more than 250 pounds of pure muscle, but he moved with a subtle grace, dancing between animal and man. What was surprising to most was that he was the head of one of the most powerful packs in the country. The Savannah pack wasn't the largest—that honor belonged to a pack in Montana—but its members had been carefully bred, trained, and in some cases selected for their strength, speed, and intelligence.

And at the top of the heap was Barrett Rainer with his burnished gold hair and copper-colored eyes. Like his predecessors, Barrett had been groomed since birth to assume his current role. Of course, the Savannah pack was unusual in that since its very beginning, it had always been run by a member of the Rainer family.

It was this steady consistency over the years that had enabled me to strengthen the relations with the lycanthropes in the area. In most cases, nightwalkers and shapeshifters didn't generally play well together, as each side attempted to carve out a territory of its own. Only through steady negotiations with Barrett, his father, and his grandfather had I been able to work out a stable peace. That's not to say we didn't have our occasional scuffle, but at least it wasn't the secret wars and strained truces found in other regions around the world.

Barrett dragged his stubby fingers through his short hair, leaving it standing on end and slightly disheveled. He wore a gray suit, but his tie was missing and the top two buttons of his shirt were undone. It was nearly two in the morning. Judging by how quickly he had gotten there, I was willing to guess I'd caught him as he was leaving his restaurant, Bella Luna, on the other side of town.

"You look like hell," he said after Knox shut the door, leaving us alone.

"Nice of you to notice," I replied with a smirk. "You're looking a little ragged as well."

"It was summer high moon a few nights ago. We're all still trying to bounce back." Barrett gave a little shrug, but even that motion seemed somewhat stiff and slow.

I wasn't particularly clear on the details, but summer high

moon was the full moon that fell between midsummer and autumn harvest, and tended to pack a little extra punch for all the lunar shapeshifters such as werewolves. From what I understood, it was a three-night frenzy of hunting, fighting, and sex. I used to tease Barrett that nightwalkers didn't need the moon to tell them when to have an orgy, we were always ready. However, I didn't feel like joking tonight. I needed the pack at peak strength.

"How's the family?"

"Sated," he said, his voice sounding heavy as he rubbed the bridge of his nose. "What's going on, Mira? You generally don't feel the need to check on the shifters at two in the morning."

"Several humans were murdered at the Docks tonight. The club was partially burned before I arrived," I began, carefully weighing each word. Barrett said nothing as he nodded, but I listened to him draw in a deep breath. He abruptly halted in the midst of drawing in air, his thick brows snapping together over his nose. He quickly released the breath and drew in another, scenting the air, but confusion was still written across his face. He smelled Nerian on me but couldn't identify the scent. I doubted if his father could have. There were so few naturi left, and it had been years since the last one was seen in the area.

I paused, not even wanting to breathe the word that could potentially shatter his world, but I had no choice. I had brought him here so he could at least try to protect his people. "The naturi struck—"

"That's what I smell!" he snarled. His nose crinkled, Barrett took two steps toward me. His wide eyes glowed slightly as they swept over me, his hands were open at his sides, with fingers curled like claws. "You reek of naturi."

"A hunter is in town. He gave . . . he gave me a naturi from my past." I paused again, licking my lips. I mentally sorted through the intimate details of my captivity at the hands of the naturi, trying to decide if there was anything that he needed to know. "That naturi is dead, but there are at least two others searching for him or the hunter. They are the ones that struck at the Docks."

Barrett paced away from me to the opposite wall, the heels of his palms pressed to his temples as if he were suffering from an intense migraine. "Mira." My name escaped him in a low growl.

"Do you have an emergency plan?" I asked, trying to keep my voice calm.

Barrett whipped around to face me "An emergency plan?" he repeated. "That's like me asking if you've got an emergency plan for a day when the sun refuses to set. Of course not! I don't know of any pack that has faced the naturi. Hell, I only know of them because of you and my great-grandfather."

I could feel the anger rising in him, but he fought back the panic and won. To the naturi, the lycanthropes were little more than slaves, foot soldiers in their war against the bori and mankind. Trapped between animal and man, the lycans had no choice but to answer the call of the naturi and obey.

"Pull your pack together, hold them, and make them fight this. I—I have to leave town for a little while."

"You're leaving now? This is your domain! The vampires are the only ones who can fight the naturi," Barrett shouted as he closed the distance between us with a few long strides. I barely resisted the urge to put my hand on his chest to keep a semicomfortable distance between us. I didn't want to feel crowded. My nerves were already frazzled from Danaus and the naturi; an irate werewolf didn't exactly put me at ease.

"I have to stop this from growing worse, and I can't do that here," I snapped. I didn't want to leave. I didn't want to leave my people seemingly defenseless. Unfortunately, I'd heard nothing from the Coven regarding Danaus. I couldn't sit there on my hands, waiting for them to send word regarding the naturi. What's more, I was not only one of our strongest fighters, but I also had experience dealing with the naturi. I knew I would be of more use in the Old World than in the New. I had to leave.

"Worse?" Barrett said.

The left corner of my mouth twitched as my eyes darted away from his direct gaze. I didn't know what the lycans knew of the seal or what happened at Machu Picchu so many years ago, but it was a rule that nightwalkers didn't speak of it to anyone outside our species. We might have all been on the same side when it came to the naturi, but nightwalkers by their very nature were all about power, and information was the richest form of power. We didn't tell others more than they absolutely had to know. And regardless of how much I respected and trusted Barrett, I couldn't fight six hundred years of conditioning.

"There are trying to return," I quickly said. "I'll tell you more when I know more."

My only warning was a low growl that rumbled deep in his chest before his right hand swiped across my midsection, his fingernails replaced with long black talons. I jumped backward, my shoulders slamming into the wall behind me. While I was fast, the wall kept me from escaping him. Four furrows slashed across my ribs and down my stomach. My leather halter top kept the cuts from running too deep, but my stomach had been completely bare.

Before I could slam Barrett with a few blistering comments, I saw him stare at his trembling hand, now flecked with my blood, and then turn confused eyes up to my face.

"I'm s-sorry, Mira. I—I don't know what happened," he said, his voice low and rough. He blinked once, his eyes glowed a deep copper, and then he blinked a second time, erasing the glow. A knot twisted in my stomach.

"Barrett?" A part of me wanted to reach out and lay my hand on his shoulder, but my body was still pressed against the wall as I balanced on the tips of my toes, struggling for those few extra centimeters of space. It didn't feel safe to move.

"I—I think they're here." And then his eyes glowed again. The naturi were here and they had Barrett, the Alpha for the Savannah pack, under their control.

"Shit!" I hissed between clenched teeth.

As he reached back with his right hand to take another swipe at me, I jumped forward, throwing all my weight into his left shoulder. I knocked us both to the floor, but quickly rolled to my feet. I squared off against him, putting my back to the only door in the room. Barrett returned to his feet and crouched in an aggressive stance. Beside his glowing eyes, his face was completely expressionless. He had no idea what he was doing. He would destroy me because that was the command implanted in his head, regardless of what he felt about me.

"Barrett, can you hear me? You have to fight this," I said in a hard voice, while I scrambled for a way to subdue him without hurting him too much. Other than the fact that I didn't just kill for the sake of killing, I needed him alive to help preserve the local pack.

In the main room, faint sounds of fighting drifted to me. Quickly sifting through my memory, I could recall seeing only two werewolves in the bar when I walked through, not counting the bouncer at the front door. I could only hope that Barrett had not brought more when he arrived. Unfortunately, I couldn't afford to divide my attention between scanning the area and watching him. I would have worry about it after I managed to take care of the Alpha.

My gaze darted around the room, taking in a quick inventory. Leather sofa, chair with ottoman, floor lamp, two end tables, two iron wall sconces. I didn't have a lot of choices. I needed to knock his ass out so I could settle the main room and take out the naturi.

Barrett lunged at me with a snarl, both hands now tipped with long claws. I sidestepped him, ducking under his outstretched hands. As he passed me, I kicked out with my right leg, knocking him into the wall. I needed some distance between us. Barrett wouldn't shift. It would take too long and it would give me a chance to attack. But it wasn't as if human form would leave him at a disadvantage. He was extremely fast and strong.

He pushed off the wall and threw himself into me. I was a half second too slow. We fell to the floor in a tangled heap, his elongated teeth instantly clamping onto my throat. I felt his teeth sink in, sending pain screaming through my frame. Yelling, I jerked my left arm free from beneath his body and punched him in the side. At least three ribs snapped beneath my fist, but I held back enough to keep from punching straight into his chest. He groaned, but clamped down harder, teeth sinking deeper into my throat.

My vision swam. I reached back and hit Barrett again, but this time I hammered his kidney. He yelped, finally releasing my throat. With a soft gurgle, I shoved him off me, sending him skidding a foot across the floor. Tapping down a fresh swell of pain, I pushed to my feet and grabbed him by the lapels of his jacket. His handsome face was covered in my blood and his eyes radiated with an eerie copper light. His large hand clamped on my wrists, threatening to snap them, but I didn't give him a chance. I slammed him into the wall, trying to knock him out.

It didn't work. Either his head was too thick or his lycanthropy made him too strong. I pulled him back and slammed him into the wall again, partially pushing him through the wooden studs. A third time left him dazed but conscious.

Dropping him to the floor, I grabbed an iron sconce off the floor and clocked him on the back of the head. He collapsed like a sack of dead fish. Blood immediately began to ooze from his scalp and trickle down his temple. I had cracked his skull, but I could hear his heartbeat. He would live.

Gritting my teeth, I took a step away from him, still clutching the sconce. Blood was still leaking from the wound at my throat that was struggling to close. A low roar had begun in my chest and was echoing through my brain. It wanted blood. It wanted Barrett's blood, and it would only be satisfied when I'd finished draining him dry.

I took another backward step. It took everything within me to turn my back on him and walk to the door. The blood lust was lit and would only be satisfied when I finally made a kill, or at the very least, fed deeply.

Slowly opening the door, I peeked out into the main room. Chaos ruled. Curtains were shredded, tables overturned, and I could see at least five dead bodies. I immediately identified two of them as nightwalkers. Blocking the entrance were two naturi. Why were they there? Danaus wasn't here.

The quickest way to end this struggle was to take out the naturi. They were the greatest threat. Reaching out with my power, I quickly located Knox but hesitated making my presence known. He was fighting a werewolf. I could feel his building anger, but a cool, underlying logic still guided his thoughts.

Please, don't kill them, I whispered in his thoughts.

Thank God! Knox sighed back, relieved to find that I was still alive. *Barrett—*

The naturi. Kill the naturi and the werewolves will stop, I directed.

Tried that. Irritation filled the comment. *They've killed Roland and Adam.*

I've got it. Keep the lycans off my back.

I silently walked the last couple of steps down the hall to stand on the edge of the main room. And the battle instantly shifted. The two naturi saw me and smiled. One of them was obviously from the animal clan. He had the same wide bone structure to his face as Nerian and dark, shaggy hair. With a wave of his hand, the four lycans I could see on the dance floor looked over at me. At once, they all attempted to disengage from their opponents so they could come after me.

Unconsciously, I took a step backward, my mouth falling open. The naturi had come after me. Not Nerian. Not Danaus. They were looking for me.

Before the lycans could move more than a couple steps, the vampires surged, bringing them down. Sickly sounds of tearing flesh and breaking bones barely rose above the earth-shattering screams of pain. Knox was willing to follow my orders up to a point. He had directed the others to keep the lycanthropes busy, but as soon as it became apparent that I was the main target, the order had changed to protect me at any cost. The four werewolves were dead, outnumbered and overwhelmed.

Swallowing a scream of frustration, I conjured up a fireball in my left hand and hurled it at the two naturi who were slowly approaching. It never reached them. One of them gracefully lifted one hand. The fireball flowed to him and then disappeared. I looked carefully at him for the first time. Tall and thin like a delicate willow, his skin was snowy white and his hair fell about him in silken waves of gold. If the sun could ever cry a tear, he would have been formed from it. He was from the light clan, and I knew I was seriously screwed. I wouldn't be able to use my ability to conjure fire as a weapon against them as long as he stood.

I smiled. He would just have to stop standing.

"I've already killed Nerian tonight," I called to them from across the dance floor. There was no missing the laughter in my tone. "We've killed your poor foot soldiers. This will be your one chance to leave my domain while you can still walk out of here." As I spoke, I conjured another fireball in my left hand.

Once again the naturi from the light clan captured the fireball, protecting them both. "You're mistaken, Fire Starter. This is your one chance," he replied. His voice was light and warm, like the early morning rays from the summer sun. "Come with us now, and we won't destroy every vampire in your domain."

My smile faded. Bright fireballs consumed both my hands this time. Quickly, I launched them both at the naturi from the light clan. With a wave of his hand, he easily dispersed the fire, but it did nothing to stop the iron sconce that had been engulfed in the second fireball. The heavy piece of iron struck him in the middle of his chest, throwing him backward as it embedded itself. I had no doubt that he was dead the moment his lithe body slammed into the wall.

The remaining naturi growled at me for only a second before darting out the open front door. Without the added defense of someone from the light clan, he didn't stand a chance against fifty nightwalkers and the Fire Starter. It had been the only way the naturi could hold me during the first week. With a member of the light clan constantly hovering in my shadow, I'd been unable to use my ability against them. By the second week I was too weak to even light a candle.

Now, with the threat finally gone, I took a step onto the dance floor and surveyed the damage. I tried to shove both my hands through my hair but stopped when I encountered the dried blood left from Nerian. My body trembled in pain, exhaustion, and blood loss. But the faces of the nightwalkers watching me were worse. Haunted, confused, and frightened, many clung to each other or knelt beside the dead. The two nightwalkers I could identify as Roland and Adam had gaping holes dominating their chests where their hearts once were. Two more bodies lay in awkward positions on the ground, headless.

The bodies of the four werewolves were badly mangled and covered with blood. No one stood next to them. The lines were already being drawn, but they were the wrong lines.

"Mira?"

My head jerked up to find Knox standing next to me. His navy shirt had been ripped in several places and there were several superficial wounds healing on his arms and chest.

"What's the count?" I murmured, my gaze returning to the bloody scene before me.

"Six nightwalkers and five lycans, unless Barrett is—"

"No," I said sharply, then drew in a deep breath, softening my voice. "No, he'll recover."

"Why?" I heard someone whisper in a broken voice.

I lurched into action, my heels clicking ominously on the cold tile floor. "You know why they did this, don't you?" I demanded. My gaze slowly swept over the assembled mass, making sure that I briefly held the stare of every nightwalker. "They had no choice! That was the naturi," I said, pointing over my shoulder toward the dead naturi. "Certain naturi can control the lycans. The lycans have no choice but to obey the naturi when they are close. This is not their fault."

"But how do you stop this?" a female asked in a tremulous voice.

"Kill the werewolves," another answered in a cold, dead voice.

I surged across the open space, grabbing him by the throat as I slammed him into a divider between two booths.

"No! You kill the naturi! You kill the naturi and the lycans are free. You kill the naturi and we are free." Releasing the nightwalker only after he gave me a faint nod, I turned to face the others again. "If you kill the lycan, you still have a naturi waiting to rip your heart out."

Walking over to one of the booths that was still covered with a tablecloth, I pulled it off and draped it over one of the dead werewolves. Donald Moreland. He'd been the bouncer at the front door. "Spread the word. If anyone attacks a lycan after tonight, I will stake you out in the sun myself," I said in a low voice. "No one is permitted out into the marshlands or any other known lycan territory until I give the word. You remain in the city. No one hunts alone."

"What about the naturi?"

I looked up, my eyes locking on Knox. "I leave tomorrow to tell the Elders about what is happening. The naturi will follow me."

While the remaining vampires disposed of the various bodies, I took Barrett to my town house a few blocks away and waited for him to awaken. Distraught and heartsick after hearing everything that had occurred, the Alpha left my town house an hour before sunrise. He and Knox would attempt to maintain peace while I was gone, but we both knew the damage was done. The memories of nightwalkers did not fade. Generations of werewolves would come and go through my territory, but the trust between the two races would never be the same again. We both knew that tempers would run high during the next few years. And despite the fact that the werewolves were as much victims in this mess as the nightwalkers, someone would use the attack at the Dark Room as an excuse to lash out.

Damn the naturi! And damn Danaus for bringing them into my domain. Intentionally or not, he had destroyed a delicate balance I had spent decades building.

Settled in my hidden lair beneath earth as the sun edged closer to the horizon, I finally allowed my mind to drift back to the thought I had been avoiding. The naturi had come looking for me. Tabor was dead and Jabari missing; dead or not, I didn't know. Sadira was the only member of the triad I was confident was still alive. Of course, she was my maker. I was sure I would have felt it if she'd been destroyed. Outside the triad, there were only a few other nightwalkers that had survived the battle at Machu Picchu centuries ago. Were the naturi hunting them down in an effort to make sure we couldn't stop them again?

Danaus knew about the naturi. Danaus knew about the sacrifice in India. Danaus knew that I was at Machu Picchu and how to find me. Danaus knew too much. I would take him with me. I would discover how he knew these things. And when I was sure that I knew everything he knew, I would kill him.

Eight

The black limo glided out of the flow of traffic and pulled up to the corner just after ten o'clock. We were in what I lovingly thought of as the theater district, even though there was only the Johnny Mercer Theater in the vicinity. It was an enormous building with tall arched openings that adjoined the Civic Center Arena. The whole area was lined with beautiful parks and tall oak trees draped with Spanish moss.

Beside the historic district, this narrow strip was yuppie central. All that glittered, glowed, and drove a BMW strolled through this area. And the hunter stuck out like a dirty street urchin at the queen's diamond jubilee.

I hadn't actually meant to make him stand out so much, though a part of me wished it had been a conscious effort. The corner of Hull and Jefferson was near the edge of the historic district, and everyone knew the Civic Center. It would be easy for him to find. That had been my only concern.

Danaus stood on the corner outside the lamplight, still in his black leather duster. It was far too hot for the jacket, but was clearly the only way he could walk around the city with his assortment of weapons. A black duffel bag lay at his feet, and I had a feeling that it held a great deal more than clothes.

It was nice that I didn't have to tell him we would be going on a journey. Of course, we both knew that the next sacrifice wouldn't be here. We had to get moving so we could pull the triad back together.

The driver alighted from the limo and circled around to open the door for Danaus. The hunter's eyes darted from the car to the man, his grim face expressing his confidence that the man had lost his mind.

"Mr. Smith?" the driver inquired, motioning with one hand toward the interior of the car. I had informed the poor man that we would be picking up a dark-haired gentleman by the name of Mr. Smith at the corner of Hull and Jefferson.

Struggling to keep from laughing, I called to Danaus from the shadows of the limo. "Come along, Danaus."

The driver picked up Danaus's bag and placed it in the trunk, all under the dark gaze of its owner. When it was carefully stowed, Danaus climbed into the limo and took the seat across from me.

When he was comfortably seated against the soft leather bench he got a good look at me. I laughed when his eyes flared and frown deepened. Anyone else's mouth would have been hanging open, but Danaus seemed to be the king of composure. He would have made an excellent night-walker, but I had a feeling vampirism might not actually be an option for him.

I lounged in the seat wearing a pair of black slacks and a matching black blazer over a deep purple shirt. My dark red hair had been carefully twisted and pinned to the back of my head, showing off my high cheekbones beneath pale white skin. A pair of lilac sunglasses sat balanced on my nose. In our two other meetings, I wore my usual attire of leather, and very little of it. Unfortunately, I had to make these travel arrangements through my human assistant, and she needed the reassurance that her employer was a normal,

human businesswoman. Though her mouth did fall open
when Danaus took a seat beside her in the limo.

As his gaze moved over me, my hand drifted up, my fingers briefly dancing over the faint scar that now stretched
along my collarbone and the base of my neck on the right.
Barrett's bite had only partially healed since last night. It
was rare for nightwalkers to scar, but lacking adequate rest
and blood, it was possible. I'd lost too much blood during
the battle and hadn't left myself enough time after leaving
Barrett to hunt. The lines on my neck weren't the first scars
I had acquired since being reborn, and considering my lifestyle, I knew they wouldn't be the last.

"Mr. Smith . . . " I started then paused. Toying with Danaus was too easy, and I struggled to keep from smiling and
exposing my fangs. After the unexpected debacle of last
night, I need something to lighten my mood. "This is my assistant, Charlotte Godwin," I continued, motioning toward
the petite woman seated next to him.

Charlotte extended her hand, but Danaus only nodded at
her then turned his glare on me.

"We are dropping Ms. Godwin off a couple blocks from
here. She decided to tag along in an attempt to get me to look
over some papers before our trip."

"It's just that you are so hard to pin down for a meeting, Ms. Jones," chided the slender brunette with choco-
late-colored eyes. Her words slipped through the limo with
a sweet, Southern drawl. She wore a mint green suit, very
composed and professional, and her long fingers grasped the
stack of papers in her lap.

My gaze drifted back to Danaus, and he arched one
eyebrow at me when she mentioned my surname. So they
were obvious fakes; that was half the fun. It gave sweet little
Charlotte something to sweat about when she lay awake at
night.

With an indifferent wave of my hand, I attempted to brush off the topic. "It's completely unnecessary. You have everything well in hand."

"But the investors are demanding to know why you won't approve the mining expedition in Peru," Charlotte countered.

"They want to go digging in the Sacred Valley, and I won't have it. If they want to load up on the sweat of the sun, tell them to pick another country. Try Chile," I said. Gazing out the window, I watched as the city slid by in a motley of lights and color. I was part of a consortium of investors that ran a gold-mining company. We had made a great deal of money so far, and now they wanted to venture into the heart of the Incan empire. They had set their sights on some mountains in the shadow of Machu Picchu. I wanted nothing to do with it.

"They won't be happy." Charlotte's soft voice intruded on a set of less than happy memories.

"Tell them to take it up with me."

Charlotte quickly broke eye contact, looking back down at the stack of paperwork in her lap. Luckily for her, the limo pulled over to the sidewalk again in front of a set of office buildings in the heart of downtown. Charlotte maintained offices both in Savannah and Charleston, where she generally reigned supreme until she had to check in with me.

It had to be frustrating. She had her own assistants and made multi-million-dollar decisions on a daily basis. Most of it was my money, though she did run a few other partnerships that I was involved in. But for all she accomplished, she was still forced to jump when I asked. Last night, I'd called at four in the morning from my town house as I waited for Barrett to awaken, and demanded that she make arrangements for the trip. And I knew that Charlotte had most of it completed by dawn. No matter how high she rose or how much money she acquired, she would still be my flunky.

The delicate brunette with the pale rose complexion tidied up the papers, drawing in a deep breath. "I hope you have a good trip. I have often wished to see the pyramids." The words escaped her in a rush of air.

"Thank you," I said. "I will contact you in a day or two to arrange for travel."

Her head snapped up to meet my eyes again. "Back home?"

"Hopefully. You'll hear from me." She nodded and nearly leapt from the limo when the driver opened the door. My soft laughter followed her out of the vehicle and onto the street.

Danaus waited until the driver shut the door before speaking. "She doesn't know?"

"No, she doesn't know what I am. Her only fear is losing her job."

"It's more than that," he corrected.

"Really?" I leaned back into the corner of the seat and stretched out my legs, crossing them at the ankle. Draping my left arm along the backseat, my index finger drew a lazy infinity sign on the slick leather. "What else does she fear?"

"Losing her soul."

I laughed, letting my powers flare out from my body. It was like relaxing a muscle after holding it tensed for a long time. I tried to rein my powers in when I was in close quarters with Charlotte. Being human, she might not have been able to sense them, but that extra bit of self-preservation that all humans possess would have picked up something. She would know that something was slightly off about me.

Danaus flinched against the unexpected wave of power, his right hand flexing at his side. Being a hunter, I suspected he would have felt infinitely more comfortable with a dagger in his hand, but he'd kept up the act of being civilized in front of sweet Charlotte. In the front of the car, the sound of the driver climbing back behind the wheel snapped me from my amusement. I pulled my powers back into myself and sighed. While the pane of glass muffled our words, it would not have stopped power from eddying out beyond it.

We pulled back out into traffic and headed out of the city. I saw brief flashes of the river as we passed through wide intersections. I had scanned the area intermittently since awakening that evening, pushing my powers as far as they would reach. By sunset all the lycanthropes were outside the city limits and settled in the surrounding countryside, while all the nightwalkers were in the city. Barrett had even changed the hours of the restaurant temporarily so it now closed before sunset. As much as we both hated it, the boundaries had been drawn. When the naturi were once again defeated, Barrett and I would begin rebuilding the trust between the shifters and the nightwalkers.

"We're going to Egypt?" Danaus asked.

"I had hoped to keep it a surprise." I let the silence sink into the car for a moment, trying to see if I could get him to demand more information, but he was proving to be a very patient creature. "We are flying to Luxor with a brief layover in Paris. From there, we take a barge down the Nile to Aswan."

"A car would be faster from Luxor, or why not fly straight to Aswan?"

"True." I nodded, my gaze darting back to my restless fingers and their infinity sign. "But you are now traveling with a vampire, and certain . . . rituals must be observed. I am entering the territory of an Elder and must move slowly as a show of respect. You never go directly into the known domain of an Ancient. It's a sign of aggression."

"I thought you said Jabari was dead?"

My eyes jerked back to Danaus's face, studying his intent expression. "So you didn't kill him. I doubted the rumors."

"I was in Egypt briefly, but I have never seen Jabari." His shoulder-length hair hung close to his cheek, casting dark shadows about his eyes.

"I don't know what to expect," I said with an elegant shrug, as my eyes strayed to the window. After you reach a certain age as a nightwalker, you can make almost any gesture seem elegant. It's part of the package. "Jabari has disappeared. I don't seek him, but I think he may have left some valuable information behind; journals describing the seal and the triad. It's a starting point. However, I think it would be wise if we proceed with caution. If he does appear, I would prefer to remain in his good graces."

"My presence will not help that endeavor."

"No, it will not." There was no reason for me to tell him that I intended to hand him over to Jabari and/or the Coven if necessary. Let them extract the information his brain held. I would have preferred to handle it myself, but there was no time to waste on my own interests. My domain was beginning to tear at the seams.

I looked down to find that I had unconsciously begun to fiddle with the silver band on my ring finger. The ring had been a gift from a lover years ago, etched with what looked like ocean waves. The Greek design whispered of old, half-forgotten memories.

Danaus let the conversation drop and stared out the window. I wondered what must be going through his head. He was willingly walking into the den of the enemy. Why? He could have left after showing me the pictures, leaving it to the nightwalkers. Of course, I doubted he trusted us to handle it. I wished I knew exactly how much he understood of this whole horrible mess. Yet, any question I asked might give the vampire hunter valuable and even deadly insight into my world.

Stretching my legs, I relaxed against the seat. I would leave it for now. If I found Jabari, he would handle it. If not, I would find Sadira. I hadn't seen her since that night at Machu Picchu, and wasn't particularly looking forward to the reunion. Our relationship had never been a happy one during the century we spent together. We both wanted control over me, and only one of us could win. It resulted in some ugly battles, and there were some wounds that even five centuries couldn't heal.

"Did you encounter the naturi last night?" I asked, forcefully redirecting my thoughts away from my maker.

"No. Did you?"

My teeth clenched so tightly my jaw ached. Before I'd left the Dark Room, the final body count was seven nightwalkers, six lycans, and nine humans, against the death of only two naturi. What did we face if the naturi returned to this world en masse? "A pair attacked the Docks, killing several people. They appeared at the Dark Room later. Several nightwalkers and lycanthropes were killed."

"I'm sorry."

"Yes." Surprised by his solemn comment, I finally looked over at him. "So am I."

We traveled in silence to a nearly empty airstrip almost a half an hour outside of the city. My private jet was fueled and waiting for us. I preferred to travel this way. Items could be loaded and unloaded from the plane outside the glare of a large airport and prying eyes.

The limo stopped a few yards away from the plane and the driver hopped from the car, leaving the engine running. I was his only task of the night, and I could feel his eagerness to have it done. Picking up and dropping off strange people at deserted airfields was not a part of his normal chores. He opened the door for me and bowed his head, as if he could feel my power. I smiled and slipped a fifty dollar bill into his fingers; I liked it when my servants were quick and efficient. A brooding Danaus followed silently behind me as the driver rushed to grab our bags.

A few steps away from the limo, Danaus reached for one of the knives at his side. I laid a restraining hand on his shoulder and smiled. He had just caught sight of the two large men flanking the short staircase that led into the jet. They wore shoulder holsters with a pair of lovely guns over their tightly stretched black shirts plus a thigh sheath for a knife.

"Down, boy," I said, patting his shoulder. "They belong to me." He stopped walking, his hand resting on his knife. "I don't like to travel without protection."

He released his hold on the knife at his side and continued to walk a step behind me. I smiled at my two bodyguards and let my hand run across the chest of the one on the right as I started to climb into the jet.

"Wait," Danaus said. "We're being watched."

I turned, my right foot on the first step, my hand on the shoulder of my bodyguard. Stretching out my powers, I searched the area. Deep black night stretched in all directions for several acres, hemmed in only by a thin line of trees. All the humans nearby were employees, and the closest nightwalker was almost fifteen miles away. I sensed no one else, which sent a chill up my back. Was Rowe hunting me now?

"Let them watch," I announced. "Let's go." I forced myself to climb the rest of the way into the jet causally, turning my back to the darkness.

Once inside, I stripped off my blazer and tossed it over the back of one of the white leather chairs. An exquisite piece of machinery, the plane always made me wish I traveled more. The front had two long benches in soft white leather along the sides of the plane. A pair of chairs faced the benches in the same white leather. The floor was covered in thick, creamy white carpet, muffling the footsteps of the passengers. Toward the back was a bar with a fridge and microwave, along with another set of chairs. I never used it, but my bodyguards found it nice for the long trips. Behind all that was another room with a bed and a door that locked.

I stretched out on one of the benches while Danaus took the bench opposite me. It allowed him to keep an eye on my assistants and me. For the first time, he looked uneasy. I doubted it was a fear of flying. I think maybe everything was sinking in. He was in a dire situation and would have to fight his way out of it. And to make matters worse, he was forced to rely on a vampire to guide him through this maze of snarls.

After shutting the door, the pilots fired up the engine. My bodyguard, Michael, walked over and knelt before me. He was a handsome man of less than thirty with beautiful blond curls brushing his shoulders. They made him look younger than he was. He had served me as a bodyguard for the past five years.

Yet for the past three he had helped to keep the loneliness at bay. He gave me laughter and diversion when the nights seemed to stretch out before me like the vast Siberian tundra. But that's all there was for us. No matter how I tried, I could not give my heart to a creature I knew needed protection from me and my kind. Some nightwalkers could. The tale was older than I was . . . a centuries-old vampire falls in love with a human, and then turns him or her so they can spend eternity together. Yeah, right. Humans can't make a marriage last more than a few decades. Do you honestly think a pair of vampires can stay together for centuries? I've yet to see it happen.

Biting back a weary sigh, I smiled down at Michael, my right hand smoothing back his hair and idly touching his cheek. He reached up and pulled my hand down so my fingers rested against the pulse at his neck. My eyes drifted shut as I let its siren song beat through me for a couple of seconds. My lips parted slightly and I touched my tongue to my fangs. A hungry longing rose up in my chest, but I smothered it, lifting my hand back to his face.

"Not now, love," I whispered, opening my eyes. "When we reach Aswan, I will need you." Michael turned his head and pressed a kiss against the palm of my hand before rising to his feet. He turned, walked toward the back of the jet and took a seat across from my other guardian. Brown-haired Gabriel had served as one of my bodyguards for more than ten years, but he still could not keep the look of envy from his eyes. I'd fed off both men in the past and neither had uttered a complaint.

Danaus's dark growl drew my attention back to the hunter. "A donor?"

"I thought I'd pack lunch," I said. "It will take us nearly twenty-four hours to reach Aswan. I don't want to walk in weak and hungry."

"They both know?"

"They have both assisted me in the past when I was in need." I watched Danaus as his forehead furrowed with this bit of information. He seemed genuinely surprised. "What has confused you? That any human would do such a thing?"

He sat forward, balancing on the edge of the seat, his elbows braced on his knees. "You can feed without killing?"

"Of course,"

"I thought it was necessary for you to kill for your survival."

"If that were true, we would have completely wiped out humans long ago." I shook my head and then threaded a loose lock of hair behind my right ear. I had thought we finally put that old superstition to rest, but apparently it still lived on in Danaus, and maybe within this group that he was a part of. "Few kill, and most of the time it's an accident. In this day of DNA and fingerprints, it's too hard to kill and then deal with the body. We have a secret to keep so we feed carefully."

"But some still kill for sport." Fresh tension seemed to hum in his frame as his hands clenched the edge of the bench.

It became a fight not to clench my teeth. "Yes, and we take care of them." I had personally taken out more than my share of fellow nightwalkers who went out of control. I might like to poke the beehive of the Coven Elders, but knew better than to stir up the humans. I liked my comfortable lifestyle.

Staring at my new companion, I was surprised by the new thought that occurred to me. "You've not actually spoken with many of us, have you?"

Danaus snorted and shook his head as he sat back against the seat, resting his hands limply in his lap. "Why? So you can try to convince me that you're not soulless killers, spreading evil by converting humans? Nerian was right— you're parasites, feeding on humanity, your only drive to fulfill your own desires."

My head fell back and I laughed, my right hand covering my eyes. "How is that any different from humans?" I dropped my hand back to the leather seat, where I tapped my nails softly on the bench. "Haven't you just described humanity? Creatures surviving off the lives of others, driven to fulfill their own desires?"

He remained silent and I let the subject drop as the plane lifted into the air. We both had our own issues to work out, but I was still curious about him, and he was at my disposal for several hours.

"What are you, Danaus?" I asked. His eyes darted over to the bank of windows over my right shoulder, avoiding me. "I've been turning that question over in my head for more than a month now," I continued, as if he'd spoken. "I've known several odd creatures in my time, but nothing like you. You have all the trappings of a human—wrapped up in your very human anger—but at the same time you sit over there pulsing with power. Are you even aware that you're doing it? Your powers are so warm and alive, so wonderful. And the angrier you become, the stronger the pulse." He still hadn't looked at me, but I knew he was listening. His jaw hardened as he clenched his teeth and his eyes narrowed. I wondered how much he understood of himself.

"You know, you smell of the wind and of some distant sea. Sometimes I think it's the Mediterranean, but it has been too long since I stood where it lapped the shore. You also smell like the sun."

The description made the corner of his mouth quirk. He was suddenly fighting a smile. The description was strange, but it was the image conjured in my brain when I breathed him in.

"If you will not tell me what, then tell me how old you are."

He stared at the windows hard, and I had about given up when his lips finally parted. "I served as a guard under Marcus Aurelius." The accent I had heard when we first met flared to life again, teasing at my thoughts.

My brain shuffled through the card catalog of names in my mind, digging deeper for a time and place. It took only a moment, and when I placed it, my mouth fell open. Several minutes passed before I could organize my thoughts enough to form a coherent sentence. "You're nearly three times my age," I whispered, bringing a smile to his lips as his eyes finally returned to my face. "You look good for an old man."

The smile faded. "It also means you're Roman in the truest form of the word. You watched the fall of the empire."

"I had left already," he volunteered in a low voice. While his expression never changed, the light in his eyes seemed to dim. Had the fall of the great empire bothered him? I think I wanted it to—it made him seem a little more real.

"Where have you been?" The question escaped me in a whisper of wonder and awe. I was just over six hundred years old, but it always filled me with a childlike giddiness when I encountered a creature older than me. I envied the knowledge their brains held, the sights they had seen that were now forever gone from this earth.

"Everywhere," he replied, his own rough voice sinking into softer tones. His eyelids drifted low, as if he were reliving some old memories. "Rome, then west across the Carpathian Mountains, through Russia and south through Mongolia into China. I came back through India, the Middle East, Africa, back through Europe, where I lived with monks." His eyes flicked back to my face and his voice hardened. "And across all those countries and through all the religions, one thing held true. Vampires are evil."

"How did you capture Nerian?" I asked. He blinked at me, his mind seeming to stumble over the abrupt change of topic. There was no discussing my species' right to live. Words would not be what convinced this man: only actions would accomplish that feat. Of course, I didn't expect him to live long enough for that.

Danaus pressed his lips into a thin line as his expression hardened. I was beginning to recognize that expression; his "I don't have to tell you anything, bitch" look.

Sitting forward on the leather sofa, I balanced my elbows on my knees. "You'll be asked that again, by those who have a lot less patience than I do. You can tell me now and we move on, or we can wait and let them drag it from your lips using pain. Whether you've realized this or not, I am the only buffer between you and them."

I sat back again, draping my left arm over the back of the sofa. Danaus was a rare gift. He was strong, powerful, and intelligent. I wanted the pleasure of picking apart his secrets, and then I wanted to hunt him. The challenge he offered was worth a little work, a little risk.

Minutes ticked by with only the roar of the wind outside the plane filling the tense air. He stared at me, as if weighing his options. They weren't great and I couldn't promise to protect him even if he did deliver the information. If an Elder stepped in, I would have to back off.

"Luck," he said at last.

"Luck?"

"He was following you. I caught him off guard and knocked him out."

I smiled and shook my head. I don't know whether I completely believed it, but only Nerian would be so cocky as to not pay attention to a human that close to him. Of course, I was beginning to wonder how badly I was underestimating Danaus as well.

"How long did you have him?"

"A week."

I nodded, rising to my feet. I stood in front of him for a moment, hands on hips, my legs spread against the slight turbulence. He tensed but his hands didn't move toward the knives concealed on his body. I didn't know how much, if any, information he had dragged out of the insane naturi, but a week was enough time to get some juicy tidbits. I was going to have to kill Danaus soon. His interesting qualities would be outweighed by the fact that he was becoming too dangerous to leave alive.

"Have you learned anything about Rowe?"

"Nothing yet. My contacts are still digging," he said.

I couldn't begin to guess at whom he was in contact with or how they would acquire information about the naturi. While nightwalkers stuck to the shadows and were diligent about maintaining our secrecy, the naturi were mere ghosts in this world.

With a sigh, I walked to the back of the jet and curled up in Michael's lap. He wrapped his large arms around me and held me against his chest. I placed my ear against his heart, letting the steady rhythm soothe my mind. My right hand restlessly played with the hair at the nape of his neck while the other rested on his shoulder. My thoughts calmed as I lay in his warmth.

I didn't want to be a part of this. I wanted to live in my city and seek pleasures where I found them. My great deed had been done more than five hundred years ago, and I walked away from my kind after that, never seeking a nightwalker companion for more than a night or two. But now I was being pulled back down into their ranks, sucked deeper into the mire. I could struggle all I wanted, but there would be no escaping.

NINE

I awoke to find myself locked in a box. For a brief moment a wave of panic surged through my frame and I nearly screamed. I thrust my hands against the top, which sank against the cool, silk lining. With eyes closed and teeth clenched, I willed the wave of fear to subside. It had been a long time since I'd done the old coffin bit. Most of the time, I slept in a windowless room on a king-sized bed covered in silk sheets. I had forgotten about traveling to Luxor, about Danaus, and Nerian. By now we should be drawing close to Aswan, home to the Tombs of the Nobles, the island temple of Philae, and the doorway to the old Nubian kingdom and Jabari.

With my hands on my stomach, I relaxed the muscles in my arms, waiting for the calm to sink back into the marrow of my bones. If I was going to steer myself out of this mess without getting killed, I needed to be calm and thinking clearly. Resisting the urge to sigh, I reached over and flipped the interior locks to the coffin. I call it a coffin, but it was actually a large box made of a nearly indestructible, lightweight alloy. The interior had been lined with red silk cushions, not that it really mattered. When daylight hit, I could sleep just as comfortably on a bed of broken glass. There was a pair of locks on the interior, ensuring that no one could open it from the outside. It went with me whenever I traveled, and I kept a spare at my private residence.

Pushing open the lid on its silent hinges, I sat up, grateful to find that no one was about to see my "rising from the dead" act. The quaint little room with walls made of dark wood was empty. The box rested on a full-sized bed covered with a colorful hand-stitched quilt. The curtains on the small windows were pulled back, revealing dark skies. Beyond, I could hear an engine running and the lap of water. We were traveling down the Nile. A ball of excitement tightened in my stomach and I struggled to keep from biting my lower lip like a giddy schoolgirl. It had been centuries since I last saw the sand dunes of Egypt.

I was climbing out of my private resting spot when someone knocked on the door. A brief stretch of my powers revealed that it was Michael, right on time. "Come in." He stepped into the room, wearing the same black shirt and pants from the previous night. His shoulder holster was missing, but I could feel Gabriel taking up his post at the door.

The young bodyguard was his usual handsome self, blond hair tossed by the wind. He already smelled of Egypt, with its exotic spices and history. His sharp blue eyes swept over the room as he cataloged his surroundings before settling back on me. He was good at his job, taking my protection very seriously. It was a nice feeling to have someone who wanted to see me rise every night. Sure, it was his job, but most of my own kind would rather shove a stake through my heart.

Prior to taking up the position as my bodyguard, Michael had briefly served in the Marines, accounting for most of his training. I didn't know how he came to be recruited by

Gabriel and I'd never asked. My guardian angel had his con-
nections and I left it at that.

At first, guarding me was just been a job for Michael; a
well-paying job, but still just a job. After a couple of years
that changed. For him, I became a source of strength and
intense pleasure. I also fulfilled his deep need to protect.

For me, he became both a comfort and a distraction
when my thoughts grew too dark. There was still something
strangely innocent in his eyes and an eagerness to please
me that was endearing. He treated me as though there was
something still human in me. To him, I was never a monster,
no matter what he saw me do.

I extended my hand to him, needing the physical contact.
"Is all well?"

He wrapped his long fingers around my hand as he
walked over to me, his intense gaze never straying from my
face. "Yes."

The sound of the engine dulled and I concentrated on
the steady throb of his heart. Its pace quickened the closer
he came, causing his face to flush. "Was there any trouble
in Luxor?"

"No, everything went as Ms. Godwin instructed. We have
just come within sight of Aswan. The captain says we should
dock in another fifteen minutes."

When he stood only inches from me, I released his hand
and slid my palms up his arms and across his shoulders. I
had taken my boots off before dawn, putting me at a flat-
footed five feet six inches at best; rather tall considering
people six hundred years ago were much shorter but still
roughly a foot shorter than my guardian angel.

His warm lips brushed against my temple in a gentle caress. "I missed you." He lifted his hands and lightly placed
them on the sides of my waist as if he was afraid he would
break me with his touch.

"I guess I should travel more," I whispered, threading my fingers through his hair, enjoying the feel of his silky locks.

His lips moved down from my temple and along the line of my jaw. "We could meet outside of work."

A low noise similar to a cat's purr rumbled from the back of my throat, and I rose up on the tips of my toes so his soft lips could reach more of my flesh. I needed Michael. I needed his warmth and vitality. It reminded me of my own shredded humanity. It also fought back the darker urges that screamed for me to throw him to the ground and drain him dry.

"I think something can be arranged." My lips brushed against his throat as I spoke, teasing me. So close. Less than an inch and my fangs would be embedded.

"Yes." There was more air in the word than actual sound. His hands tightened on my waist. I could feel the trembling need in the muscles stretching up his arms. He was fighting the desire to crush me against his body, molding me to him. From past encounters, he knew I liked to prolong the moment when time allowed, basking in all the sensations flooding my mind.

"Lay on the bed," I said, stepping back from him. Michael moved around me and pushed the box to the far side of the bed. He stretched out his long body and for a moment I stood at his side, admiring his peaceful expression. I had spent the first few centuries of my existence hunting down my prey, wrestling them to the ground, and it always felt a little strange when my meal came to me with arms open. Some of the rush spilled from the moment, but my thirst was already starting to make itself known, petty thoughts pushed to the back of my mind.

Crawling onto the bed, I straddled his narrow hips. I was beginning to see a distinct pattern when it came to the men in my life, but the position made feeding easier. It also allowed me the pleasure of pressing the full length of my body against his. I leaned forward with my forearms on each side of his head and pressed slow kisses against each eyelid, his nose, and along his left jaw. Beneath me, I felt him sigh as if the tension was unraveling from around his soul. I pressed a long, lingering kiss to his lips, carefully drawing his tongue in my mouth, enjoying the taste of him. His strong hands slipped under my shirt and slid up my bare back, pulling me more tightly against him. His body hardened beneath me and I suppressed my own frustrated sigh. There just wasn't enough time for everything.

Pulling reluctantly away from his mouth, I slid my lips down his jaw to his throat. The tip of my tongue ran over the heavy pulse that throbbed there before I finally sank my fangs deep into his flesh. He stiffened against the sudden pain then relaxed again. Drawing the sweet blood into my body, I sent a warm, tingling wave of intense pleasure through his body. He moaned as it swept into his limbs. I drank deeply, pulling his life into my thin frame until I could taste his heartbeat, feel it vibrating down in my own chest.

His hands slid down over my rear, kneading my body, keeping me pressed against him. He moaned my name; his hips shifted and rose off the bed. Except for our clothes, he would have been inside of me. The thought sent a shudder through my taut body, and I twisted the blankets in my fists. The feeling of his warm blood filling my veins was already quite satisfying, but the desire to have all of him was coiling tighter in my body. I ground my hips against him, a pure animal growl rumbling in the back of my throat as I reveled in the hardness of his body.

Releasing my grip on the blanket, I slipped my left hand under his shirt, running it up along his ribs. My thumb grazed his nipple before heading back down to his flat stomach. His skin was so warm and enticing, an intoxicating combination of hard muscle and soft flesh.

My hand brushed against the button on his pants as my fingers skimmed along the soft flesh just below the edge of his underwear. His hips lifted again, pressing into me, his body demanding entrance. With every last ounce of self-control I had, I put my hand back beside his head, wrapping my fingers in the blanket. I wanted him so badly I could scream, but I wouldn't be happy with a quickie. It had been too long and I wanted to linger over him. And Michael was worth the wait.

I lifted my mouth from his neck with great reluctance and nuzzled his ear for a moment. Focusing my powers on his neck, I closed the wound, leaving behind only a slight redness in the area. "We cannot, my angel. Not this time." Leaning up on my forearms, I looked into his face. He watched me with wide, heartbroken eyes. "If sunset had come but an hour sooner I would happily linger over you, but time will not allow." I ran my tongue over my bottom lip, drawing in the last bit of his blood, and he sighed, moving his hands up the back of my thighs, keeping me pressed against him.

I laughed and shook my head as I got off the bed. "But you are a temptation," I said, unbuttoning my shirt.

"Not enough of one," he said with a little bit of a pout. He watched as I stripped down and walked over to my bag of clothes, which lay at the foot of the bed.

"Sorry, but this is not a pleasure trip. There are serious matters I must handle."

His eyes greedily followed me as I pulled on a pair of red silk panties, then a black cotton skirt that fell to my ankles. Then came a red lace bra and a black button-up shirt with short sleeves. Michael sat up, resting his back against the headboard when I sat on the edge of the bed next to his hip. He was a little paler than he had been when he came in. I never took so much blood that his life was in danger or that he couldn't fight, just enough to take the edge off of my hunger. With any luck, I would begin the return trip home tonight and hunt again in my own domain tomorrow night.

"Are you sure you don't want Gabriel and me to accompany you?" he asked as I drew on a pair of socks.

"No, I'll be fine."

That was a lie. I was anxious and confused, but telling him my fears wouldn't have made him feel any better. His job was to protect me when I could not protect myself, which was only during the daylight hours. Michael and Gabriel protected me against humans only. They were no match for any of the other dark creatures that lurked in the night. How could they hope to protect me against Danaus or the naturi?

I shoved my feet into a pair of black boots with a low chunk heel that laced up to nearly my knees. These were built a little better for the terrain than my usual high-heeled leather boots. I ran my hand through my tousled hair, wishing I had time and access to a quick shower.

"But he will be going with you," Michael said. There was something sharp and bitter in his tone that startled me, breaking my mind free of the last lingering tendrils of desire that had clouded my thoughts.

Turning my gaze back to his handsome face, I was surprised to find lines of anger and jealousy furrowing his brow. "I do as I please," I quietly reminded him.

"I'm sorry, Mira," he said, hesitantly touching my shoulder. A look of fear flashed through his pale blue eyes. We both knew this budding relationship was a strained and uneasy thing as we sought out each other's boundaries. "I didn't mean anything."

I sighed, placing my hand against his cheek. He relaxed

instantly and pressed a kiss to my palm. "I know. Danaus is part of the matter that I must take care of. Rest for a while. I am going up to the deck. I will meet you and Gabriel at the hotel before dawn."

Walking up to the main deck, I ran my hand across Gabriel's shoulder as I passed him. He followed me at a discreet distance, hanging back toward the shadows as I strolled over to the railing of the barge. The dark night sky was filled with glittering stars. It had been a while since I'd seen so many stars, but they were quickly being overwhelmed by the growing brightness of Aswan. When I had last appeared in the town, it was only a scattering of huts, low buildings, and a single wooden dock. While it was nowhere near the size of Cairo or Alexandria, it was swelling in its own right. The tourists were starting to grow weary of the pyramids and were traveling farther down the Nile to see the mysteries of Philae and the beauty of Abu Simbel.

The wind played with my hair, tossing it about my back. I closed my eyes and slowly reached out with my senses. It was like running my hands over the people in the city, gently touching each mind for less than a heartbeat then moving on. I let my senses reach out as far as the Tombs of the Nobles and down through Abu Simbel before pulling my powers back into my body. I could not feel Jabari, though I'm not sure if I was expecting to find him.

The battle at Machu Picchu five centuries ago had not gone well, despite the fact that we were the victors. Two weeks earlier I'd been kidnapped from Sadira's care in Spain and taken to the Incan city in the sky. Surrounded by members of the naturi light clan at all times, Nerian tortured me by moonlight while all-too-sweet voices promised that the pain would stop if I only promised to protect them from the evil vampires. If not for my constant thirst for blood, I would even have forgotten, under the weight of the unrelenting pain, that I was a vampire. For two weeks there was only pain and hunger.

And then Jabari arrived. The rest of the triad was with him, as well as a great nightwalker army, yet looking back, I recalled only him. His white robes seemed to glow in the firelight, his dark skin almost as black as the night itself. He had saved me and fought the naturi. But still, only the triad and a handful of others escaped that wretched mountain, while some of the naturi disappeared into the surrounding jungle.

While Jabari hunted the naturi, he left me a wounded Nerian to finish. I broke his legs and slashed his stomach open, but dawn was coming. I was out of time. I left Nerian to die while I ran from the mountain. In the jungle, I buried myself deep into the earth to escape the sun's rays, confident that Nerian had died on the mountaintop.

The next night, Jabari returned for me. Held tightly in his strong arms, he carried me off to the safety of his home in Egypt. I remained with the Ancient for one century. He helped to keep the nightmares at bay during both the night and the day, when I should have been able to escape my battered psyche.

Jabari gave me something I had managed to find only briefly during my human years and never as a vampire: a home. Within his domain, I was always welcome. I was viewed as a beloved child, a talented protégé to be taught and encouraged. Sadira had taught me to read, to play instruments, and even various languages. But with Jabari, I gained true knowledge. He taught me the history of our kind, of the naturi and the bori, and the war that consumed all of the races before the bori and naturi were finally exiled.

While I was with Jabari, he encouraged me to explore my ability to manipulate fire. For the Ancient, it wasn't about being a weapon, but honing a skill, becoming better at something. Under his guidance, I took back control of my life, no longer a pawn for Sadira or the naturi.

Opening my eyes, I frowned, a chill encasing my lungs. There were no other nightwalkers within the area. Egypt had always been sporadically populated with my kind because of Jabari's presence. No one wanted to risk catching the attention of an Elder. Yet, it had been a long time since I walked into a region that didn't have several nightwalkers lurking in the shadows. I might not seek out another nightwalker, but there was something comforting in knowing that he or she was there. That I wasn't completely alone in the darkness.

I turned my head, catching sight of Danaus out of the corner of my eye. He had approached while my focus was on the city and surrounding area. The leather duster was gone, but he still wore his black cotton pants and black sleeveless T-shirt. There were several knives strapped to his waist, wrists, and thigh. He was prepared for battle.

"I see you've fed," he said as he stepped closer to the railing. I resisted the urge to run my finger over my lips. I generally wasn't a messy eater. "You're . . . pink," he continued, filling in the silence. The word stumbled and tripped from his throat as if he struggled for an appropriate description.

Throwing my head back, I laughed, the sound drawing the attention of several deckhands. I always looked a bit flushed after a good meal, my skin taking on a pinker, more lifelike color for a few hours, but I hadn't expected him to notice. He wasn't looking particularly happy with me; not that he ever was, but his glare seemed more censuring than usual.

Leaning back, my elbows rested lightly on the rails. "Have you eaten?" He nodded, his gaze directed at the dock as we pulled in. "I bet something died for your meal."

His narrowed eyes jerked to my face. "It's not the same."

His jaw was clenched and his lips pressed into a hard, thin line. Hot, angry power bubbled within him, pulsing against me in waves that would have rivaled the midday sun that baked the Egyptian landscape. "Why not?" I turned and walked toward the bow, my eyes on Aswan. I didn't expect an answer or want one. There shouldn't be a difference. I didn't care what he thought. We both did what we had to in order to survive; it was as simple as that.

It wasn't long afterward that we docked at Aswan, our little boat skirting several larger cruise ships to settle at a less crowded berth. I jumped down to the wooden dock, not looking back to see if Danaus had followed. But I could feel him a few steps behind me, his anger simmering. I was irritated with him. At least, I think he was bothering me. It could have been that I was forced to cut short my time with Michael, or that I didn't know where the hell Jabari was. It could have even been the fact that the naturi were once again threatening and I didn't want to face them. It could have been any or all of these things, but right now Danaus was an easy target.

I paused on the Corniche el-Nil for a moment, gazing up and down the road as I tried to get my bearings. The road ran north-south along Aswan closest to the Nile, housing a variety of travel agencies, which in turn managed the various motor launches and feluccas that ferried tourists to the islands that dotted this stretch of the Nile. We had landed farther south in Aswan than I'd anticipated. Directly in front of me was the Nile and Elephantine Island, and beyond that, Kitchener's Island, with its exotic botanic gardens. One block over behind me, the rich sounds of the souq could be heard. Vendors would be at their trade for another few hours, hawking their wares to anyone who passed close enough to be considered a potential customer. Vibrant Nubian music filled the air, played on pear-shaped guitars called ouds and shallow douff drums. The sun had set, but the city was just coming alive as people finally escaped the oppressive heat of the day.

During my stay with Jabari, we had passed most of our time farther north, in Thebes and occasionally in Alexandria. Because I needed to feed more frequently than he did, the Ancient thoughtfully lingered near populous areas, though I suspected he would have preferred to move to a more remote, secluded location. On two occasions we took trips up the Nile to Aswan, where we stayed within the local Nubian villages; Jabari's true home.

Just prior to moving to the New World, I encountered Jabari in Venice during one of my infrequent visits to the Coven. He spoke of moving south to Aswan to oversee the construction of the first Aswan dam. It would flood the areas that had once been the heart of the Nubian empire. While I never had a chance to ask him decades later, I was confident that the Ancient Nubian had also overseen the construction of the High Dam and the careful moving of Abu Simbel and Philae to a safer, drier location.

Walking north along Corniche el-Nil, I weaved my way through the crowds as they stepped off their feluccas and headed back toward their hotels, with Danaus following like a dark rain cloud. The people barely looked up at me as I passed by. The city had a feeling about it that whispered of darker things than me. Jabari had spent his entire existence in this part of the world. He had ventured elsewhere, seen the green lands of South America and the cold tundra of Russia, but he always came back to his beloved Egypt. I think the people of Aswan could feel him when he was there. They never understood what it was they were feeling, though; perhaps assumed it was one of the old gods lingering in the temples or a pharaoh's ghost.

I wondered if they felt his absence. The people hurried

down the streets with their heads down, careful not to make eye contact. The Middle East had always been rife with civil unrest, but now there was an edge to the people that I couldn't understand. Maybe they knew their god was missing.

After a few blocks I finally found what I was searching for. Unfortunately, the ferry to the West Bank was closed for the night. Aswan lay on the East Bank, overflowing with rich vegetation, hotels, and shops. The West Bank was mostly desert, with only a few monuments visited by tourists throughout the day. However, all those monuments closed by 5:00 P.M., so there was no reason for the ferry to remain open past that hour.

Shoving my hand through my hair, I turned where I stood, gazing up and down Corniche for an open felucca. It was only a guess, but I truly doubted that Jabari would have settled near the busy heart of Aswan. There were two types of nightwalkers: those that ran from their past, such as myself, and those that still embraced their human history, like Jabari. I knew where he would have gone. I just had to get there.

A smile lifted my lips as my eyes fell on a young man with skin like rich coffee as he was tying up his small felucca. It couldn't have held more than six people, smaller than most used by tourists, but he could have easily advertised it as a more private excursion.

I bargained for the price of a quick jaunt across the Nile to the landing for the Tombs of the Nobles. He was polite enough to at least ask if I was aware of the fact that the Tombs were closed, but he didn't push the matter. What did he care? He would get paid whether I was turned away at the entrance or not.

Danaus and I boarded the small boat and the captain pushed off from the dock and immediately unfurled the white sail. Between the brisk wind and the swift flow of the

Nile, we were able to cross to the West Bank in only a few minutes. Something in me wished for more time, though. I would have liked to head farther up river to see the Temple of Philae in her new home, bathed in the glow of golden floodlights. Or even gone down river to Edfu and the Temple of Horus. While a Roman replica of ancient Egyptian architecture, the temple still outdated my lengthy existence and was magnificent to see. But for now, I sat in a tiny boat with a vampire hunter while I searched for an Ancient vampire that might or might not be dead.

Ten

Danaus said nothing until we hired a pair of camels and started riding northwest into the desert, past the Tombs of the Nobles. I looked over my shoulder once as we topped the massive hill to see Aswan spread out before me, glittering in the night, with the Nile gliding like a black asp toward the north. We were leaving behind the last signs of civilization.

"Where are we going?" the hunter called from his camel behind me.

My gaze remained on the rock formation to the west that was steadily growing in size. It was the western quarry. "Seeking the key to the triad."

"Which is?" he prompted after a few seconds of silence.

"Who is, you mean."

"Mira . . ."

I smiled. There weren't too many creatures that could reduce my name to a low warning growl, but Danaus was quite successful. "Jabari."

"I thought you said he was dead."

A warm wind swept across the desert from the south, carrying with it the faintest hint of the Nile. The only sound in this vast wasteland was the muffled footsteps of the camels as they steadily maneuvered through the soft sand. There was no life out here beyond the snakes and scorpions. Not for the first time, I wondered if I was gazing at the reason why the Ancients of my race were dwindling. As time passed, Jabari spent less time in the company of the living, preferring the solitude of the vast desert terrain he ruled. And while Tabor had been barely more than half Jabari's age when he was murdered, I knew he had taken to spending more time in Russia's icy tundra than in the western cities of Moscow and St. Petersburg.

While we never aged and were completely immune to disease, my species struggled to last more than a few millennia at best. What was the point of immortality if you couldn't live for more than a couple thousand years?

I bit back a sigh and absently patted my camel's neck, running my finger over its coarse hair. "I don't know. Jabari was always the strongest of the triad. If he is gone, I would like to know if the naturi are responsible."

I didn't know what had happened to Jabari. I suspected that I should have gone straight to the Coven, but I wouldn't have been able to keep the hunter at my side, and for now, I didn't want him out of my sight. Besides, my interaction with the Coven had always been through Jabari. I didn't know how to directly contact Macaire or Elizabeth, the two other members of the ruling vampire body. I didn't think anyone in the Coven would have tried to destroy Jabari. He was one of the oldest and strongest of the Elders, just below Our Liege. Besides, getting any kind of answer from the Coven was proving to be a waste of my time. And for the first time since becoming a nightwalker, I had a feeling that time was in short supply.

After a thirty-minute ride through the desert, we finally reached the great rock outcropping that rose up around us.

An anxious knot tightened in my stomach as I dismounted from the camel. The wind had stopped and the desert seemed to hold its breath as the shadows created by broken slabs of rock watched us in silence.

Danaus started to walk around me and enter the quarry, but I placed my hand in the center of his chest, stopping him. One last time I stretched out my powers, scanning the area. I reached out into the desert and back toward the Tombs and to Aswan, searching for any sign that a nightwalker was near. There was nothing, and it hurt. It hurt more than I wanted to admit. There was no Jabari. Only something dire would draw him away from this area for so long. Maybe he already knew about the naturi and was with the Coven, but for some reason, I didn't believe it. I'd left messages with every contact I had with the Coven and heard nothing. I'd even checked one last time when I awoke in Egypt, but no one responded. With a slight shake of my head, I headed into the quarry with the hunter close at my side. We were on our own.

Slowly, we picked our way around giant boulders and slabs that had been smoothed with ancient hammers and chisels but never taken to the monuments they were intended for. I paused beside an unfinished obelisk. Three sides had been smoothed and carved with hieroglyphics and other images. The fourth side was still unfinished after countless centuries. Abandoned.

"Why here?" Danaus said, standing beside me. "Of all the places in Egypt, why would he be here?"

My hand slid over the unfinished obelisk, images of the last time I had walked through this quarry flashing through my brain. I could recall it as if it had happened only moments ago. I'd been feeling restless then, in no mood to be around the peoples of Alexandria while memories of the naturi haunted my daylight rest, and Jabari brought me down to Aswan. We'd wandered up one side of the Nile and down the other, allowing the quiet to seep into our skin. Walking beside me, Jabari had explained all that went into creating an obelisk of this size.

"Jabari was one of the chief architects for Amenophis II. He designed parts of Karnak," I told Danaus, pride bringing a wavering smile to my mouth as I stared into the emptiness. Jabari had told me of a trip he made to Aswan when he was human, and to two of the quarries here to inspect the stones that would be shipped back to Karnak. Though he never spoke of it, I always got the impression that he never had the chance to finish his life's work at Karnak because his human life had ended somewhere between Aswan and Luxor.

"What are we looking for?" Danaus asked.

Holding out my left hand, I conjured up a small flame, which flickered in the breeze that begun to stir once again. "A sign." Closing my hand around the flame, I tossed it out into the night before us. The flame split into six separate balls of fire and shot out into the deep reaches of the quarry. Shadows danced and retreated around us, revealing their secrets. If Jabari had fought the naturi here, there would be signs of a battle. The rock wall would have new scars, the earth gouged, but above all I would have been able to sense Jabari's death. I was around when nightwalkers were destroyed, had even killed a couple Ancients myself. I knew that a ripple of magic was left in the air when a nightwalker was destroyed, and it lingered for years. The older the nightwalker, the thicker the mark. If Jabari had been destroyed here, I would see it and feel it.

"This is unexpected," stated a deep voice from behind me. We both spun around to find Jabari standing at the top of the unfinished obelisk.

At just over six feet, he was an impressive figure in his traditional robes. Even for a vampire, his skin was still dark, midnight hair cut short on his head. His almond-shaped, mahogany eyes watched me, questioning. He hadn't directed his gaze at Danaus yet and he wouldn't. To recognize Danaus's presence was to give him importance.

Despite the fact that he was standing just a few feet away from me, I still could not sense him. It was like he wasn't really there. I hadn't moved from the base of the obelisk, couldn't even drag my voice past the lump that swelled in my throat. It was like staring at a ghost.

His eyes softened and he raised a hand toward me, beckoning me to his side. It was all the encouragement I needed. I scrambled up the obelisk until I nearly collapsed against him. Wrapping my arms around him, I pressed my cheek to his shoulder. My teeth were clenched so hard my jaws ached as I swallowed the sob that had knotted in my throat. He hadn't been destroyed. He was real and right here.

For a moment my world threatened to crumble. Centuries had passed since I last stood with him in his beloved Egypt, held in his benevolent arms. He had helped me recover from horrors I thought would plague my dreams for all eternity. And then one day I left and never looked back. I stood on my own two feet. But now I stood there holding him as if he were my last tie to sanity.

"Welcome home, my little one," Jabari whispered as he pressed a kiss to the top of my head. His beautiful accent skipped to my ears, seeming to caress my frazzled nerves. He wrapped his strong arms around me, holding me tightly against his chest. "The Old Kingdom has missed you."

Jabari represented more than just a mentor. In many ways he was also the voice of the Coven when Our Liege deigned to remain in the background. During the past few decades, I had been absent from Europe and the Coven, preferring to direct my focus to establishing a steady, consistent balance in my own domain. While nothing negative was ever said about my choice, a dark undercurrent had started to form, strengthened by the growing silence I was receiving from Venice. I needed Jabari to protect my back.

"I feared things must be bad to drive you back here, my desert flower," he murmured, running one hand down the back of my head, smoothing my hair.

I shuddered, struggling desperately to pull myself back together. Jabari was the only vampire in this world that I trusted. He was all I knew of safety and love among my own kind. "Why can't I sense you?"

"I did not wish to be found." There was no censure in his voice, just a statement of fact.

"Forgive me," I said, reluctantly releasing him. "I had few options."

Taking a few steps away from him, I ran a trembling hand through my hair to push it back from my face. My thoughts were coming back into focus. With a wave of my hand, I extinguished the balls of fire that flickered around the quarry. I hadn't expected to find the Elder. Hoped and wished, but never expected it. Yet, he was here now, and he would fix everything.

"You are forgiven," he said, bowing his head in a single, regal nod. "What has brought you to my lands?"

"The naturi."

Those two words sounded flat and dead to my ears. Something seemed to die inside of me every time I mentioned them. I watched Jabari's face, but there was no change in his expression. There was nothing to reveal that he was surprised by what I'd said, or that he had known the naturi was once again threatening to return.

"How?"

"Their symbols have begun to appear on trees, and there was a sacrifice at the Indian Temple of the Sun, Konark." I paused and licked my lips, forcing myself to hold Jabari's piercing gaze. "Nerian was also following me. The naturi attacked us—"

"How is that possible?" Jabari interrupted, though his voice remained even and calm. "You were to kill Nerian more than five hundred years ago."

I took a hesitant step forward, holding both hands out to him. "I thought he was dead."

"Thought?"

I never saw Jabari move. One second he was standing still more than three feet away, and in the next I was flying through the air. My back slammed into the wall of broken rocks. Stars exploded in front of my eyes as my head hit half a breath later. I slid down the wall, my left shoulder striking the ground. Blinking, I looked up to see Jabari step off the obelisk and walk toward me. His expression was still calm and emotionless, but the air tingled now with his anger.

"You were ordered to kill him."

"His legs were broken and his intestines had spilled onto the ground. I didn't think he would survive." I pushed myself off the ground. In my haste, my hand slid in the dirt and rocks, tearing at my palm. Pain screamed through my shoulder and down my spine as I moved.

"The naturi held you captive for two weeks," Jabari argued. "We never could discover all that they did to you. You were a threat to all nightwalkers and were only permitted to live because Nerian was dead. You should have made sure."

"It was dawn!" I screamed. Panic fluttered in my stomach, begging me to run. It was only years after Machu Picchu that I discovered Jabari had defended me from the rest of the Coven, which demanded my destruction. He had saved my life not only from the naturi, but from my own kind as well.

"That's not an excuse." Jabari's right hand lashed out,

grabbing me around the throat. I didn't even have enough time to claw at his hand before he tossed me against another outcropping of rocks like a rag doll. "You failed me."

Pain slashed like lightning through my back as I hit the wall and fell to the floor. "He's dead now," I whispered, doubting I had the strength to rise before he attacked again.

"Centuries too late." His sweet features hardened and his brown eyes had darkened to black clouds in a midnight storm.

My eyes fell closed, holding back the tears that started to gather. I had failed him. Jabari had always been able to depend on me for any request, no matter the task. He had given me so much, and I'd failed him. And now he was going to destroy me just like any other nightwalker who failed to live up to his expectations. A part of me welcomed it, an escape from the pain, but a faint brush of Danaus's power quickly reminded me why we had traveled to Egypt; the naturi. If Jabari destroyed me, no one would be able to protect my home, my people. It was enough that I had failed Jabari, I wouldn't fail all those who had come to rely on me.

I opened my eyes at the sound of a foot scraping in the dirt. Danaus suddenly stepped between Jabari and me, the blade of an eight-inch knife glinting in the faint starlight. My body was sore and protesting, but I pushed to my feet. This was not the wisest decision on Danaus's part nor could I even begin to understand it. Jabari would destroy him before the poor creature could draw a breath, and I still needed Danaus alive.

"This does not solve the problem of the naturi," Danaus said, his hard voice calm.

"Not only do you fail me, one whom I trusted above all others," Jabari began, finally beginning to shout, "but you bring this . . . this human into my domain!"

Standing beside Danaus, I tried to edge in front of him

and keep Jabari's attention on me. "He was the one who captured Nerian. He showed me pictures of the symbols and the sacrifice."

"You betrayed me!" Jabari closed the distance in a blur, grabbing Danaus by the throat. He pitched the hunter a hundred feet across the quarry as if he were tossing garbage out to the curb. Danaus crashed into a smooth wall of rock, cracking and crumbling stone. I winced, gritting my teeth. The impact alone should have shattered the man's spine and broken at least one of his shoulders. I started to drag my eyes back to Jabari, the muscles in my body tensed and waiting for the attack, when I saw Danaus pick himself up off the ground. He rolled his shoulders as if shaking off the momentary pain.

Something in my blood froze. After that bone-crushing impact, Danaus should not have been able to move, let alone stand and prepare for yet another attack from Jabari. My thoughts tripped over themselves as I tried to understand how he was now standing. I didn't know of any creatures other than nightwalkers that might be able to shrug off such a blow. Even a lycan would have been slow to regain his feet.

I think the realization also alarmed Jabari, because I felt the power in the area increase until it was a physical pressure weighing against my chest. The hunter had been upgraded from "bug to be squashed" to "threat that must be eliminated," regardless of Danaus's potential uses. I wanted the hunter dead as much as any other nightwalker, but we needed to get some information out of him first.

Jabari lunged at Danaus again, but despite the Elder's alarming speed, Danaus managed to sidestep him so that the nightwalker's attack was reduced to more of a glancing blow. However, it was still enough to knock Danaus back a step, sending him down on one knee, his knife clenched in one hand.

I balled my fists at my side. What the hell was going on? Danaus wasn't using his knife. He was doing what he could to defend himself without attacking Jabari outright. I didn't know if Jabari had noticed or if he just didn't care. At least Danaus had realized that we needed the information from the Elder, and so wasn't trying to kill him. Yet, if this continued, he would have no choice and one of them would end up dead.

While Danaus was still kneeling on the ground, glaring at Jabari, I rushed over and stood in front of the hunter. Rage now burned on Jabari's face, and I knew I had only seconds to get through to him.

"Jabari, I have not betrayed you," I said, no longer trying to keep the fear out of my voice. My hands trembled uncontrollably and my knees threatened to buckle. "I made a mistake with Nerian, and if you wish to kill me for that, I accept my fate, but bringing Danaus here was not an act of betrayal. I want you to see how desperate we are. The naturi are coming again. If the seal is broken, they will destroy not only the humans, but the nightwalkers as well."

"Do not lecture me!" Jabari's upper lip remained pulled back, and I fought to draw my gaze from his long fangs. He was going to tear my throat out if I didn't think of something.

"Danaus is a hunter, and yet he came to me looking for a way to stop the naturi. I remember so little of that night, and I don't want to remember. I came here hoping to find you, needing you to reform the triad that stopped the naturi the last time."

Behind me Danaus had risen and took one step forward, as if trying to move around me. He apparently wasn't the type to let anyone protect him, but he was going to get himself killed before I could get any more information out of him. I sidled so that I was standing directly in front of him. Reaching back, I grabbed a wrist in each hand. He stiffened at my touch, but I could still move his arms. I pulled his right arm around my waist, his knife still clutched in his hand. I drew up his left arm between my breasts so his left hand was holding my right shoulder. If Jabari was going to kill Danaus, he would have to go through me first. I wasn't completely sure that it would stop him, but I was hoping to buy us a couple more seconds.

The muscles in my body spasmed for a second when Danaus's left hand closed over my shoulder like a circuit closing, wrapping me in his powers. Between the weight of Jabari's powers and the tense strength charging through Danaus, a hand seemed to clench around my soul. A sharp little cry broke from my throat as I struggled to pull my thoughts above the flow of power. A second later I managed to surface and blink, focusing my thoughts again.

Jabari stared at me, his lips pressed into a hard, thin line. The anger had not completely ebbed from his eyes, but something else had distracted his thoughts. He took a half step backward, his brow furrowed. I could only imagine he was shocked to find I was willing to risk my life for a hunter; someone who would cut out my heart before saving me. I couldn't blame him. I was more than a little surprised myself, but the threat of the naturi had put us in an awkward position.

"It does not make sense to kill him when he has information that could be useful," I said. "I came to you because you were at Machu Picchu. You have always been the strongest of the triad. I came to you because I trust no one else."

The silence stretched and twisted in the quarry, the wind dying back down to nothing as the Ancient stared at me, his expression dark and unreadable. "You defend him as if he means more."

Something jerked in my stomach, a new, dark fear springing to life. This was bad. Had Lucas already been whispering to the Coven about me? Were rumors spread by Lucas the reason why I had heard nothing back from the Coven during the past couple of nights?

"I defend him because it is the wise thing to do. I will not throw valuable information away because I do not like its messenger." I definitely didn't like where this was going. If I had learned anything in my six centuries, it was to never prick the ego of a vampire. And the older they were, the worse it would be. I had managed to calm Jabari, and I thought he might have even begun to see the wisdom of what I was saying, but that didn't change the fact that a creature well beneath him in age and power had corrected him. He still had to exact his retribution.

"Would you turn on your own people to protect this hunter?" His deceptively calm voice wrapped around me before sliding into my brain. The peaceful tone of the question belied the underlying menace that lurked in the shadows.

"My loyalty belongs only to those who have earned it."

"Has he? A destroyer of our kind?"

An overwhelming urge to take a step backward trembled in my limbs, but with Danaus behind me, it was difficult to move. "I protect him to save our kind from the naturi, nothing more."

"And when the naturi are gone?" His voice had become calm and even. So much so that we could have been discussing the weather. He had straightened from his previously aggressive stance, his thin body perfectly erect.

"Then I will deliver his life to your hands. I will deliver us both if that is what you wish." Behind me, I felt Danaus stiffen, but he never made a sound, leaving me to my desperate pleading. "You have been both a friend and protector, Jabari. If it is my life you want, then it is yours, but I do not think it will save us from the naturi." I wanted to reach out and cup his face with my hands, to kiss his neck and swear my complete devotion to him, but I couldn't move. I knew I had already lost him.

Jabari approached us, each step careful and precise. He stopped less than two feet away and his voice was barely over a whisper. "It is not your life I want, my Mira." His words were coated so thickly with ice, I shuddered and closed my eyes. Danaus tightened his arms around me, pulling me harder against his chest. His warmth seeped into me through my bare arms and the cotton material of my shirt. The panic faded, enough so I could speak.

"Do not say it, Jabari."

"It is my right to ask."

But that was the big joke; it wasn't a request. When an Elder asked to make you a Companion, you had no choice but to accept. Refusal only meant death. Most would not hesitate to accept such an offer. Though the position was dangerous, it was prestigious. But it also took away all independence, all individual will and rights. This was the punishment Jabari had chosen. Not death. He would wear me down until I was a pale shadow of my former self, driving me to the point where I lay down in the dawn light.

"You know my answer," I said in a low voice. My hands tightened on Danaus's arm to the point of my nails digging into his flesh.

"Mira—"

My head snapped up and I knew my eyes were glowing, a strange blue-purple like bittersweet nightshade. Death in battle held its own honor, and I could face that. What Jabari offered was slavery. My power welled up inside my chest until it was pressing against the inside of my skin, desperate for release. "Do not place us on this precipice," I warned, my tone taking on a hard edge. "I will destroy us both; to hell with the naturi."

Without actually conjuring the thought, a deep blue flame sprang from the earth at my feet. It quickly circled Danaus and me, then rose in intensity until the flames reached my chest. Never had I created a fire against Jabari, but I would not become his slave.

He stared at me through the flickering blue flames, holding his ground. He would never forgive me for this, I knew it. Anger had made his face pale and drawn.

"Let us save our race now," I bargained. "We have all eternity to destroy each other."

The tension was making me a bit hysterical, and the power in the quarry was crushing my brain. My thoughts were scattered and broken at best. I needed to put some distance between these two men or it would drive me mad.

A frigid smile grew on Jabari's face, and he bared pristine white teeth at me. "This is not over."

"I have no doubt," I snapped.

Jabari nodded once and then turned his back on us. He walked over to the end of the unfinished obelisk, his hand running reverently along its smooth surface. The flames shrank back down to the ground and disappeared. Danaus released his steely grip on me and I fell forward to my knees. A chill ran up my arms and I felt as if I'd been dragged through the street behind a runaway carriage.

I forced myself to stand. My knees threatened to give, but I didn't sway as I turned to look at Jabari. He was staring down at the obelisk, a fragment from his past. His face was once again calm and completely unreadable.

"I will think on what you have told me. We will talk again

tomorrow." He reached up and ran one hand over his close-cut hair, his gaze out into the night. I had been dismissed.

"May I find rest in your lands?" I asked. A new fear twisted in my stomach as he remained silent. I was a stranger in his domain and I had to ask his permission to remain. All vampires had to present themselves before the Keeper of the domain. If he refused, I had to leave his lands before the sun rose. This would be particularly difficult considering that Jabari's domain encompassed most of Northern Africa and a scattering of islands in the Mediterranean.

"You may rest here," he slowly said, as if he doubted his decision.

"Thank you." I looked over at Danaus and motioned for him to leave. He hesitated a moment, his eyes darting from me to Jabari. Then without a word he slipped past me and headed toward where the camels had settled.

I stared at Jabari, his body straight and almost painfully erect. I wondered if he hurt as badly as I did. Tonight my heart had shattered in a way I hadn't thought possible after all these long centuries. He still thought I had betrayed him, and whatever wonderful thing that once existed between us had died. He would never forgive me.

"I love you, Jabari. I have loved and trusted you above all else," I whispered. "And even after what has happened to-night and with the knowledge that you will one day kill me, I still love you and will never stop." I don't know if he was listening or if he even cared. I had to say the words. I had to release them into the air so I could be free of the terrible weight on my heart.

Turning, I walked out of the quarry. I wanted him to call for me. I wanted to hear him say that he had loved me too, or that he forgave me, but he didn't make a sound; didn't move as I walked away from him. As I exited the quarry, I conjured up a small flame on the palm of my hand against the overwhelming darkness. I watched it wriggle and dance for a moment. Staring at that tender bit of light, I realized why I had retained this power even after death. If there were such a thing as fate, I had been put on this earth to destroy and not to create.

Eleven

The moon hung pale and swollen overhead in the night sky.
Clouds crept over the stars, blotting out their glittering
light and holding in the oppressive heat of summer. I stood
in the main square, the low gray-white stone walls circling
about me like the sun-bleached bones of an extinct monster. Farther away the mountains rose up, great monoliths of
stone and earth that had survived dynasties and would still
be prodding the sky when my body had turned to dust. The
air smelled thick with vegetation, and the faint tang of blood
was carried by the wind. I followed that wonderful scent up
the stairs, passing through an arch into another temple.

I paused, my heart lurching in my chest. A woman lay
stretched out across a low, large gray stone. Her head was
tilted back so her long black hair flowed from the stone and
brushed the ground. Her brown eyes were wide, trapping me
in their liquid gaze. Standing over her was a man clutching a
knife in one hand. I hadn't made a sound, but he knew I was
there. He looked up at me and I saw Nerian smile.

I tried to take a step backward, but hands grabbed my
arms, forcing me to stay where I was. Struggling, I attempted to look around me at the people holding my arms,

but I couldn't see them. Footsteps echoed through the silence of the night, rising off the stones; more were coming to hold me. I looked back up and Nerian was walking toward me, dagger still in hand. I jerked and twisted, fighting my captors, but I couldn't escape. Cold sweat slithered across my skin. Panic was throbbing in my chest faster than my own heartbeat.

Beyond, I could hear the woman repeating, "You betrayed me," in a soft voice that held an accent long dead from the earth. I pushed backward against my captors, digging my heels into the stones, trying to catch on the small crevices between the bricks, but I couldn't gain any leverage. I pushed, but I couldn't move. Nerian kept coming. His white teeth gleamed in the darkness.

I screamed and jerked but could find no release. He stopped inches from me, his laughter cutting into my skin like little razors. If I looked down, I would find that I was bleeding. He was supposed to be dead. I knew I had killed him. I had incinerated his corpse, leaving behind only a small pile of white ash in Danaus's basement. But he stood before me now, smiling. I could feel the heat of his body, smell his woodsy scent. He pulled back his arm, his laughter rising, growing almost frantic in its pitch. As the dagger plunged into my stomach, my eyes opened and I screamed again.

The sound filled the box, but I couldn't stop. I kept screaming, my hands clawing at the red silk lining the top of the box until it was shredded. I screamed until I choked on a sob lodged in my throat.

With my fingers clenched around the torn silk above my head, I lay still in my protective little box. The muscles in my arms were painfully tensed and my jaw was starting to throb. I was gritting my teeth, trying to keep from screaming again. Bloody tears streaked down the sides of my face.

I swallowed a second sob and forced myself to relax. It was just a nightmare. Nerian was dead and I was safe.

Releasing my death grip on the silk ceiling, I roughly wiped the tears from my face with the heels of my palms. It had all felt so real. I could remember smells and the feel of their hands biting into my flesh. Worst of all, I could remember the beating of my heart. I laid my trembling right hand on my chest, pressing against my sternum, but felt nothing. Things like breathing and a heartbeat were tricks, illusions used by vampires to give the appearance of life. But things like that took power and energy, so we rarely bothered with it unless we were trying to fool humans. I never resorted to such tricks, but lying there now, I wondered if my heart had been beating while I dreamed.

I had not had a nightmare about Machu Picchu in a very long time. They once nearly drove me mad, but Jabari helped me, protected and guided me from my nightmare. After I'd left Egypt centuries ago I thought I also left his protection, but now I feared that I had been wrong. Maybe he helped me during my daylight sleep during all these years, and now that we'd parted ways, he had lifted his protection. Did I now face an eternity of waking with a scream on my lips?

Or worse, had Jabari sent the dream? Would he torture me until I was finally broken and came crawling back to him? I closed my eyes and folded my shaking hands over my stomach. I forced my thoughts away from the rising panic. The nightmare could be nothing more than what it was: a nightmare. I was upset about Jabari and the naturi; both had invaded my rest.

I lay there, fatigue creeping into my frame. Nightwalkers generally didn't dream during the daylight hours. We had no memories of those hours when the sun hovered above the earth. It was dangerous for me to dream. It used up energy that I was supposed to be conserving for the night, for the hunt.

It wasn't impossible for nightwalkers to dream, but it was extremely rare. As far as I knew, it only happened to those of us known to as First Bloods. They were rare simply because most nightwalkers couldn't be bothered with spending several nights to several years carefully working a spell to bring over a human. First Bloods rose stronger and more powerful than our more common brethren, those lovingly referred to as "chum." While crass and insulting, the nickname fit. Chum was quickly made and little more than bait for a true predator.

As my thoughts calmed, drifting away from the nightmare, a deeper sense of foreboding seeped into my bones. Hesitantly, I stretched out my senses, but I didn't have to go far. Michael was leaning against the box and he was hurt. Someone else was in the room. I unlocked the box and threw back the lid, sitting up. My eyes easily located Michael, who was sitting on the floor near my feet, clutching his right arm to his chest.

Jumping to my feet, I turned to find another man, standing near the wall, a gun in one hand. My muscles tensed at the sight of Omari and I bit back a low growl. The dark-haired, dark-skinned man who served Jabari lowered the gun to his side but didn't put it in his shoulder holster.

"He came to protect you," Michael said in a rough voice before I could lunge at the human. I hadn't told him about what occurred with Jabari, but I had no doubt that my astute assistant could easily read my tense posture.

"What happened?" I said, pivoting slowly on a heel as I gazed about the room. We had been lucky enough to secure a corner suite at the Sarah Hotel on the southern edge of the city. I took a couple steps forward, glass crackling under my feet. The pretty little room had been turned into a war zone.

Furniture was broken, pictures pulled or knocked off the wall, and curtains torn. There was also a splatter of blood against one white wall, while the others were peppered with bullet holes. The hotel was located on a clifftop overlooking the city. With any luck, the distance had helped insulate us from drawing the attention of other city dwellers. However, I knew that both the hotel owner and the police had to be taken care of financially before we left the city.

"Four men attacked a few hours before sunset. They were well-trained hunters," Michael said. He reached a hand over and closed the lid of my coffin. In the center was a deep dent, as if someone had taken an axe to it. I gritted my teeth as I stared at it. The dent was over where my heart would have been.

"I arrived shortly after them," Omari stated, his words rolling to me like a low rumble of thunder.

My narrowed gaze snapped to his tense frame. "How did you know?"

Dressed in a pair of jeans and a plain, white button-up shirt, he had the polished look of an executive on holiday. Of course, the splatter of blood on his shirt and the tear in his jeans near his right calf destroyed the effect.

"Jabari doesn't trust the one called Danaus. He sent me to watch over you, and Jamila was to follow Danaus if he left the hotel during the day," Omari said, finally holstering his gun under his left arm.

"Where is the hunter?" The muscles in my shoulders tightened into a hard knot. Danaus had not been there when I was attacked.

"He left the hotel about an hour before the attackers arrived," Michael said. "He hasn't returned yet."

I stared down at my protector, relieved that the scent of his blood wasn't clouding my mind. After reaching the five-century mark, I discovered that I could go several days without needing to feed. With the meal Michael had provided for me the previous night, I was still feeling quite sated.

"Where is Gabriel?" I demanded, suddenly realizing his dark form was missing from my chambers.

A frown pulled at the corners of Michael's full lips. "He's following the men to find out who they are and where they have hidden themselves. I haven't heard back yet." He was worried, and I couldn't blame him. Gabriel was good at what he did, but four against one was a little much even for him. I gazed out the window, taking in the murky gray sky. I was awake earlier than usual. Quickly, I mentally searched the city for Gabriel.

"He's safe." My voice sounded as if it had crossed a vast distance before reaching my ears. "He's returning to the hotel." I reached out a little farther and discovered Danaus was several blocks away toward the northeast but had not yet begun moving toward the hotel.

"If I'm not needed, I'll return to my lord," Omari said, drawing my gaze back to his face.

"Is Jabari near?"

"Yes, he keeps a residence within Koti."

I nodded, recognizing the name of one of the Nubian villages on Elephantine Island. "Will you take Michael with you; tend his wounds?"

Omari stared at my bodyguard then looked up at me before briefly bowing his head. "Yes, I will take him with me."

I pressed my lips into a firm line as I looked back over at my angel. "Take Gabriel with you. I will come to Jabari after I deal with the hunter."

"Are you sure you will not need us?" Michael said, wincing as he pushed to his feet. He was hurt, but Omari and Jamila would see that he was properly stitched up. I needed to travel fast and I did not want them in my way when I faced Danaus.

"I'll manage," I said, failing to keep my fangs from peeking out when I spoke. "Go now."

I walked over to the small balcony that looked down on the city and the Nile. Nearby was the first cataract with the outcropping of stone that had once caused a series of rapids in the Nile. With the addition of the High Dam in the seventies, the rapids had been largely tamed. I waited until I sensed Gabriel meeting Michael and Omari in the lobby before putting one hand on the balcony railing and vaulting smoothly over it. Before I hit the ground four stories below, both my invisibility and cloaking spells were in place. I could not be seen by humans nor sensed by other magic using creatures. I didn't know what Danaus was capable of, but I wasn't taking any chances. He had been conveniently gone while someone attacked me while I slept and endangered the lives of my angels. I struggled to believe that he might have been kidnapped while this all occurred, or that it was coincidence that he just happened to be away from the hotel at that moment.

Cutting down the road that led back into the city proper, I ran toward the north, slowly working my way east. I slowed my gait every few blocks to check Danaus's location, but he hadn't moved yet. The city streets were still crowded with a mix of locals and tourists, enjoying the cooling temperatures now that the sun had set. After less than a mile, the tall white buildings and shorter tan square homes gave way to a vast expanse that looked like the ancient ruins of a forgotten city. It was Fatimid Cemetery. The old Muslim burial ground was filled with small, square mausoleums with domed tops and arched entries. However, the sun, wind, and sand that had ravaged the country over the long centuries took its toll on the monuments here. Names and inscriptions chiseled in the stones were worn away. Stone paths into the cemetery were broken and mostly covered by sand and dirt.

The sounds of the city died off here, falling to a soft hum of noise. Pausing at the entrance, I reached up and brushed some hair from my eyes. The wind had picked up, carrying with it the smell of the Nile. It wasn't all that pleasant a smell, but it carried good memories with it. Some nights Jabari and I would follow the winding river north, walking along as close to the banks as possible. He would tell me tales of when Thebes was the capital city of the Egyptian Empire and how he designed great monuments for the pharaoh.

Danaus was on the move finally. He had been with a group of three humans. I sensed him headed in my direction, with the other humans headed northwest, back toward the city and the river. With a smile, I silently darted over to the shadows of a large mausoleum. After I dealt with Danaus, I would go after the humans.

Leaning one shoulder against the smooth white stone wall, it surprised me that I was amazingly calm. I knew I was going to kill Danaus. I was going to put my hand into his chest and pull out his heart. It was all quite simple. It might not be his style to stake vampires during the daylight hours, but he apparently had no problems sending in others to do the job. None of it made any sense, but that didn't matter. He wasn't there when I was attacked. That was damning enough for me.

Barely five minutes passed before Danaus finally walked past me. "Where were you?" I said, dropping the cloaking spell at the same time. I tapped down the urge to sink my teeth into his throat as I watched him skillfully spin around to face me while pulling a dagger from a sheath at his side.

"Out," he snapped. He straightened his stance when he realized it was only me, and put the knife back in his sheath. That was a mistake, I mused.

"Where were you?" I repeated, pausing between each word. I was still lounging against the side of the mausoleum.

He stood only a few feet away, his feet wide apart and his hands hanging at his sides. Despite the fact that he'd put away his knife, tension ran through his frame; alert and ready. "Seeing the city."

"While you were *conveniently* gone, attackers appeared." I pushed off the building and stepped away from it into the open. Danaus took two steps to the right, maintaining a comfortable distance between us. "Four hunters, well trained. Just . . . like . . . you. Did you send them?"

"No."

"Did you know they were coming?"

"No."

I launched my body into his, and we crashed into the side of another worn mausoleum with a heavy thud. "Lies," I snarled, my fangs bared. I might not be hungry, but I would happily drain him before ripping his heart from his chest.

Danaus pushed me away and drew his knife again, narrowing his eyes at me. We had danced this before, but now there were no more games.

"I didn't know they would come."

"But you know who they are, don't you?" Kicking out with my left foot, I clipped his hand, but he held tight to his knife. I wished I had changed from the previous night. While the skirt was slit on both sides up to the knee and provided ample ease of movement, I never liked fighting in a skirt. "You know them because you're one of them. They knew how to find me because you told them."

"I didn't know they would attack." He edged away from the wall so he had more room to maneuver, but it wasn't easy. The ground was uneven, filled with graves and large cover stones, not to mention random chunks of rock broken off from other monuments.

"You sold me out!"

I grabbed him. His knife sliced my upper right arm, but it

didn't stop me from throwing him into the wall. The impact knocked the air from his lungs, and I was there before he could suck in the next breath. My hand locked around his throat, pressing into his esophagus. He struck at me with his knife again, but I caught his wrist. With few options left open, he kicked at me. The force pushed me backward, but I used the momentum of my falling body to pull him with me to the ground. Danaus landed on his side next to me.

Frustrated, I released my hold on his throat. I needed a better approach. Rolling back to my feet before he could, I kicked him below the chin, snapping his head back as he got to his knees.

"I defended you from Jabari!" Circling him, I could barely hear the crunch of rock and sand under my feet over the pounding fury in my head. "I defended you and now I have lost him forever." Stopping in front of him, I grabbed his shirt in both hands. I pulled him to his feet so he was staring me in the eye. "My life is forfeit because of you. My domain is lost, *because of you*."

"I didn't send them," he repeated, his eyes narrow, glittering slits. "Why would I send someone else when I'm looking forward to cutting your heart out?"

I tensed the muscles in my arms, preparing to slam him into a nearby pile of jagged rocks, when something shot through the slim distance separating our faces. I jerked my head backward, my eyes widening. We both looked at the mausoleum wall beside us to find a small arrow shivering in the tan brick wall. A bolt from a naturi wrist crossbow.

Danaus reacted before I could, throwing his body into mine. We landed in a heap on the ground behind the tall sides of a grave cover stone. He lay on top of me as I heard three more arrows ping against the stone and bounce off. The naturi had found us. I loosened my grip on his shirt and slid out from beneath him, trying to edge around the side of the grave enough so I could see around the cemetery.

"How many are there?" I demanded, as another arrow whizzed over the top of the grave. I lay flat on my back in the dirt, straining to hear any indications that they were close. I looked back at Danaus, who was regarding me with a confused expression. "In case you haven't caught on, I can't sense them."

"How has your kind survived so long?" he said with a slight shake of his head.

Glaring at him, I pulled back my lips enough to angrily expose my fangs. I was in no mood to exchange barbs when I had the damned naturi trying to kill me and I still had to kill him before the night was over.

The wind shifted and I caught a light smell of trees and water, the green smell of the rich earth after a rainstorm, all scents that had no business being in Egypt. They were close. I reached over and pulled a sword from a sheath on Danaus's back. Facing a member of the naturi unarmed was never a wise choice.

"Seven," Danaus said. "Four are in the cemetery, approaching fast, and three are on a rooftop outside the cemetery."

I nodded. The three outside the graveyard were to keep us pinned down until the ones in the cemetery could reach us. I rolled to my knees at the same time I heard the ultrasoft footsteps of the approaching naturi. We had visitors.

Leaping to my feet, I raised the blade so it was in front of my heart. Two naturi stood a couple dozen yards away with their arms raised toward me. Bolts sped across the expanse, aimed at my chest. I deflected them, wishing I had something with which to return fire. I didn't carry a gun. No nightwalker carried a gun. There had never been a need until now. With any other creature, it would have been a matter of knives or our bare hands. It had been five hundred years since we'd had a series of encounters with naturi before this, and guns hadn't been the models of efficiency and accuracy that they were now. I was learning the hard way how to deal with the naturi. If I survived this, Gabriel would have to give me a quick lesson on how to fire a gun.

Without bothering to reload their crossbows, both naturi drew short swords and rushed me, clearly realizing that a gun would be relatively useless. The blade I held had more reach, but I knew they would waste no time coming in close to make good use of their steel.

"Nerian?" demanded the one closest to me, his hazel eyes narrowed. He had the same bushy hair and thick frame as Nerian, indicating that he was probably with the animal clan as well.

The smile grew across my face before I could stop it. It was a smile similar to one I'd seen on Jabari's face in the past, one of peace and joy and malice. "Ashes," I replied in a voice that could have frozen the Nile. "And you will join him soon."

They both attacked at the same time, forcing me to dodge the blade of one while blocking the other. Across the cemetery I could hear the sound of steel clanging against steel. Apparently, Danaus had made some new friends. I kicked one of my attackers in the chest, sending him tumbling backward over a raised grave, while I blocked two more slashes from the naturi aiming to take off my head.

I would have to get rid of one of my attackers if I had any hopes of incinerating the other. Unfortunately, creating and controlling fire took a great deal of energy and concentration, particularly with the naturi. With houses, and sadly with vampires, all you had to do was start the fire. Humans took a little more work, but for some reason the naturi were the worst. Something about these creatures didn't want to burn. That's not to say they couldn't, with the exception of a conscious naturi from the light clan. Overall, the naturi made nice kindling; it just required extra effort. And with one aiming to cut me into multiple pieces, I couldn't be distracted with cremating my foes.

I turned, careful to keep my back to the wall of one of the larger mausoleums. If Danaus lost his battle or if one of his attackers abandoned him and attacked me, I didn't want him to suddenly appear at my back. The naturi thrust his blade at me. I blocked it. As he drew it away, he flicked the tip so the edge grazed the bottom of my arm. A long red line appeared, sending a sharp, burning pain up my arm. It was a sensation I had forgotten about. All the naturi weapons were charmed, a special poison that screamed through the body.

I kicked at him, but he sidestepped my blow. What he didn't expect was my fist landing on his nose the next second, snapping his head backward. Beneath my knuckles I felt bone break and flesh give. He staggered a couple steps backward, blood pouring down his face. He cursed, which always sounded strange to me. Their language was so beautiful and lyrical that curses came out sounding more like compliments, which is how I took it.

Across the graveyard a groan broke above the sounds of fighting. I couldn't chance a look over, but it wasn't Danaus's voice. The hunter rid himself of one of his opponents. I attacked my bloody opponent before my other foe returned. Lucky for me, pain from his broken nose clouded the naturi's judgment, and it was only two seconds later before my sword was buried in his chest. Grinning, I drew the blade upward, ripping through his vital organs and snapping bone until it broke through his collarbone and shredded the muscles and tendons in his shoulder. His eyes glazed over and his short sword clattered to the ground. Before he could collapse, I slashed my sword through the air, freeing his head from his neck.

I looked up to find my other playmate coming at me, rage glittering in his green eyes. His anger gave him more strength and speed than his companion, but I still had an edge. Nerian haunted my thoughts enough that I knew I had to kill this naturi or I would be in their hands once again—a fate I would not repeat. The brown-haired creature slashed and blocked with ease, forcing me to circle away from the wall, exposing my back. I tried to circle around so I didn't have to worry about anyone plunging a blade in my back, but he was good.

We exchanged glancing blows so that after a couple of minutes we were both bleeding small streams from half a dozen little cuts. My body burned and my arms trembled from the pain. The naturi's leather jerkin was soaked with blood and sweat, but his eyes were narrowed and keenly focused on me. Clearly, his goal was to kill me.

Gritting my teeth, I blocked another series of blows aimed at my heart and slashed at him, backing him up a couple feet. With a little space between us, I lowered my eyelids until my eyes were reduced to narrow violet slits. He took a step toward me with his sword raised but lurched to a sudden stop, eyes widening. His irises seemed to be swallowed up by the whites of his eyes and his mouth opened as a low, strangled cry echoed through the strangely quiet graveyard. I lowered my sword, focusing all my energy on his body. It took only another couple seconds for the flames to peek through his flesh, blackening it. The sound of sizzling skin and tissue hissed in the air, while the smell of burning hair and leather overwhelmed any lingering scents of the Nile and the city. I stepped back as his clothes ignited and he crumbled to the floor. He never screamed and it was a bit disappointing, because it had been such a painful way to go. But what do you expect when you start a fire in someone's lungs?

When the naturi was reduced to a clump of blackened

pieces, I withdrew the power, extinguishing the fire. Exhausted, I crumpled to my knees in front of the corpse. The sounds of fighting had died off and I could vaguely feel Danaus nearby. I needed to rest for a moment before turning back to my dilemma with him. Summoning a little power, I pushed out and touched the minds of any humans who had wandered close at the sounds of fighting or the sight of the brief fire. It took a little effort, but I erased the image, convincing them to turn around and return to their homes. Our secret was still safe.

"There's the little princess," announced a bold, mocking voice into the growing silence.

Spinning around, I landed on my butt in my haste. The last naturi had forced me to turn, leaving my back to the vast expanse of the cemetery. The last three naturi from across the street were cautiously drawing closer.

Seated on the ground with my back pressed to the sand-worn wall of one of the crumbling, red brick tombs, my eyes were locked on the center naturi, who was staring at me. I had never seen a naturi like him. Well over five feet, he had hair so dark that it looked black, where all the naturi I had ever seen before were either blond or light brown. His right eye was covered with a black leather patch, while his right cheek and jaw were crisscrossed with rough, jagged scars. The naturi healed from nearly everything, their warm beauty seemingly protected for all time.

The one-eyed naturi took a step closer, edging around the dead bodies of his companions with his sword tightly clenched in his right hand. "Time to go."

"Not a chance." Something in his voice teased at my memories, as if I should remember him, but I could not recall ever seeing a naturi like him.

"But I have such plans for you." He took another step closer. Digging in my heels, I prepared to leap to my feet.

Out of the corner of my eye I saw the other two naturi turn toward Danaus. They would keep the hunter occupied while this naturi took care of me.

Yet, again his voice and words haunted me, bringing back images of Nerian and our final conversation. "Are you Rowe?"

His grin widened and he threw open his arms in a shallow bow. "At your service." His dark red button-up shirt was open at the collar, and when he bent forward, I got a clear look at the scars that streaked across his muscular chest. As he straightened, he paused and his grin faded. "You don't remember me, do you?"

"Nope."

"We'll fix that." Rowe brought his sword down, but I blocked it with my own. Seated on the ground, I was at a definite disadvantage. I was too tired and hurt to try to burn him. I needed to get to my feet.

Rowe was about to bring his sword down again when a pair of high-pitched screams rent the air. A chill went up my spine and I flinched against the sound as if it were slicing through my skin. We both looked up to find that the other two naturi had dropped their short swords and were clawing wildly at their arms and face, pulling at their skin while screaming. I didn't have a clue what was happening to them. They collapsed to the ground then, their lithe bodies jerking and arching in pain. Suddenly, the tanned skin split and blood poured out, hissing and bubbling. Their blood was boiling. If I hadn't seen it, I wouldn't have believed it to be possible.

"I'll catch you soon," Rowe said, pointing his sword at me. The sole surviving naturi then darted across the graveyard and down into the shadowy street.

My stomach twisted as it tried to turn itself inside out, my eyes falling back on the dying naturi. It was only then that I felt the enormous press of power filling the graveyard, pushing against my skin like a hand on my chest. My gaze jerked around the area and I found Danaus focused on the two naturi. He was on his knees, one hand outstretched toward them. He was doing it. This creature I had threatened and taunted was boiling the blood of his enemies from inside.

There was a brief moment of awe as I sat there watching their blood cool in the night air. My trick was good, but his was better. And what was to keep him from doing the same to me and the rest of my kind?

Twelve

When the naturi stopped writhing on the ground and were silent except for the occasional pop and hiss of melting bone and tendon, Danaus lowered his shaking hand. In the light from a distant street lamp, sweat glistened on his hard face and ran down his arms. The power he had called forth flowed out of the cemetery and a cool breeze swept in. He looked exhausted and a little pale. That unique ability obviously took a lot out of him.

He looked up at me and our eyes locked, both thinking the same thing. Did I have enough strength left to kill him before he could kill me? We were both exhausted, but if it meant our lives, I knew we both had the energy to crush one another. I had felt his power, let it wash over me when we were close, but it never occurred to me that he could do something like this. He could kill nightwalkers without ever getting close. And yet I'd never heard anyone mention such a unique gift. Of course, the hunter would have quickly become the hunted if we had known he was this dangerous. The Coven would have sent scores of vampires after him and we would not have rested until his existence was wiped from this earth. We could not afford such an enemy.

I don't know how long we sat there staring at each other, waiting for the other to flinch first. Time seemed to stretch and twist in that graveyard filled with naturi corpses. We both had these horrible powers, which created a great amount of fear in those around us. For centuries Jabari was the only thing that kept me from being crushed by the Coven. And now I knew Danaus's secret. One word from me and he would be hunted by vampires from all over the world until he was dead . . . if he didn't kill me first.

Yet, sitting there in the dirt in that lonely Egyptian cemetery, I wasn't sure I would ever speak of what happened. He saved my life when he had absolutely no reason to. I didn't think it was possible, but I was even more confused than I'd been twenty-four hours ago.

"Who are you?" My voice sounded rough and ragged to my own ears. The various cuts and strains were coming back into focus, until I was nearly drowning in the pain. My grip on the sword in my right hand relaxed and I let it slip from my limp fingers. A breeze stirred, sweeping up from the river and weaving its way through the city before finally reaching us. Rich spices mixed with the thick smell of humanity drifted toward us, freeing us from the pall of death that had blanketed the graveyard.

Danaus sat down and was swallowed up by a deep shadow thrown by one of the mausoleums, becoming little more than a dark figure. A nightmare.

"I am a member of a group called Themis." His breathing was still labored and his arms trembled. There was a long cut across his left bicep, leaving the arm nearly covered in blood. Something in me stirred at the sight of the blood, but after what I had seen him do, I would not try for the temptation.

"The same as the men who attacked before sunset?"

"Since leaving the U.S., I haven't had a chance to get a message to them. Tonight, I finally met with my contact at the Officers' Club at the far north end of the city." Each word that passed his lips was slow and hesitant. He looked down at the ground, his brow furrowed. I suspected he didn't want to tell me anything, but knew that if we were going to move forward I had to know more. "I didn't know they were sending anyone here. When I met with my contact, I discovered they thought I had been captured and was being held against my will. There are some in Themis that don't ask questions. They were to rescue me and kill you."

"And now?"

"They have been informed that we are . . . working together." A wry, almost bitter smile quirked one corner of his mouth. His deep blue eyes flicked up to my face briefly and I had the impression he was fighting a laugh.

"I'm sure they are pleased with that." A faint noise jumped from the back of his throat that almost sounded like a laugh. Apparently, I wasn't the only one skating on thin ice at the moment. "Is that who you were meeting with here?"

"Yes, I caught them as they headed back north."

"Has Themis called off its dogs?" I inquired, idly picking up a small rock and turning it over with the tips of my fingers.

"The hunters will be on a plane out of Egypt within the next hour."

"Smart."

I would hold off from killing Danaus for now. He had used his power to not only destroy the naturi attacking him, but also successfully scared off Rowe, incidentally exposing his unique ability and saving me from a fate potentially worse than death. However, I wouldn't mind taking a chunk out of the hides of those who had hurt Michael. Nothing could light my temper faster than the thought of being attacked while I slept. I had no respect for cowards who attacked a person while he or she was defenseless.

I rose to my feet, wincing and gritting my teeth as I moved. My body hurt, and it would continue to hurt until I either fed or slept for the day. Both possibilities were still a way off, unfortunately.

"Who was your friend?" Danaus asked, slowly pushing to his feet as well.

I shook my head as my eyes danced over the remains of the naturi. "The naturi Nerian had mentioned, Rowe."

"They want you again?"

"So it would seem," I whispered. I wanted to make some witty remark about how they should have learned their lesson the first time, but I couldn't form the words. Something inside me was screaming in mindless terror. *Not again.* I couldn't let them take me again.

"Drag the bodies over to this mausoleum," I said, motioning with my head toward a large, crumbling building with its dome roof still intact. The arch opening was cracked and broken: the years had not been kind, but I was hoping the neglect meant that it was abandoned by the owner's family. Grabbing the arm of the headless naturi, I bent down and picked up the head by the hair, then pulled them into the tomb.

Danaus followed my lead and pulled over the bodies of the two naturi he managed to boil from the inside. After wrestling a little with limbs, we got the mangled remains of the six bodies piled inside the tomb.

I stumbled backward a couple steps out of the mausoleum, my vision blurring as I struggled against growing fatigue. Danaus caught my arm and steadied me.

"You're still bleeding," he said as he took his hand away and looked at the dark blood smeared across his fingers.

"Charmed weapons," I said in a low voice. "It takes longer to heal."

"You need to feed."

"You offering?"

Danaus took a step away from me and shook his head once. "No."

With a slight shrug of my shoulders, I looked out across the graveyard. The air was silent again, no one wandering close to this resting place for the dead. "I am going to Jabari's. I can manage until then."

"I'll get a car—" he began, his footsteps heading toward the graveyard entrance.

"You're not going." I shook my head, trying to clear the fog. Jabari was waiting for me. I needed my wits about me. Hiking up the left side of my skirt, I grabbed my cell phone from the garter that kept it strapped to my thigh. I had put it on the previous night upon our return to the hotel. I wanted to keep it close after Michael and Gabriel decided to do a little exploring in the city. Danaus looked at the thing like I had just pulled a rabbit out of my ass.

"We are not all fearful of this century's technology." I grabbed his wrist and slapped the phone into his palm. "Call Charlotte. Her number is programmed into the phone. Tell her I need to see if she can get my plane down to Aswan tonight. We're leaving."

"Where are we going?"

"Tell her home. I'm done. Jabari knows of the naturi. He will take care of it." I paused for a moment and stared at the hunter. I couldn't believe what I was about to say, but he'd just saved me from the naturi. Staring up at Rowe tonight, I realized that I'd been spending much of my energy blaming Danaus for everything that had gone wrong recently. In truth, it was a fair mix of my own stupidity and the naturi. Danaus didn't bring back the naturi. He was just the poor schmuck that got stuck with the job of telling someone about it. "You can hitch a ride with us back to the States. After that, you're on your own." I knew I couldn't leave him here with Jabari.

Danaus arched one eyebrow at me in mocking question, but I imagined that was all he could manage. We were both exhausted. I ignored the expression and pushed on.

"When you get back to the hotel, settle up our rooms. If Charlotte can't get the plane here in the next few hours, tell the hotel manager that we need to rent or buy a truck. We have to drive to Luxor tonight and be on a plane before sunrise."

"That may be difficult."

"I know, but I can't travel without my box," I said. While my jet was specially designed for me and could afford me some protection, I couldn't be sure the other places I might be forced to stay would be enough protection. "Money is no object. At the foot inside the box is a leather case. There's cash inside. It won't take long to find someone who can help."

"And you trust me not to double-cross you?" he asked, shoving his hands into his pockets.

"Not really." I shrugged, taking a step closer. "But if you steal the cash, my phone, and dispose of my box, that won't destroy me, just slow me down. And before I come after you for that betrayal, I will hunt down those men that attacked me tonight and hurt Michael. Help me now and I'll forget about that attack and even get you out of Egypt alive. I think that's a pretty fair trade considering the attack made by your little Themis friends. Agreed?"

Danaus stared at me in silence for a full minute before he finally spoke. "Agreed." And even then, the word escaped him in a low grumble.

I smiled. I still had an even better bargaining chip in my pocket, but I was saving that one for a rainy night.

"And speaking of your friends," I started, strolling even closer to him. "I want you to call Themis. I want a meeting." While I was more than willing to hand the naturi problem over to Jabari and the Coven, I wanted to know more about this little group that had made a hobby of hunting nightwalkers.

His eyes snapped back up to my face. "They won't do it."

"I don't care what you have to say to arrange it. Before the sun rises, I want a promise that I will meet with a member of your little group," I said, unable to stop myself from clenching my teeth. My anger was building, which was good because it was giving me a little burst of energy. "I still have to meet with Jabari and I haven't a clue as to what I'm going to tell him. I want to know what the hell is going on. I want a meeting or you're not getting any more information out of me. I am tired of my ass being the only one in the fire."

Frowning, I swept past him and stalked toward the entrance of the graveyard. Yet, I stopped only a few yards away from Danaus. It galled me to ask, but I was exhausted and unarmed. "How many naturi are left in the city?"

Silence stretched between us for a few seconds, but I refused to look back at him. It would do him no good to get me killed now after he had expended so much energy to save me earlier in the night.

"There are two more near the river, heading north." His voice was quiet and low, like distant thunder.

If I were lucky, I would have enough time to get to Jabari and return with my angels before I ran into Rowe and his companion. "How far did you search?"

"All of Aswan, from the High Dam to the Tomb of the Nobles."

"Can . . . can you sense Jabari?" My insides clenched and twisted as I waited for his response.

"No."

I nodded once, a part of me relieved. I didn't want him to be able to sense the Elder when I could not. "I should be back inside of an hour."

Thirteen

Rock crunching under my boots, I headed out of the cemetery to the northwest and the heart of the city. Pain swept through every movement, as my body attempted to heal the array of wounds and poisons left behind from the naturi blade. After only a few blocks I was weaving through the crowds on the street. I expended just enough of my powers to make myself invisible to the people passing by, but Jabari would be able to sense my approach. I could feel Gabriel and Michael across the river on Elephantine Island. They would be at the home the Ancient kept there.

It was relatively early in the evening, and the local souq was still open and would remain so into the late evening hours. Colorful fabrics danced in the spice-rich breeze. A knot of eight boys ran by me with a burst of excited chatter. The leader of the pack carried a scuffed and worn soccer ball under his right arm. Just one quick game in the fading evening light. I briefly walked through the souq, noting the pyramids of fruits carefully stacked in brown baskets and arranged according to color. Colorful signs were written in Arabic, drawing the eyes of the evening shoppers. There were a few women in the souq, but they were either accom-

panied by a man or traveled in tight knots of three or four
women to a group. It was a different world from the one I
had inhabited in the States or even in Europe during the past
centuries.

Some of the tension eased from my shoulders as I watched
the early night life of these people go on. The air was filled
with their animated chatter, and someone softly picked out
a melancholy tune on a stringed instrument, a counterpoint
to the harder murmur of noise created by cars. Here, at this
point, the naturi had not touched humanity yet and my kind
was just a silly myth no one actually believed anymore.

Slipping down to the Corniche el-Nil, I directed the felucca captain to take me across the river to Elephantine Island. The poor man never even saw me. I slipped into his
mind before even stepping onto the small white boat with
matching white sail. Sinking down in a seat at the bow, I
closed my eyes, listening to the creak of the wooden boat
and the splash of the water as we cut across the Nile. The
wind dropped to kiss the water before rising again to sweep
past me, carrying with it secrets from the Nubian kingdom
from the south and other stories from deep in the heart of
Africa. I listened to the wind and water, wishing I could
understand them, wishing they had the answers to this
dilemma.

Stepping off the dock, I instructed the captain to wash off
the smear of blood I had left on the white paint of his boat
before heading toward the southern tip of the island and the
village of Koti, near the Ruins of Abu. The path was com-
pacted dirt, and trees and broad-leafed plants crowded the
lane. I stared into the darkness that filled in the open areas,
wondering if the naturi had followed me across the Nile to
the island.

I relaxed slightly as I walked past the seven-foot rock
wall that surrounded the village of Koti. The naturi could

still follow me into the village, but I was closer to Jabari. At least, I hoped the Ancient was in the village, but I still could not sense my old mentor.

At the end of a narrow alley flanked by two tall buildings that rose up like yellow tulips was a two-story square building painted bright blue. All the homes in the Nubian village were painted bright, cheerful colors—sunny yellows, cool blues, and sweet pinks dotted the landscape like stone flowers in an enormous garden for the gods. As I approached, the ornate door opened and Omari stood in the doorway. He couldn't see me, but I suspected that Jabari had alerted him to my approach. I removed the invisibility when I was still a couple yards from the door, startling Omari, who then moved out of the doorway and motioned for me to enter.

The main chamber was bathed in the warm glow of candlelight, a hint of burning incense in the air. Jabari looked up when I entered, his gaze hardening when he took in my appearance. I sensed Michael and Gabriel also jumped to their feet from where they lounged on a pile of cushions on the floor to my right.

"Naturi!" I shouted, the word exploding from my chest.

"Here?" Jabari demanded. He leapt smoothly to his feet, his face furious, white robes swaying around him.

"No, they attacked me at Fatimid Cemetery. Seven of them. None appeared here?" I thought going after me had merely been a pit stop on the way to Jabari. The Ancient had to be their main target. He was the strongest of the remaining members of the triad.

"No one has come but your protectors and you." The Ancient shook his head in amazement. "How?" The word was one of the few I knew in Ancient Egyptian, despite both our efforts, but his meaning was clear: How had I survived? Even a vampire as old and powerful as Jabari would have been hard pressed to come out with his head still attached.

"Just barely," I said with a weak chuckle. Two on one had been a close match, but seven on one would have been impossible. "Danaus saved my life. I don't know why and at the moment I don't care. We need to get out of the city. There's one called Rowe—he's been in contact with Aurora. He tried to take me, possibly to make sure they would have a clear shot at you."

"I've not heard of this Rowe," Jabari said with a shake his head. He stared at the ground in thought for a moment, potentially digging through volumes of old memories.

"I hadn't heard of him until Nerian mentioned him. He's scarred and wears an eye patch. He pretends to know me, but I don't remember him."

"Not from Machu Picchu?"

"No. I would remember a one-eyed naturi that dresses like a pirate," I said, a smirk briefly twisting on my lips before fading away.

"Maybe you are the reason he possesses only one eye," he said, lifting his gaze back to my face.

"No, I would remember him."

"And his goal was to capture you?"

I shoved a shaking hand through my hair and nodded, unable to say the words through the tremor of fear that sapped my strength.

"You're right," Jabari said. "The naturi felt they had to get you out of the way so they could destroy the members of the triad. They were successful in destroying Tabor. They will also go after Sadira. You must go to her, protect her."

My brows bunched over my nose and I could not stop myself from shaking my head. I didn't want to leave him unprotected, even if he still wanted my head on a pike. "What about you?"

"I will go to the Coven. They must know what is going on. I shall be safe."

"But—" The words died on my lips as the room swayed. Whatever energy I'd scraped together to get me from Fatimid to Koti had run out and my vision was growing black. I put my hand out to try to steady myself on anything I could find and came in contact with a soft, warm shoulder. Blinking, I found myself looking into Michael's concerned eyes.

Jabari's deep, soothing voice floated into my ears and wrapped itself around my thoughts. "The naturi poison is still inside you. You have to feed to cleanse yourself."

My stomach twisted and knotted, attempting to turn itself inside out in hunger and pain. The muscles in my legs quivered, demanding I sit down.

Michael took my hand and placed it against his neck, once again offering himself to me. A weak smile lifted my trembling lips, but my eyes were closed again. "This will hurt, my angel," I warned. "I can't spare the energy."

"You need me."

That was enough. In a surge of raw need, I pulled him down to me, sinking my fangs deep into the vein in his throat. A rough cry escaped his parted lips as the pain tightened the muscles in his body. His hands grabbed my arms, but he didn't struggle. Forcing him down to his knees, I leaned over him and slipped my fingers into his blond hair, holding him captive.

Fear exploded in his chest and ran through his bewildered thoughts, speeding up his heart, pumping his wonderful blood into my body that much faster. His fear was almost as intoxicating as his blood, awakening something that lay curled up in a dark pit in my stomach. The creature unwound itself and swam up the river of blood. It roared inside my head, demanding more, demanding I take it all.

The hand entwined in Michael's hair tightened and a small whimper escaped him, sending fresh pleasure skipping through me. I kept his neck pressed to my mouth even as his heart began to grow sluggish. I didn't care. There was only the warmth flowing into my cold limbs and the ball of energy swelling in my chest. My fear and the pain were finally gone. I felt alive and powerful.

"Mira." Jabari's firm voice somehow broke through the haze of blood and power, but I tried to ignore it. "Release him, Mira." Instead, my free hand gripped Michael's shoulder, locking him to me.

"Release him, Mira, or you will kill him."

I jerked my mouth away from Michael and loosened my death grip. My guardian sank back to sit on his heels, blinking in a desperate attempt to stay conscious. I had taken more than I had planned to and yet the creature inside still howled for more.

When I finally looked up, I found Jabari standing beside his wooden, high-back chair. His right hand rested on the back, gripping it so tight his knuckles were turning white. His brown eyes seemed an eerie yellow in the flickering candlelight. He had heard the creature's cry inside of me, felt the same blood lust. The Ancient blinked once, releasing his grip on the chair.

Michael touched my hand timidly and flashed me a crooked smile, searching for the reassurance that everything was okay. Smiling back at him, I gently ran my fingers through his thick blond hair before pressing a kiss to his forehead. My right hand slid down to cover the bite mark on his neck. With a brief swell of power, I healed both this fresh wound and the one from the previous night.

Something inside of me trembled when I looked down at my angel. A quick search of his thoughts revealed he had no idea how close he came to dying. But Gabriel knew. When I released Michael, I felt a wave of relief wash from Gabriel as he put his gun back in its holster. A bullet from Gabriel wouldn't have killed me, but would have succeeded in loosening my hold on my bodyguard and saved his life, at least until I reacted.

It had been a long time since I last succumbed to the blood lust. A well-fed vampire was a vampire in control. But the pain and poison had shattered that hard-won control and nearly cost me my angel.

"You must go to Sadira," Jabari said in an even voice, as if we hadn't just been interrupted by my desperate need to feed.

"I can't." Shaking my head, I took a step back, away from Jabari. "Send someone else; someone older and stronger than me. Have the nightwalker escort Sadira to rest with the Coven. They can protect her." I walked over to a low bookshelf and picked up a small statue of a man seated on a throne. By the arrangement of the hands and the facial structure, I determined that it was a piece of Nubian art, though very similar to some of the pieces of work that came out of the Middle Kingdom.

I think I would have said anything at that moment—not only to avoid Sadira, but also the chance of meeting the naturi again. My good deed was done. The Coven now knew of the growing threat. Hell, I'd destroyed four naturi in as many nights, and I was willing to wager it had been centuries since the last nightwalker could make such a claim. Now, I just wanted to go home.

"Protect Sadira while I hunt this Rowe. You failed me once with Nerian. I am willing to give you a second chance. Will you fail me in this request as well, my Mira?"

A string of curses in three languages exploded from me as I slammed the stone statue on the bookshelf and stomped away from Jabari. It was a mix of gutter nonsense, but it didn't matter. The Elder's deep laughter rumbled over my curses. He'd won and he knew it. He was the only one who could convince me to face the naturi yet again.

"Where is she?" I said, unable to keep the distaste out of my voice as I turned back to face him. Jabari stared at me a moment, surprise filling his dark brown eyes. "I won't do it," I snapped. "I won't reach out for her."

"She is in London. I imagine she will come to you after you arrive," Jabari said after letting me twist for a moment in the silence. I had not seen or talked to Sadira since Machu Picchu. I didn't want to see her now, but I didn't have much choice.

However, I couldn't stop the instant curiosity that furrowed my brow at his answer. "England?" I asked before I could stop myself. The British Isles were a hotbed of magic, which nightwalkers tended to avoid. We had our own problems without heading to a place beloved by witches and warlocks. "Has she moved from Spain?"

"No, her main residence remains in Spain. I do not know why she has gone to the island." His tone was neutral, but something in his eyes made me think Jabari was laughing at me.

Shaking my head, I turned around the room again and stared at my angels. Gabriel had helped Michael onto the pile of cushions. My wounded bodyguard was a sickly shade of white and his arm was wrapped in a white bandage. I knew this was part of their job; protecting me meant that they put their own lives in danger. However, the past few years had been quiet, each of my random trips without incident. The relentless peace had made us all soft in a different way.

"Omari," Jabari called, breaking the silence that had stretched in the room. "Take Mira's companions down to my felucca. I will bring Mira down in a moment, and then you will take them back to Aswan."

I nodded when Gabriel glanced up at me for direction, and then watched as he and Omari helped Michael back to his feet. Michael would bounce back from this encounter soon enough, but I knew it was weak and stupid of me to take so much blood. Such behavior only endangered both our lives.

"Walk with me, Mira," Jabari said, extending his hand toward me after Omari and the others disappeared out the front door.

I hesitated a second, stunned by the gesture. The pain of the fight from the previous night was still fresh in my mind. My body was still recovering from the fight with the naturi too, and I didn't need any more fresh wounds. But it was Jabari who reached for me. With my lips pressed into a tight line, I took his hand.

There was no warning. The world around me slipped away and was consumed by complete blackness. I tightened my grip on his hand and felt him pull me to him until I was pressed against his strong chest. One second there was only blackness, and in the next the world rushed back, golden sand and towering walls bathed in a warm yellow light. We were at Philae, several miles south of Elephantine Island and just north of the High Dam. Not far away, a large chattering group of people gathered for the nightly light and sound show.

Jabari tightly gripped my hand, threading his long fingers through mine before turning his back on the crowd and leading me toward the Temple of Augustus. It was darker in this area, and it appeared that the nightly tour would stop at the Temple of Isis before winding south back to the Hall of Nectanebo and the boat landing.

I gazed around, admiring the way the lights and shadows washed over the high walls. The regal faces of gods and pharaohs watched as we passed by in silence. "They did a good job," I ventured as we neared the temple hidden in darkness. "I really can't tell the difference."

Before the High Dam was completed, the government had been forced to move the Temple of Philae from its original island to Agilkia Island, to the north, or it would have been permanently submerged beneath the deep blue waters of the Nile. They had obviously been careful to reconstruct the temple and the surrounding flora almost exactly as on the original island.

"Hmmph," Jabari snorted. "The island is too small. The temples are too close."

"Better too close than underwater," I softly said, but instantly regretted it. When had I become so careless with my comments? Valerio. I blamed Valerio. He had been a bad influence, and too many years at his side made me careless when it came to speaking to other nightwalkers. "I'm sorry, Jabari."

"No," he snapped, and then stopped. He sighed heavily, running his free hand over his head as he stared at the Temple of Augustus as it rose up before us. "I am the one who is sorry, my young one." He pulled me into his arms, releasing my hand so he could wrap both arms around me. I flinched at the contact, but relaxed a moment later when he brushed a kiss across my temple.

"Last night I overreacted when I saw you standing in the quarry with the human. Egypt was always our home until you left, but then you returned . . . with a hunter of our kind and word of the naturi. I didn't mean to . . . " His voice drifted off as I let his words soak into my brain, completely stunned. I don't know which part took me more by surprise—that he referred to Egypt as "our home" or the quiver in his voice when he spoke of me leaving. There had been no question of me leaving Egypt centuries ago. I told the Ancient that I wanted to return to Europe, and he made no move to stop me. I had no idea that he was bothered by my choice to leave.

Taking a step back, out of his arms, I reached up and cupped his face with my hands. I brushed my thumb over his lips, loving the feel of his smooth skin beneath my fingertips again. "It was time for me to leave," I whispered in a choked voice.

Jabari took my right hand and laid it on his chest. "I know you are right, but my heart did not wish for you to leave." There were no heartbeats beneath the palm of my hand, but I understood the gesture.

Leaning forward, Jabari kissed me. At first it was just a light brush of his lips against mine, soft as a baby's breath, as if he were testing my response. I instantly went up on the tips of my toes, pressing closer to him. He deepened the kiss as I wrapped my arms around his neck. The kiss quickly became hard and possessive, claiming me back from the hunter, my domain, and the wide expanse of years that had separated us. He tasted me, as if trying to relearn me.

I pressed close to him, welcoming him. As he deepened the kiss I also felt him slip into my mind like a finely sharpened blade. For the first time in so long, I could finally sense him. I could feel the presence of his soul, and some tension I hadn't been aware of eased around my own soul. Jabari was everywhere, everything, for a brief span of time. The world slipped away and the years rewound. I was home and safe.

And then it was over. Jabari slowly pulled away, slipping out of my mind. Yet, my lips tingled and something in my chest burned. I felt as if he had branded me, marked me for all the nightwalkers to see. It screamed, "Mira belongs to Jabari." Not a Companion, never that, but something . . . different.

The Ancient reached up and touched my cheeks, wiping away tears I hadn't realized were falling.

"What is going on, Jabari?" I inquired, unable to completely purge the fear from my voice.

"The naturi have found a way to weaken the seal." His voice was calm again, the emotion wiped away as if it never existed. Our world had been put right and we were back to the business side of our relationship.

"How?" I asked, struggling to hit the same unemotional calm that he possessed. "It can't be because of Tabor's death. That was more than fifty years ago. Why would they have waited so long to strike?"

"I do not know how they have done it. It is one of the reasons that I go to the Coven. Our Liege may know something." For some reason, I wasn't sure that Jabari believed it. There were other things troubling him, something dark and grim enough to make my beloved mentor shield himself even from his own.

"How do we stop them?"

"We will reform the triad and destroy Rowe."

Oh, yeah. Just like making the bed or tying my shoes. "How?" I countered, frustration rising in my voice. Damn it, I was starting to sound like a bad fifties cowboy and Indian movie. *How? How? How?* "Tabor is gone."

"Your task is to protect Sadira and reform the triad while I speak with the Coven and Our Liege. The three were chosen by bloodlines . . . find someone of Tabor's bloodline and the triad will be reformed."

"None of this makes any sense," I complained, wandering a short distance away from Jabari, back toward the south. I could see the golden lights shining up at the tall walls that comprised the Temple of Isis. A soft breeze picked up, stirring the trees that ringed the island.

"It does not have to make sense to you." His voice lashed at me like a whip, halting my complaints. "Leave now with your people. I will contact you soon in London."

This was the other reason why I left Jabari, more than the need to finally take control of my own life. No matter how much I loved him, I would never be viewed as an equal in his eyes. Jabari loved me in his own way, but I would always be his subordinate, beneath him even if I earned his respect. I couldn't live like that. It would have broken my heart.

With the long-lived, there were various hierarchies and layers of discrimination. For some, it was the Old World versus the New, or the discrimination of First Blood versus chum, or man versus woman, or ancient versus fledgling. But with Jabari the only creatures above him were Our Liege and his gods. And those not by much.

"As you wish," I said, bowing my head stiffly. I had forgotten myself—he was an Ancient and an Elder. Regardless of what had occurred between us, I still owed him my respect, and in many ways my life. For now, it didn't matter if I understood what was going on. All I needed to know was that I had to keep Sadira alive and find a replacement for Tabor. After that, I was done and headed home. The Coven and the triad would handle the naturi.

"What about Danaus?" I asked, looking up at the Elder again. "He knows about the naturi and he knows about Machu Picchu. He also knew where to find me. Sometimes I think he may be a spy for the naturi, and then other times . . . "

"Yes?" Jabari prompted when I drifted off in thought.

"I have seen him kill at least four naturi, and he has stood by while I killed several myself. He saved me from the naturi tonight when he had absolutely no reason to. I—I don't know what to think about him."

"Keep him close, Mira," Jabari said, putting a strong hand on my shoulder. I suddenly felt very small next to his ancient height. "I do not think he is with the naturi, but we have other enemies. He may lead you to them."

A half smile lifted one corner of my mouth as I looked up at my old friend and mentor. "You make him sound like a bori spy."

A ghost of a smile slipped across Jabari's face, but it could have just as easily been a trick of the light. "At least we know *that* is impossible. I do not know what secret he holds, but he needs to be watched for a time."

"But will it be safe for him to be with me while I protect Sadira and search for the third member of the triad?"

"What better way to draw out our enemy?" Jabari asked, titling his head as he gazed down at me. "Besides, you will not fail me a second time by not protecting your maker."

I resisted the urge to touch my neck, searching for the noose I swore I felt tighten there. I nodded, trying to smile up at Jabari but not quite succeeding.

He gathered me close again and I felt the world fall away. I closed my eyes against the darkness and only opened them again when I heard the splash of the Nile. Michael was being helped into the felucca by Omari. We were gone only a few minutes, but it felt like hours. I gave Jabari's hand one final squeeze and then boarded the felucca behind Gabriel.

I didn't know any more now than when I had first arrived in Egypt, but at least something was being done about the naturi. It was a start. Maybe not much of one, but at least there was the promise of progress.

I also had the possibility of a meeting with Themis. And while I might still be their enemy, we were both threatened by the naturi. The old "an enemy of my enemy is my friend" routine. This little shadow group might know more of what was going on with the naturi, and I needed any information I could get my hands on.

Fourteen

We made our way slowly back across the river. Less than two hours had passed since sunset and the streets were still crowded, but no one took notice of us. Usually I'd be rising from my daylight nap about now, but my nightmares had woken me early that evening. Or perhaps some deeper sense of self-preservation allowed me to wake as soon as the sun slipped below the horizon.

"So, we're off to London now?" Gabriel asked.

"And we get to meet your maker," Michael said with a wide, playful grin. "I always wondered what she would be like."

"She didn't birth me." The words came out sounding sharper than I'd intended. I didn't want them to meet Sadira. She was evil and I was not like her.

"No, but without her, we would have never met you," Michael said, drawing my wandering gaze back to his face. I looked down at his bandaged arm resting in a sling fashioned from a black silk scarf.

Without Sadira, Michael and Gabriel would not be here in Egypt, fighting hunters and the naturi. But I shook off the thought as quickly as it appeared. They had made their own choices. They knew what they were getting into and were free to leave at any time.

"We go to London and protect Sadira," I repeated, as if saying the words over and over again would give me courage. "I wonder if we could lock her in a box for a few days. Just until the Coven destroys Rowe and the rest of the naturi." Sadira would never go for it, but I was sorely tempted to try.

The smile died on my lips before it had a chance to grow. We had gone one block in from Corniche and were walking past the giant souq in search of a private taxi to take us back to the hotel toward the south when I looked up to find a naturi staring dumbfounded at us. His hand rested on the knob of a door leading into a flat-fronted, two-story building. By his stance, he had been in the process of either entering or leaving the building when we turned the corner and caught him by surprise.

Muttering something under his breath, he pushed open the door and disappeared inside, slamming it shut behind him.

"Stay here," I ordered, grabbing the knife from the sheath on Gabriel's waist. I would have preferred the gun, but it didn't have a silencer and any shots would catch the attention of the crowds still lingering in the market. I couldn't afford to divide my attention between fighting the naturi and trying to cloak the fight from the humans.

"Was that . . . ?"

"Naturi."

"But—"

"Walk down through the souq. Stay in the more crowded area." I laid a restraining hand on Gabriel's shoulder, pulling his gaze back to my face. "Protect Michael. He's weak. Keep one eye on the door. There should be two in there. If one slips past me, I will need you to tell me which way it went."

Frowning, Gabriel nodded. He didn't like the idea, but he would follow my directions. I wanted to flash him a cocky smile to ease his concerns, but I couldn't. For the second time tonight I was going to be outnumbered by naturi. Sure, I could torch the building, but without going inside, I couldn't be sure that I'd gotten both the naturi Danaus sensed earlier in the evening.

With the knife tightly gripped in my right hand, I kicked open the door. The scent of blood, death, and excrement smacked me in the face, causing me to hesitate. Humans were inside. At least, they had been at one time. I rolled inside, followed by the sound of darts hitting the wall where I'd just been seconds ago. I paused behind a chair. The spindly thin naturi I followed in was shouting something to Rowe. I couldn't tell what they were saying, but I was willing to bet it had something to do with the vampire crouched behind the hideous patterned chair.

Pushing to my feet, I was prepared to hit both naturi with fireballs. No fighting. No taking chances. But I froze when I finally saw the room. I was standing in what had been a living room, but it looked as if hosed down with blood. There once were four humans in that room; maybe more, maybe less. Their appendages had been hacked off and strewn about. By the smaller torsos, I could identify at least two children.

Rowe was in the far corner, up to his elbows in a man's chest. The human's head was still attached, his eyes staring blindly up at the ceiling. The black-haired naturi was drenched with blood, his red shirt sticking to his narrow frame. I lurched forward when the blond naturi I had followed in leapt onto the chair I was behind. With one foot braced on the back, he used his weight to topple the chair, attempting to bring it down on top of me. A short sword was raised in his right hand, ready to take off my head.

Stumbling backward, I fell away from the chair. My right

shoulder slammed into the end of a table before I hit the ground, sending a shockwave of pain through my back. The naturi tried to fall on me, the sword aimed to bury itself deep into my chest. With the pain slowing me, I only managed to get my knees up between us. Dropping the dagger, I grabbed his wrists.

"Come now, vampire," he said. "I only want your tongue." The naturi struggled, trying to break my grip.

With a grunt, I shoved him off me. He flew across the room, hitting the door and slamming it shut. "How funny." I pushed into a sitting position and raised my left hand. "I only want your life." With a thought, the naturi was engulfed in flames. He lurched about the room, waving his sword about in a last desperate attempt to kill me. For a moment it looked as if wings were sprouting from his back, but the fire quickly consumed them. Had I finally met a member of the elusive wind clan?

I would get no answer from him. Flailing, the naturi slipped on the blood-soaked tile and fell, cracking his head. He stopped moving.

The sound of crinkling plastic caught my attention. I looked up in time to see Rowe darting across the room with a black, plastic garbage bag tucked under this arm. I tried to hit him with a fireball, but it struck the wall as he disappeared into the next room. I could only set him on fire if I could see him.

Muttering a cruse, I climbed over the overturned chair. I slid across the blood-covered floor, knocking limbs out of my way until I hit the opposite wall. So much for catlike grace. Pushing off the wall, I ran through the tiny kitchen and out the open back door. We wove our way through a maze of garbage-choked alleys and narrow streets that fluttered with laundry overhead. I couldn't see Rowe, but I followed the scent of the blood that still coated him.

Coming out of one alley, I skidded to a sharp halt. The alley opened into the busy souq, several blocks down from where I'd left Gabriel and Michael. The crowded marketplace hit me with a barrage of scents, spices, cooking food, coffee, tea, and the redolent scent of men smoking sheesha. A brisk wind swept down the street from the south, carrying with it cloves, cinnamon, ginger, and the sweat of man, all mixed together to mask the scent of blood. A quick scan of the thoughts of the gathered people revealed that no one had noticed a blood-covered, one-eyed naturi carrying a garbage bag filled with human organs. Like a vampire, he had cloaked himself from their sight. And now he was gone.

Biting back a scream, I jogged back to the house. Without Danaus, it would take me hours to track down Rowe. Time I didn't have. I shut and locked the back door before trudging back into the living room. The scent of burnt flesh mingled with the blood, leaving a rancid taste in the back of my throat.

It took every bit of willpower I possessed to walk over to the body Rowe had been digging in. Squatting down, I tried to ignore the fact that my skirt was growing heavy with the blood. A quick examination revealed that the man's tongue and lungs were missing. Scanning the room, it was hard to miss that the chest cavities of all the humans were cut open.

I'd walked in on a harvest. I hadn't seen one in centuries. Jabari and I stumbled across one a few years after Machu Picchu, in which nearly twenty humans had been slaughtered. But back then the naturi were greater in number and desperate to free their captured queen. Typically, they relied on earth magic for their spells. Yet, with time, they learned to use magic based on blood and the soul. It was just as powerful. Of course, their attitude was always, "Why kill a flower when you can kill a human instead?"

Standing, I leaned against the wall and closed my eyes. When I finally succeeded in clearing my mind of the horror around me, I reached out and touched Gabriel's mind.

Gabriel?

Mira! Are you hurt? His thoughts rushed into my brain, hot and frantic. Through his eyes, I could see him, across the street, staring at the door of the building I was in. Michael was leaning against the wall beside him. Gabriel wasn't telepathic, but after several years of training, I had taught him to focus his thoughts into precise sentences so I could read his mind and project into it my own response. It took us a while to perfect, a task I had not yet begun with Michael.

I'm not injured. Something in my soul had been hurt by what surrounded me, but I was not physically hurt.

Should I come in?

No! I paused until I regained my composure. *No. Start walking toward the hotel. I have to burn the place. I'll catch up to you in a couple blocks.*

Be careful.

I waited until he pushed off the building he was leaning against and started down the street with Michael at his side. When I opened my eyes, my gaze fell on the blood-streaked face of a girl with long, black hair. She couldn't have been more than six. I set her on fire first, wishing the flames would erase her wide brown eyes and tender face from my mind. But I knew better. I always remembered their faces.

Lingering in the house only long enough to see the bodies blackened and shrivel in the fire, I left through the back door, cloaked from human sight. I walked along the alleyways until I caught up with my angels. With a single touch on Gabriel's shoulder, I made my presence known, but no one spoke. We managed to grab a private cab another block away, and took it the last few miles to the Sarah Hotel.

In front of the hotel, we found Danaus working with a

short, thin man as they attempted to strap my coffin to the roof of a dilapidated taxi that looked as if it could have been around during the time of the pharaohs. At the sight of him, I sensed a rush of anger fill both of my guardians. Danaus might have saved my life from the naturi, but he was still the cause of the attack prior to sunset.

I laid a restraining hand on the shoulders of both Michael and Gabriel before I stepped between them. Their protectiveness was warming, but a fight on the street would not speed us from this city. "I don't think this will make it to Luxor," I said as I walked up to him.

"It doesn't have to," Danaus replied without looking up at me. He tested one of the ropes to make sure it was properly secured. "Your assistant contacted the pilots and they are bringing the jet to Aswan. It should be landing within the next half hour."

"Excellent." Charlotte was good at her work. I had thought it might be too difficult to get the pilots ready in time, but apparently she'd left them on standby. The vast majority of my trips were short, and she must have grown accustomed to my desire to leave quickly. "And the hotel owner?"

"Happy to be rid of us," Danaus said in a low voice, finally lifting his eyes to meet my searching gaze. He returned my leather case, which felt significantly lighter. With an amused smile, I tossed it over to Gabriel. I was still in my skirt from the previous night, leaving me short on pockets.

"And my meeting?"

"Later." His eyes darted over to the driver, who was staring at me with his mouth hanging open. He had noticed me when I started talking to Danaus, breaking the spell. The little man in the stained cotton shirt looked terrified, but I couldn't blame him. My clothes were full of cuts and tears, and what could be seen of my flesh was covered in dried blood and black soot. Of course, Danaus looked the same as I did, with an assortment of cuts that were healing much faster than would be considered normal. His face and arms were smeared with blood and ash.

"The airport," I said in badly accented Arabic, a jaunty smile directed at the driver. The little man bobbed his head and jumped behind the wheel. He was muttering under his breath as he went. I couldn't understand it, but I doubted it was complimentary. I motioned for Gabriel to precede me into the backseat so I could sit on his lap. Michael took the front seat while Danaus was forced to sit in the back with me. It was a quick, twenty-minute ride across town to the airport, and we didn't speak again until my coffin was safely loaded into my jet. I paused at the bottom step and gazed across the airstrip. The black night sky was dotted with the dark shadows of looming palm trees. I could still smell the Nile and the hint of foreign spices. I wished I wasn't leaving like this. Despite the fact that I had escaped death and aided in the destruction of seven naturi, it felt like I was running with my tail between my legs. Rowe was still out there, hunting me and killing humans.

I was running, and time was nipping at our heels. I'm not sure how or why I knew, but I could feel it bearing down, threatening to crush us all.

After bitterly informing the pilots that we would need to land in London instead of heading home, I moved to the private room at the back of the jet. Danaus followed me back while my two guardians settled into the comfortable leather chairs near the door. During the night hours, they were generally off duty. Besides, I was in better shape than either of them at the moment, though I know I didn't look it.

Flipping on the light in the tiny bathroom, I winced at my reflection. For once I didn't look pale—my skin was covered with ash and blood. My blue-violet eyes looked nearly black and my hair was a matted mess. Turning on the faucet,

I rubbed the cool water over my hands and up my arms. I wouldn't be able to properly wash until tomorrow night, when I was in my hotel room. For now I just wanted the grime off my hands and face.

"What did you find out?" Danaus asked, not venturing far from the door that led to the rest of the jet. He didn't look much better than me, with his soot-streaked body, assorted cuts and bruises, and sweaty, matted hair. He was tired as well. I doubted he was sleeping much since joining me on this little escapade either. At night he was surrounded by nightwalkers, who would rather drain him dry. During the day he was faced with my angels, who would rather see him dead than threaten me. And then there were the naturi, who could come out to play whenever they wanted. The shadows around his cobalt blue eyes had deepened and his movements were a little slower. There was now a thick growth of black whiskers on his chin and filling in the hollows of his cheeks.

"Not much," I said, splashing some water on my face. "I am to locate a nightwalker and protect her while Jabari hunts Rowe."

"Where are we going?"

"London."

"Directly?"

"Yes. Tell Michael to contact Charlotte on my cell. She'll have the hotel arrangements made before we land. We'll be in the city for a couple days." I rubbed my skin hard in a vain attempt to scrub off the blood. All my wounds had healed, but my body was covered in long lines of dried blood.

"What's going on? You look worse than when you left the hotel."

"Just give me a minute. Give the phone to Michael."

"Mira—"

"Please, Danaus!" My voice jumped and trembled in the tiny room as my composure splintered.

Danaus stepped out of the room for a moment, and the soft murmur of his voice drifted back to me as he relayed my wishes to Michael. Charlotte wasn't going to be happy with all these interruptions, but I was trying to keep her kind alive. Sure, I was trying to save my own skin as well, but my survival would benefit her. The hunter returned to the room, shutting the door behind him. He walked over so he was standing near the bathroom door.

"Did he attack you again?"

Looking up, I caught my reflection in the mirror. I hadn't summoned my powers, but my eyes glowed. I closed my eyes and shoved my newest set of memories away as I gripped the edge of the sink.

"What happened?" His deep voice was soothing, a gentle hand massaging my frazzled nerves.

"Have you ever seen a harvest?"

"No."

"I have, a couple of times. The naturi will attack a family or a small village. They kill all of its inhabitants and harvest certain organs and body parts for the magical powers they possess." The words slipped from me, dry and quiet, but the explanation failed to numb the pain and horror.

"In Egypt?"

"Four people. Two children."

"Mira . . . " Danaus's voice drifted off under the weight of the images I painted.

"They were butchered. Innocent people. Just a means to an end."

"And we'll get them."

A derisive snort escaped me before I could stop it. Turning my head, I was halted by the sadness in his eyes. "Then what? I know what you think of my kind, and you're partially right. We are capable of that kind of brutality, but not all of us."

Danaus reached for me and I jerked out of his reach. If he

touched me, I would crumble and the tears burning behind my eyes would break free. I refused to cry on the shoulder of a man who planned on killing me at the first opportunity.

"It doesn't matter. What of my meeting?" Releasing the sink, I grabbed a creamy white towel that lay folded on the counter. I wiped off my arms and face, feeling a little cleaner than before.

"When and where?"

"Tomorrow night. Your contact can pick the place, but this person must appear alone," I said, tossing the rumpled hand towel back on the counter. I leaned against the sink, folding my arms loosely over my stomach.

"He won't meet you alone." He shoved both of his hands through his hair in a restless gesture, pushing it out of his face. The movement pulled his body into a single long line, flexing muscle and sinew in a tempting picture. I had been so focused on peeling his skin from his bones that I'd almost forgotten he was a man. An attractive one. Danaus was all muscle and tanned skin, telling tales of a long, hard life. I wondered about this ancient creature that walked around in the shell of a virile man.

"You can come too, but no one else," I said after a moment. "And trust me, I'll know. The naturi are the only ones I can't sense."

"Anything else?" Danaus folded his hands, resting them on the top of his head. With his black shirt tucked in, the fabric pulled against his chest, accentuating his flat stomach. If I hadn't known better, I would have said he was trying to distract me on purpose.

"Just that it may be a good idea to make the place private. I don't mind an audience, but I imagine your little group doesn't want to be a part of a scene."

Shaking his head, I saw a smile playing on his lips as he turned and left the room.

"Get some sleep, Danaus," I called after him. "I promise Michael and Gabriel won't bother you."

"They think I tried to have you killed," he replied, looking over his shoulder at me, his hand on the doorknob.

"They also know you saved my life." I shook my head and frowned. "Even if you hadn't, my angels only defend, never attack. They also won't harm a creature when it's defenseless."

Danaus turned around to face me, his brow furrowed. "A vampire with a sense of honor?"

"There are a few of us," I whispered. "There are some ideas that not even death can kill."

The hunter nodded once to me and left the room.

Kicking open my metal box, I lay down with one booted foot still on the jet floor. I wasn't tired and it was still hours away from dawn, but I didn't want to join the others. It had been a long time since I last spent this much time surrounded by humans. Of course, there were my nightly trips to the clubs, theaters, and other amusements, but when I had my fill of them, I was always able to walk away. I could return to my quiet sanctuary and let the silence fill me. Now I was up to my ears in vampires, humans, naturi, and whatever the hell Danaus was.

To make matter worse, I still didn't understand what was going on. The naturi were attempting to break the seal and open the door between our two worlds. I didn't know how they were doing it. All I knew was that I had to reform the triad and keep Sadira safe. Not a particularly enjoyable task, but it wouldn't last long. Jabari would find Rowe and kill him. There would be no need for the triad. Soon it would all be over. I would go home and try to forget about it.

I ran my hands over the red silk that lined the side of the box, enjoying its smoothness. A part of me wanted to call for Michael. I wanted to feel his warm arms around me, reminding me of home and my life before this nightmarish escapade began. I wanted to make him moan and to erase the memory of the pain I'd caused him earlier.

But I couldn't. I couldn't even raise my voice to utter his name. I had come so close to killing him. I hadn't drained a human during the act of feeding since I was a fledgling. Yet my fear of the naturi and the taste of Michael's blood fueled something in me. It had given me back a shred of power and control when it all seemed to be slipping from my grasp.

I could tell myself I would have stopped in time, but that did nothing to erase the knot of doubt in my stomach. No matter how much I cared for him, I would always be a threat to him.

With a sigh, I pulled my leg inside the coffin and stretched out. I needed to sleep. I would need my strength for London, and I wasn't completely healed from my encounter with the naturi. And truthfully, I didn't want to think anymore.

Fifteen

Danaus was near me. It was the first thing I thought of when consciousness slipped back into my brain. He was in the same room, somewhere close. I moved my left hand, feeling for the side of the coffin so I could unlock it, but instead my hand came in contact with a thick velvet cover. My eyes snapped open, a snarl lunging forward behind clenched teeth. I was lying on a large bed in a luxurious bedroom, with dark, heavy furniture and thick curtains pulled across the pair of windows on the wall to my left. I sat up, my fists grasping the wine-colored comforter. Danaus sat in a chair set against the door, his arms folded over his chest. He was staring at me; his intent gaze taking in my expression, the movement of my muscles beneath pale skin. Wrapped in his blanket of power, he sat there like some reluctant guardian.

"Why was I taken out of my box?" I was as angry with myself as I was at my companions. I had fallen asleep with the lid open, so it hadn't been locked from the inside. But I had been moved. *Someone had touched me while I slept.* A cold chill of fear gripped my frame in a tight fist. No one saw me during the daylight hours; not servants or guardians.

The complete vulnerability during that long stretch of time was the only thing I loathed about being a nightwalker.

"Michael said you don't sleep in a coffin when you are home," Danaus said. "He also said you were screaming when you awoke last night."

"It was a nightmare." My eyes darted back to the subdued pattern on the comforter. I'd had a blissfully empty day this time, but I could clearly recall the nightmare from the previous day. Pushing the thought aside, I looked back up at Danaus. "Who moved me?"

"I did," he said, holding my gaze.

"Why?"

"I wanted to see you sleep." His eyes never wavered from my face. There was a strange intensity to him that set me ill at ease. "You never moved. You're just a corpse." His eyes seemed to harden as he spoke but he sounded confused. It was as if he couldn't reconcile the fact that moments ago I was cold and stiff and now I was sitting in bed talking to him. "Can you awaken during the day?"

"Not yet. Someday, maybe. The Ancients sleep less, but we all lay down when the sun rises in the morning. Vampires are remnants of an old war," I explained. This line of questions was unexpected.

"What war?"

"The eternal battle between the sun and moon."

Danaus nodded and rose from his chair, which he pulled to one side. "I don't harm creatures while they are defenseless."

"A hunter with honor."

"One of the few. The meeting is in an hour," he announced, then left the room. I stared at the closed door, feeling him moving about the hotel room. He was uneasy as well, some part of him simmering. I couldn't read his thoughts, but I could pick up on his emotions. So much anger and turmoil stewed in his chest. He also had questions with no answers, and I was at their center. He had spent years of his life killing my kind, but I think he was beginning to question his choices. Maybe a part of him was starting to see we weren't all mindless killers, and it bothered him.

Grinning, I sauntered into the pale yellow bathroom off the bedroom and turned on the shower. I might be able to use this to my advantage. I wasn't sure how, but it was an interesting development. Hell, at that point I was happy to have anything resembling useful information.

Scrubbing off the layers of blood and soot, I hummed an inane little tune to myself, glad to finally be free of the last remnants of naturi. After blow-drying my hair, I pulled on a pair of black leather pants and a long-sleeve silk shirt. This one was a brilliant blue, nearly matching the shade of Danaus's eyes. It would establish a subtle tie between us. I wasn't confident my new friend from Themis would pick up on it, but I had plans for this evening. As a finishing touch, I added a pair of rectangular sunglasses with blue lenses. I turned in front of the large mirror, taking in my appearance. A warm meal, a good day's sleep, and a hot shower had left me feeling upbeat. I could finally see an end to this winding road. After my brief meeting with this Themis character, I would locate Sadira and find a replacement for Tabor. When that was done, I was headed home and the Coven was on its own. I was back in control of my life and it felt good.

My intrepid companion didn't give me a second glance as we left the hotel and climbed into a taxi. We were silent as the little car swept us across the city to Mayfair. My trips to London had been infrequent over the years, but I'd been here often enough to recognize the various boroughs regardless of what century it was. And for as long as I'd known, Mayfair was the posh center of the universe for the monied elite. Alighting from the cab, I paused and looked up at the beautiful brick town house with its flower boxes overflowing with blooms. This was not what I had expected. I thought we would find ourselves in a seedy part of town, the back room of some disreputable bar or grimy warehouse with its family of oversized rats.

Directly across from us was Grosvenor Square, with its old trees reaching up at the night sky. The landscape was dotted with old brick facades and black iron fences, keeping the common rabble at bay. Matching black lamps stood at the corners, attempting to beat back the fog that had already begun to roll in from the Thames as the temperature dropped for the night.

The city felt vastly different from Savannah. Old Europe was quieter, more subdued, as if its dark history demanded that a hushed silence be observed in the dark hours of the night if you were out on the street. As if, otherwise, any one of the ancient myths of the fey or even my own kind might creep out from the shadows and strike. Europe held onto her old tales and superstitions longer, weaving them into the histories they had witnessed as if they were truths as well. The New World proved to be vastly different, with her shorter memory and fast-paced lifestyle that wouldn't slow down for anyone, not even an old ghost story like a vampire.

Shrugging, I followed Danaus up the front stairs and into the house, trying to ignore the way the air seemed to tingle around me. Too much magic in the air, too much old magic in this hallowed isle.

I noticed that he didn't bother to knock, but walked into the foyer. Without pause, he continued down the hall to a door on the left of the stairs that led to the second floor. He had been here before.

The building was the typical English town house, with

shining hardwood floors and Oriental rugs. The paintings on the walls were of hunting scenes and wild gardens set up against dark woods. There were no photographs of family and friends. I reached out and found only one other person in the house; a man, extremely nervous. I couldn't stop the smile that lifted my lips, leaving the tips of my fangs poking out just below. Danaus paused with his hand on the brass-handled double doors and looked back at me. He felt the slight sweep of power as I searched the house, and frowned. I like to think he knew better than to ask me to behave.

Pushing open the two doors, we stepped into a brightly lit library. The man sitting behind the desk jumped at the sound of the doors opening but quickly covered it up by rising to his feet. He was wearing a dark brown suit with a creamy white shirt and brown patterned tie. A pair of gold-rimmed glasses was perched on his sharp, straight nose.

I laughed. I laughed so hard and deep that I leaned forward on Danaus's shoulder, my hand pressed to my stomach. This was not what I had expected. My experience with Themis was Danaus and hunters like him. I had naturally assumed this was a trained group of assassins; cold, hardened mercenaries. The confused man standing behind the large desk looked like a librarian. Still laughing, I watched him out of the corner of my eye. He sucked in a harsh breath as the power layered beneath the laughter brushed against him like a cat wanting affection. Interesting. He shouldn't have been able to feel that unless he had some experience with magic.

Then I stopped laughing. It was like I flipped a switch. One moment my laughter filled the room, and then it was gone. There was no gentle ebbing of the sound, just complete silence, except for the man's harsh breathing. I glanced at Danaus. No frowns. No glares. No unspoken warnings. In fact, his face was completely expressionless. I almost started laughing again. In his own way, he had given me the green light to have some fun. He, of course, would try to rein me in if I went too far, but until we reached that point, I had carte blanche.

"Enough games," I announced with a weary air, still leaning on Danaus. "I've had my laugh, but we don't have time for this. Where is the contact from Themis?"

"I –I am from Themis," the man, still standing, stammered, lifting his chin a little higher into the air.

"I don't want to talk to its accountant."

"I am a full-fledged member of Themis and have been for almost ten years." His voice gained strength as anger crowded his words. His brown eyes flicked to Danaus for half a breath before jumping back to me, as if urging the hunter to speak up.

"Really?" My gaze swept over the room. The library was a nice large room, with floor-to-ceiling dark wood shelves running the length of two of the walls. Floor lamps with beaded fringe shades stood guarding the four corners, beating back the darkness to its hiding place behind the sofa and under the large desk at the opposite end of the room. What little could be seen of the walls revealed a deep hunter green that was also in the Persian rugs that covered the hardwood floor.

I stepped around Danaus and approached the desk. Behind me, I heard the hunter step out of the line of fire to the plaid-patterned sofa that rested near the back wall.

The librarian tensed, but he didn't back up, as I strolled closer. "In what capacity do you serve Themis?"

"I'm a researcher, like most members of Themis."

"Most?" I turned sideways so I could look at Danaus, who was watching me. "What about Danaus? It was my impression that you were all like him."

"Oh, no," he said. He shook his head as a condescending

smile lifted his thin lips. "Danaus is part of a small group of enforcers within Themis."

"Don't you mean trained murderers?" I corrected, my words cracking across his chest like a whip. This time he flinched. He tried to take a step backward, but ended up falling back into his chair. He paled and struggled to form words. His eyes darted over to Danaus as if seeking protection, but his enforcer never moved.

"We have to protect ourselves," the librarian said at last.

"You've had creatures killed that were no threat to you," I said evenly. I paused beside one of the pair of chairs positioned in front of his desk, my hand resting on the back.

"You've killed humans!" he said.

"Humans kill other humans every day in order to survive." I shrugged my slim shoulders as I strolled closer, my hand slipping off the chair.

"But you feed on us."

A smile flitted across my lips as images of Michael danced through my thoughts for a moment. "Only those who permit me."

"But—"

"In two days, she's fed at least twice." Danaus's presence and his deep voice almost cast a shadow over the room; a part of me wanted to step back into that bit of darkness. "No one has died."

"That's impossible!" the man said, jumping to his feet and slamming his palms on the empty surface of the desk. His eyes were wide and glittering in the bright light. "You just haven't seen the bodies. It has been well documented that vampires must kill their prey to sustain their existence. It's not really the blood they survive on, but the death that gives them power."

I laughed again, shaking my head. He sounded like he was

quoting from a textbook. "How long have you studied my kind?" I inquired, wiping a tear from the corner of my eye.

"Themis has watched vampires for almost three centuries."

"And how many have you spoken to?"

"Personally? None." His voice lost some of its confidence and he sat back down again, seemingly shaken. His brows were gathered over his nose and his lips were pressed into a thin frown. "Until now."

"What about the others?"

"We don't talk to vampires. It's . . . too dangerous. You . . . kill," he said, struggling to find the words.

Smiling again, I paced around the desk until I was standing behind his chair. He twisted around so he was looking at me. Folding my hands on the back of his chair, I rested my chin on my hands. His fear was so thick and heavy I could taste it. My eyelids drifted closed and I drew in a deep breath, letting his fear swirl around me like an expensive perfume.

"So, you've decided to slaughter my kind based on myths and false information."

"But—But you kill," he said, as if it was the answer to everything.

"So do you," I whispered, staring deep into his eyes before I continued the circuit around to the front of the desk. Walking over to Danaus, I removed my sunglasses and hooked them over the top button of my blouse. I could feel the librarian relax in his chair as I moved away from him. Putting my right knee on the sofa next to Danaus's left hip, I sat down beside him, throwing my left leg across his lap. His hands remained limp at his side. He didn't touch me, but, more important, he didn't push me off away either. I leaned close, putting my left arm across his chest, resting my hand on his shoulder. Out of the corner of my eyes I could see the other man watching us closely, his forehead furrowed with a look of absolute confusion and shock.

Luckily for me, Danaus had bathed and changed into a clean set of clothes. He had rid himself of the smell of the naturi, reminding me again of a warm summer breeze dancing across the whitecaps in the Mediterranean. His chin and cheeks were free of dark stubble and he looked as if he'd actually caught a few hours of sleep.

I leaned in so my lips lightly brushed Danaus's ear. His muscles tensed. "Does Themis know what you can do?" I whispered. His powers flared around me in response to some emotion I couldn't quite place. I don't think it was the question that bothered him, but some deeper thought. I could understand that. We all had something to hide.

"No."

"So I thought," I murmured. I started to lift my left leg from his lap when Danaus grabbed my calf with his right hand, holding me in place. His touch was warmer than I'd expected, almost burning through my leather pants. Shocked by his sudden willingness to touch me, I went completely still.

Turning his head to look at me, my lips brushed his cheek and we both froze. Danaus exhaled slowly and I found myself drawing in his breath, holding it inside me. If one of us moved less than an inch, our lips would meet. But we sat like two stone statues.

"Jabari?" he finally asked, his whispered question deep and husky.

I stared at the hunter's chiseled profile, nearly drowning in his deep sapphire eyes. I hadn't told Jabari. It hadn't even occurred to me to tell the Ancient. Of course, if I had, Danaus would not have left Aswan alive. Why hadn't I told Jabari? If he didn't kill me over the whole Nerian fiasco, my existence was definitely forfeit for this little oversight.

Why didn't I tell him? Was it because I didn't like to share? Jabari would kill Danaus and that would be the end of it. He wouldn't appreciate the challenge the hunter represented. Or was it that Danaus was like me, an outcast among his own kind? Of course, I didn't know what he was, so that line of logic was a dead end.

"No," I said, unable to keep from coating that single word with my obvious surprise.

Danaus arched one dark brow at me, mocking one of my favorite expressions. Yeah. I was just full of surprises.

"Lilacs," he suddenly said. When my only reply was confused silence, he continued. "You smell like lilacs. No matter what you've been doing, you smell like lilacs."

Moving my head slightly, I brushed my lips across his chin. Every fiber of my being was screaming for a kiss, just a taste of his lips and his mouth. My hand tightened on his shoulder and I pressed my body a little closer. "Like you smell of the sun and sea?"

"Yes." His hand squeezed my calf again, but it wasn't a warning. His strong fingers kneaded the muscle in a deep massage, keeping me pressed tightly against him.

"Is that a bad thing?" My lips rose, skimming across his jaw to the corner of his mouth.

"No. Just . . . unexpected." With the speed of a glacier, Danaus turned his parted lips toward mine, his hot breath caressing my face.

A pen clattered to the hardwood floor, jerking us apart. We had forgotten about the gawking librarian. My head swung to the man behind the desk, a low growl escaping me. Danaus tightened his grip on my leg while his other arm wrapped around my waist, holding me in place.

"Let me throw him out the window," I said in a low voice.

"Mira . . . "

My eyes jerked back to his face, searching his gaze for any sign of frustration. I couldn't see it in his eyes, but the evidence pressed against my thigh, which was still draped over his lap. "I'll be gentle."

"With me or him?" I don't think he meant to say it out loud because his eyes widened with surprise. I leaned in to finish the kiss that had been rudely interrupted when he said, "The naturi." The only two words that could instantly kill my libido.

My head fell forward and I rested my forehead against his shoulder. "Bastard," I muttered softly. Danaus rubbed his hand up and down my back once, as if trying to soften the blow. Now was not the time.

I turned my gaze back to our spectator behind the desk, my cheek grazing Danaus's jaw. The librarian shifted in his chair, attempting to square his shoulders. I slid my hand back across Danaus's chest as I rose from the sofa as if pulled by marionette strings.

"What are you called?" I asked, strolling back over to the desk.

"James Parker."

"I am Mira." Taking one of the seats in front of his desk, I put my right heel on the edge of his desk and crossed my other foot over it at the ankle. He frowned at my feet.

"The Fire Starter," he said, dragging his eyes from my boots. His long, nimble fingers snatched up a fountain pen that had rolled off the ink blotter.

"Perhaps not all your information is bad, after all. Your group seems to be relatively well informed about the naturi—tell me what you know."

"About the naturi?"

"Start with your opinion of them," I commanded, inspecting my fingernails.

"Well, they are nothing like the fairy tales that are based

on their race; all that nonsense about elves and fairies," he began. Withdrawing a small square of cloth from this pocket, James removed his glasses and started to clean them. I had a feeling that this was more of a nervous habit than any actual need to remove dirt. "They are cold, ruthless, and view humans as a plague on the earth. Their power lies with the sun and the earth. We have evidence that says the naturi are the reason for several lost civilizations through time, up until about five hundred years ago."

"What happened five hundred years ago?" I tried to keep my voice bland and uninterested, but my eyes flicked back up to his face. His hands stilled for a moment as his brown eyes met my deep violet orbs.

James licked his lips and drew in a deep breath before speaking again. "Our information is sketchy at best, but I was under the impression that you were there," he replied. "I was hoping you would be able to tell me."

"I want to hear what you know first," I hedged, smiling wide enough to reveal my fangs.

"Not much." His hands started to work over the glasses again. "We interviewed some Incan descendants a long time ago. It's all legend and myth now. They said children of their sun god came down to Machu Picchu one day. They were holding captive a daughter of the moon god. The people of the sun were preparing to sacrifice several of the Incans in the Sacred Plaza when more than a score of the children of the moon god arrived, and freed the captured moon daughter. The Incan descendents mentioned a great battle.

"We've not been able to make that much sense out of it. It was obviously a battle between vampires and the naturi. After that night, the door between the naturi world and this one was closed, defeating the naturi. I was hoping that you would be able to tell me more." James inched forward a little to sit on the edge of his chair, glasses forgotten in his hands.

"I can't." And it was the truth. I couldn't tell him because I wasn't sure. I couldn't remember any of the other night-walkers at Machu Picchu. I knew others had been there; the greatest gathering I had ever seen, but even now I couldn't recall a single face beyond the triad: Jabari, Sadira, and Tabor. "The naturi were never defeated." Putting my booted feet back on the floor, I restlessly pushed out of the chair and paced over to one of the bookcases that lined the wall. "The queen of the naturi still lives. The final battle was simply postponed."

My eyes flitted over the various leather-bound volumes, reading the titles. They were all books on the occult. Books on vampires, lycanthropes, magic, and obscure bits of history lined these shelves. It would have taken a lifetime to accumulate this extensive a collection. I glanced over at James for a moment, taking in his clean-shaven face and eager eyes. He looked like he might be in his late twenties, early thirties at the absolute latest. This either wasn't his house or this was a family occupation. Curious.

"But you will find her in time?" he asked, rising from his seat again.

I turned back to the shelf and pulled down a large volume on nightwalkers. I opened it in the middle and let my eyes scan over the page. With an angry growl, I pitched the book over my shoulder and picked up another.

"Stop!" James said before he could stop himself. "That one's rare."

Ignoring him, I opened another book on vampires. I tossed this one aside before reaching the bottom of the page. Overriding his fear, James came around the desk to my side as I was grabbing a third book. I dropped it over my shoulder, but he caught this one.

Turning, I grabbed his jacket lapels as he cringed. Behind me, Danaus's powers brushed against me, warning me. "Is this what you have been reading about us? Has all of your kind been soaking in these lies?"

"They can't be. These journals were written by people who have survived encounters with vampires," he said. "You can't deny that you kill; you treat us like cattle."

"You paint us as mindless killers, monsters in the darkness." I released him suddenly as if he were something dirty. "Humans are remembered for more than the wars they wage and the lives they take. We create things of beauty as well." I took a step closer to James. He inched backward but was stopped when his back hit the bookshelf. I smiled at him, careful not to reveal my fangs. Lifting my hand, I held it barely an inch from his face. He flinched, his wide eyes darting between my face and hand. Lowering my hand with infinite care, I drew my fingers across his forehead to his temple and into his hair. "We feel pain and joy. We feel sadness and love just like you," I whispered, my voice like a caress. "We can give and take exquisite pleasure."

"E-Even with humans?" he asked, stumbling over the words.

I chuckled, pulling my hand back to my side. "Some of my favorite lovers have been human males. You're very . . . attentive."

Turning, I walked away to the other side of the room. As I passed Danaus, I shoved my hands into my back pockets and winked at him. He looked back at James's desk, but I caught the slight quirk of one corner of his mouth. He knew the game I was playing, and at the moment, after the questionable information they had supplied him with, he was not pleased with Themis.

"But there is one thing I am confused about." I turned back. "Despite all the horrible things you believe about my kind, Danaus was sent to find me. I don't think he was sent to acquire my assistance, just information. Why?"

"If the stories are to be believed, vampires stopped the naturi once. I thought you could do it again," James said, still clutching the book to his chest.

"I? Not we?"

"Some of the others . . . did not see the wisdom in this idea."

"And do they know about this meeting?"

He looked at Danaus, then back to me. "No." His grip on the book pressed to his chest tightened, as if it could protect him from the wrath of his superiors.

"You are a brave one. Of course, you do have Danaus here to protect you from me, but I have a feeling your little friends aren't going to be too happy about this. Interesting."

"What are you planning?" Anxiety spiked his voice.

I strolled back over to the chair I'd been sitting in and plopped down, propping my feet up on the edge of this desk. "Nothing at the moment. It's just interesting information. Do you have anything else interesting to tell me?"

"A-About what?" he said, walking back over to his chair behind the desk. He sat down and reluctantly laid the book down on the surface.

"About the naturi."

Pulling open one of the drawers to his right, he withdrew a manila folder and handed me what looked like a thin stack of photographs. I had to force myself to reach for it. The last photograph I'd been handed had sent me on this fool's errand. Gritting my teeth, I took the glossy pictures and nearly screamed in frustration when I saw more naturi symbols, each smeared in blood.

I lurched to my feet, struggling to keep from igniting the picture in my hands. "When?" I heard Danaus stand and walk over, his heavy steps echoing off the hardwood floor. I handed him the pictures, my eyes never leaving James's pale face.

"They've started appearing during the past couple of days."

"Where?" I needed him to confirm my suspicion.

"I—I'm not completely sure. I think one was in Spain," he said, running a nervous hand over his tie.

"The Alhambra," I confirmed. "Where else?"

"Another was in Cambodia."

"At Angkor Wat." I grabbed the pictures out of Danaus's hands and laid them out across the top of James's desk. "There are six pictures here. We have Angkor Wat and Alhambra." I put the two that I was sure had been identified aside. I knew these places. Jabari had drilled them into my head. I picked up another with rose-colored stone and added it to the pile with Angkor and Alhambra. "That's Petra and this is the Palace of Knossos on Crete." I added the fourth picture to the pile, flipping it over and laying it down with a slap. I'd known that place before Jabari. I'd been born in Crete.

"Oh, I remember this one." James picked up a picture of a plain dark brown sign set against a backdrop of trees. "They said it was on the back of a sign in Yellowstone National Park."

"And the last one?" Danaus asked, picking it up.

"Mesa Verde, Colorado." I recognized the stonework. Turning my gaze back to James, I fought back a knot of panic that was starting to twist in my stomach. "What about the other five sites? Have your people checked them?"

"Other five?"

"The holy cities of the naturi. I assumed you were checking those." I turned my gaze on Danaus, clenching my teeth. "You said your people were watching potential sites for the sacrifices. Did you lie?"

"We are watching them," he snapped, taking a step toward me.

"All twelve?"

"Twelve?" He looked genuinely puzzled for a moment. "There has to be more than twelve. We're watching all the ancient temples and structures that have been linked to ancient myths."

I shoved both of my hands through my hair, swallowing a scream of frustration. I knew I should have asked for more clarification sooner. He seemed to know so much when we met that I assumed he knew all about naturi history. I was wrong, and it might just cost us.

Drawing in a deep breath, I turned back to the desk and picked up the pictures. "A quick lesson on the naturi," I said, then looked up at James. "You might want to take some notes."

The Themis member immediately plopped back down in his chair and pulled out some paper and a pen.

"There are twelve so-called holy sites for the naturi spread around the world, based on the energy that culminates in the area. In North America, there is Old Faithful and Mesa Verde. In South America, it's Easter Island and Machu Picchu. In Europe, we have Stonehenge, Alhambra, and the Palace of Knossos. In Africa, there's Petra, Dead Vlei, and Abu Simbel. And in Asia, there's Konark and Angkor Wat."

Danaus shook his head, frowning. "That doesn't make any sense. Some of these places aren't that old, and Abu Simbel has even been moved from its original location. The naturi are older than all of those structures."

"It's not the structure that makes a place holy to them, it's the power emanating from the earth in an area that makes it special." I grabbed the pictures again and spread them out across the desktop. "Humans have created amazing structures at these locations. Why? Because they are drawn to these places. Some part of their brain senses something, even if they can't recognize it."

"Abu Simbel was moved."

"Only two hundred meters. It's still close enough to the original location, which is now underwater and only of use to the water naturi."

"What about the marks in the trees," James said, his head snapping up from the paper where he was furiously scribbling notes. "They weren't anywhere near these locations."

I shook my head, nibbling on my lower lip. I was getting into shaky territory. Nowhere in the histories I'd read of the naturi did I encounter tales of them making marks in the trees like the ones I'd seen. "Those feel different than the ones at the holy sites. More permanent, but I have no idea what they are for."

Danaus leaned his hip against the edge of the desk and folded his arms over his chest. "And the blood marks?"

"They weren't made from human blood," James interjected before looking back down at his notes. "We had it tested. It was all animal blood."

My gaze drifted back down to the pictures. "They're testing sites," I murmured.

"What do you mean?"

A half smile lifted one corner of my mouth. "It's old magic. You'd think you would know a little old magic, Danaus," I teased. "The next sacrifice is to break the seal, and they will need as much power they can get. With Aurora stuck in the other world, they'll need to draw as much power as possible from the earth. To do so, they have to locate the site that has the best charge. So, the naturi are testing sites with minor spells, looking for the best location."

"But Danaus said there would be a total of three sacrifices," James said, his brows meeting over the bridge of his nose.

"There will be if we don't stop them. The first was sort of priming the pump, pulling the power up from the earth.

The second will break the seal, and the third will open the door."

"And you don't think they will use any of the sites that had the marks?"

"No, they would have covered their tracks. Cleaned off the blood and immediately ended the spell. Konark has been used and the other six marked."

"So, there are just five possibilities: Stonehenge, Machu Picchu, Dead Vlei, Abu Simbel, and Easter Island," James read off his list.

"Contact Themis," Danaus ordered. "Get people to those locations now."

The hunter then turned his grim eyes intent on my face. All lightness and entertainment for the evening had been sucked from the room.

I sighed. "We have to find Sadira now." We couldn't sit by and hope that Jabari located Rowe. We were nearly out of time. If the naturi were actively searching for another site, it meant that they were likely to complete the next sacrifice soon. But it didn't make any sense. The next new moon was nearly a week away. I had a dark suspicion when they planned to strike, but I needed to confirm it, which meant I needed Sadira.

"Wait!" James said, hurrying around his desk. "I can help."

I paused at the door, my hand resting on the doorjamb. "Go back to Themis, James Parker. Go back and warn them." My voice suddenly sounded very tired. I pitied this young man who had devoted his life to studying the things that crept by in the shadows. That was one of the greatest differences between the naturi and nightwalkers. Unlike the naturi, we could feel pity on occasion.

Sixteen

We grabbed a taxi back to the hotel. Huddled in the darkness with Danaus beside me, I reached out into the city and for the first time in almost five hundred years searched for Sadira. It should have been an easy task. With any other vampire, I would have had to search slowly, letting my powers creep over the earth until I finally reached him or her. But Sadira was different. She was my maker. My connection with her would always be strong, no matter the distance or time. I should have been able to find her immediately, like lightning being drawn to a lightning rod. Yet, it felt as if she didn't exist. But I would have known it if she was dead; I would have felt it. Something was wrong. First Jabari, and now Sadira. I could feel the nightwalkers in the city, but not these important two.

"Are there naturi in the city?" I asked. Silence filled the dirt-encrusted taxi, broken occasionally by the scratchy, distorted voices from the cab radio. I stared out the window at the assortment of town houses and shops as we headed back toward the Thames and the Savoy Hotel, near Charing Cross.

"Not in the immediate area." Danaus's voice rose, as if

we were waking from a dream. "I think near the outskirts of town."

"You're not sure?" I turned my head so I could see him out of the corner of my eye.

He grimaced in the darkness, his features drawn in concentration. "It's hard to tell. It's like trying to see through a thick fog." Frustration edged his voice and hardened the line of his jaw.

"It's this island." Sinking back into the dirty backseat, I leaned my shoulder against his strong arm. I was sure he'd run into other magic-related problems while staying in Great Britain in the past. There was too much old magic in these lands. Too many old gods had been born and died on this island; too many powerful warlocks had stretched their arms here. Magic doesn't just die—it fades into the air and seeps into the earth. After centuries, this ground was saturated. Many magic users came to Great Britain because they could tap this well of power.

"Who's Sadira?" he asked, changing the topic.

"She was one of the three to form the seal centuries ago."

"Jabari and Tabor were the others?"

"Yes."

"Were you a part of it?"

"No, just a recovered prisoner." I was barely a century at the time, still a child among my kind. I had been captured two weeks before and tortured. The naturi wanted to use my unique ability to control fire as a weapon against the nightwalkers.

"Do you think the naturi will come after her?"

"Yes. Enough naturi were left behind in our world who would be able to identify the members of the triad." I just didn't understand how they would find her, when we couldn't sense them and they couldn't sense us.

Leaning my head back, I placed my right ankle on my knee, which brushed against his with the movement. Neither of us stirred for a moment, almost as if we waiting to see who would flinch first. What did it matter? I had crawled all over him on more than one occasion. And right now I wanted the reassuring warmth that washed off of him . . . it was better than the cold reality of the naturi.

"Is this how you expected things to progress?" He turned his head to look at me, his blue eyes catching a shaft of light as the taxi lurched into motion again.

"No." I slumped in the seat and crossed my arms under my breasts. "Finding Jabari was supposed to improve the situation, not make it worse. I should be home looking after my domain, not searching for Sadira. It's all a mess." Beside me, I could hear the steady rhythm of his heartbeat while his powers brushed against my cheek. His power might not feel human, but his heart did. I had been out of contact with Knox for several nights now, and a part of me was desperate to know how things were progressing with him and Barrett. I needed to be home to help suppress any fires should they spring up between the nightwalkers and the shapeshifters.

"Is this how you planned it?" I asked. Sitting so low in the seat, I was forced to tilt my head up to meet his gaze.

"No."

"Oh, really?"

Danaus leaned toward me as he whispered, "You should be dead."

I chuckled and threaded my arm through his. He stiffened but didn't jerk away. "But we work so well together," I said, earning a soft snort. "We worked quite well together in Aswan."

"You mean when you stopped trying to kill me."

Leaning my head against his shoulder again, I let my eyes

drift shut. "Well, I thought you tried to kill me while I slept. I was understandably upset."

"It's my job."

"Get a new job, like being a florist." I snuggled a little closer, trying to irritate him now. The night air was warm and we had our windows down, allowing the fresh breeze to circulate through the stale car. Yet, the warmth and strength rolling off Danaus would have been comforting no matter the season.

"I can't."

"Why?"

"You're evil."

My whole body stiffened at those two cold words and my eyelids lifted. I stared blankly at the back of the front seat. "Prove it."

"Come into a church with me tomorrow night."

I couldn't, which was the point. "Why haven't you caused my blood to boil? If we're so evil, why haven't you destroyed us all that way?" I asked, attempting to dodge his question as I sat up, pulling away from him.

"The same reason you haven't set me and every naturi you meet on fire," he said. He shifted in his seat so he could pull his wallet out of his back pocket.

"Because it lacks style and finesse?"

Still balanced on his left hip, Danaus leaned over, his mouth hovering just a few inches above my face. "Because it's exhausting. If you don't kill everyone, you're left vulnerable. In a fight, our powers are a last resort."

As the taxi pulled over to the curb, he sat back in his seat and began to shuffle through his wallet to pay the driver. I slid out of the car, grateful to be back out in the night air. There was nothing to say. He was right. With time, I gained more strength, more endurance, but the use of my unique ability would always be exhausting.

We walked up to my hotel room, lost to our own dark thoughts. I was only vaguely aware of the looks that we were earning from the other guests. Charlotte had picked the Savoy, with its palatial elegance and gilt ornamentation. Its guests were the upper crust of society, and I was wearing leather pants, silk shirt, and blue-tinted sunglasses. I think I looked like a rock star, which was amusing. Clinging to that rationale, the observers naturally assumed that the heavily muscled, darkly handsome man at my side was either a bodyguard or a lucky lover. Danaus had wisely decided to leave the scimitars in the room, and instead had an assortment of knives concealed about his body. Walking around armed in Aswan was one thing. London at least kept up the pretense of being a little more civilized.

When we reached the double doors that led to my private suite, I stopped sharply. Something was wrong. A brief touch of Gabriel's and Michael's minds revealed that someone else was in the room with them. They were tense and anxious. However, a light scan of the room turned up only my two human angels.

With a playful smile, I threw open the two doors and walked in. But all playfulness was ripped out of my body as my eyes fell on Sadira. I hissed at her, my lips drawn back to reveal a perfect set of white fangs. My hands clenched into tight fists, my nails digging into my palms until I was drawing blood.

"Such manners," she chided with a shake of her head. Her soft sweet voice was hypnotic, seeking to burrow down into my brain. She sat with her back ramrod straight and her chin up, as if she were a regal princess on her throne.

I straightened my shoulders, sending a warning look to the nightwalker. I knew my first encounter with her after all this time wouldn't be good, but I hadn't expected to react with such uncontrollable hostility.

"Why couldn't I sense you?" I demanded, failing to un-clench my teeth.

"Jabari contacted me. He said to hide myself, and that he was sending someone for my protection. I had no idea it would be you." Her voice was calm and cool. Nothing seemed to ruffle her perfectly groomed feathers.

My skin crawled as I stared at her. Everything about Sadira seemed to be one great lie, and I hated her for it. At just under five feet, she looked like someone's sweet little mother. Her long dark hair was streaked with gray and pulled up into a bun. Her features were soft and rounded, leaving nothing alluring or threatening in her appearance. She wore a long black skirt and a pale yellow shirt with pearl buttons. She looked prim and proper, safe and almost fragile.

But it was all a lie. I had seen her tear out a man's throat while she fed, the blood dripping down her chin. I had seen her plunge her hand into a woman's chest and pull out her heart so she could drink the blood directly from it. Yet, even when she was killing these people, she never looked like a predator. Just a hideous nightmare.

"Who is your dark shadow?" she inquired, smoothing over the silence that filled in the places where the tension had yet to reach. Her accent was haunting, an exotic flavor no longer on this earth. Ancient Persian. After more than a thousand years, Sadira had come no closer to shedding her accent. Most of us relinquished our old ties, preferring to blend in. Even Jabari's accent faded when he was away from Egypt. But Sadira kept hers.

"He's not your concern." I took a step to my left so I was standing directly in front of Danaus. "The naturi are com-ing. They're planning to break the seal."

"How?" Surprise lifted her thin eyebrows and extended the wrinkles that stretched from the corners of her almond-shaped eyes. Her pale hands clenched in her lap, twisting her slender fingers.

"The usual way—blood and magic. Jabari said I am to protect you and reform the triad."

"Has he been selected to protect you, then?" She refused to drop the issue of Danaus, intrigued by the fact that I was traveling with this stranger.

She never questioned the assistance of my daylight warriors, Gabriel and Michael. When a nightwalker acquired a certain level of power and frequently traveled into the domain of other powerful vampires, he or she would enlist the services of such guardians. Danaus, however, was distinctly different from these protectors. It wasn't that he stood there exuding his own dark power. It was his confidence and the fact that he seemed completely at ease in a room with two nightwalkers. He had also been out with me at night, so keeping him at my side meant that he carried a different kind of importance to me. He was an equal, not a servant.

"I do not need nighttime protection," I told her.

"Oh, my Mira," Sadira said, her voice filled with warmth and concern. "You need protection more than me or Jabari."

"I can take care of myself. I was never as weak as you liked to pretend."

"I never thought you weak, my dearest child." Pushing smoothly to her feet, she took a couple steps toward me, but I stepped away from her, the two of us circling in the small living room. I wouldn't, couldn't, let her lay a hand on me.

Sadira stopped, a look of patience filling her warm brown eyes. "I feared you would grow to be too confident in your powers. I didn't want to see you hurt. I wanted to protect you."

I blinked, and images of her castle in Spain sprung to life.

She was in my head again, manipulating my thoughts like the early days. Mentally, I reached for her to shove her back out, but it was like grabbing smoke. The memories blurred, and then abruptly focused. I was back in the dark dungeon with its damp, crumbling walls. I was lying on the cold slab, hovering somewhere between life and death, with only the sound of Sadira's voice to guide me back from madness.

Most nightwalkers are made in a night. A kiss of death, an exchange of blood, and the deed was done. But Sadira had wanted something more than when she made me. She wanted a First Blood, and thus she spent ten years—night after endless night—nursing me into her world and bringing me into the darkness. And when she was done, I was her greatest creation.

Our years together were ugly. She wanted absolute control over me; the same control she had over the other dozen vampires that resided in her castle. She had created a few others, but I was her only First Blood. They all flocked to her, clinging to her image of the caring, protective mother, but I never believed those lies, and only stayed because I thought I had no other option.

Now, however, I was free. Clutching that thought, I finally shoved Sadira from my mind and threw up as many metal barriers as I could. I pushed her back until she was just a vague shadow at the edge of my thoughts.

"I did not come here to fight with you, my Mira." Sadness tinged her voice. "When I felt your presence, I thought you had come to talk."

"Did you think I had come back to you?" Dragging my eyes back to my maker, I shook my head. "How could you believe such a thing?"

Sadira smiled at me, her head tilted to the side. The look a parent gave a foolish child; one of infinite patience and love. "Why do you still harbor this hatred for me?" We were circling each other like cats, waiting for an opening. "Does it chase away the nightmares? Does it help you to forget about Crete . . . and Calla?"

"I warned you to never speak her name." My low voice crouched in the shadows, watching. I stopped circling, my whole body painfully tensed.

"You left her and now you find it easier to blame me for your regrets. You can't run from us both forever," Sadira said, taking a step toward me. She lifted her hand to touch my cheek, but I raised my hand, just an inch from her face. Flames danced over my fingers and slithered down to my wrist. Her eyes widened.

Before Sadira, I had a life. It was a short, fragile human life, but it was my life nonetheless. I'd had a family that I loved and a place in my small corner of the world. My world didn't include nightwalkers or torture. It didn't even include my own powers, since I'd chosen to hide that unique ability and start fresh.

But Sadira slipped into my world one night centuries ago and stole me away, threatening to kill all those I loved if I did not remain at her side. So I stayed through the humiliation, pain, and seemingly constant fear. She kept me at her side as a human for roughly four years. During that time, I discovered that I would make a better vampire than I could ever be as a normal human. The nightwalkers surrounding her feared me, feared my powers. And for good reason: Sadira had taught me everything she knew about torture and manipulation. When the Black Plague swept through Europe, she offered to make me a nightwalker in an effort to save my life. I agreed, walking away from any hope of returning to the life I'd lived before.

I hated Sadira for stealing me away. I hated myself for saying yes, because I could not be what I wanted—normal. Human.

Lifting my open hands, a pair of flames danced on my palms, flickering yellow and orange. I lowered my hands again, but the flames remained hovering in midair like little balls of light. Sadira took an uneasy step back, unable to drag her eyes from the flames. She had seen my tricks with fire before, even commanded me to perform, but I'd learned a few things since I was last with her. She had never seen me burn the air itself.

With the barest nod of my head, the flames streaked toward her. Less than a foot from her chest, they split in two different directions and started to circle her. She pulled her arms against her chest, her head jerking from one side to the other, desperately trying to keep the fire in sight at all times. She was terrified . . . and with good cause.

"I left her because I had no choice. You would have killed her," I said, unable to even speak Calla's name. I hadn't thought about her in centuries, but Sadira's cruel mention brought a fresh rush of pain, as she'd no doubt intended. "I left you because I would have killed you had I stayed. You made me, so I spared your life as an act of gratitude. I owe you nothing now."

Sadira lifted her eyes to my face, and I could see a mixture of anger and genuine confusion in their depths. A part of her honestly could not understand my hatred. She did everything in the name of protecting her children, but that also meant controlling them. And no matter how hard she tried, she could not completely control me. In the past, she could make me bow under the pain and anguish she caused, but it was always short-lived.

Danaus purposefully entered my line of sight, standing behind Sadira's left shoulder and frowning. He didn't have to say anything. This argument was wasting time we didn't have. I would have to add Sadira to my list of unfinished business. If naturi didn't kill me first, I would finally deal with Sadira and my past.

"Enough of this." Waving my hands in the air, the flames vanished with a puff of smoke. I paced away from Sadira, over to the windows that looked down on the city. Pushing aside the gauzy white curtains, I looked down on the busy street as a steady flow of traffic rushed below us.

When I turned back around, the tableau looked exactly as it had when I entered the room. The moment had been erased. Sadira's face was expressionless, but that did not mean I'd been forgiven. A vampire never attacked another of her kind that was twice her age. And you never attacked your maker unless you were sure you could kill them. While Sadira worked under the pretense of love and protection, she was no different than the others. She would strike out at me at her first chance, but I wasn't particularly worried. She could hurt me but would not try to kill me. I was a valuable pet, and she wanted me at her side, broken and obedient.

"One sacrifice has been completed at Konark, and the naturi have attacked me twice," I said, trying to boil down everything that had happened recently into a concise description. It wasn't easy. Was it fair to leave out the dead in my domain or the fear that seemed to burn in me every time I stepped outside? "We think they are going after anyone who survived Machu Picchu."

"We?" Sadira said, cocking her head to the side as he eyes slid back to Danaus.

"Jabari and I," I sharply corrected her assumption. "Tabor is dead. That leaves you and Jabari as part of the triad. I don't remember who else was at the mountain that night, but not many of us survived."

Sadira's dark brown eyes narrowed on me as she frowned. Resting her right elbow on the arm of the chair, she settled her narrow chin in the palm of her hand. "What do you remember of that night?"

"Not much after you arrived. I remember Jabari rescuing me, holding me, with you and Tabor standing nearby. And then nothing . . . just light and . . . pain." I struggled to pull the memory loose from the jumble of thoughts crowding that night. "Why can't I remember? What happened after you arrived?"

"Have you asked Jabari?"

"He said he would tell me later." Frustration and anger crept back into my tone. I shoved my right hand through my hair, pushing it from my face.

"Then I will leave it to him," Sadira said quickly, with a relieved look. She was obviously glad to wash her hands of the ordeal. "I don't wish to talk about that night."

"Why? What happened? It couldn't have been that bad if we won." Taking another step closer, I moved around the coffee table in the center of the room in front of the sofa.

"No, Mira, please. You may doubt me, but I do love you. Even after all these years, the sound of your screams still haunts me at night. It is a sound I know I shall never forget."

"You never heard my screams," I said in a low voice. "The naturi had stopped torturing me before you arrived." Her eyes darted away from me, locking on a point somewhere over my shoulder. A heavy knot twisted in my stomach as my mind pushed against the dark shadows that crowded my memories of that night. "How could you have heard me screaming?"

"It's not important right now. There is nothing we can do until the triad has been reformed." Her voice wavered before she could bring herself to meet my gaze. I stared into her brown eyes for a long time before I spoke again. She'd made her decision and I couldn't move her.

"Fine." I shoved my hands into my back pockets in an effort to keep from sending another fireball at her. "Jabari said to reform the triad I needed to find someone of Tabor's bloodline. I don't know Tabor's maker so I guess we need to find one of his children."

"And there you are in luck, though I wish one of his other children were closer," Sadira announced, a light frown pulling at her full red lips.

"Why?"

"His name is Thorne. He is a little . . . different from what we have known. He appears to be a part of a new breed of nightwalker. He's rather open about his condition," she said delicately.

"Whatever. I'll deal with him," I said with a dismissive wave of my hand.

"He's not likely to come with you."

"I'm sure I can handle him." And I was sure. "Have you met him? If he's going to be difficult, I would prefer it if he didn't know I was looking for him."

Searching the area for a nightwalker I had never met before would take time and be invasive—rather like bending every vampire over and checking the initials in their underwear. If Sadira or I had met Thorne before, I could feel for him more discreetly.

"We have not been formally introduced, but I recently tracked him down to a bar on the outskirts of the city called Six Feet Under."

"I'll find him," I bit out. Turning, I was about to stalk out of the room, happy to finally be leaving Sadira, when Danaus moved toward the door as well. "No, you're staying," I told him, placing a restraining hand on his chest, ignoring his dark looks. "Someone needs to stay here and protect her."

"What about the naturi?" he asked.

Fear lurched in my stomach, wrapping itself around my heart. "Are they close?"

"Not that I can tell, but you wouldn't know it until they were standing next to you."

I glanced over at Michael and Gabriel seated on the sofa. If our enemies attacked as they had at Aswan, they wouldn't have a chance. They were no match for the naturi.

But by that logic, I also couldn't drag Sadira behind me through the bowels of London. She would be too much of a distraction if I were forced to try to protect both her and Thorne. I was trapped. I couldn't imagine how Jabari had expected me to manage this. He could have just commanded Thorne to appear using his telepathic abilities, and Thorne would have appeared. Easy as that. Unfortunately, I wasn't that intimidating yet.

I paced away from the door, desperately trying to find a new solution. I didn't know any other nightwalkers in London I could call on and trust them to defend Sadira with their lives. And Danaus wasn't about to stay behind when we both knew I needed him at my back to tell me if the naturi were closing in. I was about to give in and have Sadira accompany me to the pub when I felt someone else.

My hand flew to my mouth, but a chuckle still escaped. It was crazy and desperate, but I was completely out of options. I spun around sharply, facing Danaus. He jerked back a step, surprised by my quick change of direction. "Could Themis protect her?" I asked. His dark brows snapped together and he looked at me as if I had suddenly gone mad. "Do they have the firepower here in London to protect her?" I repeated a little slower.

"Yes, but—"

"We don't have any other choice. I'm not thrilled about the idea, but I can't be in two places at once."

A long, heavy silence stretched through the room as Danaus stared at me. When he finally spoke, it sounded as if he'd ground up the word with his back teeth before releasing it: "Agreed."

"Great. Now go fetch James. He just came up on the elevator," I said with a laugh at his surprised look. "He followed us to the hotel and has been searching for us."

Danaus hurried out of the room, a dark look filling his eyes. I don't know whether he was upset that James had followed us or because he hadn't noticed earlier. I had a feeling Danaus was so focused on the nightwalkers that surrounded him and the naturi that he forgot to pay any attention to the humans lurking on the fringe.

He reappeared a minute later, dragging a flustered-looking James in by the arm. He gave the young man a shove into the center of the room as he slammed the door closed again. It was nice to see Danaus angry with someone other than me. James ran his hands over his jacket as he eyes quickly surveyed the room. He stiffened at the sight of Michael and Gabriel, but when his eyes fell on Sadira, he stumbled backward a few steps, running into Danaus. Stepping away, he found himself that much closer to me.

"This was what you wanted, wasn't it?" I said, taking a step even closer to him, my hands lightly clasped behind my back. "I felt you bumbling through the hotel. You had to know I would be aware of your presence." I circled behind him as I spoke. I gave him credit for not trying to run as I heard his heart thudding like that of a cornered hare.

"I—I want to help," James said, struggling to keep his voice from breaking. He wasn't wearing his glasses now and I noticed his eyes were more copper than an ordinary brown; an odd shade with an almost red highlight in their brown depths. Trapped in that room, surrounded by monsters, he was younger than I initially thought; definitely mid- to late twenties.

"And so you shall," I whispered in his ear. I quickly moved away, then stepped in front of him again. "James Parker, may I introduce Sadira," I grandly announced with a flourish of my hands as I bent in a mocking bow.

"A pleasure and an honor," he said with the kind of grace and aplomb everyone had come to expect of the British. He gave a slight bow of his head out of respect, but nothing more. I was impressed.

Sadira smiled at him, a picture of sweetness and gentility. "It is good to meet you, James Parker." Her soft accent made it sound like she was almost purring. She then looked at me, and the warmth was replaced by a look of extreme caution. "What games do you play, my daughter?"

"No games. I have a task to be completed and I cannot drag you along, yet I can't leave you behind either. My new friend James will see to your protection while I am gone."

"I beg your pardon." His eyes widened until I feared they would roll from their sockets. "How can I possibly hope to protect her?"

"Take her to the Compound," Danaus responded, his deep voice sweeping unexpectedly through the room like a bitter winter wind.

James spun around to look at the hunter. "Have you lost your mind? No vampire has ever been permitted inside the Compound."

Danaus just stared at the young man. He obviously didn't care about precepts and traditions.

"James, she is one of the three nightwalkers that can stop the naturi," I said, placing an arm around his bony shoulders. He stiffened at the touch but didn't try to pull away. "I must go fetch one of the others and cannot protect her at the same time. So it is in everyone's best interest that she remains alive and well guarded. Your little group can do that." I leaned close so he could hear me when my voice dropped to a whisper. "Besides, after all the damage your group has brought on my kind, you owe us this one."

James turned his head to look at me. I smiled, letting him get a good look at my fangs. He jerked violently backward, stumbling into Danaus again. "But what if—I mean, if she—" he started, but halted each time as he struggled to form the sentence without completely insulting Sadira in the process.

I chuckled, shaking my head. I'd put him in an awkward position. Less than two hours ago he had never spoken to a nightwalker before, and now they surrounded him.

"She'll behave herself."

"Mira!" Sadira gasped, sounding appropriately scandalized.

My name only earned her a dark chuckle.

"Where are you trying to send me?" Sadira demanded, her hands tightening on the arms of her chair. There was no threat or warning in her voice, but it held none of its usual sweetness either.

"The safest place I can think to put you." I paused, stepping away from James, to stand directly in front of her. "In a den of hunters."

Sadira came out of her chair instantly, her body rigid. "Are you mad?" Her eyes were wide and sparkling in the pale yellow lamplight.

"I have no other options. They won't harm you as long as you don't attack them."

"Can you promise that?"

"No," I admitted with an indifferent shrug. "But it's in their best interest that you remain alive since you're key to stopping the naturi. Of course, if you threaten them, I'm sure they have ample stakes lying around."

"You can't do this, Mira!"

"Do you have a better idea?"

She stared at me, impotent rage and fear blazing in her eyes. Her small hands were balled into fists at her side.

"I didn't think so. I'm sending Michael and Gabriel with you as well, to help act as protection and a buffer between you and Themis. Don't think to strike at me through them . . . you have your own string of pets that I can go through too."

Sadira sat back down, lifting her chin a little higher. "You'll regret this."

I laughed at her. "You're not the only one who wants my head on a pike at the moment. Take a number and get in line." I turned my back on her and walked over to the windows, still shaking my head.

"Themis will never let them in." James's voice was fragile, as if he was terrified I would rip his throat out at any second.

"Call Ryan." Danaus said before I could speak. The two members of Themis just stared at each other.

"Use the phone in the bedroom," I said, pointing toward one of the doors in the two-bedroom suite. "I'll have my limo brought around to the front while we wait."

Finally, James frowned and left the room, closing the door behind him. Michael had already risen from the sofa and was calling down to the front desk for a limo, while Gabriel sorted through weaponry.

"Take it all," I said. His head snapped up, lines of confusion digging furrows in his forehead as he looked at me. "You may not be returning here again. I want you and Michael prepared for anything. Set up sleeping shifts when you arrive at this Compound. I want one of you awake and with Sadira at all times."

"But at dawn . . . ?" Gabriel started before the words seemed to die in his throat.

"I'm not sure where I'll be. Hopefully, I'm being overly

cautious." Gabriel frowned, his gaze darting over to Danaus for a moment. I noticed that his hand tightened on the dagger he'd been about to place in a belt sheath. "He will not kill me while I sleep," I told him.

"But will he protect you?"

"Yes, I think he will." The idea was amusing, lifting my mood a bit. I looked over at Danaus, who stood stiff and expressionless. He was completely unmoved by Gabriel's glares and our conversation. "I think he would much rather kill me himself than allow someone else to do it."

"That is not much comfort," Gabriel said, a wry smile briefly touching his lips.

I looked away from my guardian, my eyes falling on Sadira. She had been closely watching the conversation, a smug smile lifting her lips. "Now you have your own," she said. I had always mocked her about her need to be surrounded by pets and puppets.

"It's not the same." My momentary amusement drained from my body. "Their job is to guard me when I cannot protect myself. Nothing more."

"Really?" Her smile grew as her eyes slid over to Michael sorting through the pile of weapons at Gabriel's side. She could tell that I had fed off of him. The faint mark we left behind was a warning sign to other nightwalkers. If I did not feed off of him again in a week's time, the mark would fade.

"Only when I travel," I said. "And they are still human. When they return home, they have other lives in the sunlight. For your *pets*, there is nothing for them beyond you."

James picked that exact moment to come out of the bedroom. I hadn't wanted to continue this conversation with Sadira anyway. She had a knack for twisting things, and I didn't need to justify my actions when it came to my guardian angels.

"We can go," James said, his shoulders sagging a bit. "They are expecting us."

"Good. The limo is waiting. With any luck, Danaus and I should be no more than an hour behind you."

"Wait!" Sadira suddenly cried, drawing my gaze back to her face. "If I am to go to this Compound, you must fulfill a request for me."

"We don't have time for this, Sadira," I growled.

"You know you have no choice. They cannot keep me where I do not want to stay," she reminded me with a small smile.

She was right. She was an Ancient nightwalker who would be surrounded by humans. If she didn't want to stay at Themis, she could leave regardless of the fact that she would be risking her own life. "What do you want?"

"There is another nightwalker traveling with Thorne; tall, brown hair with blue eyes. Tristan belongs to me. Bring him back with you as well."

"If he belongs to you, why is he with Thorne?"

Sadira dismissed the question with a wave of her slender hand. "Just a little misunderstanding. Bring him back to me and I promise to behave."

I stared at my maker, my teeth clenched. I didn't like this. Why was this nightwalker with Thorne if he actually belonged to Sadira? Was I about to step into a battle between two Ancients? Or was Sadira playing some other game? Damn it, I didn't have time for this nonsense, but if I didn't protect Sadira and reform the triad, Jabari was going to have my head.

"Very well," I snapped, looking away from her.

"Thank you, my daughter," Sadira purred. I wanted to shove a fireball down her throat.

I turned my attention to Danaus again. "Anything?"

With his arms folded over his chest, he closed his eyes,

his thick eyebrows drawn over his nose in concentration. His powers filled the room like warm sunlight, but no one's expressions changed, not even Sadira's. Was I the only one who could feel the wonderful wave of power bathing the room?

Out of the corner of my eye I saw him lift his head, his eyes opening. "No naturi in the immediate area. They should be able to make it to the Compound safely."

"Go now," I said, resisting the urge to shake my head in an attempt to shed the last tendrils of warmth still clinging to my brain. James led the way out the door, and Sadira didn't look back as she followed. Michael and Gabriel both nodded to me once, then left without a word. A part of me wanted to hug both my angels. I wanted to hold them and then send them straight back across the ocean. Their job was to protect me during the day, with the expectation that it would only be against any human that found me. My intention had never been for them to face anything like the naturi. It was more than either had ever bargained for, and I had not wanted this for them.

Biting back a sigh, I followed my angels down to the lobby with Danaus at my back. I had just handed Sadira over to a pack of vampire hunters while crawling through the bowels of London looking for Tabor's replacement. I doubted this was what Jabari had in mind when it came to protecting Sadira.

Seventeen

Every city has a section that police seem hesitant to enter, even ultracivilized London. In my own beloved Savannah, these dark streets, which housed the Docks, were among my favorite to stroll down. In London the dark section was far from Mayfair and Hyde Park. It grew out on the fringes of the city, filled with tightly packed, brick tenements. The air was thick and heavy in the summer heat, filled with ghosts and old, grim memories. I doubted there were many psychics in that part of town; the dead would have given them no rest. But the air pricked my skin and tingled with anticipation. You came here to get problems taken care of, one way or another.

Our taxi driver seemed grateful when we let him drop us off a couple blocks from the pub. He snatched up Danaus's money and turned his car around, heading back to the bright lights and busy hum of traffic. We continued the rest of the way to the pub in silence, our eyes scanning the area for anything that might offer a potential threat. Beside me, I could feel the gentle throb of power emanating from Danaus. It pushed and brushed against my skin, probing as if it were trying to figure out exactly what I was.

Trying to ignore it, I felt outward with my own powers. While I couldn't sense the naturi, in this small, six-block region I counted more than a score of magic users, even a couple of full-fledged warlocks and witches. They took note of me in the sense that they were aware of something powerful passing through their part of town, but nothing more. There were only a handful of nightwalkers in the area, all significantly younger than I was. As vampires go, I wasn't particularly old, but finding those that had walked the earth longer had become more difficult recently. There was something very unsettling about that fact.

Six Feet Under was a dive in the truest sense of the word. It had once been a mortuary with its own crematorium, but apparently the previous owners had moved on. A neon sign flickered over the entrance of a corpse clutching a lily to his chest, a tombstone resting at his head. A bit cliché for a vampire hangout, but who was I to scoff? One of my favorite haunts back home was a vampire-owned bar called Alive One. Its clientele was almost all human, with a few of us stopping by for laughs. Pickings were better next door at a nightclub called Purgatory. Alive One was a place to warm up for an evening of feeding and debauchery.

With a name like Six Feet Under, I expected the normal goth scene of black clothes and pale skin. What I got was wall-to-wall London punk.

We elbowed our way through the crowd outside the club to the front door, where I cleared the mind of the bouncer. I wasn't about to spend the next hour waiting in line to get into a club while the naturi were lurking. Just inside, I'd pulled my leather wallet from my back pocket when it dawned on me that I was only carrying American dollars. I'd had Charlotte procure me some Egyptians notes before leaving but no other currencies because I wasn't sure where I would end up.

Before I could say anything, Danaus reached over my shoulder and handed the bored-looking doorman with purple hair a folded twenty-pound note. Enough to get us both in with no questions.

"Don't worry. I'll pay for our next date." I walked into the bar before he could retort.

He and I paused just inside the pub, gazing over the crowd. The people were packed so tightly it was amazing anyone could breathe. It looked as if all the walls had been knocked out of the place, making it into one huge room. A long bar dominated the right wall, with customers lining the edge more than three deep. On the back wall stood a stage where a band was currently screeching and a pale waif of a man screamed into the microphone. I'll admit I'm no great fan of punk, but fan or no fan, this was just noise.

I let my eyes dance over the crowd, looking for any sign of our prey. Before entering the pub, I had picked up the presence of two nightwalkers, but I didn't try to identify them. Yet, in this crush, I knew I would have to use my powers to find them. There were too many people here to try to pick out Thorne and Tristan quickly by sight. Stifling a sigh of frustration, I reached out a little. It took only a second and I didn't like what I found.

"Damn it," I said through clenched teeth. I couldn't catch a break.

"What?" Danaus said, turning to look at me. "Did you find him?

"Yeah, I found him." Tristan had been easy enough to locate. The pale brown-haired vampire was seated in a circular booth off to the left of the stage. He was also the only one I could see in this place who was fashionably dressed, no doubt thanks to Sadira's tastes for expensive things.

But the other nightwalker was just as easy to spot; I had no doubt that the pale singer clutching the microphone was

Thorne. How was I supposed to get him now? I could push my way through the crowd, jump onstage and throw him through the nearest window, but I was trying not to make a scene.

"We wait," Danaus announced in a low voice after I pointed out the singer in disgust. He muscled his way through the crowd along the back wall. Ignoring the fact that the floor crunched beneath my feet, I followed in his wake, watching the dislodged people look up angrily then sidle away when their eyes touched his face and bulging form. It was an interesting twist. For me, brute force was saved for my own kind. When it came to humans, I needed only sensual allure and a slight threat of something dark and powerful to get them to do what I wanted. But Danaus could stand in a room, and its occupants would begin to squirm. He had become what the humans equated to the grim reaper: walking death.

Ensconced in a shadowy corner, I leaned back against the poster-covered wall with my arms folded across my chest and watched our prey. It was all wrong. I checked again and again to the point that Thorne stuttered in mid-song and scanned the bar. He felt me but hadn't pinpointed my exact location yet.

A vampire singing on a stage in front of a crowd of screaming fans. How could this have happened? From the moment we are reborn, we are all taught one thing: *Stay in the shadows. Never draw attention to yourself.* The longer the humans look at you, the more they will see and sense that there is something different about you. They will know you're not human. They might not be able to comprehend what you are, but they will know.

At the end of the song, Thorne leaned forward, balancing some of his weight on the microphone stand, and hissed at the crowd, pulling back his lips and flaunting his fangs. I lurched forward, but Danaus's hand stopped me from getting more than a couple steps away from the wall. The crowd went insane, their cheers rattling the windows and pushing me back a half step. They knew what Thorne was and they loved it. I scanned the spectators, taking in their expressions. There was no fear; just excitement and pleasure. It would have been intoxicating if it didn't seem so wrong.

"They know?" I asked, turning to look at Danaus. The hunter stood beside me, continuing to stare up at the stage as he dropped his hand from my shoulder.

"They think it's just an act," he said, nodding to the undulating crowd. I looked back, my stomach twisting. If they knew the truth—that three real nightwalkers stood in their midst—would they still be celebrating? Or would they run screaming from this place that still smelled faintly of death under the layers of sweat and alcohol?

We hung back as Thorne stepped down from the stage. Followed by the rest of the band, he waded through a surge of the crowd, laughing as they ran their hands over his body and reached for him. He settled into a circular booth next to Tristan, surrounded by his fellow band members and a smattering of female groupies. I took the lead this time, threading my way there, with Danaus following close on my high heels. I needed to have this done now.

Standing in front of him, it was still hard to believe Thorne was a nightwalker. Without the slight flow of power leaking from his body, I would have said he was only a sad, thin human. He looked like someone had animated a skeleton and then carelessly thrown a draping of skin over his bones so that they would hold together. His flesh was almost a powdery white, nearly matching the bleach-blond hair that stuck out in all directions on his head. He wore a pair of skintight leather pants that only accentuated his thinness. His chest was bare, revealing every rib and bone.

He wasn't even bothering to breathe. Any other human would have been winded after singing a full set, but he didn't even pretend, and the people around him didn't question it. It was like momentarily slipping into someone else's dream. A vampire sat, open about what he was, and no one noticed or cared.

On the other hand, Tristan was what I'd come to expect a nightwalker to be. He appeared to have barely escaped his teens when he was reborn. His dark brown hair hung down to brush against his thin shoulders and his pale blue eyes watched the crowd, but his gaze seemed distant, as if his thoughts were somewhere else. He was nicely dressed in Hugo Boss, Ralph Lauren, even a little Armani, in the luxury Sadira swathed herself and those around her. Looking at him, I wondered if I'd had the same grim and unyielding appearance near the end of my first century.

"Bugger off," snapped one of the band members. My eyes never left Thorne, who had yet to notice me. He was too busy whispering sexual promises to the pink-haired girl sitting next to him. Tristan had looked up and was closely watching me, but no expression had yet to appear on his handsome face.

"Are you Thorne?" I demanded, preferring to ignore everyone else.

The nightwalker reluctantly pulled away from the woman and looked up at me. A broad smile lit his face, revealing his fangs again, as his eyes slid down the length of my body. "For you, I can be anybody," he said in a thick, cockney accent.

The line would have been far more effective delivered by the likes of Pierce Brosnan or even with a lovely Scottish burr, like Sean Connery's. From Thorne it was just pathetic.

"Are you Thorne, child of Tabor?" I demanded. That

definitely caught his attention. He stared at my face, his eyes narrowing as he concentrated. There was a faint surge of power from him for only a second before his eyes widened.

"Bloody hell, another vampire!" He laughed, throwing his head back. Everyone at the table looked at me in a new light, questioning. They were weighing me, wondering what Thorne had meant. The tension around the table grew slightly, but not enough to indicate any real concern. The bassist narrowed his gaze on me then looked over at another band member, trying to decide if they should be worried. To them, I was another imposter.

"We need to talk," I said over his laughter. "Now."

"As you can see, I'm a mite busy." Lounging insolently in the booth, he linked his hands behind his head and stretched out his legs beneath the table. The pink-haired woman in the ripped white T-shirt leaned over and placed her head against his chest, wrapping her arms possessively around his waist. She shot me a dark, warning look. I wanted to laugh. How could I want some toothpick when I had Danaus hovering in the shadows? Of course, my "plaything" could boil my insides with a thought. But that play date would come only if we survived the next few days.

"Send them away."

"Who the hell do you think you are, you damn wanker?" he demanded, sitting up.

I leaned forward, slamming my hands down on the dirty tabletop with enough force to rattle the pints of beer. The amber liquid sloshed a bit on the table and everyone jumped backward. "I am Mira, and your better." He jerked back suddenly, his heels digging into the floor as he half stood. He was trapped between the booth and the table, looking like he was about to start climbing the wall to get away from me.

"Fire Starter," Tristan whispered in a tone that sounded

a touch too much like awe. His eyes widened and his pale lips parted slightly as he stared at me with new interest. I ignored him for the moment. My main concern was that I now had Thorne's attention.

"My reputation precedes me," I said tightly. "Get rid of them before I throw your bony ass through the wall."

"You wouldn't dare," he snickered, his eyes darting off toward the huge crowded that danced and screamed behind us. Sticking to the creed of remaining in the shadows would not include throwing a person through a brick wall, but what Thorne didn't know was that I had a penchant for pushing the limits of the shadow dance we maintained.

"She'll do it," Tristan said evenly, his wide eyes never leaving my face.

Thorne hesitated a moment, staring at me through narrowed, beady eyes. "Get out of here," he grumbled in a low voice. I glared at him, resisting the urge to grab for his throat when he looked over at his companions. "Get out of here!" he repeated. He gave the woman at his side a hard shove, sending two people to the floor. The others scrambled out of the booth, grabbing their drinks as they pushed their way into the crowd.

Eighteen

I slid into the seat to Thorne's left while Danaus walked around the booth and sat across from me, trapping Thorne and Tristan between us. The faded maroon plastic seat sagged in certain places and had been mended more than once with silver duct tape. The music spun by the DJ crowded the dance floor with scantily clad people. It was a good turnout and would have been a nice place to spend a few entertaining hours if I wasn't already previously engaged.

Thorne stared at Danaus for a long time, his eyes pinched and narrowed. He sniffed the air, then jumped backward, hissing. He tried to stand in the booth, but I grabbed his arm and jerked him back down.

"I know your smell. You're the hunter." His voice was choked as he slid closer, his haunted gaze then slamming back, confusion twisting his features into an ugly knot as he picked up Danaus's scent on me. "But . . . why are you traveling with him?"

"Not your concern," I said, but the sound came out sounding more like a growl than actual words. "Why didn't you try to protect Tabor when he was attacked? Wasn't that your job?"

"I wasn't there," he said, wrenching his arm out of my grasp. He picked up the mug of beer in front of him and emptied the contents before slamming it back on the table. It was sort of strange. He didn't expend the energy to breathe but would use the energy to digest alcohol. As far as I knew, no vampire could digest solid food, but we could do liquids. Unfortunately, no amount of alcohol would intoxicate us, but drinking the blood of a drunk human would give you a nice though extremely temporary buzz. Intoxication for nightwalkers had nothing to do with alcohol.

"Where were you?" I laid my hand on the table, then quickly lifted it in disgust when I discovered that the surface was covered in a sticky film.

"I was on loan." The right corner of his lips twitched as if in a suppressed smile. I nodded, while Danaus stared hard at me, expectant.

"I'm always surprised at how little you know," I said, setting my hands back in my lap. "It is a common practice among nightwalkers to loan out their pets to others of similar strength. It's called being polite."

"And they let themselves be used like that?" There was a curl to his lip as he spoke in distaste. Resting on the table, his left hand tightened into a fist.

"You make it sound like we have a choice," Tristan softly interjected.

A sharp, bitter laugh escaped before I could clip its wings. "When you are young and weak, you go where you are told and do what you are told. If you're lucky, you survive the encounter and return to your maker."

"And if you are killed while you were *on loan*?" Danaus's hard blues never wavered from my face.

"Then your maker gets to kill one of the other vampire's pets. A fair trade," Thorne said with an indifferent shrug.

"Why? Why do this?" Even as Danaus shook his head,

his gaze still never left my face. He watched me closely, as if seeing me or my kind for the first time. I think whatever little bit of respect I had earned was dying before my eyes.

"Why else?" My laughter spiked higher, trying to hide an unexpected stab of pain and embarrassment. "Pleasure and entertainment." It was time Danaus understood us a little better; the good and the bad.

I looked over to Thorne, who was staring out at the crowd, dancing to the music. His gaze was distant, a smile teasing at his thin lips. His thoughts were lost to another place and time.

"Who did you go to? Claudette?" I prodded. She had a reputation for sampling the children of the Ancients. I'd had the pleasure of visiting with her once. Luckily, it was a brief visit.

"Macaire." Thorne blinked twice as if trying to free his thoughts of some old memories. "I was sent to help break in his newest Companion." A smile blossomed on his thin, angular face, his fangs poking a little against his lower lip.

"Lucas is a fool," I muttered under my breath.

"True," he chuckled. Thorne stretched out his legs again, toying with a stray bottle cap on the tabletop. "He won't survive long. He thinks too much on his own."

It was a sad but true thought. Good servants did exactly what they were told and nothing more. You start thinking and trying to predict the needs of your master, and you'd get crushed when you made a mistake.

"Of course, Tabor said the same of you," he continued.

My eyes jerked back to his face but I kept my expression blank. "That I think too much?"

"No, that you wouldn't survive." Thorne's brown eyes seemed to dance with malicious glee for a second in the faint undulating light. "He said that without Jabari, the Coven would have killed you centuries ago."

I had suspected this for a while, but to actually hear the words sent a chill down my spine. "I'm no threat to the Coven." I tried to sound as if none of this made any difference to me.

"So you say, but Tabor is dead and a seat is still open on the Coven. I may be in London, but even I hear the occasional whispered thought or rumor." He leaned forward, his chest nearly brushing the edge of the table. "Everyone is watching, waiting for you to make your move."

Sitting up in the booth so my nose was mere inches from Thorne's, I tightly gripped the edge of the table for balance. "Well, tell everyone that I don't want it."

"No, you just want the colonies." He snickered, flopping back against the booth, his amusement unbroken. He elbowed Tristan once in the ribs, flashing him a wide grin that the other nightwalker didn't return.

The colonies had become the last refuge for my kind. The Coven and the Ancients dominated Europe, Asia, and even down into Africa. South America had been abandoned by nightwalkers because of what happened at Machu Picchu . . . the death and pain that still lingered was too unpleasant, even for my kind.

That left the United States. It was an enticing place, with its lax morals, hypocritical philosophies, and fast lifestyles. In the West, all was still new and precious. It was an exciting place to be, especially when there was little to no threat of encountering an Ancient. I had been part of the wave of young ones to leave Europe in search of my own home, moving out from beneath the thumb of the Coven.

But the newness of the colonies was a curse as well. It lacked the history and long memory of Europe and Asia. The colonists didn't realize that there were dark corners that should not be illuminated and questions that should not be asked. There was no doubt among my kind that when the

Great Awakening arrived, it would start in the New World.

The nightwalkers in the States were different from those in Europe. We were younger on average, and quiet. The families were fewer and smaller in size. We did what we could to safeguard our secret. But our numbers were growing, and the Coven knew it. It didn't help that I was one of the oldest among those across the ocean. There was some speculation of a coup, and my stubborn silence didn't soothe any of the frayed, anxious nerves.

"I'm surprised the Coven has not come down on your head," I said, desperate to change topics. I sat back in the booth and let my hands fall back into my lap. It was one thing to open the door to our world to Danaus; it was another to let him see into the politics. I didn't want anything to do with the Coven. And I certainly didn't want to play Keeper for all of the States. I just wanted my little city with its cramped alleys, trendy little bars, and quiet, tree-cloaked neighborhoods.

"For what?"

"Your little show." I waved my arm to encompass the dimly lit pub filled to the brim with waiting victims.

Of course, I was sure part of the reason Thorne had been overlooked so far by our kind was because he'd settled in London. Between the wellspring of magic that had soaked into every inch of the island and the constant flow of witches and warlocks passing through the city, the whole place was a powder keg waiting for a careless match. No vampire stayed in the city long. If anything went wrong here, we all knew a vampire would play the scapegoat. Few older vampires would hang around, and definitely not long enough to bother with him.

"You know it's our law to stay in the shadows and never reveal yourself to more people than necessary," I continued. "I'd wager this crowd is a little more than necessary."

"Why?" Sitting up, Thorne crushed the bottle cap between two fingers and dropped it on the table. "Why keep hiding? These humans have seen more horrible things in their lives than us. I've seen monsters in their movies and on their newscasts that were ten times worse than what I've done. It's time they knew."

"It's not for you to decide."

He hit his fist on the edge of the table, knocking over his empty mug. "Then who?"

"I don't know. It's coming, but not yet. There is more at stake than just the nightwalkers. There are things these humans aren't ready to face."

"I don't think they'll have much choice. Besides, they accept me."

"They think you're a fraud," I reminded him. Slouched in the booth, I tried to avoid kicking Danaus in the shin, but the booth was crowded with long legs.

"Not for long. It's time we stepped forward. Let them bask in our power. I'm tired of hiding."

"But it's what we are, what we've always been. We are just shadows and nightmares to these creatures. Nothing more." I recited words I had heard a hundred times over. I sounded old even to my ears. My rationale was a tired one, clinging to the ways of my kind. I had seen this longing in many of the younger ones as they walked among the humans. Movies were made about us, with only small nuggets of truth permeating their depths. Humans gobbled up books about nightwalkers and magic users, looking for an escape from the mundane. But what if they woke up one morning and realized those things that thrilled and secretly enticed them were real and living next door? Would they still look at us with the same interest, or would we become vermin to be exterminated, like rats or cockroaches?

"Yeah, but it's like you said. It's coming."

"Enough!" I shouted, scratching my nails on the table, picking up a gooey layer of grime underneath them, causing me to grimace. Watching Thorne peripherally, I began to clean out my nails with a matchbook lying in the center of the table. "None of this matters. It's not why I've come. What did Tabor tell you of the naturi?"

At the mention of the naturi, Thorne stiffened beside me.

"He rarely spoke of them and only when he was in a black mood," he said, his voice barely more than a whisper as he gripped the edge of the table. "It was always at the same time of year; new moon in the middle of summer. He would stay locked away in his private rooms for several nights on end." His accent had grown thicker and older again.

I paused. "What did he tell you?"

"Nothing that made any sense. Just that if I ever saw one, I was to run. Don't try to fight. Just run." He raised haunted eyes to my face. I understood his fear. Tabor was not only his master and creator, but had been an Ancient and an Elder on the Coven. Thorne knew that for something to unnerve Tabor so thoroughly, it had to be bad.

"More than five centuries ago, a triad sealed most of the naturi from this world. They are trying to break through. We need your help to seal them again."

"My help?" A nervous laugh escaped him and skittered under the table to hide. "What the hell can I do?"

"Tabor was part of that triad. He's gone, but he made you. As part of the same bloodline, we think you can take his place in the triad."

"And do what? Tabor was more than three thousand years old when he made me." He stared wide-eyed at me, confident that I had lost my mind. I couldn't blame him. Even though I'd said it, I was having trouble believing it myself. Thorne wasn't a particularly strong nightwalker. He had probably stayed alive this long only because of Tabor's protection and his own smarts.

"I don't know. This wasn't my idea. Jabari sent me to find you," I admitted, frowning.

"Bloody hell," he muttered. Slumping back in the booth, he pushed the overturned mug with his index finger, making it rock. Any hopes he might have had about escaping me dissolved to dirty slush. He might have hoped to talk his way out of my grasp, but if an Elder had sent me, there was no escape. I would hunt him until I expired. And in a fight, he had no chance.

At that moment, a waitress in a tight black tank top brought over a tray laden with three mugs of ale. It was the dark type that reminded me more of motor oil than any liquid a human might actually want to imbibe. She leaned forward as she placed the mugs in front of each of us. Around her neck dangled a pentagram; she wasn't the first one I'd seen in London wearing such an item.

"I thought you might want another pint before going on again," she said, picking up Thorne's empty glass. She shuffled away, squeezing between the band members who had come back over to the table.

"We got another set," announced the man with a purple mohawk who had been playing the drums when we walked in. His brown eyes shifted to my face in an appraising manner, but I could also feel his anxiety. I was threatening his meal ticket.

"We have to go," I said, drawing Thorne's gaze back to my face.

"Y'got me," he snapped. "I can't outrun you. Let me finish this set before you take me to Hell."

Frowning, I looked expectantly over at Danaus. He knew what I wanted to know, and I was getting sick of asking. The sooner the naturi were taken care of, the sooner I could go back to trying to kill him instead of depending upon him to watch my back. Danaus shook his head at me, his eyes narrowing.

"Fine. Go. Just a couple songs. It's late," I said, irritation clipping my words as I slid to my feet so I could let him out of the booth.

Avoiding Danaus's gaze, I watched as Thorne quickly downed half of his beer. He slammed the glass mug down on the table, his face twisted in disgust. "Blast, that's a nasty brew," he groaned, then said nothing more as he slipped out of the booth. But as he turned to follow his band mates up to the stage, Thorne grabbed my right wrist. He gave my arm a little jerk, but I didn't move. "Come on," he said, motioning with his head for me to follow him up to the raised platform.

"I can't sing." A swell of panic rose up in my chest and I pulled against his grip, but he didn't release me.

"You call this singing?" He laughed, his smile widening. Around us, the crowd was screaming and jumping as the other members of the band picked up their instruments. The shouting throbbed and crashed against the walls, threatening to topple the place. Their excitement was a live thing in that large room, pushing against me. Thorne stepped close, pressing his cool, bare chest against my arm. "Come up there. Show them what you are. It's the next best thing."

I looked down at his brown eyes, which were now glowing, the irises overwhelming all other color. He was riding the wave of their emotions, and for him it was the next best thing to actually feeding on them. The idea of standing on that stage and screaming into the microphone, purging all the anger I had carried around during the past few days, was tempting. But it would be more than that. I would bare my fangs to them, and those humans would scream for more. They would love me for being a nightwalker. Deep down, they would think I was a phony, but for a moment I wouldn't be hiding.

"What were you before?" I asked suddenly.

Thorne cocked his head to the side, the glow vanishing from his eyes at the strange question. "Before Tabor?" I nodded. "I walked the boards at Drury Lane," he said, smiling. For that sentence, the cockney accent disappeared. It was still British, but cultured and precise. Tabor always had snobbish tastes, so I imagined that Thorne had been born to a life of privilege and luxury. I wondered what his companions would think if they knew where he came from. Of course, that would all be moot once they discovered he was roughly two hundred years old.

"Go now before I change my mind," I said, stepping away from him as I pulled my arm free. Sitting back down in the booth across from Danaus, I watched Thorne jump back on the stage. I wasn't surprised. He'd been an actor before Tabor turned him. He had been accustomed to being the center of attention, pretending to be something he wasn't. Watching him now, I wondered if I might have seen him during my brief visits to London during the late eighteenth century. At that time, there were only three theaters: Drury Lane, Haymarket, and Covent Gardens. On several occasions Drury Lane had played host to Edmund Keane, the preeminent actor of his day. And now the emaciated Thorne stood shrieking before a crowd of disillusioned teenagers.

I looked up to find Danaus watching me, his expression again unreadable. A part of me wished I could crawl around in his brain, wrapping myself around his thoughts. The longer he stayed with me, the more he saw of my world, and I wanted to look at it all again with the eyes of an outsider. There was so much I had grown numb to during my long existence. Before Sadira changed me, I'd marveled at her strength and power. I sat in awe of her, amazed at the sheer number of nightwalkers that came to her side and bowed to her. Even before I was reborn, I grew inured to the killing and torture. I had been a gift to those who pleased her and an instrument of torture for those who disappointed her.

With my maker still lingering in the background of my thoughts, I looked over at Tristan, whose interest was starting to make me extremely uncomfortable. He was younger than Thorne, maybe a century, at best, judging by the quiet throb of power that rolled off of him.

"So, where do you fit into all of this?" I asked, dropping my hands down to my lap.

"I don't," he replied with a faint shrug of his shoulder.

"Why are you here?"

"I came for the entertainment. Thorne said it would be interesting."

Danaus snorted and looked back out at the crowd. Interesting. That was an understatement. The screaming crowd wasn't so much dancing as it was writhing in a giant mass. The array of clothes and colors bore no resemblance to anything I had ever seen in nature.

"Why does Sadira want me to take you to her?" I asked.

Tristan flinched at the mention of the Ancient and lines of tension tightened around his eyes and mouth. "You've spoken with her?"

"I saw her less than an hour ago. I came here for Thorne, but I will be taking both you and Thorne back with me to where she is hiding."

"No," he whispered. Some of the light that seemed to burn in his eyes when he discovered who I was had died, and a knot twisted itself around my soul. When he spoke again, his voice had hardened with a mix of anger and fear. "No! You can't! I won't go back. Mira, please." He leaned forward and held my gaze when I would have looked away from him. "You know what it's like. You remember. I can't go back."

I sat back against the booth and closed my eyes as it finally dawned on me. "She made you," I murmured softly to myself. Sadira had made Tristan, and he ran away after being her pet for roughly one century.

"I've known about you since almost the beginning," Tristan said. He reached under the table and grabbed my left wrist, forcing me to open my eyes and look at him. "You were the one that got away. You escaped our maker and have lived your own life. That's all I want."

I gritted my teeth and swallowed the snarl rising in my chest. That bitch! That manipulative, evil bitch! I didn't want to shove a fireball down her throat now. It was too kind a death for her. I wanted a baseball bat. A baseball bat and one endless night.

In one swift move she would accomplish an amazing coup over both Tristan and me. I had no choice but to retrieve the wayward vampire for her. Sadira wouldn't believe any excuse I gave for not bringing him, and she would disappear from my grasp, putting my head back on the chopping block with Jabari and jeopardizing all the people in my domain. However, if I brought Tristan back to her, it would not only crush his one shining hope of ever escaping her, but prove to everyone that I was still a servant to my maker despite my "escape."

"I didn't escape Sadira. I was with Jabari," I said, but quickly stopped. It wasn't an escape. Jabari just took what he wanted and that was that.

"So you escaped an Elder?"

"No, it wasn't like that." I shoved my hand through my hair and looked around as I quickly scrambled for a way to explain this. Danaus smirked, watching me with his arms crossed over his chest. I wasn't sure if he fully understood what we were talking about, but he could tell that I was digging myself in deeper.

Dropping my hands back down to the table, I turned back to Tristan, who was watching me with desperate eyes. "This isn't about me. I can't help you. Right now, the naturi are making a mess of things. I need Sadira cooperative if we're going to stop them, and that's only going to happen if I bring you back to her. And conscious or not, that's what I'm going to do."

"Mira—"

"The naturi are my concern right now, not a nightwalker that hasn't learned to take care of himself," I snapped angrily, hating Sadira and myself more with each passing second. I wasn't made of stone. I remembered what it was like living with Sadira. The nights of screams, fighting to stay in her constantly fluctuating favor, abandoning all semblance of pride and dignity just to survive until the dawn. But now wasn't the time.

"What about after the naturi are defeated?"

A part of me wanted to smile at his innocence. To him, there was nothing so strong that could defeat our kind. Of course, he had yet to face any member of the naturi.

"If I stand with you against Sadira, I would be claiming you," I said with a weary shake of my head. "I don't keep a family."

"But you have a domain."

"That's different, and you know it." Ruling a domain, you were the peacekeeper and arm of the Coven for a specific area. The head of a family was more than that—in general, a family unit protected each of its members against other nightwalkers or families, and none more so than its head. Of course, the family itself could be more dangerous than any other vampire outside the family. There were several families within my domain, and they all answered to me if there was a problem.

I didn't want my own family. It was enough that I watched

out for a large group of nightwalkers within a single area. A family evoked a certain type of intimacy and dependence I continued to eschew. Anyone you took into your family generally lived with you and looked to you for direction. I was still able to keep a distance from the nightwalkers in my domain. Sometimes, weeks passed between my meetings with Knox.

"Tristan, I can't fight this fight for you," I replied. But even as I said it, I wondered if I should. Hadn't Jabari fought for me in his own way when he took me to Egypt and away from Sadira?

I was snapped from my thoughts when a scream tore through the air above the shouts of the crowd, one of flesh-searing pain. My head jerked back up to the stage to see Thorne stagger backward, his left hand grabbing at his chest. His sharp fingernails left a trail of jagged lines in his flesh. Dark blood oozed from the wounds, leaving almost black streaks down his pale white skin. His gaze darted back over to me, filled with pain and confusion. Around us, the crowd went wild. They all thought it was part of the act.

Lurching to my feet, I took a step forward, but was stopped by the press of screaming fans as they crowded the stage. Danaus stood behind me, his body humming with tension, ready for action. Unfortunately, I didn't have a clue as to what we were fighting. My eyes never left Thorne, who had crumpled to his knees with another scream. His face was now streaked with dark, bloody tears. The cuts on his chest were not healing. By now they should have stopped bleeding and started to close, but the thick liquid continued to seep down his chest.

Reaching out with my powers, I scanned the bar. There were a couple magic users, but not one of them could have taken down a vampire, even one as weak as Thorne. I couldn't understand what was killing him.

"Naturi?" I shouted over my shoulder at Danaus.

"None near," he replied without hesitation. Apparently he'd had the same thought and had scanned the area. "How?"

"I don't know." My voice sounded dazed and lost as I watched Thorne fall the stage with a thud. He was dead. I couldn't sense him anymore. The end had come quite suddenly, as if it had crushed his very soul. He was dead before his head hit the stage.

"We have to go," Danaus said as the rumble of the crowd started to change to fearful questioning. The act had finally gone a little too far for them, and they could sense that something was off. We had to go before they started to think about with whom Thorne had last been talking. I turned and started to walk past the table when my eyes caught on the mugs of beer. My right hand snaked out and snatched up Thorne's half-empty glass. Dipping a couple fingers into the dark liquid, I dabbed it on my tongue. I spit the vile liquid back out and threw the mug against the wall with enough force that it shattered in a starburst of glass and dark amber beer.

"Poisoned!" The drink had been laced with enough naturi blood to poison Thorne. Thanks to my lengthy captivity with the naturi, I would always be able to recognize that wretched taste. However, most nightwalkers wouldn't. The naturi were too few in number, and it had been centuries since I last heard of a nightwalker being poisoned.

"The barmaid," Tristan snarled as he slid around the booth to stand directly behind me.

The barmaid with the pentagram stood behind the bar looking in my direction. I wasn't sure she could see me, but she didn't have to. She knew she had succeeded. Growling, I launched myself into the crowd, tossing people out of my way as I waded through the sea of flesh. Bodies flew through the air, limbs askew as they crashed into the undulating hoard. I was halfway across the room when Danaus finally caught up with me.

"There isn't time!" he shouted, grabbing my arm.

My gaze never wavered from my prey. Jerking free of him, I roared, "She's dead!"

"We're leaving now." Danaus wrapped one of his arms around my waist and lifted me off my feet. Balanced on his hip, he turned and carried me toward the door. Tristan was right behind us, looking unsure about whether to follow Danaus or go after the barmaid. I screamed in frustration and clawed at Danaus's arm, but he wouldn't release me. I was stronger but couldn't get the leverage I needed to free myself.

Looking up, my eyes met with the blue-haired woman that had killed Thorne. She was smiling triumphantly at me. I should have let the naturi she served have their fun with her, as I knew they would. But I couldn't. I smiled back at her, my eyes glowing in the semidark. Behind her, dozens of bottles of alcohol exploded in a wall of fire. Glass and liquid fire rained across the bar, raising the volume in the pub to hysterical levels. Thorne's killer shrieked, her body engulfed in flames.

As Danaus pushed his way toward the double doors, I grabbed the edge of one of the square columns that rose up to support the second floor, abruptly halting him. I pulled my body back into the crush of people running for the exit. We were being pushed and elbowed, but we managed to shrug most of it off. We'd both be a little sore for a while, but I had bigger fears.

"The body!" I shouted above the thunder of cries and screams. Danaus carried me back in so we were pinned against the column, ignoring the angry cries of confusion. "Lift me up!"

Without question he boosted me up so I was sitting on his shoulder. If not for his strength and my superior balance, it would have been an impossible task in this crowd. I looked over the writhing wave of bodies to the stage. Thorne had not been touched and his band mates had disappeared. I still had to see what I was burning if I couldn't specifically sense it. Frowning, I focused on his body and it was instantly bathed in dancing flames.

Flames were already starting to eat at the walls and lick at the ceiling. In a few minutes the fire would consume this place, but I couldn't take any chances. I had to be sure the body was destroyed before the local fire department managed to extinguish what I started. They'd have trouble discovering why the fire started, but I was more concerned with Thorne's corpse. Jumping down from Danaus's shoulder, I grabbed his forearm and pulled him out the exit door to the left of the stage, bypassing most of the people who crowded the exit at the front of the building. I looked back once to find Tristan following us, thankful that he wasn't trying to escape in the chaos. At the moment I think he was too shaken up by the attack and death of a fellow nightwalker to be concerned with his own freedom.

In the distance, the high-pitched whine of approaching police cars and fire trucks echoed in the night. We weaved our way through the crowd and down the dark streets, then ran for blocks until we were bathed in the bright lights of Piccadilly.

Nineteen

Darting down one of the few dark, empty alleys I could find, I stopped running, letting the shadows wrap their arms around me. At the back of the narrow passage I howled into the night. The horrible sound bounced off the brick and stone walls before finally flying free into the black sky. My hands were shaking with frustration and fear. The one person that was supposed to fix all of this, that was supposed to make the naturi go away, was now dead. To make matters worse, it was because I had failed to protect him. I should have expected the naturi to pull such a trick. I should have grabbed Thorne and dragged him out of that place. I couldn't fathom how they knew to kill him, that he would be the one I would need. It didn't matter. It could have just been my usual rotten luck. It didn't make Thorne any less dead.

Silence consumed the alley again until all I heard was Danaus's labored breathing. Our run had left him winded. It was a strange reminder that I was still dealing with a human, or at least someone part human. I walked back toward the hunter, who was leaning against the wall, struggling to catch his breath. My gaze briefly tripped over Tristan, who stood against the opposite wall, shaken by the unexpected turn of events.

"What happened?" Danaus demanded between ragged breaths.

"The waitress poisoned Thorne. She spiked his beer with naturi blood. She probably spiked all the beers she brought over," I said. My anger flowed from my tensed muscles, leaving behind only the cold, lead weight of fear in my stomach.

"Why?"

"She was a pagan. They're usually naturi sympathizers." Frustration crept back into my tone as I paced to the back of the alley. "They believe the naturi are sweet and peace-loving like all those asinine fairy tales. They've struck out at my kind before, but most don't have access to naturi blood."

Jerking my head around, I turned my narrowed gaze on the young nightwalker. He was squatted down with his elbows on his knees, his fists tightly clenching his hair, as if trying to hide from me or the naturi. "How long had Thorne been going to that pub?" I asked.

Tristan flinched and then turned his face up to look at me. "I—I'm not sure exactly. He knew a lot of people there so I think he had been appearing there for a while."

"I wasn't looking for a damn insider!" The comment escaped me in a low growl as I paced a couple steps away and then returned.

"How did she know to go after Thorne?" Danaus's breathing had returned to normal. He was recovering from our little run a lot faster than he should have. But that was my mysterious Danaus. The long scratches I'd left on his arms were long gone and there was only a light crust of dried blood running across his tanned skin.

"I don't know." I threw my hands up in the air as I approached him. "Less than a dozen people would have known about my search for Thorne." The moment those words drifted past my parted lips a horrible thought dawned on me. I stared at him. "And you're the only outsider in this whole mess."

Closing the distance between us in a flash, I slammed him back against the wall. His arms were pinned between our bodies, keeping him from drawing any weapons. Of course, he didn't need his arms to kill me, but that was the least of my concerns at the moment. Jabari was going to rip me in half, if the naturi didn't get to me first.

"You knew about the naturi first. You knew I was at Machu Picchu and hoped I would give you more information about the nightwalkers. Once you learned that we could rebuild the triad, you alerted your people to Thorne's existence," I snarled, my words lashing at him.

"Then why did I save you in Aswan?"

"Because you need me to lead you to the other members of the triad so you can finish them off." I felt a sickening lurch in my stomach as my mind continued on that line of thought. "And I put Sadira right into your hands."

"What?" Tristan gasped. Despite his desire to escape his maker, the reflex loyalty was always the hardest to get over.

Releasing my hold on Danaus, I stumbled backward. "I left Sadira with his people as protection," I told him. "I couldn't protect Sadira and come after Thorne at the same time." I could care less if Sadira lived or died, but I couldn't keep burning through triad members if I wanted to defeat the naturi. "Why?" I asked, looking back at Danaus. "Why would you help them? Is that what you are? Part naturi?"

"I'm not helping them," he said, taking a step away from the wall toward me. I sidestepped him, keeping a comfortable distance from him. "Think, Mira. They tried to kill us both in Aswan."

"Of course they did. It's what the naturi do—kill anything that is not their kind. Surprised that they would betray you?" I cried, still circling him. My foot kicked an empty aluminum can, sending it skidding around the dirty alley. "Your connection to the naturi also explains how you got Nerian. He would have fought you and you would have had to kill him. You can't capture the naturi."

"Nerian was insane," Danaus said, his voice edged with what was beginning to sound like desperation. "While I had him, he ranted endlessly about you. He spoke of Machu Picchu and things that had been done to you. Even if less than half the things he spoke of were true, how could I help monsters like that?"

I shivered, breaking eye contact for a moment. Pacing back down the alley, I ran my left hand along the rough brick wall to steady myself. Danaus had dredged up thoughts that had no place in that dark alley. I didn't know whether to believe him. I had absolutely no reason to believe him. But I was also desperate and running out of time.

"I would love nothing more than to see all vampires wiped from existence," he said, "but right now vampires are the only ones who can stop the naturi from destroying mankind. I can put my hatred aside for now. Can you?"

"Mira?" Tristan's questioning voice was little more than a soft whisper, searching for a little direction, reaching for something he could cling to in the swirling maelstrom that was sucking us in.

My gaze slid around the deep shadows of the narrow alley as I reviewed Danaus's actions during the past few days. When we weren't bickering, he had proven useful. Had he actually put his hatred of my kind aside? I didn't want to believe him.

"How?" I whispered. My voice was on the verge of shattering. "It's like they're one step ahead no matter where we go."

"I don't know," Danaus said softly. I looked up. He sounded tired for the first time. His shoulders were slumped and his voice soft, almost fragile. I watched him for a couple seconds. He was worried, and maybe even a little scared. I still didn't trust him, but I believed his fear. We were all about to get crushed by this army that was grinding away toward oblivion. I didn't know whose side he was on, but we were all in its path regardless.

None of it mattered, though. I needed to get to Sadira. After that I would figure something out.

"There's the little princess." Rowe's voice danced down the dark, narrow alley, shimmering out of nothingness. I spun around, my eyes scouring every inch of the alley before shooting up to the rooftops. The naturi couldn't use glamour against nightwalkers; we could see through it. At least, we always had before, but I couldn't see him.

"Danaus?" My right hand fell to my hip, searching for a weapon, only to discover that I was unarmed. Danaus wouldn't allow me to attend my Themis meeting armed, and I hadn't thought about grabbing anything before leaving to fetch Thorne. Walking around armed was no longer a normal occurrence for me.

"Who was that?" Tristan demanded, pushing away from the wall. He circled past Danaus, looking around the area, though he had no idea who he was looking for.

"Rowe, a naturi," I bit out. My hands were out to my sides, ready to attack.

"I can't sense him," Danaus said, slowly turning as he peered into the deep shadows.

"What?" My gaze jerked to his face, but he wasn't looking at me.

"I can't sense any naturi in the immediate area." The hunter's jaw was clenched and his power beat in thick, heavy waves against me. He was pouring everything he had into locating the owner of that voice. A knife was gripped in his right hand, ready.

"Maybe he's not here. He might have projected his voice from another location to scare us," Tristan suggested.

Danaus paused for a moment and looked over at me. "You think so?"

"Not really, but I'd rather not stick around to find out," I muttered. "Let's just get going."

"Not yet, princess," Rowe said with a chuckle. This time his voice sounded as if it was coming from behind me. I turned to see the brick wall quiver as if made of water, and then Rowe stepped through, smiling at me.

"Shit!" Turning, I tried to run. He was less than a foot away from me, too close. It would be too easy for him to stick a blade through my heart before I had a chance to act. I needed distance, but there wasn't time. Rowe grabbed a handful of my hair. With a quick jerk, I fell backward, my shoulders slamming into his chest.

He didn't waste a second. He released my hair and his left hand snaked around my waist, up between my breasts, to roughly grab either side of my lower jaw. Tilting my head back, he pried my mouth open with his fingers and thumb. I blinked once and my eyes focused on the open vial filled with red liquid. Rowe held it balanced over my open mouth. If I jerked or moved, its contents would dump straight down my throat.

"Hold, all of you!" he commanded, his light voice hardening for the first time. "Or we find out if the little princess can survive a heavy dose of naturi blood. We've already proven that the albino couldn't."

I jerked my head in anger without thinking before I reacted. He had killed Thorne. However, my rage was over-whelmed by fear once again when a drop of blood fell on my lower lip and slowly ran down my chin. A faint trembling started in my limbs that I couldn't control and slowly spread through the rest of my body. I couldn't move or he would destroy me.

A low growl rumbled from the other end of the alley and I could feel the cool breeze of Tristan's powers as he stood poised to attack. I prayed that he wouldn't move, as I was in no position to start shouting orders.

Rowe leaned his head down so I could feel his hot breath against my neck. "Tell me you remember the taste of my blood, Mira. Tell me. Of course, you've tasted more than just my blood." A strangled cry erupted from the back of my throat as he ran the tip of his tongue up my neck to my earlobe.

"Let her go!" Danaus shouted, taking a step forward. Dragging my eyes from the vial over my head, I looked at the hunter. His face was twisted with rage and his heartbeat pounded in the silent alley. But the knife pointed at Rowe was steady.

"Go on, misfit. Kill me like you killed the others. But can you do it before I drop this down her throat?"

"What do you want?" Danaus bit out each word, holding his ground.

"I've got what I want." Rowe chuckled, his grip tightening on my jaw. My blood filled my mouth as my teeth dug into the sides of my cheeks. "She goes with me."

Rowe pulled me backward as if he meant to go back through the wall. I dug my heels into the concrete as best as I could and stiffened my whole body. My hands grabbed his pant legs near his knees, holding him trapped. If he tried to jerk me backward again, he would either stumble or be forced to drag me, causing the blood to tip into my mouth.

If he moved, he'd kill me. So be it. I would rather die a relatively quick death than be held captive by the naturi again. I wouldn't go with him. I wouldn't let him have me.

"Move, princess, or I dump the blood down your throat." Rowe brought his face close again, his cheek pressing against mine. "I want you alive purely for my own pleasure, but you are just as useful to me dead. Either way, I win."

My gaze darted from Danaus to the vial. The hunter could do nothing without killing me. The angle of my head made it impossible for me to see Tristan, but he was still a way off, closer to the entrance of the alley. His low growl had stopped, but I would sense his powers.

I would not go with Rowe. Death was a better option. Closing my eyes, I forced my shaking hands to release Rowe's pants.

"Mira, don't." Those two words drifted from Danaus, nearly breaking the thin barrier that held back my gathering tears.

As Rowe took a step back, I focused my powers on the naturi blood within the vial. The liquid and glass ignited in Rowe's hand. Screaming, he attempted to tip it into my mouth when the vial exploded from the extreme heat, raining down glass and boiling blood. The distraction allowed me to pull from his grasp. My knees slammed into the concrete, sending a shock wave of pain through my legs.

Glass and blood were splattered across my face and eyes, blinding me. I threw a fireball behind me, hoping to hit Rowe. At the same time, I heard metal clatter against brick.

"He's gone," Danaus said as I prepared another fireball in my hand.

Extinguishing the fire, I raised my hands, trying to wipe away the blood burning my face and eyes. I cried out, jerking away my trembling hands. The shards of glass had cut both my fingers and face. "I can't get it off! I can't get the blood off!" I screamed, panic taking over.

"Stop, Mira," Danaus commanded, his voice closer now. "I'll help you." A whisper of cloth and the scrape of his shoes revealed his approach. I put my hands out, feeling for him, not sure if I wanted him close since I couldn't see him. Danaus took my left hand in his and squeezed it. My other hand brushed against warm skin, his bare chest. I froze, my mind stumbling. To my right I felt Tristan approach. He knelt beside me, his cool presence brushing against me while one of his hands came to rest on my knee.

Danaus released my left hand and placed his hand under my chin, gently tilting my head up. "Hold still. I'm going to wipe your face off." A soft cloth slowly swept over my face, wiping away Rowe's blood and the bits of glass. Danaus's scent filled me. I could smell smoke from the fire at the club, his sweat, the soap he used, and deep down I could smell him now on my skin. He had taken off his shirt and was cleaning my face with the same gentle care one would show a baby.

When he was done, he swept his shirt over my hair, smoothing it back from my face, shaking out any remaining bits of glass. Blinking a few times against the last of the blood that had seeped in, I lifted my eyes to his face. His emotions were clear—fear and anger. Beneath my hand, his heart still pounded like a jackhammer.

"Better?" he asked, his voice deceptively calm.

I tried to speak but the sound cracked before I could form a single word. Jerking from him, I attempted to crawl away from him and Tristan. I couldn't let them see me cry. They couldn't know that terror still hummed in every muscle and screamed like a madwoman in my brain.

"No!" Danaus grabbed my wrist and pulled me back.

Seated on the ground in the middle of the alley, he held me in his lap, his strong arms forming a protective cocoon around me. Burying my face in his neck, I sobbed. It felt as if my very soul had shattered. All my strength and power had been stolen away the moment Rowe touched me.

"I can't go with them again. I can't do it again. Not again," I pleaded mindlessly, as if Danaus could save me in some way. Images of Nerian and Machu Picchu danced through my head. The memory of my screams and Nerian's laugh rang in my ears. And now there was Rowe. His scent, the feel of his skin, the heat of his breath, were all imprinted in my brain. *I couldn't escape them.*

"Never," Danaus whispered, his voice breaking through the barrage of memories in my brain. "Never again. I won't let it happen. The naturi will never touch you again."

I believed him. From Danaus, it was a vow. If it was within his power, he would not allow the naturi to capture me again. Regardless of what happened between us as vampire and hunter, he would not allow me to fall into the hands of the naturi.

The silence of the alley crept into us as we sat on the ground. With one hand over Danaus's heart, I pressed my head to his chest with my eyes closed. Tristan sat beside us, his long fingers now entwined in the fingers of my right hand. His presence was a cool, calming balm, while Danaus's warmth acted as a safety blanket. Listening to his heartbeat, I let its steady rhythm wash through me, cleansing me of the fear and the pain. Danaus rubbed his jaw against the top of my head as his hand ran down my hair and back in a soothing caress. Surrounded in their combined power, for a brief moment I felt protected. But it couldn't last. The night was dying and we still had to reach Sadira before Rowe found her.

"Thank you," I whispered, rubbing my cheek against his warm chest before slowly pulling out of his embrace. I gave

Tristan's hand a quick squeeze before pulling my fingers free. My knees shook as I stood, but I managed to keep from falling on my ass.

I walked over to where Rowe had held me. Behind me, I heard Danaus rise and pull his shirt back on. Tristan stood beside me, a soundless shadow. I kept my eyes on the ground. Shards of glass sparkled as they caught some distant shaft of lamplight.

"How was he able to sneak up on us and walk through the wall?" Danaus asked.

"Spells," I murmured. "I think it's why he risked a harvest in Jabari's domain. Certain human organs are needed for some extremely powerful spells. Rowe knew he'd need these spells if he was going to succeed in grabbing me." Lifting my eyes, I reached out, my fingers hovering mere inches from the brick wall he had come through, but I couldn't bring myself to touch it. The wall appeared solid, but I half expected to see Rowe's hand reach out and pull me in.

Danaus walked up beside me and picked up his dagger, which lay on the ground next to the wall. He'd apparently thrown it at the naturi at the same time I blindly threw my fireball. "When you broke the vial, you expected to die," he said, drawing my gaze. His hair hung down around his face, cloaking his features. "I saw it in your eyes."

"Yes." I couldn't lie. I hadn't wanted to die, but death was preferable to being held by the naturi.

"Don't ever do that again." Anger vibrated in his tone. A long, heavy silence settled between us, holding us still before he finally spoke again. "I will not let you escape me so easily."

Biting back a smile, I bowed my head slightly. "As you wish."

I glanced back at the brick wall one last time, my would-be smile fading to a frown. I was tired of being the prey in this little game of cat and mouse. It was time to turn the tables on the naturi.

"Was it just Rowe you couldn't sense or can't you sense the naturi at all now?" I asked, cocking my head to the side as I looked at my semihuman companion.

Danaus's warm powers swept out of the alley and pushed out through the city for almost a full minute before they finally dissipated. "I can sense the naturi, but I cannot tell if one of them is Rowe."

"How close?"

"Outside the city," he said with a shake of his head. "To the north."

"You have any more weapons?" The naturi were killing my kind, killing people in my domain, and Rowe was trying to kidnap me. It was time to strike back.

"We don't have long until sunrise, Mira," Tristan interjected.

I nodded, glancing over my shoulder at the young nightwalker. I wanted revenge, but I wasn't about to get caught out in the open without a safe place to go to ground during the daylight hours. "How far away is this Compound?"

A half smile tugged at one corner of Danaus's mouth. "Less than two hours away. To the north."

"So, you're saying it's on the way . . . "

"Possibly. I won't know until we get started."

We had time. Not a lot, but there was a window. We could strike quickly, cut down some of their numbers, then make a run for the Compound. It wasn't much, but I just needed to reduce their numbers. Hopefully, I would get another shot at Rowe.

Danaus nodded and led the way out of the alley. If I had any shred of luck left in this pathetic existence, Sadira was still alive and staying out of trouble. But I wasn't betting on it at this point.

"Mira." A catch in Tristan's voice stopped me from following behind Danaus. The nightwalker didn't need to say anything. I could feel his fear. "I can't fight them. I mean, I've never—"

"I need you," I said, laying my right hand on his shoulder. I needed every spare hand I could find when it came to taking on the naturi. Right now all I had was Tristan and Danaus. "We have to stop them or they're going to make living with Sadira look like a Sunday garden party."

His large blue eyes darted away from my direct gaze and he stared down at the ground. I was losing him. "Stand with me now, Tristan." I paused for a moment, searching for some words of encouragement. I knew what I needed to say, but it took a moment to finally force them out. "Stand with me now, and I swear, I will help you find a way free of Sadira."

His gaze snapped back up to my face, questioning and distrustful. I couldn't blame him. We both had the same manipulative maker. "I swear. I don't know how, but I will help you," I repeated.

Tristan nodded and turned to follow Danaus out of the alley. I was still cursing myself when I fell into step behind them. I don't know whether he had just manipulated me, but it didn't matter. I needed his help, and there was a good chance both of us weren't going to survive this little escapade, making my promise moot.

Pausing at the mouth of the alley, I glanced up. The night sky was a murky midnight blue in the lights of the city. Dawn was just a few hours away. I could sense it like an old man could feel a storm brewing by the ache in his bones. From the first second we are reborn, nightwalkers can sense the night. After the sun set, I could feel the night swelling around me, oozing into every crevice and dusty corner. The burgeoning night flourishes toward its midpoint, which is so rarely midnight, and then it wilts. As the night dies, time crumbles around me. I can feel it waning like the steady flow of sand in an hourglass.

And now that I was desperate for time, I felt it slipping that much faster out of my grasp. I clenched my fist at my side and swallowed a curse for the sun. Even immortal, I was still a slave to time.

Twenty

Less than two hours later I was kneeling with Tristan in the outer fringe of a thin copse of woods just northwest of London. There was a scattering of farmhouses close by, their fields outlined by spindly wooden fences and stone walls. According to Danaus, we weren't too far from Stonehenge and less than thirty minutes from the Themis compound.

For a July evening, the air was crisp and heavy, as if the skies would soon open up with rain. Beside me, Tristan drew in a deep breath, relying on his hunting skills to track his prey, but they wouldn't help him with the naturi. They smelled of the earth, holding none of the musky scents and pheromones found with other living creatures. I bit down on my lower lip as I watched the woods through narrowed eyes, trying not to think about Tristan's inexperience. But that kind of inexperience was rampant among my kind. It had been five hundred years since any of us faced a serious battle against the naturi. Since Machu Picchu, we had been content to fight among ourselves, with only occasional incursions against the lycanthropes and the warlocks. But even those amounted to little more than beating chests and gnashing teeth.

"Remember what I told you," I whispered. "Shoot them in the head or in the heart. Once they go down, take off the head as a precaution." I looked down at the gun tightly clutched in my right hand. Danaus had supplied us both with handguns and, when we both looked lost, a quick lesson in using them. Vampires didn't use guns. Up until now, the old ways were always more efficient . . . and more fun.

"Do you honestly trust the hunter?" Tristan hissed, turning his head to look at me. Danaus had dropped us off near the entrance to the woods and then drove on a couple more miles. He was going to circle around and find a perch on higher ground. He had a rifle and planned to pick off some of the naturi from a distance while Tristan and I attacked.

"No, but he's had more than one opportunity to kill me and hasn't taken it. It doesn't make any sense to do so now." I scanned the area, picking up nothing but small flashes of wildlife. Danaus was about a quarter mile away to the east, no longer moving. It was time. I couldn't sense the naturi, but he had said he would attempt to put them directly between us. All we had to do was walk through the woods toward him and we should trip over them.

"Let's go," I murmured, standing and silently walking deeper into the woods, ignoring Tristan's soft comment under his breath. Something about me pushing my luck. Yeah, that went without saying.

I wasn't counting on the element of surprise as we moved soundlessly through the woods. While the naturi couldn't sense us, they would know something was approaching as we unavoidably disturbed wildlife along the way. Furthermore, after our time in the pub, we smelled of smoke and human sweat, which would also give away our position. But with Danaus playing sniper, I was hoping to at least keep them confused, earning us a slight and very brief edge.

We moved in the woods, picking through the underbrush.

What little noise we did make sounded like the wind running its fingers through the leaves. While nightwalkers preferred the city, we all spent a little time out in nature. It was a good way to hunt; to stretch our powers, our senses, our bodies to their limits.

And tonight we were hunting naturi.

After a few minutes we stopped at the low murmur of voices in quiet conversation. I couldn't make out any of the words but seriously doubted they were speaking any language with which I was familiar. Their comments were quick and sharp. I had a feeling they knew we were close.

Crouched low in the dirt, Tristan and I crawled closer, sticking to the thick undergrowth in an attempt to remain hidden as we got as close as possible. I paused for a second as a branch snagged the left arm of my silk shirt. My leather pants afforded me some protection from the rocks and dirt, but this wasn't exactly the best attire for crawling through the woods. Neither were my leather boots. My heels had sunk into the soft earth and small holes on more than one occasion.

We finally halted a few yards from a small clearing in the woods. There were ten naturi scattered before us, four from the animal clan. Other than those from the water clan, with their blue-green hair and gills, the animal clan was easiest to identify. They wore their dark brown hair long and shaggy. The structure of their faces was wider and harsher, with sharp cheekbones and a hard jaw. At least two more were from the earth clan. They seemed the exact opposite of the animal clan, with their tall, willowy frames and dark, earthy skin. Their hair color was a broad array—purple, blue, yellow, green—all the colors of the flowers.

What had me worried was the other four I couldn't identify. Their height and build varied, as did their hair color. They could have been from the wind clan, which I had little experience dealing with, or the light clan, which would take away my special gift as an advantage.

Of course, I was coming after the naturi on their own turf. If we were going to survive this, we had to strike fast— the longer the fight lasted, the more chances the naturi had to take advantage of their surroundings.

I was also worried that I had yet to see Rowe. The pirate wannabe had been so good at finding me so far, I just assumed that he'd be with the nearest group of naturi. Or that he'd come to me.

Looking over at the white-faced Tristan, I flashed him a broad smile full of fangs and joyful menace. It was time to go. I just hoped Danaus stuck to his end of this bargain.

As I stood, I flicked off the safety and widened my stance while holding the gun with both hands. I would have only enough time to get off a few shots, and I'd never used a gun before—I had to make each bullet count. Tristan rose smoothly beside me at the same time, a low growl rattling in his throat.

We squeezed off six quick rounds, and the two naturi standing closest to us went down. The report of my gun and Tristan's was almost immediately answered by a shot from farther away. Danaus took out one of the earth clan and two of the unidentified naturi. In less than three seconds we had taken down six naturi with guns. From there, it got hard.

Overcoming their initial shock, the four remaining naturi scattered. Tristan and I continued firing, but they were on the move and our aim wasn't that great despite our superior reflexes and speed. The last remaining member of the animal clan lunged at Tristan, while I saw the earth naturi simply sink into the ground as if she'd stepped into a quicksand pit. I couldn't see the other two naturi, and in the distance the mournful cries of wolves were raised in chorus. The damned naturi had already called for backup.

I snarled as I turned on a heel to grab for the naturi wrestling with Tristan. But I never got there. Vises wrapped around my wrists, jerking my arms over my head. I was dragged backward into the center of the clearing before being pulled into the air.

Looking up, I found the two missing naturi. There was one holding each arm as they pulled me higher in the air. Given their enormous iridescent wings, I assumed they were members of the wind clan. Where the hell humans got the image of six-inch, half-naked pixies with a golden trail of magic dust I'll never know.

"I guess Rowe missed the Fire Starter," giggled one of the naturi in English, for my benefit.

The other gave an inelegant snort, tightening her grip on my right wrist, her long nails digging into my flesh. "She wasn't so hard to catch."

I tried to jerk free of their grip, but their fingers were like metal shackles that tightened until I was sure my bones would soon break. Narrowing my gaze on my two captors, I summoned up my powers, preparing to set their lovely wings on fire, but something else grabbed me, shattering my concentration. Twisting as best I could, I looked down to see what had grabbed my right ankle. A long, thick vine had wrapped around it and was snaking up my calf.

"If he is so fond of her now, won't he love her more if we make her taller?" chuckled a third, saccharine-sweet voice to my left. I looked around to find the earth naturi standing on a tree branch, her shoulders propped against the tree trunk as she did her best "Tarzan meets Jane" impression. Out of the corner of my eye I saw her wave her hand, a second vine wrapping around my left ankle a moment later.

"Or he might love her twice as much if there are two of her," suggested the first wind naturi. Meanwhile, the wind naturi continued their ascent, and the vines attempted to pull me back down to earth. A scream erupted from my throat before I could stop it. My body was being stretched and pulled in two separate directions. Their nails dug into the soft part of my wrists, sending tiny rivers of blood down my arms while the vines tightened around my ankles. I vainly attempted to twist in their grip, but neither the naturi nor the vines loosened their hold.

Closing my eyes against the rising pain as my shoulders threatened to dislocate, I focused on the creatures I could feel holding my arms. Heat built in my limbs, crawling up to my fingertips. My eyes flew open and I directed the fire at their wings. The tissuelike substance went up in a bright ball of orange flames before jumping to their lithe bodies. They instantly released me and we all plummeted back down to the earth.

There wasn't time to scream. Pain ripped through my body as I came to a sudden halt. Something plunged through my back and tore through muscle and organ before finally punching through my chest. The world swam. The darkness crowded my eyes for a moment, and I fought back against the wave threatening to consume me. Clenching my teeth, I looked down, ignoring the fact that my feet were dangling in the air, to find a piece of wood sticking out of my chest. I had been staked from the back by a branch. The naturi had staked me. The only reason I was still alive was that she'd managed to miss my heart, barely. Blood was pouring out of me at an alarming rate, soaking into my clothes and running down my legs.

Discovering that I was still alive, the earth naturi screamed in frustration. A second later the vine tightened around my ankles and resumed its attempt to pull me back down to the earth. I screamed as the branch pulled on muscles and tore at organs. My weight finally overwhelmed the branch and it broke, sending me back to the earth with a heavy thud. The impact sent a shock wave of pain through my tortured body, further loosening my hold on consciousness.

A gunshot cut through the night then, and I heard something fall near me. The air carried with it a puff of earth and wind. The naturi. Either Danaus or Tristan had shot the naturi. One less thing to worry about, but it didn't matter. I was running out of time. I couldn't lift my arms to try to push or pull out the branch. I couldn't move.

My eyes fell shut, riding the next wave of pain that threatened to swamp me. I had to think of what I needed to tell Danaus or Tristan. Someone had to tell Jabari, Sadira, the Coven, about the attacks. Someone had to tell Knox that I was gone and that he needed to watch over the nightwalkers in my domain.

"Mira!" Danaus barked my name.

My eyes fluttered open again and I saw the hunter kneeling next to me. One of his hands was cupping my cheeks, tilting my head so I could look up at him, but I couldn't feel it. My entire world floated in a sea of pain.

"Tristan?" I roughly whispered.

"I'm here," he said, suddenly coming into my line of sight. He was a mess of cuts and scratches, and bloody matted hair.

I closed my eyes, trying to find the strength to continue talking. Some of the pain was beginning to recede, and that worried me. The branch was still embedded in my body. "Naturi?"

"They're gone. Dead."

"Wolves?"

"Mira, we have to get this stake out of you and get you somewhere safe to heal," Tristan said, a soft waver running through his voice.

"Wolves?" I knew they were coming. Even with the last of the naturi dead, they would continue to come and attack, clinging to the last command shoved into their brains.

"Damn it!" Tristan snarled when the air was once again filled with the forlorn cries of the approaching wolves. "Hunter, take care of the wolves. I will help Mira." I saw Danaus nod at Tristan before carefully lowering my head back to the ground, then disappearing from my line of sight.

Tristan moved behind me and knelt behind my head. Over the pain, I felt him grip my shoulder, his thumb sweeping back and forth a couple times in a gentle caress. "I'm sorry," he whispered, then jerked the branch out of my body. Every muscle in my frame clenched and I screamed again. I hadn't thought the pain could get any worse. My thoughts were scattered to the wind, swirling around me in ragged fragments.

" . . . losing blood . . . need to feed . . . " Tristan's words were coming to me in bits and pieces. I tried to focus. There were things I needed to tell him, but I couldn't concentrate, couldn't remember anything that had seemed so important just minutes ago. Or was that hours? Time was slipping away from me.

Danaus's name suddenly popped up in Tristan's diatribe about me needing to feed. I fought back the wave of pain and managed to open my eyes. Tristan was still behind me but was leaning over so I could look him in the face. He was pushing something into my back, keeping the pain screaming through my body.

"Danaus?" I murmured.

"Fighting the wolves," Tristan confirmed. "When he comes back, you will feed from him so we can get you somewhere safe."

That's what I thought he had said. "No," I choked out, letting my eyes fall shut again.

"Mira, we have no choice. My blood won't help you."

I licked my lips and gathered up my energy again. I was in no mood to die, but drinking from Danaus seemed like a very bad idea. Even as I appeared to be facing my final hour, the hunter didn't seem the type to give such a donation. "No . . . dangerous. Bad blood."

"What? What are you talking about?"

"His blood is dangerous . . . Don't feed from him." I didn't have the energy to explain it, but I was still conscious enough to know that until I knew what he was, drinking from the hunter was a bad idea. While there was a chance his blood could heal me, there was also a good chance it could kill me faster than the hole in my back and chest.

"Mira—"

"No, Tristan," I bit out around clenched teeth.

The young nightwalker heaved a heavy sigh, looking away from me. "We need to get you to Sadira," he muttered. As much as I hated it, he was right. Our maker was the only one who had a chance at keeping me alive.

"Leave me now," I whispered, "and not even death will stop me from collecting your head."

A fragile smile played with the corners of his lips as he looked back down at me. "Very frightening, Fire Starter," he murmured, smoothing some hair from my face.

I wanted to smile and say something reassuring, but I was just too tired and had no doubt that I looked as threatening as a half-downed kitten.

"Is she dead?" Danaus's voice intruded in the growing silence.

"Asshole," I grumbled.

"We need to get her to Sadira," Tristan said, his hand tightening on my shoulder.

"Take her to where I dropped you off. I'll bring the car," Danaus instructed.

"How do I know you won't abandon us?"

"Because I need her alive," Danaus growled, stepping away from me.

I wanted to think about that comment, turn around what he meant, but I didn't have the chance. Tristan picked me up, sending a fresh wave of pain through my body, and then the world went dark.

Twenty-One

The world slowly swam back into focus, and I instantly wished it hadn't. Pain washed through me in sickening waves, threatening to pull me back under into the thick darkness. I resisted the desire to let unconsciousness sweep me under again. Tristan and Danaus were arguing about something, but I couldn't quite catch the thread of their discussion. I could make out the low growl of the car engine. A window was open, and a breeze slipped across my skin, chilling the blood that was drying on my arms and stomach.

Cracking my eyes open, I found myself lying across the backseat of a small car. I was on my side, my head in Tristan's lap. He was still pressing what I guessed was his shirt into my back in an effort to slow the flow of blood, while his other hand was pressed to my chest.

"How the hell should I know?" Tristan angrily snapped, his voice finally pushing through the fog of pain slowing my thoughts. "The Ancients never talk about Machu Picchu. We don't talk about the naturi. The naturi are gone. They were gone . . . " His voice faded toward the end to a low whisper.

I closed my eyes again, his words echoing through my brain. He was right. We didn't talk about this ugly part of our

past, running from the horror, the moment that brought my
kind to the very brink of extinction. We ran from it, afraid
mentioning it would conjure up our enemy once again.

"Why? What happened there? Why is it so important?"
Danaus fired back from the front seat, where he was driving.
"They've killed Tabor and they continue to go after Mira.
Both were at Machu Picchu."

"Machu Picchu is important because it was the last battle," I said in a low voice. I felt Tristan flinch beneath me,
surprised that I was conscious again. "It was the last in a
long series of battles against the naturi."

"What happened?" Danaus inquired, his voice softening
somewhat.

"I don't remember anything about that night."

"It's understandable," he murmured under his breath.
The words had nearly been stolen away by the wind, but I
caught them before they flew away.

"Why?" I tried to turn my head to look up at him, but it
felt as if it weighed the same as a baby elephant and I gave
up the attempt.

"Sometimes the mind forgets things to protect itself."

A chill slithered across my skin that had nothing to do
with the wind. I wished I could fold my arms over my stomach, fighting back the black memories of the naturi. "What
did Nerian tell you?"

"Enough to haunt me."

The truth was, I didn't want to hear the details about that
night. I still remembered the naturi with startling clarity, as
if the memories had been charmed so I could never escape
the pain. And now there was Rowe, with his voice teasing at
my brain as if I should remember him.

"I remember Nerian." My words barely inched over a
breathy whisper. "I remember what the naturi did to me.
They held me for almost two weeks. They wanted to use me

to kill the nightwalkers when they arrived at Machu Picchu. We had been battling them off and on for several centuries. Prior to Machu Picchu, they managed to break the seal using the energy at Petra. They had come to Machu Picchu to open the door between the worlds and finally free the remaining host along with their queen, Aurora." I paused for a moment, trying to force my eyes open so I could look around, but it just took too much energy. I felt lucky to be talking.

"I remember seeing the nightwalkers arrive, but I can't recall their faces, except for Jabari. It was the first time I had ever seen him. And then, nothing. I can't remember anything after seeing them appear."

"What is the next thing you do remember?"

"Standing over Nerian. Sunrise was near and he was dying. I escaped into the surrounding jungle for the day. The next night Jabari came for me."

"What about Rowe?"

"I had never seen Rowe before the attack in Egypt," I said with a sigh.

"He seems to know you."

"I know, but I don't know him. I'm pretty sure I'd remember a one-eyed elf." It didn't make any sense. I had dug through my memory during the past couple days but couldn't recall anything about a naturi named Rowe, or any naturi that resembled him. "At Machu Picchu, I remember feeling Sadira, though I can't recall seeing her. I also remember hearing Tabor's voice. Before leaving, I heard him speaking with Jabari. He sounded tired . . . and angry."

"Where are we going?" Tristan abruptly demanded. I could feel the tension running through him increase. Unable to move, I gathered up what energy I could and dipped into his mind. It was relatively easy since he was holding me, but I didn't have the strength to maintain the link for long. I managed to pick up flashes of trees from his mind, edging closer to the road. The area seemed desolate and lonely, perfect for an attack.

"The Themis Compound. Sadira is there," Danaus said.

"What's Themis?" Tristan asked.

"Vampire hunters," I muttered.

"That's not the goal of Themis," the hunter snapped.

I didn't try to stop the snort of disbelief that escaped me, despite the fact that I was currently in no shape to pick a fight. "Enlighten me. From what I've seen, it doesn't make much sense. There's you—a nightwalker hunter—and James, a bookworm who seems to be completely out of touch with reality."

A deep silence settled into the car, and I sat patiently, feeling it gently take each dip and curve in the road as we headed closer to the Compound, which housed more humans that had hunted my kind.

"The goal of Themis is balance," Danaus volunteered at last. "Most of the members of Themis are like James Parker, scholars who study the occult. They watch from a distance, cataloging events and creatures. And then there are those who are hunters. They are sent when your kind threatens mankind. We are trying to keep your secret, and the secret of all the others, from leaking over into the world of man."

"And are you sent to destroy my kind by wise, knowledgeable men like James?" I demanded, sarcasm dripping off my words.

"No, the leader of Themis is the only one who can dispatch a hunter."

"Ryan?" I asked, recalling the name that Danaus had tossed out earlier that evening when persuading James to take Sadira to the Compound.

"Yes."

"I look forward to meeting him," I said, trying to sound confident, though my blood was soaking through Tristan's shirt and into the cloth car seats.

An odd sound came from Danaus. It sounded broken and rough, as if his voice were dragged over sandpaper. He was laughing at me. I tried to smile as well, though it was a struggle to get all the right muscles working. It didn't matter. The sound helped push back some of the pain for a brief moment. It was like catching a shaft of sunlight between shifting thunderheads, and I wanted to bask in it before the black clouds stifled the golden light.

"You will not be able to intimidate and manipulate Ryan like you did James," he said in an amused voice.

"How about seduce him with my feminine wiles?" I asked in a low voice. Tristan let out a rough sound that could have been a laugh, but he quickly covered it up by clearing his throat. I knew there wasn't much attractive about me right now. If I didn't get to Sadira in the next few minutes, there wouldn't be anything left of me but a blood-covered corpse.

"Doubtful," he said.

I sighed dramatically, my eyes managing to flutter open for a moment before I gave up the fight. "I guess I shall just have to figure out what he truly wants."

"How will you do that?"

"I haven't a clue," I admitted, which earned me another chuckle.

"And you're not concerned?"

"It's less than one hour until sunrise, and I'm riding in a car with a hunter toward a conclave of hunters. The naturi are breathing down my neck, literally, and my last hope for defeating them was killed while I stood watching. Just supposing that I survive the next hour, I still have Jabari, who will rip out my throat because I failed to protect Thorne. At this point, I think the least of my concerns is a human with his own agenda."

There was a soft creak of plastic as Danaus tightened his hands on the steering wheel. "I hope you're right."

"With my recent track record, I doubt it. But what have I got to lose?"

"True," he conceded in a low voice.

As the silence slipped back into the car, I felt Tristan shift beneath me. I knew why. I could feel it too. We were running out of time. If Sadira didn't have enough time to properly heal me before the sun rose, I would not reawaken when the sun set again. Both the blood and life would drain completely from my body and I would be dead.

"How much farther?" Tristan asked.

"Not far."

Dawn was drawing too close and I didn't like the options Tristan and Sadira would be left with if I didn't make it. Would Danaus defend them against his brethren? It wasn't an issue I wanted to contemplate.

"How long have you been with Themis?" the young nightwalker asked, trying to redirect his thoughts.

I managed to move my right arm enough so my hand came in contact with Tristan's left leg. I touched his ankle, rubbing it in an attempt to ease some of the tension that flowed through him.

"A few centuries."

"Why did you join them? You don't seem to be the type to fall in with a cult," I teased, my hand falling away from Tristan.

"They're not a cult."

"Answer the question."

"Because I seek balance," Danaus said, to my surprise.

He rarely answered my questions about himself, but apparently I had not dug too deep. I wondered if his powers had kept him out of balance.

"And what did you do before Themis?" I wanted to know about the shadows that lurked in his beautiful eyes. What horrors had he witnessed, and had he ever been the cause?

The steering wheel creaked again. "I hunted and destroyed evil."

"That's rather vague." Tristan stirred beneath me. "Whose definition of evil are you going by?"

"God's."

"Great. So you've spent your life hunting nightwalkers because some human decided we were evil." Whatever momentary warmth there had been between the three of us shriveled and froze as I balled my right fingers into a fist, my nails digging in my palm. For a time we had forgotten who we were.

"You kill," Danaus snapped.

"You're beginning to sound like James." For a time, I think we forgot that we were still on opposite sides; that we were working under a temporary and fragile truce. "Humans kill. You kill. So do we. It may not be right, but we do what we must to survive."

A tense silence hung heavy in the air as Danaus turned off the main road and the car seemed to grow darker. I opened my eyes and peripherally could see only flashes of sky through the trees that thickened around us, blotting out the remaining half of the moon.

Before me, Danaus's powers flowed out from his body, bathing me in its warmth, easing my tension. "There are no naturi here."

"Are you sure? You couldn't sense Rowe," I said, wishing I could sit up and look around.

"There are no naturi here," Danaus repeated calmly.

"Why can you feel them while I cannot?" Tristan demanded.

Loosening the tension from my fingers, which had been balled into a fist, I forced myself to relax. I needed to conserve my energy if I was going to make it through the next few minutes. The darkness was crowding in again, and I could no longer hold my eyes open. My body had tried to heal itself, but without more blood, it was hopeless. As it was now, I was using up most of my energy just to stay alive.

"Because they are the essence of life itself and you are no longer alive."

"But I can sense you and other living things," I whispered.

"You can sense all things that are human, or at least started human, because a part of you is still human. The naturi world is closed to you." His voice was strong, like a hand massaging the tension from my shoulders.

"Then how is it that nightwalkers can seal them away from this world?"

"That, I do not know."

"Just keep working on that, will you?" I said, my words fading toward the end.

Danaus parked the car and turned off the motor. I gave up trying to look around and slipped back into Tristan's mind. He was terrified but was holding together for now. He looked up at the enormous mansion that loomed before us. Every window was filled with light despite the late hour. Apparently, their unexpected guests were causing a bit of a stir.

Tristan had already scanned the manor, easily finding both Michael and Gabriel. While Tristan had never met either human, I knew both extremely well and could recognize them in his thoughts. The other humans were a hive of chaos; anxious, fearful, but also curious. Sadira remained hidden, and Tristan was reluctant to step out of the car.

She has been told to hide herself, I said softly in his mind. *She is here.*

Are you sure?

Positive.

I slipped out of Tristan's mind but still felt something else humming in the air. For a moment I thought it was Tristan or Danaus, but the signature of the power was different. There was a magic user inside, a very powerful one.

Danaus heard me softly chuckle as he opened Tristan's door. "What?" he asked. He probably thought I'd finally lost my mind.

"Some interesting occupants. I look forward to meeting them," I replied. Of course, that was assuming Sadira could put me back together again.

Twenty-Two

Blinking against the bright entrance, I tried to raise my hand to cover my eyes, but it was too heavy to move. Instead, I pressed my head into Tristan's bare, blood-smeared chest as he carried me into the great manor. It seemed they had flicked on every light in the place, much like James had earlier in the evening, attempting to protect themselves against the dark creatures entering their sanctuary. Before closing my eyes, I caught a glimpse of the enormous marble and wood staircase that dominated the main hall. On both the left and right of the hall, doors were pulled open and footsteps scraped and echoed off the hardwood floors as people stepped out to inspect Tristan and me.

"Sadira," I murmured softly against Tristan, my lips lightly brushing the cool skin of his chest. I wasn't sure if anyone could actually hear me anymore. The world was fading away—the pain had dimmed and I could no longer feel Tristan's arms holding me.

"Mira?" Tristan's worried voice demanded an answer, but I simply didn't have the energy to reply. "Sadira! Where is she? We're losing Mira."

The young nightwalker's question was answered with a horrible sound, a mix of scream and snarl. It was Sadira. I knew her voice, its every tone, pitch, and nuance. For years it had echoed through my brain, a singsong chant I could never escape.

Soft hands touched my face, turning my head. "Mira! Open your eyes and look at me now!" Sadira commanded.

My eyelids fluttered for a brief moment before I finally gave up the attempt. Licking my lips, I drew in a slow breath. "We had . . . problems," I whispered.

A snarl of low curses escaped Sadira in a rough voice, but she was very gentle when she pressed a kiss to my temple before resting my head against Tristan's chest again. "I need somewhere to work undisturbed. There. In there."

My thoughts drifted away for a while. I was vaguely aware of Tristan carrying me somewhere followed by a flurry of angry voices and some slamming doors. A soft whimper escaped me as Tristan set me down on a hard surface that I could only guess was a long tabletop. The bright lights were banked at last and I was able to force my eyes open a crack. Tall bookshelves lined the wall to my right, broken only by portraits of grim-faced men with gray and white hair.

"They found us . . . " I forced out as my eyes fell shut again. There was no more time. I had to tell Sadira what happened so she could tell Jabari. The Elder would fix it; he'd be able to stop the naturi. "They killed Thorne. N-Need another."

"I know," Sadira whispered. I could only guess that Tristan had caught her up on the evening's events while I drifted in and out of consciousness. She was standing beside me. Her small hand swept over my forehead, pushed hair away from my face. "But we need to heal you now."

"Triad—"

"None of that matters. None of that matters without you."

Sadira pressed a kiss to my cheek and then my forehead. "I need you to relax your mind."

"Tired. So . . . tired." I was exhausted. Tired of fighting, tired of the pain.

And then something stirred. Swamped within the pain, I felt something faint shift in my thoughts, but as I tried to focus on it, it slipped away, pulling back into the swirling mist that consumed my thoughts. I reached out again, searching for the movement, and then the pain was gone.

My eyes flew open and I screamed. My thoughts came to a screeching halt as I looked around me. The wall of books and stern-looking men was completely gone. The gleaming hardwood streaked with my blood was gone. Around me were cold stone walls and wooden torches held in wrought-iron sconces guttering with firelight in the large room. It was a dungeon. It was the dungeon below Sadira's castle in Spain. It was the room where I'd been reborn.

Another scream of panic rose up in my throat as I sat up and twisted around to thoroughly scan the room. It couldn't be the same place. When I closed my eyes, I'd been dying on a boardroom table in England. Sadira didn't have the ability to instantly flit from place to place like Jabari. It couldn't be real.

"It's not real." Her disembodied voice floated through the air for a moment before she came through the stone wall to my right and stood beside where I sat on the long stone slab. "The pain was taking you away from me. I needed to take you away from the pain so I could heal you. The damage is . . . extensive. Organs have been shredded and your heart has been punctured. You're dying."

"I guessed as much," I sighed. Anxiety crawled up my spine, digging claws into my back. I could tell my brain that it wasn't real, but rising panic wasn't buying it. It looked real, it felt real, it smelled real. "But why here?"

"I need you to trust me," Sadira said with a soft smile, tilting her head to one side. "This is the one time in your life you trusted me completely."

A snort escaped me as I swung my legs over the side of the stone table and dropped to my feet, putting the table between us. "I have never trusted you."

"That is an interesting lie," she chided. "You lay helpless night after night for ten years, completely dependent upon me to keep you alive. I was in your mind; you never doubted that I would return each night to you."

I stood with my left hip pressed against the stone slab, my arms crossed over my chest. Out of the corner of my eye I could see Sadira watching me, waiting for my response. I knew she was right. I had trusted her to bring me into her world, not to abandon me. But at that point my only other option was death.

For a moment Sadira's image wavered, and I turned to face her, automatically reaching for her, but my hand passed through her. "So much damage . . . " Her voice whispered through the air, but her lips never moved. She was having troubling repairing the damage and maintaining the fantasy world. Pain cut through my chest, doubling me over, my forehead pressed against the stone table before me. I felt nothing but the pain for several seconds before it faded again like a wave pulling back out to sea.

When I stood again, Sadira was before me. Her face was strained and pale, but she was with me again. "There is so much damage. I wish I could reach Jabari," she absently said. She wasn't looking at me, but down at the table that stood between us. "But then he may use that as an excuse to take you back."

Something twisted in my stomach that had nothing to do with the wound she was fighting to close. Jabari couldn't help her. Only Sadira could heal me. She was the one that made me a nightwalker, and only her blood could repair the wounded flesh she'd helped to create. I hesitated to ask. Sadira was very careful with knowledge, well-aware that controlling the flow of information was the easiest way to control her children. Despite her distracted demeanor, she didn't drop that information without a very good reason.

"Only you can save me." Even if it was all an illusion, the words tasted bad on my tongue as I said them.

Laughter danced in Sadira's eyes as she looked up at me. "How I wish that were true." She chuckled even as the light seemed to die from her expression. "Jabari has watched you from the moment I found you in Greece. I was *allowed* to keep you only if I promised to bring you before him whenever he commanded. And when the time came to bring you into the darkness, it was agreed that you would be a First Blood."

"What do you mean 'agreed'?" The statement implied that others were involved in the discussion about my fate, but there was never anyone but Sadira and her children around. As a human, I was occasionally brought before the Coven and other Ancients as a form of amusement, but Jabari had never been around then.

"Jabari and Tabor discussed it." Sadira reached across the table and took my right hand in both of her hands. Turning my arm over, she ran the fingers of her left hand down the inside of my arm. "My blood runs in your veins—shaped your organs and gave you an immortal life—but so does Jabari's and Tabor's."

"No!" I jerked my arm out of her grasp and took a step back. "I don't remember either of them."

"You were barely alive. It was easier to manipulate your memories then."

"I don't understand," I said, pacing away from the table.

There was no sound in the room, not even my footsteps on the stone floor. There were only our voices, because that was the point of bringing me here, not helping me to escape the pain. There was something she needed to tell me regardless of whether I wanted to hear it. "Why?"

"You were different, Mira." Sadira walked to the end of the table and started to come around it but stopped when I backpedaled, trying to keep some distance between us. "There was no human like you. It was more than your ability to control fire. We could sense an energy in your soul that we had never felt before. So, we decided to make you into a nightwalker, but we knew you would have to be a First Blood if we were to have any chance to preserve this energy."

"So you made me into a First Blood. That was part of our agreement. What about Jabari and Tabor?"

"Do you think Jabari would allow me to make a creature that could potentially destroy him?" Sadira demanded, incredulous. "Of course not. But if his blood flowed in you, he was sure you would feel bound to him, protecting him from your temper. It would also enable him to know your location at any time."

I turned my back on Sadira, a chill sweeping through me as a slight pain throbbed in my chest. It was nowhere near as intense as before, but was a subtle reminder that there was another world I had to return to. I stared down at my bare arm, my pale, white skin unmarred and unbroken. The reality of my raw and bruised wrists did not bleed into this illusion. It wasn't important. My focus was on the blue veins below my skin. Jabari's blood filled my veins in some way, had helped to give me this life.

"Yet things did not go how he had hoped."

Sadira's words jerked my head up. She had silently walked

around the table and now leaned back against it. Her small slender hands were folded before her stomach.

"What happened?"

"You remained . . . you," she said with a smile, while an odd glow grew in her eyes.

"What the hell is that supposed to mean?"

"It means he assumed that you would be easier to control as a vampire because you could be subjected to more intense forms of punishment without being killed due to your human frailties. But you refused to obey me. You refused to obey any Ancient that crossed your path. Also, I refused to give you up, so you were stolen."

I forced out a sharp little laugh. This was where her little story took a wrong turn and I was no longer buying it. It was a good try up until then. "I was kidnapped by the naturi, and we both know it."

A look of pity crossed her pale face as she shook her head. I longed to smack that look off her face but remained standing where I was, my fists clenched at my sides. "Think, my Mira. Before you were stolen, we were traveling west, heading back from Vienna. It was only you and me. We had gone to ground just before sunrise in a tiny village just west of the Pyrenees. No one knew where we were. The only ones who could have found you were those who made you."

"No!" I shouted, flinching at the faint echo that seemed to bounce around in my brain. I knew what she was saying and it was impossible. Jabari could have handed me over to the naturi five centuries ago. And he could have done it now. After the battle at Machu Picchu, I collapsed in his arms for a century, leaning on his strength. Then, centuries later, the naturi found me in my own domain and again in Egypt, driving me into Jabari's waiting arms.

The pieces fit, but I didn't trust them. Jabari hated the naturi. He wouldn't use them against another nightwalker.

He didn't have to. If he wanted something, he simply commanded and the nightwalker obeyed. Except for me. I didn't accept a direct order from anyone . . . but Jabari, and that was only because he had saved me from the naturi.

Gritting my teeth, I shoved both my hands into my hair and paced away from Sadira. My thoughts were swirling in an endless circle. Was she telling the truth? I knew she couldn't be trusted.

"Why are you telling me this?" I growled, refusing to look at her.

"Because he's searching for a way to replace you," she whispered.

I dropped my hands back to my sides as I turned back around to look at my maker. "How?"

"The same way we made you," she said, shrugging her slim shoulders. "I have helped with ten others, and I know there have been some I was not a part of. Not one has survived beyond the first year."

"Why? What happens?"

Sadira shook her head, her eyes dropping down to her folded hands. "That's not important. The fear is that he may succeed one day."

"And then you think he will have no further use for me." My voice was dead. Was any of this true? I didn't know what to believe anymore. My eyes wandered around the room that was my home for ten years. It had been my entire world and Sadira my only contact with life. She had been warmth, and compassion, and love for those years. Had that been a lie too? Or was it the only thing during those years that had been the truth?

"I know you feel no love for me, but you are my child, my beloved daughter. I do not want him to end your life because he feels you are no longer useful to him," Sadira murmured.

I didn't want him to end my life either, but I wasn't about

to seek shelter in Sadira's open arms. It wasn't exactly an enticing alternative. "Why have the others died?"

Sadira shook her head and her image wavered. At the same time, the pain in my chest increased. "It's near sunrise. We will speak more later."

Before I could stop her, pain stabbed through me and my eyes popped open. The library with its tall bookshelves and grim men surrounded me again. Candlelight flickered, casting shadows around the room. Sadira sat on the edge of the table beside my hip. She was using a delicate white lace handkerchief to wipe blood from her wrist. Her skin was so pale she was nearly translucent, and her eyes seemed more sunken and shadowed. I could taste her blood in my mouth, but it hadn't been enough. The worst of my wounds had closed using her blood, but I still needed to replenish all that I'd lost.

Just the taste of Sadira's blood sent up a dull roar inside my chest. The monster that wound itself around my soul was awake and screaming for blood. I clenched my teeth and tried to push it back. I would likely kill anyone I tried to feed from right now if I couldn't get a handle on my hunger.

Gabriel.

I whispered his name in my mind, sending the soft plea out to his brain. A wave of his emotions pushed back through me; fear, relief, worry, and joy all came rushing back in the wave of my mental touch. I wrapped my mind and heart up in his concern, holding them close to me as he entered the room and pulled me into his arms. I used those emotions as a way of protecting him from me as I sank my fangs into his throat and drank deeply.

The monster roared and clawed at my soul until I was sure there were only jagged shreds left, but I refused to give in to its demands that I take it all. I drank only enough to get me through the day. When I awoke at sunset, I would have enough strength to hunt and replenish all that I'd lost.

Lifting my mouth from Gabriel's neck, I instantly healed the wound and rested my head against his chest as he continued to hold me. His heartbeat was strong, seeming to vibrate through my weakened frame. He smelled of spice and cotton and steak. A smile teased at my lips and I relaxed in his arms. Themis had been kind enough to supply my angels with dinner. At least they'd been safe here.

"That was too close, boss," Gabriel murmured, rubbing his chin against the top of my head. He tightened his arms around me, keeping me pressed close but still trying to be careful of my tender wounds.

Tipping my head back, I pressed a quick kiss to his cheek before gently pushing out of his arms. The room spun slowly and my limbs trembled. I was weak and my whole body hurt. Hunger still roared in the back of my brain, but I had pushed it down so it was now little more than low white noise mixing in with all my other aches and pains.

"Sunrise," Sadira murmured, and I nodded as I swung my legs over the edge of the table. We were running out of time. Sunrise was less than fifteen minutes away and we needed to find a secure location to sleep.

I looked down at myself for the first time. My silk shirt was a mess. Both sleeves were shredded and the front was torn open from the waist down. What remained of the cloth was soaked in my blood, as were my leather pants. In fact, my blood was everywhere; my hands, face, the table, Sadira, and now Gabriel. It had been too close.

As my feet touched the ground, I felt my knees give out on me, but Gabriel grabbed my elbow, helping to steady me as he came to stand behind me. This was going to be tricky. I needed rest.

The sound of footsteps on the hardwood floor was my only warning before the door to the library swung open. Tristan stepped into the room, followed by Danaus, Michael, and James. Sadira extended her hand to Tristan. The young nightwalker hesitated a moment, his eyes darting to my face before he finally walked over to her, allowing Sadira to wrap her arms around him. Stiff, he stood with his arms lightly around her waist, his eyes closed. She was in his mind, not mine, but I knew she had already begun the task of drawing him back to her side. I had a promise to keep, but not now. I was in no shape to help anyone right now.

Michael stepped around Danaus to approach me. His handsome face was heavily lined and pale from worry. He wrapped his one good arm around me, pulling me as close as he possibly could to him. His large body shook slightly as I touched him, a shiver of relief running through him. Unfortunately, I was forced to release him almost as soon as he touched me. I was still too starved. I needed to feed, and his heartbeat combined with the sound of Gabriel's was slowly driving me mad.

Stepping away from my two angels, but keeping one hand on the table for balance, I looked over at Danaus, who was watching the little reunion from the doorway. "Sunrise is close. We have no choice but to stay here. We need a windowless room, preferably in the basement with a door that locks from the inside."

"I have something," he said with a nod.

James stood just behind Danaus's shoulder, his eyes dazed as he surveyed the room.

"James, could you fetch some food and drinks for my guardians?" I said to him. "They will be locked with us for the daylight hours. I don't want them becoming weak."

The Themis member nodded, snapping from his trance

at the sound of his name. "I will go prepare something," he said before hurrying from the room.

Sadira, Tristan, Gabriel, Michael, and I followed Danaus out of the library and down the hall toward the back of the manor. As we trooped slowly through the house, I was vaguely aware of the people lingering in doorways and down long hallways, watching our progress. My gaze swept over them, causing a frown to pull at the corners of my lips. Most were older gentlemen in their late forties and fifties, looking the same in their drab suits and neckties. There were a smattering of women, but they looked equally bookish, with their pale skin and pulled-back hair. I was beginning to wonder if these people saw the sunlight as infrequently as I did.

"You let me leave Sadira with a convention of librarians," I groaned, shoving both my hands through my hair in frustration. I swallowed a whimper as the movement pulled on the newly mended tissue and skin that stretched around my stomach and chest. I had lost my mind.

"She was safe." Danaus glared at me over his shoulder, his jaw clenched.

I looked back at the others, who remained in the doorways staring at me, their faces a mixture of fear and curiosity. "Don't you people sleep?" I snarled, then stalked off down the hall after Danaus, trying to ignore the spots that passed before my eyes. I needed to go to sleep before I fell over.

But beyond the pain, an odd feeling crawled over my skin. I had never been gawked at like that before. These civilized British librarians were watching me like I was a sideshow curiosity, or a monster. Or an evil miracle, considering the slow dance with death I had just survived.

The basement was unlike most I had known—dry and lacking an overwhelming smell of mold. Floor-to-ceiling bookshelves covered most of the walls, overflowing with books and ancient scrolls. I would have liked to linger down there, looking over the various stories these people had collected. Most of it was probably biased and terribly misguided, but it would have been interesting to see how humans viewed the other creatures surrounding them. I kept walking, my heels echoing off the tile floor as I followed Danaus.

At the end of the room was a wall with a thick, heavy wooden door held together with iron bands. The type of door that would lead to a dungeon. Danaus pulled the door open, the muscles in his arm jumping and dancing under the strain. Running his hand over the right wall on the inside, he flicked on the overhead light to reveal a single bare bulb glowing in the darkness. Inside, I saw several dusty crates and boxes, no doubt holding whatever strange artifacts these people valued. The room was used for storage and was obviously not visited often. Sadira stepped inside, frowning.

"It's just for one day," I wearily reminded her.

"Do you need blankets or anything?" Danaus asked awkwardly.

"No," I said with a soft chuckle. For all purposes, Sadira, Tristan, and I would be dead when the sun rose. We had no need for such comforts, though they were always nice to wake up to. "Just the food for Michael and Gabriel; I would appreciate it. This isn't the best way to spend the daylight hours."

He stared at me for a long time, his eyes weighing me. "You actually care for them," he murmured, as if his brain couldn't comprehend the idea.

"Very much," I half whispered, my gaze following my angels for a moment. "I'm not a monster from your nightmares. As you said, a part of me is still human." I was too tired to pound my fists against his stubborn misconceptions about what a nightwalker was supposed to be.

James appeared then, scurrying to the door of the basement room, an enormous basket on his arms. I stepped out of the doorway and allowed Gabriel to take it from him. James stepped back, running one hand through his hair. It had grown somewhat disheveled from the long night's adventure, and his tie was now missing.

"If you want, we can rotate in others so they can have a break," Danaus offered, instantly regaining my attention.

"No!" I said sharply. The fresh surge of fear snapped me awake. "No one else comes in or out of here." I turned my gaze over to Michael and Gabriel, who were inspecting the room. "And you do not open the door for anyone besides Danaus. No one!" Both gave me a slight nod before resuming their inspection.

I hesitantly stepped inside and turned to face Danaus, who had moved back out of the room. He pulled the heavy iron key out of the door and handed it to me so I could lock the room from the inside. I didn't ask him if it was the only copy. I didn't want to know the answer or to see him lie to me if it wasn't.

"Sweet dreams," I said. I tried to smile but knew it never reached my eyes.

Danaus reached up and slowly moved a lock of hair from where it had fallen in front of my eyes. His beautiful sapphire eyes caressed my face as if he were trying to memorize my features. "You too," he finally said before closing the door.

My hand was trembling when I put the cold key into the lock and turned it, the metal grinding against metal. It had been a while since anyone bothered to lock this door. Moving into the room, I tossed Gabriel the key. In one corner, Michael was already sifting through the large basket of food. It

had been a long night already, and I hoped they could catch
a little sleep in shifts, having no idea what tomorrow would
bring for any of us.

On the opposite wall, Sadira and Tristan lay on the dusty
floor, wrapped in each other's arms. Their eyes were closed,
already giving over to the daylight sleep. We could sleep at
any time but had no choice when the sun rose. It was the
tradeoff we all had to face. During the long night hours, we
were practically gods among the humans, with abilities beyond their comprehension. But as the sun touched the earth,
we were reduced to helpless husks, completely unable to protect ourselves. I sat on a crate against the wall and stretched
out my legs. With my arms crossed over my chest, I waited,
staring at the opposite wall. I didn't want to close my eyes
regardless of how tired I was. I didn't want the dawn to come
and take away my ability to defend myself.

But it came despite my protests. I could feel the night
give one last feeble gasp, clawing at the earth as it finally
shriveled up and died. The light crept steadily toward the
horizon, the gray sky giving way to the warm yellows and
pinks that I had watched paint the clouds in my youth. Despite the fact that I had not been reborn until I was twenty-
five, all my memories of the dawn came from my youth.
I could recall walking down to the shore to watch the sun
lifting into the sky, its delicate rays jumping and dancing
on the waves. The cries of the gulls filled the air as they left
their nighttime perch.

As the light broke across the sky, my body clenched,
struggling to hold my powers locked within this poor frame.
Yet, no matter how hard I tried, still it slipped through my
skin and down into the earth. As my eyes fell shut, the last
thing I recalled was the feeling of Danaus. Strong and powerful, his warmth washed through me, protecting me as he
stood guard outside the door. I tried to reach out with the

last bit of my powers to touch his warmth. The hunter was still protecting. He could have so easily left Tristan and me in the woods, allowing me to slowly die while he returned to Themis to destroy Sadira. Despite his angry protests about my kind being the root of all evil, he had saved me twice from Rowe and now stood guarding me from his own people during my weakest moment.

Twenty-Three

A scream erupted from my throat as my eyes snapped open. Machu Picchu rose up around me and Nerian stood close with knife in hand. This time I had been lying on Intihuatana as he prepared to remove my heart. It took a moment for my vision to clear. Blinking again, I found Michael standing before me, his warm hands cradling my face. I pulled away, moving out of his grasp, and pressed my back into the cold stone wall. The weight of Sadira's worried gaze pushed down on my tense shoulders. I couldn't blame her for her fears. I was supposed to protect her, and I was slowly being driven mad by nightmares that I shouldn't have had in the first place.

"I thought you had escaped the nightmares," she said, her voice a soft caress that reminded me vaguely of flannel pajamas. She was standing near the door. Tristan hovered close by, his arm around her slim shoulders. His body and face had become as still and stiff as a marble statue as he tried to mentally remove himself from Sadira, but I saw a flicker of concern flash through his eyes before he could squash it.

"They're back." I was only mildly surprised that she'd

asked Jabari about me. I jumped down from my resting spot on top of the crates, wincing at the movement. My body was mostly healed, but I was still sore. "It's nothing. It will pass. What time is it?"

"Two hours past sunset."

I barely stifled the curse that had risen to my lips. I was a late sleeper, but I'd never slept that late. The nightmares combined with the injuries were draining me, forcing me to sleep later into the night. That left me vulnerable not only to humans and naturi, but also to other nightwalkers.

"Let's get out of here." I held my hand up and Gabriel tossed me the key. He looked rumpled and a little weary, but otherwise fine. Michael wasn't wearing his homemade sling and seemed to move a bit easier. Both of my angels had also regained their color from my previous feedings. I unlocked the door and pushed it easily open, the metal hinges groaning in the silence. My little band trooped across the basement and up the stairs, where James met us. I was surprised to find him wearing a pair of jeans and a hunter green T-shirt. It was a little disconcerting to see him looking so casual, even though his hair was still perfectly arranged and his shirt neatly tucked into his pants. His brown belt even matched his dark brown shoes.

"Nice outfit," I said with a half smile.

James flushed, his hand absently reaching for a tie that wasn't there. "I had a feeling I was a bit overdressed for assisting you."

"No doubt."

"Are you leaving now?"

"Soon. Where's Danaus?"

"Resting, I believe. He stood guard in the basement all day." My stomach muscles twisted and knotted at the thought of him sitting outside my door while I lay helpless. Yet, instead of fear gripping me, I was surprised to feel my cheeks flush. I felt important . . . almost cherished. I hadn't expected the hunter to stay all day.

"Do we need him anymore?" Sadira asked from behind me, shaking me from my thoughts and reminding me that she was the valuable commodity here, not me. I was just part of a game Rowe was playing.

I turned my head so I could see her out of the corner of my eye. "No, I guess not," I said, disappointment threading itself through each syllable. I had become accustomed to having him there, someone protecting my back—even though he meant to stick a knife in it the first chance he got. "We need to find Jabari and a replacement for Tabor. We might as well stay while you search."

"And then where?" Sadira's soft voice was edged with fear and doubt.

"Back to London. My jet is still there, and we can take it to the Coven. If Jabari is not there, one of the other Elders will be. It's also the safest place I can think of. You can stay there while I fetch Tabor's replacement or search for the location of the next sacrifice."

"I will show you to a comfortable room you may use," James said, leading us down the hall. He opened the door and my two guardians entered first, sweeping the room, one hand always on the butt of one of their guns. They were good at what they did and I felt a small swell of pride as I watched them. I entered only after Gabriel gave a single nod, indicating that it was clear.

Sadira settled in an ornate chair in one corner of the room, allowing her to survey the entire room and keep her back to the wall. We hadn't survived this long without learning to be cautious. Of course, in my case it also helped to be lucky.

I looked around the cozy room, taking in the pale yellow striped wallpaper and antique furniture with its slightly faded flower print. Lamps dotted the room, casting the area in a soft, warm glow while sweeping back the shadows to the far corners. There were a few landscape portraits and bookshelves set into the walls.

"Is there anything I can get you?" James inquired, drawing my attention back to him. He was so eager to be involved, to help in some fashion, even if it was only fetching food, that I wanted to smile. By the sheer fact that we hadn't drained him dry yet, he was willing to give me and my kind a chance. I wished more humans could view us with the same open-mindedness.

"Do you have any more hunters lying around?" I asked, knowing Danaus couldn't be the only hunter lurking around this rambling old house. "I'd like at least a pair at the door."

"Of course."

"And a meal for my companions."

"Food for Michael and Gabriel will not be a problem, but . . . " He hedged nervously, his gaze darting to Sadira, who smiled. While she would never admit to it, she was enjoying James's discomfort.

"Sadira and I will hunt outside of the Compound later this evening," I said, then looked over at Tristan. He was still young and I had no doubt that last night's confrontation had left him feeling like he could use a bite. I didn't want a half-starved nightwalker on my hands when I was having trouble myself, particularly around this many humans. They were hell to control and extremely dangerous.

"I'll feed later as well," Tristan volunteered, his voice soft but firm.

"Very good," James said with a quiet sigh of relief. "Anything else?"

"Yes, a shower."

"I beg your pardon?"

Pushing him back out the door, I rolled my eyes toward

the ceiling. "I'm a vampire, James, not a self-cleaning oven," I said. I turned my gaze to Sadira for a moment. "Find me another Tabor. I'll be back soon." Closing the door, I looked at James again, who was blushing.

"Forgive me, I just never thought . . . " he stammered, resetting his gold-rimmed glasses on the bridge of his narrow nose.

"Yeah, all us undead don't need to bathe. Our magic keeps us clean." Laying my hands on his shoulders, I gently turned him so he was pointed toward the main hall. "Find me a shower and then fetch the food. If you're lucky, we'll be out of your hair in less than an hour."

James silently led me up the stairs to the second floor. Down the hall to the left, he opened the third door, revealing a beautiful bedroom decorated in mint green and gold. A large four-poster bed dominated the room, and a heavy walnut desk lounged against the far wall. The room was neat and clean, with its books properly arranged. I paused at the bureau to look at the row of pictures, all of smiling family and friends.

"This room belongs to Melanie Richards. She's currently in the States visiting family," James explained. "I would give you a spare room, but we're a little crowded at the moment."

"Had to call in reinforcements?" I teased. His mouth bobbed open and closed for a moment, but I had pity on him. There was something a little endearing about this poor human. Maybe it was just the fact that he didn't resemble a librarian at the moment, like all the others. "I don't blame you," I whispered, with a secret little smile.

I turned my gaze back to the pictures, wondering if any of the females was the room's owner. "I bet she's going to be upset to discover she missed out on seeing the vampire circus sweep through."

"That's an understatement," James muttered, earning a light chuckle from me.

"You'll just have to tell her that I used her shower. Maybe that will placate her," I said, feeling supremely absurd. I walked into the bathroom off the bedroom. It was small, with a set of green towels hanging on the towel rod. Most of the personal items had been removed, but I was relieved to find some shampoo and bath gel. I smelled of smoke and felt grimy, coated in a thick layer of my own blood.

"Is there anything else I can do?" he offered, his hand resting on the white marble sink.

"No, I can handle this, unless you want to stay and wash my back?"

This time James smiled and shook his head. I think he was beginning to catch on to my teasing. "I shall leave you and take care of the other items." With that, he headed out of the room.

I closed the bathroom door and looked at myself in the mirror. I looked like a nightmare. My red hair hung about my face in matted clumps, filled with dried blood, leaves, and dirt. My face and body were streaked with blood and dirt. I looked like the hideous, blood-sucking monster vampires were proclaimed to be. And yet none of my own fear was showing beneath the blood and dirt. The world couldn't see that I didn't have a clue about what I was doing. Most of my decisions were made on the fly, and the fact that I was still alive was a testament to my own stupid luck.

Turning away from the mirror in disgust, I turned on only the hot water and stripped out of my clothes. I climbed into the tub and sighed as the steaming hot water heated my cold flesh and turned my complexion pink. It was the quickest way to gain warmth without feeding. The feeling was always short-lived, but I enjoyed it while it lasted. Relaxed again, I washed my hair and scrubbed off last night's encounters at the pub, in the alley with Rowe, and in the woods.

With my hands braced against the tile wall, I let the hot water pour down on my head and over my body, rinsing off the dirt and soap. I closed my eyes and stretched out my senses. I started on the first floor, pausing for a second. While I couldn't feel Sadira, I could pick up the swell of power emanating from her. So much for hiding. Hell, let her blame it on me. Jabari had plenty to be angry with me for. Why not add one more thing? I had a few things I was eager to discuss with the Elder.

The members of Themis were still anxious, running about the large mansion like a hive of angry bees. There was a large group meeting at the opposite end of the second floor. I didn't pause to hear what they were discussing. I didn't care. We'd be gone soon and I'd never have to deal with these people again.

On the third floor, I located Danaus. He was so calm and at peace, I could only guess he was asleep. He was more difficult to read than humans and other nightwalkers. Much like most magic users, his powers seemed to muddy things. I could pick up on emotions but not specific thoughts. I lingered over him, soaking in his calm the same way I had soaked in the warmth of his powers. Reluctantly, I moved on and was about to pull away when I picked up on the other strong magic user in the house. He was on the third floor in what felt like a large room. He was calm as well, but there was a deeper sense of concern and anticipation curling around him. This had to be the illustrious Ryan.

With a shake of my head, I closed the connection and turned off the shower. Wiping off the excess water, I toweldried my hair as best as I could. Reluctantly, I pulled on my pants, shoes, and bra. The shirt was ruined. I would have to borrow something from Miss Richards for now. If we had time, I hoped to stop at the hotel in London and pick up my things before we flew out. Locating a brush under the sink, I ran it through my hair, getting rid of the tangles as best as I could. When finished, I at least felt like I carried the semblance of average humanity.

Reaching for the doorknob, I suddenly stopped. Michael was waiting for me in the bedroom, his heart thudding fast in worry. I jerked open the door to find him pacing the room, clenching and unclenching his hands at his sides.

"What's wrong?" I demanded in a harsh voice, making him jump.

"Nothing," he quickly answered, his hand automatically reaching for his gun in his surprise. A spastic smile jumped across his lips as his hands returned to his sides.

"What are you doing up here?"

"I didn't think you should be here unprotected."

"I'm fine. Your job right now is to protect Sadira. I can manage," I reassured him, running my fingers through my damp hair. Fear unknotted in my stomach, leaving the muscles trembling for a moment.

"Do you need anything?" His eyes were wide as he watched me.

"No, I'm fine."

Something about him was making me ill at ease. He seemed nervous and extremely tense. I could only guess that it was the constant traveling and the threat of the naturi. While I'm not sure he completely understood the danger, he'd overheard enough conversations to catch a solid glimpse.

He walked over to me and placed a trembling hand on my cheek. "I'm worried about you. You nearly died last night and you're still in danger here," he murmured, pressing a gentle kiss to my temple. "This place is wall-to-wall vampire hunters and God only knows what else. You know I'll do whatever it takes to protect you, but . . . " His strong voice drifted off, suffocated by his doubts.

"But you and Gabriel are outgunned," I finished, running my hands up his strong chest. Lacing my fingers behind his neck, I pulled him down so his forehead touched mine. Michael wrapped his arm around my waist, enveloping me his warmth. "Right now, these hunters are not the threat that concerns me. Besides, they seem to follow Danaus, and he needs me alive."

He pulled away so that he could look me in the eye. "He tried to have you killed in Egypt," he reminded me, with barely caged anger.

"He claims it was a misunderstanding. They were trying to rescue him."

"And you believe him?"

"No." I laughed, pulling his head down to capture his soft lips in a quick kiss that lasted a bit longer than I initially intended. Michael's arms tightened, pressing me against his strong body. His skin was warm and his heart pounded against my breast, proclaiming his life and strength to my own cold form. I started to break off the kiss, telling myself that I had too many things to take care of, when Michael deepened it, running the tip of his tongue along the seam of my lips. My own body instantly responded, my mouth opening so his tongue could dart in, tasting me.

French kissing a vampire was an art form that Michael had mastered during our years together. He could kiss me without pricking his tongue on my fangs, but there was never anything hesitant or careful about it. He explored my mouth, opening up senses and feelings within me I hadn't realized were laying dormant, waiting for him and his touch. In his hands, I felt almost human again.

I moaned softly against his mouth, my fingers threading through his hair. With a little pressure he guided me backward until I felt something pressing against the back of my knees. Running his hands up and down my back, he slowly pulled his mouth away and smiled down at me, his eyes sparkling with some kind of mischief. It was on the tip of my tongue to ask what he was thinking when he gave my left shoulder a little shove, pushing me onto the bed.

"Make time stand still, Mira," he murmured in a low, husky voice that sent a shimmer of warmth over my body. "Give us tonight."

Parting my knees so he was standing between my leather-clad legs, I sat up and grabbed a fistful of his shirt. As I lay back down, Michael crawled onto the bed, placing his elbows on either side of my head as he leaned down and reclaimed my lips. My eyes fell shut as he wrung another moan out of me, my body instinctively arching against his. I wanted to feel all of him. I needed to feel all of his soft, warm skin pressed against the length of my body, but I would follow his lead. Michael was in control and I was enjoying every second of this escape while I could.

Moving his lips along my jaw, Michael shifted his weight onto his left arm, allowing him to slip his right hand between our bodies. His nimble fingers slid over my ribs and up to cup my breast, his thumb rubbing over my nipple through the rough lace of the bra.

"Have you missed me?" he asked in a harsh, breathless whisper, running his lips over mine.

"Very much." My hands fumbled for a moment, searching for the edge of his shirt. I finally found it, allowing me to run my hands up his back. His muscles flexed and danced beneath my fingers. He kissed me again as his fingers pulled down the bra, freeing my breast for his teasing fingers.

"Not nearly enough, I think." Changing directions, he ran the tip of his tongue along my flat stomach from my belly button, up along my ribs, skirting along the edge of the red scar left from last night's wound before finally settling on my bare breast. His tongue swirled around my hardened nipple, his teeth grazing it.

My eyes fell shut again. My fingers dug into his blond locks, twisting to get a better hold. I arched against him, my heels digging into the edge of the bed. I needed to be closer, to become a part of him.

"You're driving me mad."

Michael chuckled, his hot breath dancing across my damp flesh from where his mouth had been just moments before. "That's the point." My angel moved back up to my lips, kissing me deeply.

Wrapping his arms around my waist, he rolled over onto his back, pulling me on top of him. "Bite me, Mira," he said, moving his lips to kiss down my jaw to my neck.

"Not tonight, my angel," I said, lifting my face so I could kiss his lips again, but he kept his head turned so his neck was before me. The main artery throbbed at me, beckoning. The darkness stirred inside me, but I struggled to push it back down again. I was still half starved, needed to gorge myself on blood not only to heal but to regain my full strength. But I wouldn't feed off Michael. I had taken too much of his blood too often. His warmth and laughter kept any lingering pangs of hunger at bay.

"Please, Mira. Bite me. I need this." His words escaped him with a harsh, desperate quality that sent a chill through me.

I sat up so I could look down at him, my desire suddenly cooling. "Please, don't push me, my angel," I said wearily. "I need you strong."

"I can handle it." His right hand cupped my cheek. He tried to pull me back down but I wouldn't budge.

"No. You should go back downstairs." I moved so I was now sitting beside him, my hip pressed against his.

"Please, Mira," he said, his voice wavering. Something in his tone finally caught my attention and I stared into his eyes. They looked a little glassy, as if he was sick. Frowning, I pushed into his thoughts. Jumbled and fragmented, it took me a couple seconds to make sense out of them, but there was one repeating one; the need for the pleasure my bite brought him.

I pulled loose of the tangle of thoughts in his brain and smacked him hard enough to snap his head sideways. "Enough!" I was more frustrated with myself for letting this happen than at him. Michael had become addicted and come begging to me for his next fix. His interest in sex had nothing to do with me and everything to do with my feeding off of him.

He looked at me like a wounded puppy and I bit back a groan. "I need you to be focused. I can't get Sadira out of here safely without you," I continued in a soft but firm voice, resisting the urge to cup his cheeks with my hands. Pushing off the bed, I got to my feet and paced away from the bed, readjusting my bra so my breasts were covered again. A horrible, hollow ache throbbed in my chest. I had fooled myself into thinking that I'd held his interest.

When I turned back, Michael was standing beside the bed, straightening his clothes. His eyes still looked hurt, but he had pulled himself back together. At least for now. Maybe he wasn't too far gone yet. It didn't matter. I was done with him. When we reached the Coven meeting place, I was putting Michael and Gabriel on the next plane home. They would be of no real help after that, and keeping them at my side would only put them in unnecessary danger. I wouldn't ruin what was left of Michael's life.

"Go downstairs. I'll be down in a minute," I directed, forcing the words up my raw throat. Michael nodded again and left the room. I sat on the end of the bed and followed him with my mind. He did as he was told and went directly to the room that held Sadira and the others.

Putting my elbows on my knees, I leaned forward and rested my forehead in the palms of my hands. I was destroying Michael by being in his life. Why had Gabriel's mind come through this so unscathed? He was always a solid rock at my back. I had fed from him in the past and yet his mind suffered none of the damage I apparently had wrought with Michael.

But there was no answer. Michael was crumbling before me and it was my fault. I'd thought I was someone important in his life. I would never be so foolish as to describe the emotion as love, but at least some emotion that would be used to describe a person. But to him, I was just the source of intense pleasure, like a drug.

Being addicted to the bite of a nightwalker was a common enough occurrence, but it was also easy to avoid. If you never fed from the same person more than once, or if you did and always wiped his memory, the problem was avoided. But eventually we all ended up with a human companion that we drifted back to for a long span of nights in the name of pleasure and companionship. In time we drained them. We drained them of more than just their blood, but their willpower, their dignity, and their lives.

My thoughts were scattered again when someone knocked on the door. I looked up at the mirror over the bureau to find my face blissfully blank. It was nice to look so unaffected when I felt like screaming.

"Come in," I called, rising from the bed.

"Sorry to disturb you," James said as he entered. A deep flush stained his cheeks when he saw me standing by the edge of the bed without a shirt. He quickly averted his eyes.

I walked over to the closet door and pulled it open. "I was

just heading downstairs," I said, riffling through the clothes I found hanging there until my eyes fell on a plain black button-up shirt.

"If you have a moment, Ryan has requested a meeting with you before you leave," James said, obviously expecting me to turn down the invitation.

I paused in the act up buttoning up the shirt, grateful that Melanie and I were roughly the same size. "Just me? Not Sadira?" I was surprised. Sadira was the oldest of the trio of nightwalkers in the compound, making her the natural superior.

"He asked only for you."

"I guess I can spare a few moments," I said with an indifferent shrug as I attached the last two buttons. I was going to finally meet the big boss man. I wasn't sure how much new information he would be able to provide, but so far Themis had been most helpful. Far more helpful than Jabari and Sadira, who were working very hard to keep me out of the loop, while someone was trying to kill me. And this time it didn't appear to be a hunter.

Twenty-Four

Ryan was a warlock. I had suspected it before arriving at the Compound, but it was blatantly obvious when I walked into his private office on the third floor. He leaned against the front of his large walnut desk, his long legs stretched out before him and crossed casually at the ankle. He had been expecting me. Of course, I'm sure he could feel every move I made in his manor without straining himself.

He was a handsome man, standing just over six feet, with a long, lean body that somehow managed to exude a beautiful grace rather than being awkward. He wore a dark charcoal-gray suit with a black undershirt. Unlike his brethren, he wasn't wearing a tie, and the top two buttons of the shirt were undone, revealing an expanse of nicely tanned throat. In fact, his tanned skin and dark-colored suit stood in sharp contrast to his long white hair. Falling somewhere past his shoulders, it was pulled back with a narrow, black ribbon; a throwback to an era long past.

His face had a strange ageless quality to it. There were no wrinkles or deep lines, making him seem to be in his early to mid-thirties at first glance. But his gold eyes held a depth that one could only earn through years of experience. He was old; older than any human was meant to be.

Magic had a distinct effect on a human's physical appearance. And the deeper and more skilled a warlock or witch became in the use of magic, the more profound the effect. His power was etched into his features and imbued every inch of his being. It sizzled in the room like a current of electricity, making my skin crawl.

Most humans that used magic did it by accident. Events sometimes happened in their favor and the human simply chalked it up as a run of good luck. Only the ones who actually studied magic and attained some basic understanding were called witches and warlocks. And then there were those like Ryan, who made the study of magic a life's pursuit. *They* were simply called dangerous.

After James wordlessly shut the door, leaving me alone with this strange man, Ryan rose to his feet without pushing off the desk. He stood in the same, seemingly boneless manner that vampires could. I had known a few warlocks in my time, but never saw a human pull a trick I always thought exclusive to nightwalkers.

"Impressive." I said, lightly applauding. "I guess pulling a rabbit out of your hat is too mundane."

He smiled back at me; a warm, friendly smile that seemed open and guileless. That was almost more impressive that his earlier trick. How could someone who wielded as much power as he did seem so nice? The same way the naturi seemed so harmless—centuries of practice.

"My name is Ryan," he said, extending his hand toward me. I stared at it a moment, admiring his long fingers, but never touched him. It was a good, strong hand, the type of hand that could comfort as easily as it could punish.

Stepping around him, I looked at some of the bookshelves that lined his wall. I glanced over the old spines, but my attention was still completely on the room's only other occupant. I preferred to keep a little space between us for now. "I know your name," I replied blandly. "I also know what you are. My question is: Do your associates know?"

"They know I'm a warlock," he said, drawing my eyes back to him. His smile grew a little wider. "However, I imagine your assessment of my powers is a little more accurate than theirs."

Arching one eyebrow at him, I smiled. "So you've purposefully kept them in the dark." There was no anger or accusation in my voice. Just honest curiosity. I wanted to understand his motives and the situation I had walked into. I also desperately needed to understand the players in this little farce before it cost me my existence.

"My abilities aren't important to their cause."

"That's not what I meant," I corrected. "You've not only kept them in the dark about yourself, but also the truth about vampires. I've heard and read some of the things these people believe about my kind. Why do you allow them to perpetuate such lies?"

"For their own safety," he said. His wide smile faded a bit but still lingered on his lips. He shoved his hands in his trouser pockets, reminding me of a corporate executive after hours.

"What about mine? You've been sending hunters after my kind."

"Both of our worlds are changing; much faster than I expected, I must admit. A couple centuries ago some of the things written about vampires were true. Most were ruthless hunters that killed every time they fed, but now I have found they are using some discretion. You're still very dangerous, and without some fear of you, I worry humans will run blindly into your inviting arms."

"I may have disillusioned poor James of some of these archaic notions. Will you silence him to keep him from infecting the rest?"

"No, of course not," he said with a shake of his head, looking amused. "I won't suppress the truth within Themis. However, I want them to find it on their own."

"And the hunters? Were they your creation? Another attempt to protect your flock?" I slowly paced back over toward him, my footsteps muffled on the thick Persian rug.

Ryan had yet to move other than to turn on a heel so he was continuously facing me. "The hunters were created long before I ever joined Themis."

"But you've done nothing to get rid of them since joining this little cult, despite your enlightened view of my kind."

"What makes you think that my view of nightwalkers is so enlightened?" he countered, arching one brow at me.

"I'm here and still alive," I said, holding out my hands, palms up at him. I stood directly in front of him, only a couple feet of empty space separating us. "You could have ordered Danaus to stake me and the others during the daylight hours, but you didn't. I also know that you couldn't have attained the kind of power I feel in this room without running into things far worse than me during your long years."

"What could be worse than a nightwalker who can control fire?" he said, his smile finally returning.

"Danaus."

Ryan's smile instantly vanished and a shadow seemed to pass over his eyes as he stared at me, weighing my answer. We were both now standing in a field of land mines, each wondering how much the other person knew. His hands shifted in his trouser pockets, his eyes narrowing in thought.

I had never run across such an eye color in any creature before—not yellow, but the true, deep luster of gold.

"Danaus is an interesting . . . person," he said, pausing for a breath before continuing. "He's had a particular interest in you during the past several years."

"How long have you known about the naturi's plans?" I demanded, my voice hardening. My hands balled into fists at my sides and I resisted the urge to take a step closer.

"His interest in you had nothing to do with the naturi." Ryan's broad shoulders slumped as he seemed to relax. He moved back to lean against the front of the desk and motioned for me to take a seat in one of the leather chairs resting before it. I was feeling indulgent, so I sat to his right, crossing my legs as I waited for him to continue.

"Before arriving on Themis's doorstep," he said, "I understand that Danaus spent many years living with monks, who taught him that good and evil was a black-and-white issue in this world. Humans were created by God and were innately good. By that logic, everything else was evil and had to be exterminated. You were an interest of his because you seemed to embody the ultimate evil. A nightwalker, a human that has turned from God, that can control fire, directly linking you to Satan and all that is evil.

"You're somewhat of a mythical creature among your own kind. It took him almost a decade to track down your given name. Most still just know you as the Fire Starter."

" 'Mira' doesn't strike the same kind of fear," I said with a shrug.

"Danaus became quite determined to find and destroy you . . . " Ryan paused, staring at me. A dark shadow seemed to passed over his face as he regarded me with his too perceptive eyes, sending a chill up my spine. I suddenly wished that I wasn't seated so close to the warlock.

"And then something changed for him. In all his searching and digging, not once did he hear a tale of you killing a human. Of course, there were numerous stories of you slaughtering your own kind, particularly those who had carelessly killed humans."

"But he thought I killed when I fed," I interjected, recalling our conversation during the plane ride to Egypt.

"True, but I think he was beginning to have doubts about that old myth as well. Before we discovered the naturi's sacrifice, he had stopped his search for you. You were beginning to raise some uncomfortable questions . . . I think he was even contemplating leaving Themis. When I sent him to look for you in the States, he had regained his resolve to destroy you." Ryan paused, staring thoughtfully. I knew he must have made sure that Danaus once again had ample motive to go after my head. "But something has changed for him." Ryan said the last softly, as if thinking aloud rather than talking to me. I knew his thoughts as though I'd read them. He was wondering about that change. Danaus had more than enough opportunities to kill me but he hadn't, and protected me on more than one occasion.

"He's learned that Themis doesn't have all the right answers," I said stiffly. "He's not pleased with your little group at the moment. Danaus has been misled and used. You've lied to him."

"I never lied to Danaus," Ryan said. The warlock frowned at me, shifting his weight from one foot to the other. "If he asked, I would have told him all I knew of your kind. He had his mind made up about nightwalkers long before I was born."

"You could have told him."

"He had to discover it on his own."

"Nice excuse," I said snidely. "You had your own agenda, and the fact that you could use Danaus's misinformed conclusions to your advantage provided you with no moral dilemma." I leaned forward in the chair, tightly gripping the arms.

"Don't we all." He shrugged his wide shoulders. "I wish you would not think so ill of me, Mira. We have the same goal."

A dark smile lifted the corners of my mouth as I stood. "I doubt that."

"I'll give you that you probably have more fun at it than I do, but our goal is the same: maintain our secret as long as possible."

"Is that your goal?"

"I'm not the villain you want me to be. We've both done things to keep the humans from discovering what surrounds them. You've killed numerous nightwalkers that jeopardized the secret. I've done the same with the hunters. We're both guardians, protecting that fragile wall that separates our world from the world of the humans."

Ryan stood a step forward, closing the distance between us to less than a foot. He slowly raised his hand, with his finger bent, and held it beside my cheek. "May I?" he whispered.

"May you what?" I watched him through narrowed eyes. Warlock or not, I could still be on the other side of the room before he moved.

"I just wish to touch your face."

I stared, confused at him for a second, my brow furrowed. It seemed an extremely strange request coming from him, but I didn't think it was necessarily a trick. When a witch or warlock casts, you can feel the building of power in the air. Of course, Ryan was more powerful than any I had known before. There was enough energy in the air already that I might not notice any specific shift. But I nodded, regardless.

Noticing my wariness, he inched his hand forward until the back of his fingers gently caressed my check, sliding

down from my cheekbone and along my jaw. His skin was
warm and I felt only a slight jolt of energy from the contact,
but nothing more. It was his voice that actually held me en-
tranced briefly. "Forgive me," he murmured. "You're not as
cold as I expected."

"I find it hard to believe that you've never touched a
nightwalker before," I teased, tilting my head up so I was
looking him in the eyes.

"Once before," he said, a grim smile touching his lips.
"And that was only after he was done feeding off me."

"Yes, a meal tends to warm us up."

"But you've not fed tonight?"

"No."

"And you're still not . . . "

"Cold as a corpse?" I supplied. The darkness that had
briefly clouded his expression lifted at the comparison and
his smile brightened. "Under normal circumstances, I can
go several days without feeding and retain some warmth. A
hot shower also helps."

"Do you retain such warmth because of your ability?"

"To control fire? No. Fire does not burn or warm me.
In fact, if I use the ability too much, I grow cold because it
requires energy."

"I hadn't known."

"No human ever has."

"Why do you trust me?" he asked, sounding surprised.

I laughed deeply, the sound filling the room, shoving
aside some his energy. He shifted at the sudden intrusion,
resettling himself against his desk. "I don't." I slumped into
the chair behind me, throwing one leg carelessly over the
chair arm. "Call it a gesture of good faith. I give you a little
something . . . "

"Because you want something," he finished.

"Doesn't everybody?"

"What is it you desire?"

My voice and expression hardened instantly. "Information."

"An expensive commodity."

"Perhaps, but what you get in return is valuable as well," I said, my eyes never wavering from his face.

"And what is that?"

"Your life."

"So we've come to threats," Ryan announced, sounding amused.

"Not at all. Just a statement of fact. The naturi are a threat to both human and nightwalker. You have information that may help my kind. We are the ones risking our lives to protect you."

"Very noble of you."

"Hardly," I said with a snort. "And you know better." I looked up at him and his expression turned serious again. We had enjoyed our brief moment of levity, but time was wasting away.

"What is it you think I know?"

"I don't know, but considering that I know nothing, it has to be more than me," I admitted. "You discovered the first sacrifice in India before we even realized anything was happening."

"Are you sure we were the first?"

"No," I whispered.

Before the disaster in London and Thorne's death, I would have emphatically said yes, but now I wasn't sure of anything. The naturi knew too much, finding me far too quickly in Egypt and again in London. Someone was betraying me, and I didn't like my options at the moment. Of course, I wasn't about to voice those thoughts to a human. And if I had my way, I'd be holding the creature's heart in my hand before the naturi attempted the second sacrifice.

"But at the moment," I continued, pressing through those dark thoughts, "it doesn't matter. How did you discover the body?"

"Konark has long been the center for heavy magic use," he explained, "though it hadn't been used for a very long time. I felt the surge in power that night. I had researchers on a plane before dawn touched the Indian sky."

"What about the trees?"

"That, I fear, was just luck. One of the members of Themis was on vacation in Canada. He caught sight of a carving while hiking and took a picture. He thought it was some new branch of Wicca springing up. After that, I sent out every available operative to find more carvings."

"How many did you locate?"

"Twelve."

"Do you know what they mean? Can you read their writing?"

"Not really," he said with a sigh. "The markings on the trees mean nothing to me, but I can make some educated guesses with the blood markings surrounding the sacrifice at Konark."

"Do you think you found all the carvings?"

"Yes. I've checked every day since the first sacrifice but detected no other places I think might have the markings. Do you know what they mean?"

"The carvings? No," I said with a shake of my head. "This isn't the first time they've attempted to break the seal, but I have never seen or heard of the carvings before."

"I had thought they were used as a way of activating the twelve holy sites," Ryan speculated. With his right hand, he picked up a crystal paperweight about the size of a baseball. It looked like a crystal ball, but instead of being clear, red veins ran through the orb. He rolled the crystal between his two hands, a nervous gesture that revealed his worry, unlike the more guarded and planned expressions that crossed his face.

"No, the first sacrifice accomplished that. The carvings mean something else," I said, shoving my hand through my hair, pushing it back from my face.

"So, now we just wait for the second sacrifice."

"It will be soon. Very soon," I whispered.

Ryan put the paperweight back on his desk and stood. "Are you sure? How do you know?"

"They've begun checking the other eleven sites. Once they locate the right one, they have only a small window of time to use it. The pool of power is constantly moving. I've never heard of anyone being able to tell when it will move or where it will go to. Maybe Aurora can, I don't know."

"But the next new moon isn't for another five nights," Ryan said with a shake of his head.

"The naturi are not bound to the key phases of the moon, though it helps," I replied, fighting the urge to get up and pace. I forced a tight smile onto my lips as I titled my head back to look up at a warlock. "You know magic. It's more than just the moon, and the seasons, and the alignment of the heavens."

"Magic is also about circles and balance," he finished. His brows drew together slightly, as furrows ran through his smooth forehead.

"And the anniversary of when the last seal was created is upon us," I murmured. The thought had first occurred to me when I was talking to James last night. I too thought they would stick to phases of the moon, since it would provide them with the most power to break the seal. But destroying what the nightwalkers had wrought on the anniversary would not only be a powerful blow magically, but deal a heavy blow to the morale of my kind. "The naturi will be making their attempt either tonight or tomorrow night."

"And if they were to succeed . . . "

"Then they would be able to open the door in five nights, lining up perfectly with the new moon."

"And the pagan harvest holiday."

"We're running out of time," I said with frustration, pushing out of the chair. I paced over to the wall of books on my left and back to Ryan, my arms folded over my stomach.

"But you have everything you need," he argued, looking at me with confusion filling his face.

"No, I don't," I replied, turning to walk back toward the bookshelf. "A triad of nightwalkers stopped the naturi five centuries ago. One of the three, Tabor, was killed by the naturi several years ago. With him gone, we have to reform the triad. Unfortunately, the replacement I found was killed while I stood there watching."

"But the triad has already been reformed," the warlock said, his voice a gentle caress in the silence of the room.

I spun on my heel to look at him as my stomach attempted to turn itself inside out. "What?"

"I could feel it as soon as you entered the compound. All the pieces needed to seal the door again have been found," he said confidently.

My legs threatened to buckle beneath me when I heard this horrible pronouncement. I was supposed to be the third? It couldn't be. Sadira was my maker, putting us in the same bloodline. And if Sadira's story was to be believed, so was Jabari and Tabor. I didn't want to be a part of the triad. My job was to find a replacement for Tabor and protect Sadira. After that, I was returning to my city across the ocean and never looking back. They didn't need me for anything else.

"You're wrong," I said, nearly choking on the words. "I can't help them."

"You have no choice," he sadly said. "I—" Ryan abruptly

broke off as his gaze darted toward the door and cocked his head to the side as if listening to someone whispering in his ear. "Something is coming."

"What do you mean 'something'?" I snapped. "Is it the naturi?"

"No, something else. I don't know what. It's powerful," he said, pushing away from the desk to stand.

"Great," I muttered, already moving toward the door. "You better get your people to cover. I'll do what I can." I didn't know what I was facing, but I assumed it was at the Compound because of me and my traveling troupe of vampires and misfits.

"Thank you," Ryan called.

"Don't be too grateful. I may still need to pick your brain."

"As long as I'm alive for it," he joked, though the laughter no longer reached his golden eyes.

I paused, holding the door handle, and looked over my shoulder at the warlock. "Did you order my death?" I inquired, wondering if I would ever have another chance to ask. I needed to know exactly where I stood with this creature.

"Recently?" he asked.

"Ever."

"Yes."

Twenty-Five

I walked down the main staircase toward the first floor, my feet sinking into the thick carpet that covered the stairs. Apparently Ryan had sent out some kind of mental warning to the proper people because I heard doors being thrown open around me and hurried footsteps across the hardwood floors. I needed to get these people out of my way. If something not good was headed to the compound, I didn't want to concern myself with the stray gawker trying to collect a little valuable data.

A part of me was aching for a fight. A couple of naturi to deal with, something to rip apart; their flesh squishing warmly between my fingers and collecting under my fingernails. While I'll admit that I was still extremely hungry, more than a rising blood lust clouded my thoughts. I craved just the sight of blood. I wanted to see it splashed across the skin and soaking into torn and shredded clothing. I needed the violence, an outlet for the frustration and the fear. In the brief moment when you are struggling to stay alive, you convince yourself that you're actually in control of your life and destiny. And when you kill that which was trying to kill you, you bask in a moment of true power. I wanted that moment, even if it was an illusion.

Unfortunately, I couldn't afford a fight right now. My job was to protect Sadira, and the best way to do that was to avoid confrontation altogether. Sadira's skill lay not in physical strength, but in the horrible ways she could destroy a creature's mind. She cultivated fear and obedience in her own special way but was not a fighter. Furthermore, neither she nor I were at our top strength after last night's healing session. We both had to feed, and I still needed a couple more days of rest.

A familiar voice halted my descent at the second floor, jerking me from my frantic thoughts.

"What is it?" Danaus called from behind me. I turned on the stairs to find him buckling the last leather wrist guard on his right arm as he descended. His hair was damp and hung heavy about his broad shoulders. To my surprise, he was wearing a pair of dark blue jeans instead of his usual black cotton pants. His navy T-shirt was untucked and strapped down with a pair of sword sheaths crossing his back. I guess now that he was home, he felt he could go casual. Or maybe it was the fact that his mission was technically over. I had a tendency to forget how handsome he was when I was plotting how to peel his skin from the network of muscles and sinew that danced as he moved.

"I don't know yet," I said. "Get your people somewhere safe. I'll handle it." I continued down the stairs at a slower pace, reluctantly serious.

"They're being moved to the basement, and all spare hunters are going to stand guard down there," he replied, walking down one step behind me.

"Any naturi?"

"None that I can sense."

I think Danaus was about to say something else when the

heavy front doors crashed open against the walls. Splinters flew through the air and I barely had enough time to raise my arm to shield my face. There had been no warning, no surge of power. I stayed, unmoving, on the third step from the bottom, a gust of cold air trying to push me back up the stairs. Lowering my arm from my eyes, I saw Jabari step across the threshold, the wind dying away to a whimper.

I've heard humans say someone looked like the wrath of God. To me, Jabari looked far worse. Bare-chested, the nightwalker stared at me, his eyes glowing a wicked pale yellow, like so many fires I had conjured in my past. His cheekbones seemed more prominent than usual and his cheeks were hollows. For the first time since I'd met him, Jabari looked like the walking dead. He reminded me grimly of Charon, the ferryman for the underworld. Indeed, I believed Jabari had arrived to usher me from this life.

Some part of me still loved him, but even I was beginning to question who it was that I loved. The questions were piling up, and the one person I'd been willing to trust was holding a stake over my heart. Sadira's tale replayed in my head as I stared at him, dragging up painful questions as a knot of betrayal and anger rose in my throat. I had seen Jabari manipulate and use other nightwalkers like pieces on a chessboard, moving them about and sacrificing others when necessary to accomplish his ultimate goals. Somewhere along the way I'd convinced myself that I was different, that I truly mattered to the Ancient. Had I been wrong? Would he dangle me before my greatest fear in an effort to control me? *Yes*.

"Jabari!" I cried, throwing my arms up in sham surprise. "It's so good of you to join us. Please, come inside." If it had been at all possible, his gaze would have set me ablaze at that moment. I only widened my smile, my teeth clenched so hard my jaw ached.

"You were ordered to protect Sadira," he snarled, his voice crackling through the air like lightning.

"And so I have." My tone was still light and mocking. I had nothing to lose any longer and was tired of being pushed around.

"Here?" He threw open his arms to encompass the manor. At the same time, half of the little globes in the overhead chandelier exploded, dimming the light. Shadows lunged from the corners and clawed up the wall to slink across the ceiling.

"They've hunted us for centuries. It's time they protected us for a while."

"You go too far."

"No, not yet," I said with a sigh. "But don't worry; I will." To his obvious surprise, I came down the last three steps to the main hall, drawing closer to him. "Would you like to see Sadira?" Extending my right arm toward the hall along the left side of the staircase, I motioned for him to walk with me. His body was so stiff with rage, he could give only the barest of nods. I don't know why he didn't rip me in half then, beyond pure curiosity.

I preceded him down the long, narrow hall, keeping a slow pace, as if I didn't have a care in the world. What did I have to fear other than the rabid vampire at my back? The pair of hunters flanking the door headed toward the basement with a jerk of my head. No need for an audience. In a fight between nightwalkers, humans just ended up being props.

Opening the door, I saw the same tableau I'd witnessed before leaving to take a shower. Sadira was seated in her chair like a queen, her back to the wall. Tristan stood dutifully behind her with a blank expression, while another pair of hunters stood near the door and window. My own pair of guardian angels, pacing the room, paused as we entered.

"All humans out!" I announced as Jabari, Danaus, and I

entered. The two hunters quickly left the cheerful, buttercup-colored salon without another word, but Michael and Gabriel didn't move. "My angels as well," I added, my tone softening. Both frowned, but left without another word. I think instincts alone told them to put some distance from this lethal gathering.

I turned to shut the door behind them and found that Danaus was still in the room. My eyes moved from him to the door in a silent question. A grim half smile lifted one corner of his mouth for a couple of seconds. "I don't fit either of those categories."

"You may regret this," I muttered, shutting the door.

"Wouldn't be the first time where you're concerned."

That I believed. If he wanted to remain, so be it. My only worries were Jabari and my neck.

"He leaves," Jabari ordered, snapping my attention back to the Ancient. "He is not one of us." I flinched at the sharpness of his voice, but I tried to not let it show. The Elder wanted me groveling before him, cowed and obedient. Not this time.

"No." I stepped away from the door, to stand next to Danaus. My face was blank, devoid of servitude. I wasn't taunting or particularly begging for a fight, but I wanted Jabari to know that I was finally drawing the line in the sand.

I sensed more than saw it when the Ancient's arm snaked out with the intent of grabbing Danaus's neck. Gritting my teeth, I caught his wrist and shoved him backward, nearly throwing him across the room. Jabari slid across the polished hardwood floor and caught himself before he slammed into the opposite wall. In the far corner, I heard Sadira gasp and Tristan hiss softly at my unexpected response. Both seemed to shrink as Jabari growled, the sound resembling a tiger's warning more than anything that would emerge from the throat of something that had once been human. His powers flooded the room, nearly choking me. I mentally clawed my way back to the surface, refusing to be swamped by him. Truth be told, I would rather have been killed by Jabari than face the naturi again. But either way, I'd go down fighting.

"Is this what shall finally destroy us? This creature, I will not let you kill," I spat out, my lips drawn back to reveal my fangs. My posture was hunched as I waited for him to attack again, every muscle pulled taut and ready. The wound in my chest and back screamed in pain, but I pushed it back. The darkness deep inside of me began to rise up, swelling until it started to slowly blot out what was left of my humanity. It was the blood lust, the driving need to feel another creature's life clutched in the palm of your hand. I remained in front of Danaus, making it clear to the Elder that he would have to go through me first.

"There is always your failure to kill Nerian as I ordered," Jabari reminded me.

"He's dead now. Just a few centuries late."

"You also failed to protect Tabor's replacement," he continued, his body completely still. The quiet before the storm. Apparently, Sadira had succeeded in reaching him with the news that evening.

"The naturi knew where we were. They knew." Rowe always seemed capable of finding me easily. My voice dropped down close to a whisper. "I wonder how."

"What are you implying?" Jabari's fingers curled into fists, and the glow in his eyes flared, as if he was using all of his energy not to crush me. He knew exactly what I was saying.

"Not implying. Just curious," I hedged, trying to give myself some room to maneuver. "The naturi seem one step ahead no matter where I turn. They can't sense us, but Nerian knew where to find me. They knew to kill Thorne before I even knew who the hell he was. Rowe has come hunting for me twice now. Someone is betraying me." I moved a step closer.

"So you turn first on your own kind, when the enemy stands at your back," Jabari bellowed, pointing at Danaus. The nightwalker took a step to his right, moving away from the wall and closer to me.

"Not first. I've talked to them. I don't think Themis has been in contact with the naturi, and they're not the ones keeping me in the dark." I'd reached the point where I preferred to see both Danaus and Jabari dead than give either of them another chance to carve out my heart.

"You've been told everything you need to know. You do as you have been instructed."

"Bullshit!" I screamed, taking another step closer. "I stopped taking orders a long time ago, and I won't put up with your secrets when it's my life on the line. I was the one they were trying to kill in Aswan, not you."

"How do you know he didn't send for them? His people attacked you while you slept."

"Because the naturi don't follow orders either," I hissed. "Not from humans or nightwalker. Or am I wrong?"

Jabari's eyes widened before he lunged at me. I barely had enough time to jump out of the way. Pain flashed up my arm as his fingernails ripped through the sleeve and slashed my skin. I landed in a crouch and launched myself into him, colliding with his chest. He fell back with a heavy thud. Sliding across the floor, he crashed into a pale blue sofa with me on top of him. A small end table went over and a ceramic lamp was smashed, sending small shards skidding across the hardwood. I sat up, hissing at him, my fangs bared. Jabari backhanded me, snapping my head around. To him, I was nothing more than an annoying fly. I tumbled backward but quickly rolled to my feet, to find him standing as well.

"You've been hiding for a couple of years now," I said before he could attack again. "Why? Why hide when the naturi can't sense you? Afraid of someone else finding you?"

"I want to be left alone."

"Did you know about the naturi?"

Instead of answering, Jabari threw himself at me again. The haze of anger clouding my thoughts also slowed my reflexes, allowing him to catch me before I could move out of his grasp. His momentum carried us into the wall, and a grunt escaped me as my spine dug into it. Lifting my legs as soon as I hit, I placed my feet against Jabari's chest and kicked out with all my strength, pushing him off me. Then I pushed off the wall and lunged. Jabari was just getting back to his feet when I hit him, reaching for his throat. Once again he brushed me aside.

"Did you know?" I asked again, jumping to my feet. I shoved against the sofa, sending it skidding across the room, its wooden feet screeching against the floor. I didn't want anything in my way when I went after him again. The Ancient stood unmoving, watching me. "Did you?" My scream rattled the glass in the window.

"Mira, stop," Sadira said. I could barely feel her tension and fear over Jabari's angry powers. She'd stopped cloaking her presence when he appeared. Now I could feel all of her chaotic emotions, even hear some of her thoughts.

"Then tell me I'm wrong," I demanded, never taking my eyes off Jabari. His blank expression never changed. "Tell me."

"You are wrong," he said, carefully enunciating each word, as if talking to an addled child.

"I don't believe you." The words came out choked and broken.

"That is not my concern."

"It will be," I whispered, straightening my stance. I was no longer poised for the attack, but I wasn't relaxed either.

The fight was over for now. "I don't know who you're protecting, but I hope they're worth it."

"It should be your life you worry over. You are the one who has failed to reform the triad. You are the one who has brought your sire to this haven for hunters," Jabari said, his lips pulling back in a sneer.

For a brief moment I wondered if he was referring to Sadira or himself, but I let the thought drop. If it was true, Jabari obviously didn't want me to know, which gave me a slight edge for now. "You gave me an impossible task," I snapped. "I couldn't protect Sadira and fetch Thorne at the same time. Not with the naturi running around. She had to be put somewhere safe and this was my only option. She has come to no harm. If anything, they've treated her like a queen since she stepped foot on their grounds." Reaching up, I shoved a lock of hair that had fallen in front of my eyes behind my ear.

"You should have taken her with you. She could have saved Thorne."

"Maybe, but I doubt it," I said with a shake of my head. "I couldn't have properly protected them both. But none of this matters. The triad has been reformed."

"What? How?" Sadira demanded, springing from her chair. I could feel the hope blossoming in her chest. I clung to that light emotion against Jabari's drowning anger.

"Me. I will be the third," I said, my eyes darting from Sadira back to Jabari. I didn't want to be, and if we could find someone else, I would happily hand over the position, but that didn't seem to be an option.

Jabari laughed, the dark sound crawling across my flesh like a hundred tiny spider legs. "Where would you get such an idea?"

I glanced over at Danaus, who was standing near the door. He was returning his sword to the sheath strapped across his back. I hadn't even seen him draw it. He paused in the middle of the act for half a breath, his eyes narrowing on me. "I spoke with a warlock," I continued, returning my attention to Jabari.

"And what does he know about the triad?"

"Apparently a lot. At the very least, he knows more about what is going on than I do. He said that the triad has already been reformed."

"He said you would take Tabor's place?"

"Not exactly, but it's not like there's a lot of other vampires hanging around. He could have meant Tristan, but I didn't think so since he's still cutting his fangs."

Jabari's gaze never wavered from me as his smile widened and I saw his beautiful white fangs. It reminded me of Nerian's smile, with all the grim, painful promises it held. "You fool," he said, the words encased in a chuckle. "You believe the word of a human over your own kind."

"I'm just trying to survive, and you've done nothing to help that cause recently."

"Mira, my child, you can't be the third," Sadira whispered, as if trying to soften the blow. "It's impossible."

"Why? Because we're of the same bloodline?"

"You've turned on your own kind," Jabari snarled.

"Not yet, but I see little reason to defend them at the moment. Why can't I be the third?"

"You're not strong enough."

"Bullshit. I'm stronger than Sadira, and I'm stronger than Thorne was. Why can't I?"

"Mira!"

I turned on my heel, startled by Danaus's voice. His presence had been pushed from my mind by Jabari's attack, and now I stood so I could look at both him and Jabari, not wanting to put my back to the Ancient I no longer trusted.

"They're coming," the hunter said.

I read it in Danaus's face before he could speak. Tension had crept in around the corners of his mouth and pulled his lips into a worried frown. A thick, heavy silence pushed into the room, and it was all I could do to keep from drowning in it.

"How many?"

"Enough."

My throat suddenly constricted and I'm not sure what kept my knees from buckling. Either it was too many to bother to count or it was better I didn't know.

"Do we have time to leave?" I asked, wondering how long it would take to get everyone out of the compound.

"No, they're too close."

"Who?" Jabari interrupted.

"We'll have to make a stand here," I said, desperate to get hold of a situation that continued to spiral out of my control. "Your people safe?"

"Safe as can be expected." Danaus reached up and withdrew one of the swords strapped to his back. His deep blues flicked before he tossed it to me.

"Who's coming?" Jabari demanded again, his shout filling the room.

I slashed the air a couple of times with the sword, testing its weight and balance, purposefully ignoring Jabari for a moment. It wasn't the same one I had borrowed in the Aswan cemetery. It seemed of a higher quality. Maybe something from his private collection, kept for only special occasions? *Lucky me.*

At last I looked up at Jabari and smiled. "The naturi."

Twenty-Six

The naturi were coming. My fingers tightened around the sword and I closed my eyes for a moment, drawing the anger and tension into a single ball that resided in the pit of my stomach. I was done running.

Turning to look at Jabari, I resisted the urge to point the sword at his chest. No reason to antagonize him any more. We had enough problems. "Are you with us or against us?"

"And who exactly is this 'us'?" he sneered, his hands clenched into fists at his sides. "Humans? The hunters?"

"Anyone who wishes to stand against the naturi. I welcome both hunter and nightwalker. We can settle the question of my allegiance some other time."

The nightwalker drew up to his full height and straightened his shoulders. "I harbor no love for the naturi."

"Great. Stay here," I said, trying not to think about the fact that I was giving orders to an Elder. I had no doubt I'd pay for it later, assuming there was a later for me. Desperate to keep the situation in hand, my attention flashed to the other two vampires in the room. Tristan stood with his arm around Sadira's delicate shoulders, as if trying to comfort her, but the fear in his wide blue eyes told another tale. He had faced a small group of naturi with me last night and I barely survived. He was in no hurry to push his luck any further.

"You are expendable. Jabari and Sadira are not," I said, pointing the sword at him. "Protect them no matter what."

"Where are you going?" he asked, his grip tightening on Sadira.

"To see if I can find more help," I called over my shoulder as I marched out of the room with Danaus following on my heels.

I paused in the hall, trying to assess the battlefield, as Danaus closed the door. There were too many rooms, too many doors and windows. "How many entrances are there on the ground floor?" I asked.

Danaus stood beside me now, his eyes also scanning the terrain. "Three; front door, back door off the kitchen, and a garden entrance."

"Not to mention windows in every room," I murmured, talking mostly to myself.

"We can move to the basement," he suggested. "There are no windows down there and only one entrance."

"We would be trapped." I shook my head, my hair falling around my face. "They could wait us out until dawn, then come down and slaughter everyone. Besides, they are only after us. I'd rather keep the naturi away from your librarian convention downstairs." I continued down the hall to the front doors, which were shut again, my heels hitting the hardwood floor the only sound in the silent manor. "Where's Ryan?"

"I'm here." A weary voice drifted down the stairs toward us. I looked up to see the warlock seated at the top of the stairs on the second floor. He'd shed his jacket, his shirt-sleeves were rolled up past his elbows, and sweat slicked back the hair at his temples. His powers filled the air like an electric current looking for an outlet. I hadn't noticed the power crackling around me until I saw him, my focus having been centered on the coming horde.

"How long have you been holding them off?" I asked, unable to keep the note of awe out of my voice. The air sizzled with whatever spell he was working, but even now I could feel it weakening.

"You don't think I called them?" he asked in surprise.

"You're not that stupid."

"Thanks." His mouth quirked in a half smile. "I'll do what I can to hold them off, but I won't last much longer."

"Save it," I said, waving him off. The spell he'd worked had left him nearly exhausted and he would need his strength. "Go to the basement with your people. The naturi are after my kind, but I can't promise they won't slaughter humans just for the fun of it."

Danaus walked up the stairs past me and helped Ryan get to his feet. The warlock descended to the first floor with his hand on the hunter's shoulder. Ryan still looked a bit shaky, but appeared to be catching his second wind.

Seeing the two men standing side by side for the first time, I realized that I liked Danaus's eyes better. There was something more human in those cobalt depths than Ryan's glittering gold; something that still whispered of hope. It was missing from Ryan's eyes, creating a strange juxtaposition. Danaus was a man who said he was doomed to hell, and yet hope still flickered faintly in his precious blue orbs.

On the other hand, Ryan was a fraction of Danaus's age, with a smile perpetually haunting his lips, but he'd lost that flicker of hope that seemed to haunt all creatures. I don't know what a human had to endure to become a warlock, but was it truly worse than what Danaus could have seen in his centuries of life?

"Do you have any more magic users lurking about?" I asked, snapping back to the problem at hand.

"A few, but they're no match for what is coming," Ryan said as he reached the bottom step.

"Have them charm the door and any weapons you can dig up," I instructed. "Iron hurts the naturi. A bullet to the head or heart will work. Otherwise, you generally have to cut off their head or remove the heart to kill them."

"A lot like killing vampires," Danaus interjected.

"Or humans," I said, glaring at him. "Get Ryan downstairs and lock the door behind you."

"I stay up here," Danaus stated, earning a startled look from me.

"Apparently I'm not the only one with loyalty issues." The smile slipped from my lips before it could fully form. "You need to protect your people."

"I can do that best up here. Ryan will be in the basement should we fail." He paused, smiling when I could not. "Besides, we have unfinished business."

Yes, our great showdown. Misfit versus misfit. I had forgotten somehow. Couldn't let something else kill me before he had his shot.

"Very well," I said with an indifferent shrug. Looking over at Ryan, I bit back a sigh of frustration. "I'm sorry. I had no desire to endanger your people."

"I knew the risk when I agreed. All I ask is that you win." He turned and started down the hall toward the basement, the fingers of his right hand trailing along the wall as if to steady himself should he suddenly falter.

"You were wrong earlier," I called after him. "The triad hasn't been reformed. It can't be me."

Ryan looked over his shoulder, his palm pressed flat against the wood-panel wall. He stared at Danaus for a couple of seconds, then at me. I didn't feel any stir of power. He was just thinking, as if reassessing his earlier conclusion. "No, you have everything you need," he said at last.

I nodded, though I'm not sure I actually believed him. If it wasn't me, then it meant Tristan was seriously holding out on me. It had been a long time since I'd last underestimated the power of another vampire. It was a mistake one generally didn't have a chance to make twice.

As Ryan disappeared down the stairs, he was quickly replaced by both of my guardian angels. I shut my eyes and clenched my teeth as I bit back a curse in rough Italian. Somehow I'd managed to forget they were here. I should have sent them home as soon as we hit London.

"Where do you want us?" Gabriel inquired, a gun clenched in each hand.

"Back down in the basement," I said, waving my sword toward the hall they had just come down.

"Our job is to protect you, not these people," Gabriel replied, not moving from where he stood.

"Your job is to follow my orders, and I'm ordering you to get back downstairs!"

"No," Michael said, standing stubbornly beside Gabriel.

"I can handle things up here. I haven't survived six hundred years depending on the protection of humans. Now get back downstairs before I drain you both."

"We—" But the sound of cracking wood and shattering glass halted Gabriel's rebellious words. I was beginning to see serious drawbacks to this whole loyalty thing. Unfortunately, now was not the time to discuss some of its finer aspects. Our guests were knocking.

"Danaus!" I shouted, turning my attention back to the entrance to the manor. Facing the front doors, I gripped the sword he'd given me in my right hand, my legs spread apart as I awaited the attack.

"They're surrounding us," he said, standing beside me with a weapon in each hand. "Six at the front door, another dozen coming in through the windows."

"They're already in the room with Jabari," I told him. I couldn't sense the naturi, but I could see them through Sadira's eyes. Fear had ramped up her powers and in turn strengthened our natural connection. There was a strong link between us after I had taken in so much of her blood last night. We could share thoughts and emotions with no effort. We could also see and feel things each other felt, introducing a potentially dangerous distraction into the mix.

"Gabriel, you're in with Jabari and Sadira. Keep them alive no matter what," I shouted. "Michael, you've got my back." I didn't look at them, but kept my eyes trained on the door. Their footsteps echoed down the hall as each took up their new positions. Their fear filled the air, teasing me with its thick, heady scent. There was nothing that could excite the senses of a vampire faster. Except maybe the scent of fresh blood and a woman's silence-shattering scream, but that was on the hunt.

Twisting my right wrist once, I impatiently slashed the air with Danaus's sword. I was eager to start this dance at last. It was my turn to lead.

As if in an attempt to be courteous of my wishes, the doors exploded open. I have to give them their due. Where Jabari had thrown them open, the naturi blew them completely off their hinges. Both large oak doors flew through the air, spinning like an out-of-control windmill. I dove sideways, knocking Danaus to the floor. As I fell, I grabbed the front of Michael's shirt with my free hand, pulling him down with us in a large heap. I rolled off Danaus, careful that the dagger and sword he held didn't accidentally relieve me of my head.

Behind me, arrows whizzed through the open doorway and thunked heavily into the wooden staircase. They were trying to clear the entrance. I was on my feet when I felt a shift in the wind.

A loud cacophony of noise filled the air, a grating mix of wings, claws, and calls. Raptors of all shapes and sizes filled the large entryway, making it suddenly seem small. We remained trapped on our knees against the wall as ravens, owls, hawks, and falcons flew through the halls, heading up the staircase and then back down again. Few bothered to attack us, but that wasn't their goal. The naturi had sent the birds in as a distraction to buy them some time.

Michael lifted his gun and squeezed off a couple of rounds, picking off a couple of the larger birds when they got too close. I covered his wrist with my hand and forced him to lower the gun.

"Don't waste your ammunition," I shouted over the noise. I jerked my head to the side as a brown owl dove close enough to drag its long talons across my cheek. Pain slashed through me and I fought the urge to press my hand to my cheek. If I lifted my arm, I'd only end up with a series of scratches.

"Mira, we can't stay like this!" Danaus snapped.

With a growl, I grabbed a vase off a nearby pedestal and threw it across the room toward the largest clump of birds as they fought for space in the air. The porcelain shattered on impact with the chandelier, sending it wildly swinging overhead. Shadows lunged and stretched in a gruesome dance around the room. Several birds were knocked from the air, hitting the hardwood floor with a heavy thud.

As the birds scattered, I lifted my left hand and focused on anything that was flying. Feathers instantly caught on fire, filling the room with a horrid stench. I killed only a few, though I wished I hadn't been forced to kill any of them, but it was enough to clear the air. The birds of prey scattered, with some heading out the open door while others flew up to find sanctuary on the third floor.

With the birds preoccupied, I turned my attention back to

the entryway in time to see a naturi edge forward, his wrist
crossbow aimed at me. In a single, liquid movement I pulled
a knife from Danaus's belt and flung it at my adversary. The
blade buried itself in his throat and nearly severed his head.
He fell backward, the shaft firing harmlessly up at the ceiling. The dead naturi from the animal clan disappeared into
the dark doorway, out of sight.

"Come out and play, blood drinker," sang a melodious
voice outside the door.

"You come in. I'll reunite you with your brother, Nerian,"
I replied, tightening my grip on the sword. Some part of me
was relieved to find that it wasn't Rowe once again calling
out to me.

To my surprise, the naturi stepped into the doorway, short
sword drawn. Danaus raised his gun, but I put a restraining
hand over the top of the weapon. "Take care of our other
guests, and cover my back," I said, motioning with my head
toward the opposite end of the hall and the back door as I
rose to my feet. The telltale sound of claws clicking across
hardwood indicated that several wolves had found their way
into the manor. Danaus and Michael had their own set of
problems while I took care of the naturi in the doorway.

Barely topping five feet, he looked like a slender youth,
more akin to a young willow than the human he was supposed to resemble. His long blond hair was pulled back, revealing a face similar to that of a fifteen-year-old boy, with
its fresh sprinkling of freckles and wide green eyes. But
his appearance belied the years of experience that hummed
through his thin frame and filled his narrowed eyes.

"I thought we'd see Nerian together. I understand he had
some special plans for you." A malicious grin split his young
face. A chill crawled up my skin, sinking sharp fangs into
my muscles. He was from the light clan, I had no doubt. Neither us could summon fire to destroy the other.

Closing the distance between us, I swung my sword with enough force to cleave his body in two. He sidestepped the blow for the most part, and deflected what he couldn't escape with his blade. He was quicker than most naturi I had encountered so far, each movement precise and fluid like a dance. Was he another form of Danaus? A creature that had studied the fine art of hunting nightwalkers?

The chaos around me dulled and the sounds trickled into my ears now as if enveloped in cotton. There was only the naturi standing before me in a pair of worn blue jeans with the left knee torn out. Hatred burned in his almond-shaped eyes.

Our swords scraped and clanged, searching for an entrance into the soft, meaty parts of the body. Dodging a thrust aimed to place his blade between my ribs, I brought my own sword down. He backpedaled, moving smoothly out of danger. With teeth clenched, I tossed my head, moving a lock of hair from where it had fallen in front of my eyes. The creature tried to use the momentary distraction to his advantage, slashing at my stomach. I was ready, catching his blade with mine and pushing him back toward the opposite wall.

I screamed. A searing pain splintered throughout my left shoulder, like someone had shoved a red-hot knitting needle into it. Someone had put a naturi dart in my shoulder. The pain slithered under my shoulder blade, slinking down through my muscles like liquid fire. I barely managed to block the naturi's next two attacks as my mind struggled through the fog of pain.

"Danaus!" I shouted, kicking my blond adversary back against the front doorjamb.

"We're being overrun from the back!" His deep voice boomed over the sound of singing steel and breaking furniture. "Hurry up!"

"Fine," I growled to myself. My left arm was starting to

go numb and was nearly useless. I couldn't close my left fingers around a weapon if I had to.

"You look tired," the naturi mocked. "Want a drink?" He tilted his head to expose the long line of his throat. I feinted with my sword for his neck, then abruptly switched directions and plunged the blade into his heart up to the hilt.

"I'm not into junk food," I said as I slowly withdrew the blade and slashed it through the air, removing his head from his neck. The unattached member bounced and rolled away, his wide, gemlike eyes staring up at the ceiling, lost and unfocused. "Tell Nerian I said hi."

Spinning around, I found my companions barely holding a mix of naturi and wolves at bay at the opposite end of the hall. Inside the salon that held Sadira and the others, I could still hear the constant crash of furniture and gunfire. Sadira's thoughts were muffled but her fear was still riding high. However, that was matched by anger, which was encouraging. Sometimes the only thing that kept you moving was raw anger and hatred.

Gritting my teeth, I lifted my left arm. A low groan broke from my throat as the pain threatened to overcome my fragmented thoughts. I ignored it as best as I could and focused on a collection of creatures drawing closer to Michael and Danaus. It took only a couple of seconds for each one to explode in a glorious ball of fire. Only when they thumped lifelessly to the floor did I finally extinguish the flames. I'd taken an ugly risk using my powers. If I used them too often, it would leave me exhausted and vulnerable. Not a good combination when battling the naturi, particularly since I wasn't at full strength before this battle even started.

My left arm dropped back down to my side and I swayed on my feet. I opened my mouth to ask for a naturi count from Danaus when Michael rushed toward me. Stunned, I didn't think to move when he turned his shoulder into my chest and sent me back toward the open entryway. I stumbled over the body of the naturi I'd killed moments ago and landed hard on my butt. My left hand fell in a cool, wet spot on the Oriental rug. Glancing down, I discovered I was sitting in a spreading pool of blood that was leaking from the dead naturi. I frantically wiped it on my shirt and pants, desperate to be clean of the stuff. I imagine there is truly no stranger sight than a vampire wiping blood off like it carried the plague.

With fangs bared, I tore my gaze from the blood back to Michael, a vicious curse on the tip of my tongue, when I instantly stilled. He stood over me, his face slack. His blue eyes were staring blindly at some distant point I could not see. Something cold slipped down into my bones and knotted in my throat. A small, damp spot in the middle of his chest was growing by the second across his shirt while his skin paled to a gut-wrenching gray.

Behind him I heard the soft, liquid squish and suck of a blade being pulled from muscle and flesh. I noticed then that the door to the first room off the hall was open, when all the doors had been closed moments before.

I lurched forward on my knees, catching Michael's limp form as he fell forward. Lowering him to the ground, my eyes never wavered from my angel's pale face. Beside me, I felt more than saw Danaus attack the one that had stabbed my guardian. With a trembling hand, I smoothed his golden locks from his forehead, inadvertently smearing some of the naturi's blood across his perfect skin.

Michael's eyes drooped closed and his full lips briefly formed my name.

"Sleep, my angel," I whispered, my voice as rough as concrete. I bent down and pressed my parted lips to his. "You've done well."

The tension and lines slowly disappeared from his handsome face, as if time was kindly erasing some of the wear and tear he had suffered through his long years. He was moving away from the pain and the fear. Peace was settling inside him.

Something inside of me screamed in pain. I should have sent him home. I should have never included him in my life. Michael was a breath of fresh air. He had glowed with light and vitality, and I'd seen to its destruction.

Holding him, I could feel the life draining from his body, his heart slowing to a thick, torpid beat. His soul was pulling loose of its bonds, struggling to be free. I couldn't heal him. With all my power and abilities, I couldn't heal the human body beyond the closing of puncture wounds from my fangs. The best I could do was try to turn him into a nightwalker, but I wouldn't. His soul wanted to be free like a kite on a string. I knew I had to let him go no matter how badly I needed him to stay.

Twenty-Seven

The pain in my left arm was gone. I stood without actually using my muscles. I just pushed out with my powers until I was lifted to my feet. Around me the sounds of battle dimmed and the world faded. Time ground to a crawl, edging along the floorboards like a multilegged insect. I paused long enough to grab both of Michael's guns and my sword. Tucking one gun in my pants at the hollow of my back, I kept the other in my left hand while the sword remained tightly clutched in my right hand.

To say that I was angry would have been an understatement. I wanted to send a wall of fire through the entire building, cleansing it of every moving creature, breathing or not. Michael was gone and I wanted a gallon of naturi blood for every drop spilled of his. I wanted them dead.

Striding into the front parlor, I paused long enough to assess the scene. Furniture had been overturned and the lighting was dim as one small lamp in the far corner fought back the darkness. Danaus battled two naturi at once, a scimitar in one hand and a short sword in the other. A flicker of light danced across the steel that had yet to be smeared with blood. Three more naturi stood near the window where they had come in, watching the show. I would have normally let Danaus have his fun, but I just wanted them dead. One of them had killed Michael.

Stepping forward, I lifted the gun toward Danaus's assailants. Without hesitation, I squeezed off several rounds, putting one into the forehead of each naturi before they could turn on me. The recoil sent a shock wave up my arm and I hissed in pain, but it didn't slow me as I swung around and fired the last three rounds at the remaining naturi. Only one found its mark, briefly pinning the brown-haired creature to the blood-splattered wall before he slid to the floor.

Out of bullets, I pitched the gun at the closest naturi, shattering his nose and left cheekbone. He screamed and stumbled backward, holding his face. I closed the distance, rage bubbling in my veins. His companion stepped forward to protect him, and I left his head rocking on the floor seconds later.

The wounded elflike creature lashed out, swinging his sword wildly, half blinded by the pain. In a flash of movement I was standing behind the creature. I grabbed a fistful of brown hair and jerked his head back before running my blade across his throat. I was careful to slice the main arteries and open his windpipe. It's a subtle art; something learned through years of torture and death. If I had left him like that, he might have drowned in his own blood. Unfortunately, I wasn't sure how quickly he would heal so I lopped off both his hands. I didn't want him coming back to stab me later. This way he would at least bleed to death. He would suffer awhile longer than if I'd just decapitated him like his companion. I wanted his death to be a slow one.

Danaus grabbed my right arm as I started to leave the room, halting my progress. "He's not dead," the hunter growled. His hand bit into my flesh while his powers beat angrily against me.

"He will be." Danaus didn't release me, his gaze burning into my cold eyes. I knew what he wanted. He didn't believe in torture. "Remember, they did far worse to me. At least he knows he's going to die. I had no such guarantee." I wrenched my arm free of his grasp and continued to the hall.

I was relieved to see he followed directly behind me instead of ending the naturi's suffering. Maybe he knew this wasn't the best time to cross me. I paused in the hall, careful not to look down at Michael's cold body. Instead I gazed up the hall to find three more naturi heading toward the room holding Jabari and the others, looking to attack the small group from behind. I pulled the second and last gun from my pants and plowed through the three that were now coming after me.

"Are there any more coming?" I stepped on the body of the nearest naturi, indifferent as to whether he was dead yet, as I walked toward the closed door.

"Yes, but we have a couple of minutes," Danaus said, following close behind me. "The last of them are in with the others."

I shoved open the door and for a second my confidence slipped several notches. The room looked like a cyclone had blown through. All the furniture had been destroyed. Exquisite landscapes were ripped off the walls, their heavy frames used as weapons. The walls were pockmarked with bullets and gaping holes created by flying bodies. Corpses littered the floor, broken and torn.

Sadira stood in one corner with a wounded Tristan behind her. One of the legs of the chair she'd been sitting in was tightly clenched in her fist and her fangs were bared. Other than the fangs, she still didn't look like a vampire, just a mother protecting her child. Of course, we're talking a half-crazed, bloodthirsty mother with her blood-splashed yellow shirt sticking to her thin frame and dark hair flowing down her back.

My Gabriel still stood strong beside her, a knife in one hand and a naturi short sword in the other. I didn't want to contemplate how long he had been without ammo. His right shoulder and left thigh were bleeding, but he didn't waver, so I hoped the wounds were superficial. I couldn't lose him too.

And in the eye of the storm stood Jabari. His energy pulsed in violent waves through the room. At least a dozen bodies circled him, torn apart in various ways. The nightwalker stood empty-handed, covered in the blood of his enemies. Jabari didn't use a sword or knife. He preferred to take apart his enemies with his bare hands. It was a lost art.

Watching him face down the five naturi that currently circled him, I remembered why I had always loved him. I loved his strength and his power. I loved that I only felt anger radiating from him, no fear, no doubt, no indecision. With little effort and no hesitation, Jabari pulled the heart from a naturi's chest. He tossed the two objects carelessly aside and moved onto his next prey.

And deep down I knew I was standing in that line, no matter what happened from here on out.

"Shall we?" I said, looking over at Danaus as I tried gauge the best place to enter the fray. Relieving Sadira and Gabriel would probably be the wisest place to start. Jabari was doing fine on his own.

"After you," Danaus said, motioning for me to precede him. I was beginning to think he was enjoying himself. He was splattered with blood and a line of sweat ran from his temple to his hard jaw. His narrowed eyes were keenly focused on the naturi in the room, weighing their skills. But there was also a glitter of amusement there, soaking in the thrill of the battle and the rush of adrenaline. At that moment, Danaus was more of a predator than the naturi could ever be. He was a dark stalker riding the wave of blood and death, his human side obliterated.

With a slight shake of my head, I jumped in, lunging at the naturi that was backing Gabriel toward the wall. After a couple of exchanges he was dead, his head rolling across the room. In the spare moment between adversaries, I tossed Gabriel the gun I'd been carrying. I wasn't sure how many bullets it still had, but it was better than nothing.

"Keep back and make sure nothing comes through the door," I said over my shoulder as one of the two naturi attacking Danaus rushed me. We crossed swords, circling each other the best we could considering the floor was thick with miscellaneous body parts and slick with blood. Poorly balanced with my left foot on someone's chest while my right foot rested on another's hand, I blocked an overhead blow aimed to split my skull. I finished by swinging my blade down, cleaving my foe in two.

Half stumbling off the dead body, I looked up in time to see Danaus skillfully finish off his opponent with a neat spinning slash that not only lifted and threw the naturi across the room, but cut him clear to the spine. While I was skillful with a sword, watching Danaus was like taking in the Russian ballet. I could feel more than see the ripple of muscle and sinew dancing beneath his tanned skin. Every movement was precisely timed and balanced for the maximum effect. The light throb of his powers tumbled from him to wash through me.

I glanced around the room. Jabari was down to his last two naturi. Sadira knelt beside Tristan, her bloody hands cupping his pale cheeks. Gabriel leaned against the wall near them, struggling to catch his breath.

"How bad is it?" I inquired, looking down at the young

nightwalker. We were all covered in blood, making it hard to tell who was actually bleeding.

"The cut isn't deep, but the sword was charmed," Sadira said, flicking worried eyes over to me. There was a smear of blood across her forehead, and her blood-soaked clothes clung to her slender frame, making her look even frailer.

"It slows the healing. It's more pain than actual poison. He'll survive," I said, turning my attention to my guardian angel. He stood staring down at the gun in his hand, a frown on his full lips.

"He died saving my life," I volunteered, struggling to keep my voice steady as an image of Michael lying in my arms flashed across my mind. I should have been paying more attention. I might not have been able to sense the naturi, but I should have heard the door opening or the footsteps.

Gabriel nodded. "Then he died happy." His fingers tightened around the handgun, his expression hardening. He'd said the words as much for me as for himself. My brown-haired angel had outlived three bodyguards now. The other two had been brash and careless, picking a fight when they should have known better. Michael, in contrast, had been smart. He knew when to keep his head down and how to follow orders. In the end, I was just bad for him.

Forcing my attention back to Danaus, I pushed those regrets aside for now. They would only distract me and get me killed. Later, I would cry bloody tears for my fallen angel. The hunter was staring toward the broken window, his expression intense and drawn. It wasn't good.

"Here they come."

I was already moving before the last word crossed his lips. Jabari had just ripped the arms off his final opponent and was standing in the open in the center of the room. Much like Michael had with me earlier this horrible night, I put my shoulder into Jabari, throwing us both to the ground as a barrage of arrows entered the room through the window. These bastards were starting to become predictable.

Frowning, I looked down to find Jabari staring up at me with a stunned look in his wide brown eyes. I guess I would have too, had I been in the same position. Less than an hour ago we'd tried to kill each other.

"It's been years since we had fun like this," I said, lying across his strong chest.

Jabari gave a weary sigh, his eyes suddenly turning sad. His face had lost its walking dead look. He looked almost human, or at least a little less like a corpse. "I still do not understand you, desert flower." He reached up and tucked a dirty, wet strand of hair behind my ear. "But things have not changed between us."

"I don't expect them to. You are just one of the many people who wish to kill me right now," I reminded him as I rolled off his chest and to my feet. I remained squatting down as another barrage of arrows soared through the room. I could smell his blood now that we were so close. He had been cut. It was impossible to tell how many times or how deep. As an Ancient, he would be able to tolerate the pain better than most, but without rest or a meal, he was going to slow down. We all were.

"Promise me something," I continued, my eyes locked on the window.

"What do you desire?" He knelt beside me, his long body tensed and ready for the attack. His soft accent rippled across me like a soothing hand rubbing my back.

"I love it when you say that," I teased in a dreamy voice. He said nothing, but his expression hardened in warning. I was pushing my luck. "When the time comes, let it be between us. Don't let the Coven send one of its flunkies. I deserve better than that." I looked over to find him smiling, white fangs peeking out beneath his lips.

"As you wish." His voice was deep and solemn.

Not quite. I wished to walk away from this mess and go home. I wished that I could push the naturi, Themis, Danaus, and this whole nightmare to the farthest reaches of my mind. I wished for my fairy godmother, the good witch of the north, or some other bitch with a wand to glide in here and zap these arrow-shooting assholes. But I wasn't counting on it.

"How many?" I called across the room. Danaus frowned at me, his grip tightening on the short sword in his hand. He knelt behind some broken furniture near Sadira and Tristan. The naturi blood was beginning to darken and dry on his skin. His cobalt blue eyes glittered in the weak lamp light.

"You don't want to know."

"Tell me."

"Thirty—more or less."

I nodded, my expression carefully blank. I wanted to scream that it was impossible. I didn't think there could have been two dozen naturi on the entire island. Unfortunately, one nightwalker was already down and another was starting to weaken. Sadira could hold her own better than I'd previously thought, but Gabriel wasn't going to last much longer. I was tempted to call for Ryan, but his own people would need him. We were on our own.

As if on cue, naturi started leaping through the open window. Danaus was nice enough to take out the first one from across the room by carefully placing his knife in the creature's forehead. It was enough to startle the naturi standing next to him, buying me an extra second as I jumped to my feet. The first few fell quickly, but our little group was soon pushed back by their sheer number.

I was only vaguely aware of my companions. I just kept moving, blocking, and slashing. Yet, it seemed for every one

I killed, I was forced back a step as two more took his place. Frustration and fatigue finally got the better of me. The naturi I faced now wasn't a better swordsman, only lucky. I raised my sword to block a swing aimed at my neck and missed the dagger he plunged into my stomach with his free hand. I removed his head with a scream of frustration and pain, but the damage was done.

Crumpling to my knees, the naturi poison surged through my body, adding to the renewed throbbing ache in my left shoulder. Desperate, I did the only thing I could think of: I created fire. It was all I had left. The flames leapt up from the floor in front of me and quickly spread down the line until it separated the naturi from our little group. The naturi stepped back, watching us, possibly wondering what I would do next or waiting for a member of the light clan to appear so he could remove my final weapon.

"Burn them, Mira!" Sadira screamed from some distant point off to my right.

"I can't." The words escaped me as a hoarse whisper, but I know she heard me over the crackling flames. My sword clattered to the floor and I pulled the dagger from my stomach. The pain was already beginning to crush my thoughts, and I knew I wouldn't be able to keep the flames going much longer. Still weak from the previous night's battle, I had too little strength left to call upon.

"Burn them, Mira!" Jabari commanded angrily. "Destroy them all."

I wanted to say no, but I was too tired to even form the word. I looked up to find Danaus standing beside me, his hand extended, offering to help me to my feet.

"Let's finish this together," he calmly said. "Your life is mine to enjoy when I choose."

I wanted to laugh. Danaus would choose now to make a joke, repeating what I'd said about him days ago to Lucas.

I think I smiled. I'm not really sure since I could no longer feel my lips over the pain in my abdomen.

But most important, he was making a deal with me; one last push with us both using our powers to destroy the naturi that stood watching their prey. If we survived, we'd both be exhausted and at the mercy of whoever was left standing. Unfortunately, we were out of options.

Slowly, I lifted my bloody right hand from my stomach and placed it in Danaus's hand. And I screamed. Whatever pain I'd felt from the naturi poison was a mere bee sting compared to the power flowing through my body now. It surged down my arm and through my limbs, threatening to peel my flesh from my bones. It kept building, trying to rip me apart.

Burn them.

I blinked and found myself standing somehow, but the room was growing black. "I—I can't see them," I said in a choked voice. Panic was crowding in where the pain had yet to sink.

Yes, you can.

This time I realized the voice in my head belonged to Danaus. I wanted to curse and scream at him, but something strange caught my attention. I suddenly realized the room was more crowded now. A split-second search revealed I could now sense the naturi.

I picked through the occupants of the room as the pain built to a point where it seemed I was hanging onto consciousness by a thread. As I reached out, there was only one thought left in my brain—to kill them. I mentally tried to grab their hearts and set them on fire. It was a trick I'd used in the past that had proved effective, but something would not let me. It pushed me toward this almost wispy throb of energy in each naturi. Too weak to fight it, I gave in and wrapped the powers building in me around that bit of smoke.

Another scream ripped from my throat, louder than the first, as the energy flowed out of me. My knees buckled and I fell, still tightly clasping Danaus's hand as if it were my last anchor to sanity. As the pain ebbed, I heard the thought again.

Kill them all.

My focus cleared and I felt more naturi. Without hesitation I pushed outward, past the walls of the manor, into the trees surrounding the compound. I set aflame every throb of naturi energy I ran across, pushing the power out until I finally encountered a different feeling of power blocking my reach somewhere miles from the Compound.

Then the energy stopped. Beside me, I heard Danaus drop to his knees, my hand slipping from his to thud against the cold, sticky floor. The room was silent except for his ragged breaths. My body still hurt with an intensity I never thought possible, but my thoughts were clearing, and I wished they hadn't.

I realized with a startling clarity what I had done. I'd destroyed their souls; wiped them completely from existence. Previously, I had just set their bodies on fire. Yes, I killed them with a certain amount of glee, but their souls had been free to pursue whatever afterlife they believed in. This time there was nothing left. My eyes were closed but I could smell the charred bodies and burned hair. I had destroyed them completely. And not just the ones attacking us. I had obliterated every naturi within several miles of the Themis compound.

Twenty-Eight

The silence was overwhelming. After the heavy pound of footsteps, clang of steel, and screams of pain, the quiet was suffocating. Even Sadira's thoughts were now hushed. I could still feel her in the room, but there was only a muffled confusion. Did she know what I had done? I hated the naturi with every fiber of my being, but had I known I was capable of such utter destruction, I would never have committed the atrocity. Taking a life is one thing. The body ceases, but something of the creature still lives on somewhere. I had stopped that, done something I didn't think possible.

But how? It didn't make sense. I had never done such a thing before. Even at my peak, I should have been able to only flambé the occupants of the room, if even that. There were so many, and I was exhausted.

Something happened when I touched Danaus. Not only had I been able to sense them, which is unheard of among nightwalkers, but I could also destroy their souls.

Slowly, I opened my eyes and turned my head to the right to look at Danaus. The ebony-haired hunter sat on the floor beside me, his body hunched over. His head was bowed, leaving his face hidden behind a curtain of long dark locks.

He had been affected as much as I, his breath still ragged and uneven. When he finally looked over at me, I saw my horror mirrored in his blue eyes.

Danaus reached out to touch my arm, but I lurched across the floor, pushing away from him. "Don't touch me!" I shrieked. I cringed, nearly curling into a ball as a fresh wave of pain washed through my body. It was blinding, but my fear of what had happened was greater. I know it didn't make much sense. I had crawled all over the man on more than one occasion and nothing had happened, but the memory and pain were still too fresh.

"Mira?" Sadira said, her voice a fragile shade of its normal strength.

"They're gone." My words had been reduced to a pathetic whimper. The raw ache was starting to subside at last and my thoughts were coming together in a more logical fashion. I lifted my head and reluctantly gazed around the room. It was a disaster, something from a nightmare, with body parts strewn haphazardly around the small area. But to me, the most garish of these grisly sights were the bodies of those I'd destroyed. After their souls were incinerated, their bodies had been reduced to gray and white ash. Most had collapsed into large heaps, but a few still stood like thin, dirty snowmen. Because of me, the island was dotted with dirty snowmen, empty shells waiting for a breeze.

"Then it's done," Sadira said. She was sounding strong, more sure of herself. "The triad has been reformed."

"So you believe me now," I said, trying to force a smile on my lips. But it fell short. What I really wanted was to vomit. My stomach twisted in a desperate dance to purge itself of the violence I had been responsible for, but I'd lost too much blood during the past couple nights.

"No!" Jabari roared, his angry voice an explosion in the silent room. "It can't be him."

"Him?" My head jerked up to look from Jabari to Sadira, but both of them were ignoring me.

"He's not even one of our kind," Jabari declared.

"Apparently that does not matter," Sadira said matter-of-factly. "You felt the power in this room as much as I did."

"No!"

"You'd pick Danaus over me to be in the triad?" I demanded. While I was never one to discriminate according to a person's race, there was something that irked me about asking Danaus—whatever it is that he was—to be in an all-vampire triad of power. Particularly after he'd spent so much time killing us.

Unfortunately, it might not have been the wisest decision to call attention to myself, considering that I could barely remain in an upright position. I wanted to lie down, but the pools of cooling naturi blood and assortment of body parts made the idea unappealing.

"You're still blind to the truth?" Jabari asked incredulously. He walked over to me, his face twisted with rage. "You can never be a part of the triad, no matter how old you become or how strong you grow." Kneeling down so he could look me in the eye, he sneered. "You are just a weapon, nothing more than a sword or a gun, a tool. Your true power is in how another can use you."

"No," I croaked, but my mind was already turning over the idea. The voice in my head had been a command and I obeyed. I had no choice, couldn't have stopped what happened no matter how hard I tried.

"The triad focuses its power in you. We used you like a key to lock the door between this world and the naturi," Jabari explained.

"If I was so important to what happened, why can't I remember that night?" I asked through clenched teeth. The thought of being controlled by another twisted in my chest, numbing the pain still throbbing in my body. It seemed that from the moment I took my first gasping breath on this earth, I'd struggled for my independence, my ability to control my own fate.

"To protect you."

A snort of disbelief escaped me as I narrowed my eyes at my old friend and guardian. "I'm beginning to think that nothing you've ever done for me was for my benefit."

Jabari smiled at me, and it was unlike any other I had ever seen cross his face. It was like a mask had finally been lifted, one I hadn't even realized I'd been staring at for the past five hundred years. I had seen him smile in pleasure and in hatred, but now he seemed formed of ice, cold and unyielding. He put a finger under my chin and titled my head up. I tried to jerk my head away but I found that I couldn't. The leak of power oozing from him through his finger into my skin was slight, but it was enough to cause my already sore muscles to tense. There was a new presence in my head claiming dominion, but he had yet to speak or command me. For now, he was just staking his claim, proving he had control over me.

"You can't remember because we didn't want you to remember," Jabari stated.

"We?"

"The Coven. We needed to know who could control you. You can be quite an effective weapon."

I gritted my teeth and tried again to move my head away from his touch, and again I couldn't, which made his smile widen.

"Sadira can control you," Jabari continued. "Tabor could, and so can I. Surprisingly, a couple of Tabor's children could as well, so we naturally assumed that it was a matter of finding the proper bloodlines."

"There were others?" A new horror dug its claws into my

flesh. There were no memories to drag up, but I could easily imagine the scene: me playing the puppet for the amusement of the Coven and its lackeys.

"A few. We ran some experiments. Unfortunately, most of those we found who could control you had to be destroyed. We couldn't let our little secret out. We also had to make sure you didn't know. There would always be the chance of someone reading your mind and discovering your unique ability."

"So I've been allowed to live this long so the Coven could pull my leash at any moment," I said. Something flashed in Jabari's eyes for half a second, a random thought I wasn't supposed to know. "What?" I snapped. "Something about the Coven?" I watched him as his expression hardened, and I smiled back at him. "Not everyone can do it," I slowly said. "Not everyone on the Coven can control me." My smile widened and his expression went purposefully blank. I was right. "That must be an ugly sticking point for someone." My mind quickly rifled through the other members of the Coven; Macaire and Elizabeth. Tabor, my other leash holder, was gone. Could I have been the reason for his final demise?

"You're very lucky to have survived so long," Jabari said. "Wisely, you chose to fulfill the requests of the Coven, giving you a purpose and the illusion that you would obey our wishes."

"All the Coven asked of me was to keep the peace and protect our secret. Not an entirely unreasonable request," I replied, with a slight shrug that made me instantly wish I hadn't moved my hurt shoulder.

"And now we have this problem," Jabari growled, his eyes sliding over to Danaus, who was closely watching the exchange. The hunter pushed to his feet, wincing at the movement, but at least he was standing. I still wasn't sure I could.

"We naturally assumed that you could only be controlled by your own kind," Jabari continued. "That's not good, my desert flower; particularly since there are questions about your loyalty."

"There are few who have done anything to earn my loyalty," I replied, causing him to frown. I liked it better than his smile at the moment. "But it doesn't matter. You will only let me live until you find a way to create another like me."

"If you live that long," Jabari said, moving his finger from beneath my chin. If I still breathed, I think I would have sighed with relief. The Ancient stood before me, staring down as if weighing something. "The naturi know you are the key to stopping them. Enough of them survived Machu Picchu to know that you were the one who sealed the door. You were right. They were trying to kill you in Aswan, not me. I believe they were also trying to kill you in London, but they killed Tabor's child instead. You have always been their target."

"If I'm so damned important, why send me to protect Sadira? Why not send someone else?"

"We needed bait."

"Bait?"

"To draw out Rowe. We knew he would come after you again. The chance to kill you is too much of a temptation."

I closed my eyes, trying to ignore the knot of tears that had grown in the back of my throat. It seemed I was becoming everyone's favorite target. "And killing Rowe would end this? It would stop the naturi?" My voice trembled as I fought for control of my emotions.

"Rowe is the last known leader of the naturi," Danaus volunteered.

My head snapped up to look at him, meeting his glittering blue eyes as he watched me. "You used me too," I whispered.

To his credit, he didn't look away, but continued to hold my horrified gaze. "Yes. When he tried to take you in Aswan, I realized that you must have some other importance that you either were not telling me or didn't remember. I thought he would make another grab for you."

"Well, you both missed your chance to end this. Rowe had me in London, threatening to kidnap me," I said bitterly. "It would have meant destroying me, but I can only guess that you both have other plans for me still."

"Mira . . . " Sadira began in a placating voice.

"I've heard enough!" I shouted.

"So have I!" mocked a horrible voice from behind me. I didn't need to look around to see who had spoken. I knew by the sound, the tone, the look of complete shock on the faces of the others who had spoken. With a burst of sheer terror, I tried to lurch forward, but he grabbed me by the hair, wrapping it around his fist. Jerking me backward, he pulled me into the darkness and out of the Compound in less than a heartbeat. Rowe had finally caught me.

Twenty-Nine

The darkness gave way suddenly to a moonlit plain hugged by a desolate ribbon of road. I slowly pushed up into a sitting position so I could look around. Rowe took a few stumbling steps away from me before finally collapsing to his knees in the grass. Bent over, his fingers clutching the grass, he struggled for air. His whole body was trembling, his shirt sticking to his narrow frame as if he were sweating profusely. All this flitting from place to place was taking its toll on him.

Digging my nails into the dirt, I started to pull my legs beneath me so I could rise. My whole body screamed in pain and the world swayed slightly. I was too low on blood to pick a fight and expect to win, but at least Rowe was in ragged shape as well.

"Watch her," Rowe bit out without looking over at me.

Until he spoke, my gaze had not drifted beyond him. Now, I lifted my eyes to see six naturi of various size and clans approaching us warily. And beyond them rose the pale monoliths of Stonehenge. They were attempting the sacrifice tonight, and for some bizarre reason, Rowe had decided he needed me on hand to witness their triumph.

"Shit," I hissed, lowering my head. I was in no shape to take on seven naturi alone.

A wheezing laugh escaped Rowe. He was kneeling on the ground with his forearms in the grass in front of him. His head was turned toward me, his black hair partially obscuring his face, but I could still see the smirk twisting his lips.

"Oh, like you're in any better shape than me," I snarled.

"At least I have someone to protect me," he said, pushing into a sitting position with pain-filled slowness.

I looked back at the naturi standing before us. A female with pale blond hair that fell to her waist stepped forward. She extended one hand and flames danced over her fingers. Naturally, one of my keepers was a member of the light clan.

"It doesn't have to be like this, Mira," Rowe said.

"Go to hell, Rowe," I snapped, my gaze never wavering from the six naturi standing before me.

A harsh clutter of words jumped from Rowe that I couldn't understand. Several of the naturi briefly expressed surprise and confusion, but after a moment they backed away, returning to the inner circle of stones.

Silence crept back over the plain. The air was still, waiting. It was only after the naturi retreated back into the shadows of the stones that I noticed the soft sounds of a woman crying. The naturi had their sacrifice waiting in the darkness, surrounded by great bluestones. Where the hell was Jabari? He could move from place to place in an instant. He should have been able to locate me wherever I was. Why hadn't he appeared yet? If he were there, I knew we could stop this now. I'd even have settled for Sadira or Danaus, but I knew it would take several more minutes for either of them to reach me.

I dragged my fingers through the earth, digging narrows furrows in the soft dirt. The grass was moist, as if it had rained recently. Beneath me, I could feel the strange hum of power beginning to build. Had they begun the sacrifice already? I couldn't see most of the naturi, as they remained hidden behind the giant stones, but I could hear the faint sound of movement; breathing, the soft swish of clothing.

"You can feel it, can't you?" Rowe said. The weight of his stare was a physical pressure on my shoulders, but I refused to look over at him. "You could feel it while you were at Machu Picchu. In those last days, Nerian didn't need to touch you, the power in the mountain was enough to have you writhing in pain."

I shook my head. I wasn't going to let him play mind games with me. "Just stop. You weren't there," I replied.

"I was there," he murmured. My gaze jerked over to him at the sound of movement. He crawled a couple feet closer but remained out of arm's reach. "Every day and every night of your captivity, I was there. You just don't remember because I looked a little different back then."

"Years not been kind?" I mocked.

His face twisted into a look of anger and hatred for a split second before he could wipe it away. "I'm sure the years have scarred us both in interesting ways."

"Why bring me here? I could still stop your sacrifice, destroy all your plans." I smiled at him as I sat up. I rubbed my hands together, knocking off the dirt.

Rowe sat up as well, seeming to move with a little more ease and less obvious pain. We were both slowly regaining our strength. "Because the reward is worth the risk."

A laugh escaped me before I could stop it. "Killing me is worth that much to you?"

Rowe shoved his left hand through his hair, threading some of it behind his left ear so it no longer fell in front of his one eye. A white scar ran along his jaw and seemed to glow against his tanned skin in the moonlight. "My goal is not to kill you."

I snorted in response, and Rowe said something under

his breath in his own language, frustration filling his voice. He looked over at the arrangement of stones for a moment before turning back to me again.

"It doesn't have to be like this between us."

"What? The naturi have graciously decided to stop killing nightwalkers?"

This time he was the one to snort. "No, nightwalkers are vermin. They need to be exterminated. I meant between you and the naturi."

"I am a nightwalker, asshole."

"But you were never meant to be," he said, leaning toward me as his voice dropped to an urgent whisper. "You never should have been made into one of their kind. Your powers reach beyond their limitations. You could have been more. You still could be."

I leaned back, trying to keep some distance between us. With him sitting this close, it was hard to resist the urge to take a swipe at him, but I didn't stand a chance with his compatriots just a few yards away. "Let me guess, you can help me become more," I sneered.

"You can feel the power here, and no other vampire can. When they swarmed Machu Picchu centuries ago, not one of them reacted the way you do. You can still feel the earth despite being a nightwalker," he explained. "It's still a part of you because it's more powerful than anything you've gained through becoming a nightwalker. You belong with us, not them."

A slow chuckle built until my head finally fell backward, my laughter filling the plain, silencing the soft plaintive cries from the woman doomed to die tonight. "Save your breath. I've heard this speech before, though it was more interesting the first time. At Machu Picchu, you guys were just trying to convince me to kill my own kind. Now you want me to believe that I belong among you."

"Can you honestly tell me you feel you belong among your own kind? Hmmm, Fire Starter?"

The laugh died inside of me. "It doesn't matter."

"You can end the war tonight," Rowe softly said.

"By killing you?"

"By completing the sacrifice."

My brow furrowed as I stared at him for a long time, letting the silence grow between us. "What are you talking about?" I asked, my voice dropping to match his softness.

"If you complete the sacrifice, the seal will be broken *permanently.* You made it. If you break it, the nightwalkers will never be able to recreate it again. We end this battle forever."

"And if I don't?"

"I kill you now."

"And if I do?"

"You walk away. The naturi shall never bother you again."

"But I will be branded a traitor and will be hunted by my own kind until the end of my nights," I said with a shake of my head.

"Then break the seal and remain with us," he offered, stunning me. "I am consort to the queen, and you will be under my protection. The naturi will never harass you and the nightwalkers will never touch you."

I turned my head to look back at Stonehenge for a second before letting my eyes fall shut. In the hands of the naturi, I was a weapon against the nightwalkers. And while among the nightwalkers, I was a weapon against the naturi. Without ever knowing it, I had managed to dig a heel into both worlds.

Planting both of my hands into the dirt, I pushed off and rose to my feet. Beside me there was a soft rustle of clothing as Rowe stood. He stuck close to me as I slowly walked past the first circle of stones and into the inner circle. The other six naturi circled the woman lying on the ground. Her wrists had been bound together and then tied to a stake in the ground above her head. Her ankles were also bound together and staked so that she was stretched out, her body running east to west. She had short, dark brown hair and her round face was streaked with tears. The smell of her blood filled the air, as her wrists were rubbed raw from her struggles.

"What do you need me to do?" I asked, staring down at her.

Rowe stepped in front of me and gently grabbed my chin, tilting my head up so I was forced to look him in the eye. "You will do this?"

"It's time to end this war."

A half smile lifted one corner of his mouth briefly and he nodded. "You must cut out her heart and place it on the ground. Her blood must saturate the earth before we burn her heart."

I had to be sure. I couldn't make any mistakes now. As Rowe stepped back to my side, I took a step closer to the woman. She stared up with wide eyes, pleading silently with me to free her. But I couldn't. She was the only human in the area. As long as she lived, she could serve as a sacrifice for the naturi whatever I did. The best I could do for her was make it quick.

Staring down at her, I focused on her heart. The slender woman gasped suddenly, shattering the silence in the night air. Her body arched off the ground and all the naturi took a step backward. The woman jerked again, this time screaming.

"What's happening?" someone demanded.

"It's the nightwalker! She's killing the woman," another voice snarled, but I didn't look up. I remained focused on the woman's chest until her pale blue shirt with pearl buttons finally started to blacken and catch on fire.

"Stop her!"

Rowe grabbed me and threw me backward into one of the enormous stones, breaking my concentration. I fell back to the ground, my eyes clenched shut as I waited to see if I'd hit the stone with enough force to knock loose the other stone balanced on top of it. When I wasn't immediately crushed, I opened my eyes, trying to ignore the pain throbbing to life along my spine and in the back of my skull.

"Can we still use the woman?" Rowe demanded, looking briefly over his shoulder at the woman, who was no longer moving.

"The heart has been destroyed," someone else confirmed.

The naturi with the eye patch turned back to me, a knife clutched in his right hand. "Then we will try it with her heart," Rowe proclaimed.

I dug my heels into the earth and tried to scoot backward, but I was halted by giant stone sticking up from the earth. I had used the last of my powers to kill that poor woman, and now I had nothing left to save myself.

My only warning was a slight building of pressure, a shift in the powers that filled the circle, and then Jabari was standing beside me.

Rowe and the other naturi jumped back, gathering on the other side of the circle, the woman's corpse between us. The knife in his hand trembled as he stared at the Ancient, his breath hissing between clenched teeth.

"You cannot have her," Jabari proclaimed.

Rowe hunched forward, then a low growl escaped him as giant wings exploded from his back. As black as a moonless night, the fully extended wings were more than nine feet long from tip to tip and resembled those of a bat. "You cannot keep her forever," he snarled, pointing his knife at Jabari.

I looked up at my onetime mentor and protector to see a wide grin split his handsome face. He extended his arm so his hand was nearly over my head. Power immediately surged through my body, ripping a whimper from my throat. It was as if strings had been attached to various parts of my body and I was pulled back to my feet. There was no voice in my head commanding me, but I could feel a presence, a subtle push of power. There was nothing to fight. Nothing to push or struggle against. I was merely a spectator in my own body. Reduced to a mere marionette.

A second wave of power pushed through my body, nearly blinding me with pain. My left arm lifted and three of the naturi exploded into balls of fire. I could feel the member of the light clan trying to extinguish the fires, but she was no match. She was engulfed in flames next.

With a single flap of the enormous wings, Rowe launched himself into the air. "See you with the dead," he bit out, and then he was gone, leaving behind the last two naturi to be burned alive.

When the last of the naturi were reduced to ash, Jabari released me. My knees buckled and I collapsed back onto the ground. Pain seemed to be a living, breathing entity within my body. I didn't seem to exist anymore. There was only pain and horror.

I blinked a couple of times, trying to clear my vision, and saw Jabari extend a hand toward me, offering to help me back to my feet. I jerked away from him. "Don't touch me," I snapped.

His dark laugh rose up in the silence, wrapping itself around me like a noose. "I don't need to."

A shiver rippled through me and I clenched my teeth to keep them from chattering. No. No, he didn't need to touch me to control me.

"We go to Venice. It is the best way to protect you from the naturi," Jabari announced.

I certainly didn't want to admit it, but he was right. Venice was the one place I would be safe from them. They never set foot in the city. The old tales said that one of the naturi's gods had died in what is now the city of Venice, creating the canals that wove their way among the tiny islands. The naturi supposedly couldn't enter the city. Unfortunately, Venice was also the home of the Coven. I didn't want to be anywhere near another Ancient, let alone near at least three of the most powerful nightwalkers in existence.

I frowned, realizing I had no options. I didn't have the strength to fight Jabari, and even if I did, I didn't know how. The bastard could control me like a puppet. And if I slipped away from him, I had no doubt that Rowe would cut my heart out the first time he caught sight of me. At least Jabari needed me alive for the time being. I had stopped the second sacrifice, bought us a little time. The naturi would strike again.

But the triad was reformed, even if it now included a vampire hunter. And the triad still had me, a weapon that could kill or bind them.

The sound of a car engine jerked us both from our thoughts. It was Danaus. I knew it without using my powers. It was the hunter.

"You will travel to Venice and you will bring the hunter with you," Jabari ordered. "We will be waiting for you."

I nodded, my eyes darting away from his face. "Sadira?"

"She has already left for Italy. She asks that you bring her child." My gaze jumped back to his face, to find a mocking smile lifting his lips. She would demand that, keeping both Tristan and me on a short leash. As the car drew close, Jabari stepped backward and disappeared.

My eyes fell shut and it was a struggle just to remain upright. For the first time, I wondered if I'd chosen the right side. If I'd sided with the naturi, I would have been forced to kill nightwalkers and stand by while the naturi killed the humans. If I'd sided with the nightwalkers, I would have been forced to kill the naturi. And regardless of which side I might have chosen that night, the innocent human woman would still have died by my hand.

The car engine stopped and I could hear the sound of heavy footsteps running across the field. I opened my eyes in time to see Danaus come between a pair of large stones, a long knife in his right hand. His eyes quickly swept the carnage, pausing briefly on the woman that lay to my left, before he finally put his knife back in its sheath at his side.

I slowly pushed to my feet, but my legs buckled again. Danaus crossed the short distance separating us, grabbing my arms and keeping me from hitting the ground again.

"Jabari?" he asked.

"Come and gone already," I said. My voice was harsh and rough as I forced it past the lump in my throat. "We go to Venice." A fragile, mocking smile slipped across my lips. "We did it. We reformed the triad and even have a weapon that can stop the naturi."

I flinched as his large hands cupped my cheeks, but the power that filled him didn't try to push inside of me. It swirled around us, forming a warm, comforting cocoon.

"Don't let him beat you," Danaus ordered, forcing me to meet his glittering gaze. I knew he was talking about Jabari. He didn't know about Rowe yet, and I wasn't sure I would ever tell him. I was already enough of a danger to the world around me; no reason to up the ante.

"He already has," I murmured. "I'm a tool. A weapon."

"No, you're the Fire Starter. A walking nightmare to both vampire and naturi. We'll find a way to beat him."

I didn't even try to keep the skepticism from darting through my eyes as I stared up at the hunter. I couldn't imagine what kind of miracle he expected me to work.

"You've eluded me for the past few decades. What trouble could a few old vampires offer?" he continued, arching one thick brow at me.

Danaus was being ridiculous, but I understood his point. We had to find a way if we hoped to survive. Our fates were linked now.

"We'll find a way," I whispered. "I always do."

Danaus leaned forward and brushed a kiss against my temple, sending a wave of peace deep into the marrow of my bones, helping to ease some of the pain. "And then we'll kill each other as God intended."

Eos Books

Celebrating 10 Years of
Outstanding Science Fiction
and Fantasy Publishing
1998-2008

Interested in free downloads? Exclusive author podcasts? Click on **www.EosBooks10.com** to celebrate our 10th Anniversary with us all year long—you never know what we'll be giving away!

And while you're online, visit our daily blog at **www.OutofThisEos.com** and become our MySpace friend at **www.MySpace.com/EosBooks** for even more Eos exclusives.

Eos Books-The Next Chapter
An Imprint of HarperCollinsPublishers